Praise for

BEYOND THE WESTERN SEA
—◆ Book I ◆—
The Escape From Home

"Pulsing 1850s emigrant adventure . . .
packed with action and a huge cast
of villains and heroes . . .
every chapter ends with a cliffhanger,
and the suspense builds . . ."
Booklist

"Suspense-filled adventure . . .
the dank, dirty back alleys of Liverpool come alive
through the struggles of the three children."
School Library Journal

"YOU WON'T BE ABLE TO
STOP READING . . .
a cliff-hanging ending."
The Bulletin for the Center for Children's Books

BEYOND THE WESTERN SEA

—◆ *Book I* ◆—

The Escape From Home

AN AVON CAMELOT BOOK

AVON BOOKS, INC.
1350 Avenue of the Americas
New York, New York 10019

Copyright © 1996 by Avi
Published by arrangement with Orchard Books, New York
Library of Congress Catalog Card Number: 95-36058
ISBN: 0-380-72875-3
RL: 6.7
www.avonbooks.com

First Avon Camelot Printing: October 1997

CAMELOT TRADEMARK REG. U.S. PAT. OFF. AND IN OTHER COUNTRIES, MARCA REGISTRADA,
HECHO EN U.S.A.

Printed in the U.S.A.

For Linda Cruse Wright

CONTENTS

Wednesday, January 22, 1851

Thursday, January 23, 1851

Friday, January 24, 1851

Chapter 1
A Knock at the Door

J ust before dawn—that moment when time itself seems to stand still, when the whole world teeters on the edge of possibilities—a man looking like death's own shadow came scurrying down a bluff toward the tiny village of Kilonny in Ireland.

He was dressed in a black frock coat and black trousers. His coat was patched; his trousers fit ill; his boots were badly broken. Only his white neck cloth relieved his funereal appearance, and that was soiled from excessive use and little washing. Tired eyes, set deep in a flat, grizzled face, were mirrors of grief. But then, the man's principal state of mind these days was woe.

Though he knew exactly where he was going, knew too the path he'd trod with weariness so many times, he carried a small lantern to light his way.

Kilonny Village lay upon devastated land. Little grew in the heavy mix of clay and jagged stone that made up the valley's earth thereabouts. The trees were barren of leaves. And with its clutch of crumbling structures, the village was like a prehistoric ruin in a rank, forgotten place.

When the man reached the village, he went directly to one of the first huts, a seven-foot pile of sticks thrust up, mortared with clay, then roofed over with rotten thatch from a collapsed cottage nearby. No proper door barred his way.

1

Instead, he knocked upon a splintery slab of wood that had been pulled across the entry.

The knocking woke Patrick O'Connell from fitful sleep. Twelve years of age, small and wiry, he owned little more than the ragged clothes he wore and no shoes at all. Coal black hair framed a pinched face with large eyes that proclaimed his hunger.

"Jesus, Mary, and Joseph!" the boy whispered under his breath as he made the sign of the cross and glanced about. There were neither windows nor furniture, only a wooden bowl of cornmeal and a chipped jug a quarter full of soured buttermilk. Their other possessions—clothing, digging tools, a few odd bits and scraps—would barely have filled two bundles.

In a hole scooped from the earthen floor near the hut's center lay a turf fire whose glowing ember—the size of a thumb—offered more smoke than heat. Patrick's mother, Annie O'Connell, and his sister, Maura, were huddled together in a corner, sharing what warmth they could.

Though Patrick wanted to know who had knocked, he held back. Who could have proper business with them at such an hour? The O'Connells' lives had been miserable for so long that the only visitor he could imagine was new calamity.

The potato famine had come, bringing starving times, no employment, illness, and death. So it was that eleven months ago Patrick's father, Gregory O'Connell—Da to the children—grew so desperate he took most of the money the family still had and sailed to America in search of work. Since then there had not been one word from him. In that same period a fever had taken Patrick's younger brother, Timothy. His mortal remains lay in Kilonny's crowded cemetery. Now there was no money left to pay the quarterly rent to Mr. Morgan, the agent for Sir James Kirkle, the English lord who owned all the land around the village.

Perfectly reasonable, then, for Patrick to think the knocking meant Mr. Morgan had come to evict them. If it were so, he'd have constables and soldiers by his side to drive the family away and tumble their hut. Such things happened, and often. It was fear of eviction that caused Patrick and Maura to guard the entryway at night. This night's watch was Patrick's.

He looked around for a weapon. Spying a rock against a wall, he hefted it in the palm of his hand. Maybe—coming in the dark—the rock would scare the agent off.

"Mother! Maura!" he whispered across the earthen floor. "Bestir yourselves! Someone's at the door. It's likely Mr. Morgan."

Maura, instantly alert, started up. She was fifteen, tall and thin, with a strong, high-cheeked, and dirty face from which angry blue eyes blazed beneath a tangled mass of long, thick brown hair. It was a rare day—or night—that saw Maura O'Connell smile.

"Did you say someone's come?" she asked.

"And wanting to get in," Patrick said. A pale yellow glow of lantern light seeped through the splintery board.

Maura touched her mother gently. "Mother," she said, "you must move."

Mrs. O'Connell groaned, sat up slowly, and automatically crossed herself. Though only forty-one, she looked the flinty side of fifty. Her thin hair was streaked with gray. Her eyes were dull and sad, her cheeks haggard, her lips parched and tight. When she coughed—as she did often—a spike of pain cut deep within her sunken chest.

"What is it?" she asked half in a whisper, half in a moan.

"Someone's at the door," Patrick said with even greater urgency.

3

"God keep us from more misfortune," his mother murmured. She began to say her rosary beads.

"Go on, Patrick," Maura commanded. "See who it is."

Clutching his stone, Patrick crept forward and put his eye to a crack in the wood. "I can't make him out at all," he said.

Maura pulled her dark red shawl close around her body and moved next to her brother. At the threshold she paused and tried to steady her nerves.

"Maura," Patrick whispered, "if it is Mr. Morgan, I've got a stone for him." He held up his fist.

"Hush!" his sister cried, struggling with her own dread. "Put aside your foolishness! It'll do us no good. None! Do you understand?"

Patrick shrank down and let the stone roll away. "I'll try," he muttered, convincing no one, least of all himself.

"Mother?" Maura called. "Are you ready then?"

Mrs. O'Connell, assuming the worst, closed her eyes. With arms wrapped about herself, she began to rock slowly back and forth, praying softly.

Knowing all too well there was little she could do about Mr. Morgan if it were he, Maura faced the entryway, took a deep breath, and cried, "Who's that at the door?"

Chapter 2
The Man in Black Delivers a Message

*I*t's Father Mahoney, Maura O'Connell," came a whispered voice. "Would you be kind enough to let me in!"

"Father Mahoney!" Mrs. O'Connell cried with relief. "He'll be bringing no harm."

4

"But he might be bringing a warning, Mother," Patrick cautioned.

"Don't you speak it," Mrs. O'Connell said with a vehement shake of her head.

"It's true, Mother," Maura agreed. "You know how vicious Mr. Morgan is. He may have the father in his pocket as he does so many others."

"By the Blessed Virgin!" Mrs. O'Connell cried as she pulled herself to her feet and wrapped a black shawl tightly about herself. "Am I hearing my daughter saying such dreadful things? Father Mahoney has been a loyal friend. For Jesus' sake, open the way to him!"

Maura pulled aside the board. "Father Mahoney," she said, "you're welcome here."

"God be with you in the morning," the priest said as he stooped low and entered the hut. His fingers were raised in a blessing. The three O'Connells breathed an "Amen" but were too uneasy to speak more.

The priest set his small lantern on the ground. Rubbing his hands together to ease the chill, he searched for Mrs. O'Connell through the smoky gloom.

"Mrs. O'Connell," he said, clasping and unclasping his hands, "you'll forgive me my waking you so early."

"Has something happened?" the woman asked, alarmed by his manner. "Is it Mr. Morgan who's coming? Are we to be driven out?"

"God protect us all from such rough usage, Mrs. O'Connell," the priest replied. "Though, true enough, I was over to Skibbens way just yesterday, where Mr. Morgan was tumbling cottages. May God witness his cruelty! Faith, it's terrible to see. I'm fearing it'll happen here in Kilonny, and soon at that."

"Jesus have mercy," Mrs. O'Connell whispered. "What will the people do?"

5

"God's love will care," the priest said.

"I don't doubt it, Father," Mrs. O'Connell offered with instant humility.

Maura gave an angry toss of her head. "And in the here and now?" she asked.

Father Mahoney, alarmed by this suggestion of blasphemy, looked around with sad eyes. He waited. But when Maura said no more, he turned back to her mother.

"Mrs. O'Connell," he said, "I tried to talk to Mr. Morgan—him of the Kirkle estates—to secure the unfortunates of Skibbens more time. All the narrow man would say is, 'Orders are orders, money is money, and the law proclaims it so.' Then I—" Now it was the priest who stopped midsentence lest *he* speak in a way that would bring a rebuke. "But," he said, smiling now, "I haven't come at such an hour to bring sad news."

"Pray God, I hope not."

"No, no. I merely wanted to explain the odd hour of my coming. You see, when I got home from Skibbens, I found the post wagon had left a letter." He glanced about benevolently, first at the cowering woman, then at Maura—whose look remained hostile—and finally at Patrick, whose eyes were fixed upon him with intense interest.

"A letter?" Mrs. O'Connell said, not sure she understood.

"'Tis true," Father Mahoney explained. "It was addressed to me, but when I opened it, sure enough, it was for you."

"Father," said Mrs. O'Connell, "it's a mistake you're making. Never before have I received such a thing."

"Well, by the grace of God, you have now," the priest informed her grandly as he reached into a deep coat pocket. "I couldn't wait for the bringing of it."

"But who would be writing to me?" she asked fearfully.

Father Mahoney smiled broadly. "It's from America," he announced.

6

"America!" the woman fairly shrieked. "God have mercy! Who's it from?"

At the word—*America*—Maura pressed a hand to her heart. Patrick gasped.

"It's your husband," the priest proclaimed.

"Is it—is it something that's happened to himself?" Mrs. O'Connell stuttered, full of fright.

Father Mahoney, still smiling, produced a creased letter from his pocket. The O'Connells stared at it.

"Patrick, lad," the priest said. "Point the lamp so all can see."

Patrick snatched up the lantern and aimed its beam at the paper. Maura crept closer. Mrs. O'Connell, hands over her mouth, edged in too.

"There, you see," the priest said. He pointed to and read from the paper:

> "Father James P. Mahoney SJ
> St. Peter's Church
> Kilonny Village
> County Cork
> Ireland"

"It's not Mr. O'Connell," Mrs. O'Connell said. "He was hardly above the making of his mark."

"Someone could have done for him," Patrick said.

"But what does it say?" Maura asked in a voice quivering with emotion. "Does it tell how he fares?"

The priest drew himself up. "Gregory O'Connell, God bless the man, has sent the most extraordinary news!"

7

Chapter 3

In Which the Letter Is Read

S weet Jesus," Mrs. O'Connell murmured as she sank to her knees, "I thought the man truly lost."

"The Lord provides," Father Mahoney reminded her kindly. "And He loves most the ones with faith."

"I never doubted, Father," the woman insisted, her eyes glistening with tears as she crossed herself yet again. "But, oh, Father, with all the terrible things that have happened, a body can't help but question."

The priest held out his hand. Mrs. O'Connell kissed it fervently, then breathed a deep sigh. "Father," she asked, for she could not read,"would you be kind enough to tell us what Mr. O'Connell has said?"

"I'm proud to do it," Father Mahoney replied. "Patrick, lad, keep the lantern steady."

Trying to hold his excitement in check, Patrick drew closer as the priest carefully unfolded the letter. From it, he extracted another piece of paper.

"Now then," the priest began, "the letter's dated early November past from a place called Lowell."

"Where is this . . . Low-ell?" Maura asked.

Father Mahoney looked around. "I don't rightly know," he admitted. "Somewhere in America."

"But America is huge!" Patrick objected.

"Shhh!" Maura said, hands clasped together tightly. "Let the father read!"

The priest cleared his throat and began:

"To my beloved wife and you my three darling children."

The reminder of her lost child caused Mrs. O'Connell to moan softly. After a moment the priest went on:

"I have not spoken before, since I was unsure of my ways and not wishing to send anything but what was good tidings. I—bless God—work steady in a cloth-making manufactory in this city and have found good pay with decent lodging, far better than anything I have known before. I have a good young friend too who writes this for me."

"Merciful God!" Mrs. O'Connell broke in. "He did the right thing, and it's done well for him! Work *and* friend. And I feared him lost at sea!"

"Or that savages killed him," Patrick added.

"There's much more," the priest said, recalling them to the letter.

"But with all my struggles I have saved enough so as to pay your passage and the children's passage beyond the sea to America so we will—God willing—be together at last and in peace again."

"Dear, sweet Jesus!" Mrs. O'Connell cried, pressing her hands to her chest to suppress a cough. Maura, with a sob, turned to her mother, knelt, and hugged her about the neck. Patrick clapped his hands in glee.

"I am sending money herewith to Father Mahoney, knowing him to be an honest man who will see you get this. The draft of money is on the Provincial Bank of Ireland. Fifteen pounds."

"Fifteen pounds!" Mrs. O'Connell exclaimed in astonishment. "The man's become rich!"

"Father Mahoney will help you. Send to the address I give here the name of your ship and when you are coming, and it should be to Boston City. Then I will surely come to meet you, for I reside not so far. You must keep well in spirit and in health, and so I embrace you, dear wife and dear children, writing as I do from America.

> *Your faithful husband until death,*
> *Gregory O'Connell"*

All but laughing with pleasure, Father Mahoney lowered the letter. Mrs. O'Connell began to weep outright as Maura hugged her closer and kissed her wet face. Patrick looked down at his bare feet, at his mother, at the letter, each in turn and over and over again, trying to absorb these great tidings.

"And here," the priest cried, allowing himself a rare laugh as he held up the second piece of paper, "is the very bank draft your husband spoke about. Fifteen pounds!"

Patrick stared at it. If the paper had been a brick of gold, it could not have been more wonderful. As far as he was concerned, he could live forever on that!

"Now then," Father Mahoney said, "I congratulate you on your good fortune. Once you walk to Cork City, you'll take the boat for Liverpool, England. From there it's the packet boat straight over the sea to America. That's the way it's done. Your husband's money will see you through in perfect safety. Not even four pounds for full passage. Less for Patrick, I'm thinking. You can count on me to make arrangements."

"To America," Patrick echoed with excitement.

"America, to be sure," the priest said. "And Mr. O'Connell's place of residence is set down right here. Fifty-four Adams Street, Lowell, Massachusetts. Sure then, it must be a fine place for living."

Mrs. O'Connell drew her hands from her eyes. "But it's not a Catholic country. And God knows," she groaned, "I can't go so far from the grave of my perished Timothy."

"Mrs. O'Connell," the priest said gently, "you have my sacred vow. I'll be here in Kilonny, looking after him."

"Mother"—Maura held her tightly—"Mother, we need a place that lets us live. Haven't thousands gone before?"

"It's just as Maura says," the priest agreed. "Put your minds to a whole new life. You know the likelihood that Mr. Morgan will tumble all."

Mrs. O'Connell shook her head again. "It's as much as your life is worth to go journeying beyond the western sea."

"Mother," Patrick cried, "Da wants us with him!"

"Mrs. O'Connell, your husband is now a prosperous man."

"Father Mahoney," said Maura, her voice firm, her heart beating madly, "you shall write to Da. Tell him we'll be coming to that place called Lowell as soon as possible. And may heaven be kind to us all."

Chapter 4
January in Kilonny

G ray clouds hung over Kilonny Village. The sun, low in the east, floated in the sky as if it were a holy wafer. A cold mist, like the wet fingers of a water witch, poked and prodded into every nook and cranny.

Within the O'Connells' hut, the turf fire was dying. By the open entrance stood two small bundles, each tied with bulky knots. They contained all the family's possessions. Mrs. O'Connell, occasionally coughing, more often weeping, knelt on the earth, saying her beads. On either side, Maura and Patrick tried to soothe her anxiety.

"Now that it's time, I've not the heart for leaving," their mother whispered. "I don't, and that's God's truth." She closed her eyes and made the sign of the cross.

Maura, irritated in spite of herself, struggled to stay calm. "Mother," she said with barely suppressed urgency, "you know perfectly well what's about to happen. It's impossible to stay."

Mrs. O'Connell shook her head. "I can't believe it."

"It's true, Mother," Patrick cried, with a look over his shoulder toward the entryway. Had it been up to him, he would have left an hour ago.

"Mr. Morgan is on his way," Maura reminded her mother. "We're not the first to be tumbled, and heaven knows we won't be the last."

"Besides, Mother," Patrick urged, "haven't we promised

12

Da we'd go? Didn't Father Mahoney buy the tickets from the people and write to him, telling him the name of the ship we're taking and even the day we're getting there?"

"Aye, but, children . . ."

"Mother, we no longer have the choice!"

As if to prove Maura's point, a boy stuck his head into the hut. "The agent's coming," he cried. "With soldiers and constables!" The message delivered, he bolted away. They heard the message repeated—like a fading echo—as he went on to their neighbors.

The words were too much for Patrick. "Mother," he shouted, "we have to go this minute!" He and Maura pulled their mother up.

"I can't. I can't," the woman kept saying, coughing and weeping.

Next moment it was Father Mahoney himself who entered. "Mr. Morgan has arrived," he announced. "And with reinforcements too."

Patrick snatched up the bundles and ran out.

"Patrick!" Maura cried, but he was gone. "Mother," she pleaded, "do you want to be buried alive in rubble? For God's sake, you must move!"

Mrs. O'Connell, as though blind, groped her way out of the hut.

"Ah, Maura," Father Mahoney said, "you must be leaving too."

"Father," Maura whispered, "will you give the place a final blessing before I go?"

The priest nodded in understanding, lifted his hand, and spoke softly but quickly. Maura, eyes cast down, hands clenched before her, waited until he was done. Then she said, "Go now, Father. I'll be there in time."

He took her at her word and hurried to give service elsewhere.

Her blue eyes blurred gray with tears, Maura stood in the middle of their barren home. The floor was as cold to her bare feet as her heart was hot. She looked about to see if anything was forgotten only to realize the uselessness of such an effort. Whatever possessions they had had were long gone—sold, or broken, or taken. With an angry snort of self-mockery, she pushed the hair out of her face and wiped her eyes dry with the heel of a hand. Intense anger swept through her. "A curse on this land," she whispered, "and may I keep angry with its memory!"

Hurriedly now, she scratched at the floor and gathered enough dirt to pour over the tiny turf fire. The last ember was extinguished. Without another glance, Maura ran out of her home.

Chapter 5

Mr. Morgan Comes

*K*ilonny Village looked like an anthill overturned. People were frantically rushing in and out of their cottages and huts, trying to save what they could. With cries and shouts, with wailing and curses, they piled boxes, bundles, and pieces of furniture on the muddy road in an unruly mound.

Barely a quarter of a mile away, atop the bluff that overlooked the village, Mr. Morgan sat tall on his chestnut horse. He was a proud, stiff man, with the long face of a wolfhound. Dressed in black hat, flaming red jacket, and jack boots, carrying a whip in hand, he looked like a general surveying the site of a coming battle.

He was surrounded, on foot, by four constables and twelve soldiers. In the slanting rays of the dawning sun, the soldiers' muskets and bayonets sparkled. Each constable held a ladder. All were ready to charge on Kilonny. Mr. Morgan restrained them.

"Patience, boys, patience," he cautioned. "Show some remorse for the poor sods. The beggars are losing their homes."

It was not long before the thirty men, women, and children of the village, few dressed in anything more than rags and with bare feet like the O'Connells, completed the removal of their goods. Once that was done, they grouped themselves about Father Mahoney by the side of the road, their faces turned toward the man in scarlet.

"All right, boys," Mr. Morgan said softly, "they're ready. Don't be pushing too hard. They're agitated and might even be spoiling for a fight. The smoother, the better, and all in all the less price to pay."

The agent touched his heels to his horse. Saddle leather creaked. The mare, her nostrils blowing a mist of warm air that made her seem like a smoke-breathing dragon, cantered smartly down the slope. The constables and soldiers trotted by her flanks.

"Good morning!" Mr. Morgan cried cheerily as he approached the villagers and saluted them by lifting his beaver hat high. "A very good morning to you all!"

The crowd around Father Mahoney stared at the agent with sullen hatred.

Mr. Morgan settled his hat on his head and returned their hard looks with deliberate congeniality. "I bring you heartfelt greetings from Lord Kirkle himself, whose land agent, as you know, I am. He has begged me—out of his graciousness—to make known that it grieves him greatly to tumble these sometime homes of yours. But these are troubled days. All must make sacrifices. Rich and poor suffer alike. These dwellings that you have rented must be returned to his lordship if he's to reclaim the land for increased productivity in the interests of greater good. You may trust in his superior judgment that it's best for all.

"Notwithstanding, his lordship deeply regrets your current inconvenience and begs, as a token of his deep esteem, that each of you will accept two shillings as traveling money for your pains."

There was some nervous shifting among the villagers, but most simply stared at the agent.

"Come, come!" the man urged, his voice turning to a sneer. "I can offer the gift but once. Willy-nilly, we'll be tumbling these dwellings, so don't be standing on false pride, now. Here's your good queen's fair coin. You'll be needing it."

Still, no one stirred.

"You there, Father Mahoney."

"Your Honor."

"You should be teaching your people submission and the acceptance of charity. Charity is no sin. But surely pride is. I suppose even a papist knows that," he added sarcastically.

The priest, struggling to control his anger, replied, "Your Honor, these people have no place to go."

"Now, now, my good man. It's general news that Mrs. O'Connell has a husband who went out to America and has become rich. Hasn't he sent them money to go?"

"They are the only ones," Father Mahoney said.

"Ah, with hope, Father, it's only a start. One goes and gets rich and sends a remittance. Now three shall go and gain greater riches yet. No doubt the four will send money enough until all of Kilonny settles in America. It's the promised land, they say."

"Mr. Morgan," the priest cried, "you are cruel to speak so."

The agent tapped his hat down so it sat more securely.

"None of that, Father!" he cried. "None of that. You're edging close to insurrection! Orders are orders, money is money, and the law proclaims it so.

"Now then," he pressed, "who'll take Lord Kirkle's generous gift? All right then, a double gift to the first one who steps forward. *Four shillings!* Four shillings now! Come along, pride goes before the fall!"

He held up his hand to show the shining coins.

A grizzled old man, cloth cap in hand, hobbled out from the stony-faced crowd and moved toward Mr. Morgan. The agent saluted him. "Well done, Mr. Foggerty!" he cried. "Well done! Here's your four shillings, and welcome to them you are." He leaned down from his saddle and dropped the shillings into the shaking uplifted hand. For Maura, the chink of each coin was like a church bell tolling a death.

Old man Foggerty folded his crumpled fingers over the coins, replaced his cap, and, without a backward look, set off down the dirt road.

"No one else?" Mr. Morgan called. "Last chance."

A woman came forward. She also took the coins. Then slowly but surely the rest followed until they were standing as a group behind Mr. Morgan. Only the O'Connells were left.

Patrick, who had been staring at the ground in a torment of frustration over the money, glanced up at Maura. Thinking her gaze was elsewhere, he took a step forward, only to have her reach out and pull him back.

"No!" she hissed under her breath. "It's Judas money."

"But we need it!" Patrick said.

"No!"

"All right then," Mr. Morgan cried. "Constables!" He pointed to the O'Connells' hut. "In America, I'm told, they live in grand places. So I'll venture to say the proud O'Connells will have no more need for that. We'll start there."

While the soldiers stood on guard, muskets across their

chests, the constables darted forward and set their ladders against the walls of the hut. In a trice they scrambled up and began pulling away the old thatch and tossing it on the ground as if it were so many handfuls of weeds.

The crowd, looking on, uttered a moan, as if witnessing an execution in which death had come at last.

The sight was too much for Patrick. He ran to the side of the road, picked up a stone, and hurled it at Mr. Morgan. The agent, astride his horse, was keeping one eye on the crowd, one eye on the tumbling. The stone struck him on the arm. Red-faced, he spun his horse about.

"Arrest that boy!" he shouted, pointing right at Patrick with his whip. "Arrest him!" Two of the soldiers turned toward Patrick. The boy tore down the road.

Father Mahoney lifted his hand in horror. "Kneel!" he cried. When the villagers did as he urged, he began to pray.

"Mother, come!" Maura said. "We must leave!"

The deeply shocked woman staggered to her feet. Patrick was far along the road. Maura and Mrs. O'Connell hurried after him but could not keep themselves from twisting back to see if any soldiers were following.

Mr. Morgan spurred his horse upon the road. The two soldiers ran by his side. The agent barked an order. The soldiers halted; then each kneeled on one knee and aimed his musket.

A horrified Maura and Mrs. O'Connell froze. "Jesus protect us!" the woman cried, her hand to her mouth in terror. "They're shooting!"

The soldiers fired. The bullets sped harmlessly by.

Maura, gasping for air, realized they had been aiming over their heads. And indeed, when they lowered their muskets, they laughed and turned away. Mr. Morgan, however, galloped down the road to where Maura and her mother still trembled.

He reined in and shook a clenched fist at them.

"Begone with you!" he cried in rage. "And if you are not out of this country in two days, I'll have that boy arrested and transported!"

"But, Your Honor," Maura cried, "our ship does not leave till then."

"Two days!" Mr. Morgan replied. "Two days! I'll be coming to look for you!" So saying, he whirled about and rode back to the tumbling.

"Don't look again," Maura said to her mother. "Our home is gone. We must hurry!" They scrambled along the road toward Patrick.

Annie O'Connell did look back. And Maura did too. Thus it was that they saw the walls of their hut, with very little effort, come thudding down.

Furious at Patrick and angry at herself for watching the tumbling, Maura touched her dress where all their money and the tickets Father Mahoney had purchased were pinned for security. With a resolution stiffened by rage, she turned from Kilonny and stared down the road as if America itself were just beyond the horizon.

Chapter 6
On the Road to Cork

*M*other and daughter were breathless when they caught up with Patrick beyond the first hill.

"And now what do you intend, Patrick O'Connell?" his sister demanded. "Mr. Morgan says he'll arrest you if you're not out of Ireland in two days."

"I had to do something," Patrick said with indignation. "That Mr. Morgan has no heart."

"It's not a heart he'll be using if he intends to arrest you."

"The man's a coward, Maura," Patrick insisted. "You'll see. He'll never come!"

"But think of what you've done," Maura went on. "We're *all* at risk. Look at Mother."

An exhausted Mrs. O'Connell sat by the side of the road, fingering her beads. Now and again she coughed. Tears ran down her sallow cheeks. Her bleak eyes were staring back toward Kilonny.

Struck with remorse, Patrick swallowed hard. "I'm sorry," he murmured. "I didn't think."

"Faith then," Maura snapped, "if we're ever going to reach America, you'd best begin to. You'd also better be praying that Mr. Morgan has no time to be chasing after the likes of you."

"I'm only a boy," Patrick pointed out. "What would he get by chasing me?"

"What does he ever gain by his general meanness?" Maura replied hotly. "It's what the English are. High and mighty, all of them. We've nothing in common. Oh, Mother of God," she said in weary exasperation, "let's be finished with it. It's over and done. We need to be going."

Patrick held out his hand to his mother, and following her halting steps, they started slowly down the hill. Maura carried one bundle, Patrick the other.

The morning mists were melting, but cold gray skies remained. Though it was only twenty-five miles from Kilonny to Cork, none of the O'Connells had ever made the journey. The dirt road they followed, crooked as a lazy snake, was full of ruts and holes. Stones were sharp on Maura's and Patrick's feet. The view was hilly, with fierce streams splashing through bottomlands past empty, often blighted fields. Only now and again did truly green fields appear, patches

20

of heaven on the hide of hell. Once, twice, Maura saw a sheep, each bleating as if lost.

As they made their way, Patrick—hoping his sister wouldn't notice—kept stealing looks back for signs of Mr. Morgan. The farther they traveled—with no sign of the agent—the better he felt.

"Maura," he said after they had gone a fair bit, "where do you think the others will go?"

"That's their own business."

Patrick looked up at her. "Don't you care?"

Maura tossed her hair back. "I've but one head, and it's full of caring for us."

"How long will it be till we get to Cork then?" he wondered.

"We'll get there when we do," Maura snapped. Then, regretting her harsh tone, she added more softly, "It shouldn't be more than two days if we can keep a steady pace." She gave a knowing nod toward their mother.

For a long while they did not speak. Then Patrick said, "There, you see. Didn't I tell you Mr. Morgan wouldn't come."

"Well . . . God help us if he does."

Two hours of walking brought them to a T in the road. They halted. A white stone marker indicated Cork was to the left, eighteen miles away.

Since they had not eaten that day, Maura untied one of the bundles and pulled out a small sack. From it she scooped a handful of sour cooked cornmeal. She placed a small portion in her mother's hand and did the same for Patrick. A last bit she took for herself.

Patrick studied his helping. "It's not even fit for pigs," he said.

"There's no good complaining," Maura reminded him.

"Father Mahoney said our food must last till Cork. Once on the boat, they'll feed us. It's part of the ticket price."

Patrick ate reluctantly. "What kind of food do you think they eat in America?" he asked.

Maura held out some cornmeal. "They say this comes from there."

Patrick screwed up his face. He hated the dry, gritty texture of the meal. "Maura," he said, "is everyone in America rich?"

"I don't know."

Patrick grinned. "I intend to be rich. Can you guess what I'll have when I am?"

"No."

"Heaps of decent food. And a horse."

"And what, Patrick O'Connell, would a dirt-poor boy like you do with a horse?"

"I'd gallop past Mr. Morgan and clop off his hat!" Patrick said gleefully.

Maura snorted. "I'd leave that for others if I were you." The reminder of what had happened made her anxious. She stood up. "Are you ready, Mother?"

Mrs. O'Connell did not budge. "I have to rest awhile," she whispered. These were the first words she had spoken since leaving Kilonny.

Maura and Patrick exchanged looks. "Mother," Maura urged. "We can't stay here. We truly must hurry."

Mrs. O'Connell shook her head. "It would be better for me to die at home. The earth will know me there."

Patrick felt his stomach tighten.

"Mother," Maura said gently, "you know as well as I, there's nothing left."

She coughed. "Father Mahoney will be looking after things," she said. "He promised."

"Mr. Morgan will push him out too, Mother," Maura said.

She took her mother's arm and lifted her forcibly. "Besides, your husband is waiting."

At that Mrs. O'Connell allowed herself to be pulled up. The three started off along the bigger road.

They began to meet other travelers. Though most were walking, some rode carts being pulled by people. All were leaving Ireland. A few hoped to settle in England, others to find their way to Canada. Most, however, set their hopes on America.

"There's the place for work and food for all" was the reason always given.

Being with travelers like themselves raised the O'Connells' spirits. People gossiped about all they had been told of emigration: rules and regulations, what to do, what not to do. Some of it made sense to Patrick; some did not. It hardly seemed to matter. All that mattered was that they get there. When one of the cart haulers offered to let Mrs. O'Connell ride rather than walk, and she accepted, Maura's spirits soared. Everything seemed possible if they could only get to Cork. Mr. Morgan was forgotten.

All that day they trudged. As they walked, more and more people joined until they became almost a traveling village, some forty or more people. That night they slept by the side of the road.

"It's like a pilgrimage," Patrick said to Maura as he stared into the night sky.

"That's true," Maura agreed, trying to be hopeful, "and to the promised land."

Chapter 7
The City of Cork

*T*hey were up at dawn. But it was not until the middle of the afternoon that they reached the crest of a hill. From it they looked down into a valley. Before them was the river Lee and the ancient city of Cork. What they saw astonished them.

Cork lay upon a tear-shaped island surrounded by river. At the most eastern point of the island, a multitude of ships were moored. More were anchored beyond where the river widened as it flowed east. The travelers could just make out St. George's Channel and the sea, glimpsed along the eastern horizon.

But the city was their immediate concern. What they saw hardly seemed real. Squeezed close together were too many houses to be counted. Black smoke drifted up from hundreds of chimneys and mingled with the river mist. Piercing this dense air, church spires reached like fingers pointing toward a brighter place.

As the travelers gazed at the city in wonder, bells began to peal from the churches, clanging and banging. The noise brought bursts of birds pinwheeling up and around.

"Who would have thought that one place could keep so many people," Maura murmured.

Mrs. O'Connell shut her eyes against the vision and crossed herself.

Patrick, gazing openmouthed at the scene, hardly dared to breathe.

The travelers—awed into silence—started down the hill, crossed the river over the arching wood and stone of North Gate Bridge, and entered Cork with trepidation. Everyone felt woefully out of place. Hundreds of signs, bills, placards, notices assaulted their eyes. Buildings towered over their heads and seemed likely to topple at any moment. The sheer number of people on the muddy streets was daunting. Stores, stalls, and carts were crowded with goods. The O'Connells were wonder-struck by the quantity of food. Where did it come from? Patrick's mouth watered. How he wished he'd taken Mr. Morgan's money!

The three stayed as close together as they could. Amazed by all they saw, they kept reaching out to touch one another lest they be pulled apart.

"Look there!" Maura cried with excitement.

Mrs. O'Connell and Patrick stopped to look where she was pointing. It was a poster on a wall. Bold black letters blazoned:

CORK AND LIVERPOOL STEAM PACKET COMPANY
DIRECT TO LIVERPOOL

On the poster was a picture of a ship at sea, its smokestack pouring forth a black cloud, side wheels clearly churning. Below were smaller pictures of other boats next to times for departure. At the bottom of the bill, in the biggest letters of all, it read:

10 SHILLINGS ONLY!!!

"Are we to go on one of *those?*" Patrick asked.

Maura, after first looking about to make sure she was not

watched, reached into her dress and removed the pins that held the packet containing their money and tickets. Sorting through the papers, she tried to find the right tickets.

"Aye," she said nervously, a finger resting on one line of the poster. "The *Queen of the West*," she read. "Six hundred and thirty-six tons. Three hundred and fifty deck passengers. That's the very one," she said, thankful Father Mahoney had taught her how to read.

Mrs. O'Connell turned her eyes toward the steady flow of people passing. "Are they all going?" she asked in wonderment.

"I think so," Maura said.

"There will be no one left in Ireland," her mother whispered sadly.

Patrick said, "Hadn't we better find the boat?"

But Maura had no idea where to turn. The streets of Cork were so close, the buildings so tall—Patrick counted some of five stories—it was impossible to see any distance. Maura worried that if the other two knew how tense and confused she felt, they'd abandon their journey in an instant. She led them blindly. Suddenly Patrick halted. "Look!" he cried, pointing ahead along the street.

It was Mr. Morgan, and he was moving in their direction. With him were two armed soldiers.

"Merciful God, help us now!" Maura exclaimed. Pulling their mother along, they dived into a narrow side alley and ran its length. Mrs. O'Connell coughed and gasped for breath. The alley emptied out upon a large avenue on which a crowd of emigrants was milling with their bundles, boxes, and wagons full of possessions. Maura, hoping they would not be noticed among them, led her brother and mother into their midst. She was afraid to look at her mother. Instead, she glanced at Patrick. He was grim, white-faced.

As the crowd pressed forward, Maura began to wonder if

anyone knew where he was going. Then they turned a corner. The river—some two hundred yards wide here—was before them again. To the right were many ships tied to the quay. Some had funnels smoking like the ships on the poster. The quay itself was piled high with barrels and crates. Cattle and horses were also there, milling about. Above, gulls swooped and squawked as if scolding people for their confusion.

"Do you see Mr. Morgan anywhere?" Maura asked.

"Not a sign," a thoroughly chastened Patrick replied.

Maura searched desperately right and left. To buoy their spirits she kept saying, "This way," and continued to move with the crowd along Merchant Quay.

It was Patrick who sang out, "Look over there!" Across the river a wooden sign had been erected. It bore the name they were looking for:

CORK AND LIVERPOOL STEAM PACKET COMPANY

"Blessed Saint Anthony," Maura cried in relief. "That's where our ship should be."

They hurried back across the river, over the same bridge they had traveled before, then moved on to St. Patrick's Quay.

Sitting behind a small table beneath the sign was a burly, ill-shaven man dressed in the wrinkled uniform of a ship's low-ranked officer. His cap was perched high on his bald head. An unlit cigar dangled from his mouth. On the table before him lay a ledger and a pocket watch. A long line of raggedly dressed people filed past him, each showing him a paper ticket. Sighing with boredom, the man scrutinized the tickets, dipped the nib of his steel pen into a bottle of red ink, ticked off a number in his ledger book, then waved the people past, apparently happy to be rid of them. Every now

27

and again he turned, spit into the water, consulted his watch, and bellowed. "*Queen of the West* leaving for Liverpool in one hour."

The *Queen of the West*—a little farther along the quay—was some two hundred feet in length. She was flat decked but for her midships twin funnels from which black smoke drifted idly. There were two auxiliary masts with reefed sails. Great paddle wheels in cowlings rose on either side of the ship. They would drive her forward. On the cowling of the port-side wheel, a small deck was mounted. From this place the captain or first mate would give his commands.

After waving along another group of passengers, the ship's officer cried: "*Queen of the West* leaving for Liverpool in fifty-five minutes."

"When we're on board, Maura," Patrick asked, "will Mr. Morgan be able to get us?"

"Let's pray not," Maura told him as she readied their tickets. Once she had them in hand, they started forward. Halfway there Mrs. O'Connell halted.

"What's the matter?" Maura asked.

"I need more time," their mother replied.

"More time for what?"

"To think of what I'm doing."

"But Mr. Morgan—," Patrick began.

Mrs. O'Connell shook her head. "By the Holy Mother, I can't go on just yet," she said, and slumped to the ground.

Reluctantly, Maura put the tickets away and led them across the street from the quay.

Patrick, unable to suppress his agitation, stood on guard, searching the street in both directions. He noticed, almost over their heads, a huge sculpture atop a large stone building. It portrayed a man in ancient costume. He was slaying a dragon with a spear.

"Maura, look up," he urged, and pointed.

"It's blessed Saint George," Maura whispered, her eyes wide.

"The dragon looks alive!" Patrick said in awe. He fancied the idea that he was the one with the spear. "And, sure," he said, "doesn't the dragon look like Mr. Morgan himself?"

"Well, it's not," Maura scolded, and turned him around. "It's this way you should be minding, Patrick O'Connell. Haven't we got some real dragons to be dealing with?"

Patrick stole another glance at the sculpture and shook his head.

The man at the table called, "*Queen of the West* leaving for Liverpool in forty minutes."

"Shouldn't we be getting on?" Patrick asked. "We're like to be left off if we don't."

Maura did not respond. She had thought she felt sure of what they were about to do. Now that the ship was right before them, wanting only to be boarded, hard truth took hold. She was swept with grief and uncertainty.

Should they go? The voyage would be dangerous. America was unknown. They were cutting themselves off from all they knew, both bad and good. Then she reminded herself that Da had done it and had called upon them to follow. And here was Mr. Morgan looking for them, wanting, no doubt, to arrest Patrick. They had to leave Ireland.

Using every bit of will to suppress her turbulent thoughts and feelings, Maura bent over her mother. "Mother, are you ready now?"

Mrs. O'Connell, saying her beads, shook her head and coughed. She was weeping.

Maura stroked her mother's hair and in so doing tried to soothe herself.

"Don't you think we should be getting on now?" Patrick asked.

"*Queen of the West* leaving for Liverpool in thirty minutes."

"Maura, if we wait too long, we won't be able to board,"

the boy worried. He could not believe the numbers of people clambering onto the boat.

"As soon as Mother is ready."

Mrs. O'Connell, who had hardly spoken that morning, suddenly said, "I'll not be going."

A spasm of fear stabbed Maura. Patrick stared at his mother, the boat forgotten.

"Now, Mother," Maura said, trying to make light of what she'd heard, "you'll wear my heart down to a pip with all your nay-saying. Am I to push you every inch of the way?"

"I'll not be going," the woman said again, her voice firmer.

"*Queen of the West* leaving for Liverpool in twenty minutes."

"But we have to!" Patrick cried. "We can't stay here."

"It's you and Maura who will go," Annie O'Connell said. "I'll go back to Kilonny, and there I'll stay."

"Oh, Mother," Maura cried in exasperation. "You know as well as anyone, there's no Kilonny to go back to!"

Mrs. O'Connell stood up. The look on her face was of grief and exhaustion. Maura recognized it as the same as when her brother Timothy died.

"But what about us? And Da?" Maura asked, feeling full of tears.

"You'll ask my husband to forgive me. I cannot do it. God grant him power to understand."

Patrick, clutching his bundle, looked anxiously from his mother to Maura. "But, Mother, you have to! We can't go without you!"

"*Queen of the West* leaving for Liverpool in fifteen minutes."

"Go, and Jesus bless you both," Mrs. O'Connell said, gazing at each of her children, touching their stunned faces with the palm of her hard hand. Abruptly, she turned away and set off with an urgency and energy she had not shown in weeks.

Maura ran forward and grabbed one of her mother's arms. "Mother, you can't do this!"

"Let me be!" Mrs. O'Connell cried as she pulled away with a strength that caught Maura off guard. "I'm telling you to go."

"*Queen of the West* leaving for Liverpool in ten minutes."

"Mother!" Patrick choked, tears starting. "You have to come. You have to! You do!"

But Mrs. O'Connell was running, her black shawl fluttering behind like the broken wings of a frightened bird.

The boat whistle let forth an ear-piercing screech. "*Queen of the West* leaving for Liverpool in five minutes."

Maura turned back from the sight of her retreating mother to where Patrick stood. "*Mother!*" the boy screamed. "*Mother!*"

Maura made her decision. She rushed to her brother's side, scooped up the other bundle, and all but dragged him—weeping, straining to see back over his shoulder—to the man at the table. He was already standing, stuffing his watch into a pocket. Maura and Patrick were the last ones.

Fumbling frantically, she tore the tickets from her dress and offered the crumbled wad to the man. With a grunt of disgust he sorted through them, plucked out two tickets, and flung the other papers back at Maura.

"Move yerselves!" he ordered.

Still pulling at Patrick, Maura lunged for the boat and ran up the steep ramp. Even as they stepped on deck, the gangway was yanked free with a rattle of chains. The boat whistle shrieked. Black smoke surged from the funnels. The two great side wheels began to turn while overhead gulls screamed hideously.

Patrick, wrenching free from his sister, broke through the crowd, shoving and pushing until he reached the outer rail. "Mother!" he screamed again. "Mother!"

Mrs. O'Connell was nowhere in sight. And the *Queen of the West* was sliding down the river Lee.

31

Chapter 8
Ireland Left Behind

G ulls coasted and turned, now and again screeching out their mock good-byes. The passengers who filled the entire deck of the *Queen of the West* stared silently at the passing countryside. Some were in tears. Others prayed. No one laughed or sang.

Patrick and Maura hunched down together. They looked at nothing, not at the passing shore, not at the people about them. It was hard to distinguish their own heartbeats from the monotonous pounding of the ship's engines, which shook every timber of the boat relentlessly.

"Maura?" Patrick said finally.

"What's that?"

"What will happen to Mother?"

Maura looked at him sadly. "I don't know."

"And what will we be telling Da?"

"Just as she asked us to."

"Maura?" Patrick repeated.

She looked around to see tears coursing down his cheeks. "I'm wondering if we'll ever see her again."

"Faith then, I can't read the future," she replied.

Patrick pressed his face into Maura's lap. For a while he remained motionless. Only when the boat began to pitch and yaw did he sit up. He gazed out over the boat's side. "We're coming out upon the sea," he said in awe.

Maura looked for herself. Patrick was right. The sea was before them. As one, both turned to gaze at the retreating land. Trees and houses could still be distinguished, but soon they melded into a low mass of green. Then the green itself disappeared. Nothing remained but the sea, with whitecaps rising and rolling for as far as they could see. Ireland was gone.

Patrick turned and surveyed the crowded deck. People were so packed together there was hardly any room to sit. There seemed to be as many old people as young ones, more men than women. Their clothing was as tattered as his own. Many clung to boxes and bundles, as they did. Everybody looked scared. Patrick recalled the placard in Cork, listing the *Queen of the West* as carrying three hundred and fifty passengers. Surely, there were more.

He turned to his sister. "How long before Liverpool?"

"I don't know," she answered. "Father Mahoney said it depended on the weather."

Patrick scanned the sky. It was the same gray color as the sea, broken only by the black smoke that trailed from the funnels. "If it gets bad, will we be able to find a place below?" he asked.

"I suppose," Maura replied without much thought.

"Maura?"

She looked around at him.

"Are you all right?" he asked.

Instead of answering, she reached out and pulled him close. "Oh, Patrick," she said, her voice trembling, "I'll be needing your help as much as you'll be needing mine."

"I'll try," Patrick told her, flattered that his sister would acknowledge her need of him.

The moment passed. Maura recovered her composure. She eased her brother away.

"Do you think they'll be giving us food soon?" he asked.

"Sure, I couldn't say. Why don't you go and find out? I'll stay right here."

Patrick braced himself against the roll of the ship and then moved off.

Maura watched him go. "Jesus, Mary, and Joseph," she whispered. "Thee are three. We are two. Protect us."

As Patrick made his way through the crowded deck, the constant shifting movement of the *Queen of the West* made him feel queasy. He tried to keep his eyes on people. One or two of them he recognized from the road. These he greeted like old friends.

He found a boy about his own age, sitting forlornly on top of a large bundle. The two eyed each other with suspicion.

"Good evening to you," Patrick said.

"Good evening to you," the boy responded.

"Are you going to America?" Patrick asked.

"Canada."

"And where would that be?" Patrick asked.

The boy shrugged. "Across the ocean. I've an uncle who's there. He wrote and said a man can have as much land as he wants. No end to it, and all of it free."

Patrick nodded. "My father's been for less than a year, but he's already rich. He sent us money to come."

The boy considered Patrick solemnly. "Aye, they say it's not so hard."

Patrick looked out over the water for a moment at one huge side wheel lifting and flinging down buckets of white foam. Then he asked, "Do you know when they'll be offering the food?"

The boy shook his head. "There won't be any."

"What do you mean?" Patrick asked, alarmed.

"The only thing you get for your ten shillings is passage to Liverpool. No food. It's what my da told me. It's the boat to America that feeds you."

Patrick felt his stomach growl. "Are you sure?"

"It's true," the boy insisted.

Refusing to believe such a thing, Patrick worked his way forward again. He saw a sailor coiling and securing some rope. Near him on the deck lay a piece of bread and cheese that, from time to time, he picked up and bit into. Hungrily, Patrick approached him.

After standing unnoticed for some minutes, he said, "Please, Your Honor, will there be any food for us?"

The sailor neither stopped his work nor looked up. "Food!" he spit out with indignation. "Do you think you've boarded an inn, Paddy? We're just a channel crosser. Get off with you!"

Patrick stood his ground. "What about water?"

"Help yerself," the sailor said. "It's all around." Laughing, he turned his back. The moment he did, Patrick leaned forward, snatched up the bread and cheese, and flung both into the sea. Then he ran off before the sailor noticed.

"There'll be no food," Patrick informed Maura when he returned. "They don't give any at all."

Maura blanched. "Are you sure?"

"Two people told me so, and one of them a sailor. There's not even water."

"Then we'll have to make do with what remains of the cornmeal we brought." She made a motion toward their bundles.

Patrick restrained her. "I'll wait," he said with a shake of his head, "for Liverpool."

"You'll be waiting hours."

"I'm willing." He dropped down beside her. Gradually, his eyes dimmed and he fell asleep, his head rolling with the motion of the ship. Maura turned him gently to rest in her lap.

After some hours, the ship's pitching movement grew violent. Over and again, it rose high on a wave only to drop down sickeningly as though into a pit. Seawater spray show-

35

ered everyone. The first time it happened, there was a startled shriek from many. The second time, the cries ceased, replaced by moans. People became ill. The boat began to stink of it.

The air grew colder, the sky darker. Maura drew her shawl tighter. And then it began to rain, slowly at first, a mist indistinguishable from ocean spray. When the storm strengthened, people began to stir, struggling toward the steps that they presumed would lead them to protected areas below decks. The sailors refused to let them pass.

The crowd objected angrily. The sailors, in turn, grew hostile. "You're to stay on the top deck," they insisted, and hefted belaying pins to show they meant it. "There's no room below. No room below!"

The passengers retreated, huddling together like sheep for protection.

As the wind rose, sailors appeared with tarpaulins, sheets of old canvas sail coated with tar to make them waterproof. "Get under these," they barked as they flung the tarpaulins out.

People spread them quickly and, though already wet, crept beneath them. Heavy, ill-smelling, the sails were too small to cover everyone. Even those who managed to find shelter, like Patrick and Maura, were barely protected. It was difficult to breathe. The stench was loathsome.

Cold rain and seawater lashed the deck, soaking even those under the tarpaulins. Maura and Patrick clung to each other, engulfed by groans and the murmurs of piteous prayer.

When Patrick began to shiver violently, Maura twisted onto her knees and grabbed his hand. "Come with me," she cried above the wind.

Groping their way in the darkness, they crawled over others to get out from under the tarpaulin. The moment they emerged, Maura regretted her decision. Bad as it had been beneath the tarpaulin, the open deck was worse. Windswept rain beat fiercely upon the open deck, making it slippery under their bare feet. The only light came from a few lanterns swinging wildly as the boat heaved and tossed. Many people had found no protection from the wet. The first mate, steering the ship from atop one paddle wheel, was as drenched as any of them.

Maura retreated to the tarpaulin, plucking at the edge to lift it. Stronger hands pulled the same edge down, refusing to let them crawl back under.

"This way then," she called in desperation. Finding Patrick's hand again, she worked her way across the deck in search of stairs leading below. She found them only to discover they were covered over by a grilled hatch, and the hatch was lashed down. No matter how she pulled at it, it would not open. Desperate, she lay flat and peered through the hatch holes in hopes of seeing someone whom she might call for help. What she saw, and smelled, was cattle. They were being protected. Not the people.

Furious, Maura scrambled up and, with Patrick in tow, made her way to the ship's bulwark. She pushed her brother against it, then huddled down in front of him, to protect him as best she could. His teeth were chattering. The sound beat relentlessly upon her heart.

The storm lasted three hours. All through it Maura and Patrick endured the open deck. When the harsh weather passed, the sky cleared and they saw the moon. But soon it vanished, and only the cold, damp dark remained. Still the great side wheels churned, throbbing monotonously as the ship plowed over the sea.

Patrick slept poorly. Maura, blue with cold, her feet numb, merely dozed. "Liverpool," she chanted to herself, as if it were a prayer. "May Liverpool come soon."

Chapter 9
In London, England

*B*ut, sir," the boy pleaded, "you have no reason to whip me!"

Dressed in a black cutaway dinner jacket, bleached white cravat, and polished leather shoes, Sir Laurence Kirkle looked like a miniature adult. It was his voice—piping, almost babyish—that revealed him to be but eleven. With sandy-colored hair, rosy cheeks, and bright eyes, he seemed to be in bloom. At that moment, however, he was swallowing chest-heaving sobs, his eyes were filling with tears, and his fingers were twitching with agitation. For he was standing before his father, the Right Honorable Lord Kirkle of Her Majesty, Queen Victoria's Treasury Bench. And in his lordship's hands was the long, thin wooden cane he used to thrash his sons.

A florid fat man of some sixty years, Lord Kirkle had carefully trimmed gray whiskers and pronounced lines of age that splayed, fanlike, from the corners of red, watery eyes. The clothing he wore was similar in cut to his son's, though he had a silken waistcoat over which a golden watch and chain glistened.

"Laurence," his lordship said, his deep voice trembling with emotion, "the choice is entirely yours. You either do what you have been told or you'll receive punishment." He held up the cane to prove he was in earnest.

"But it's not fair!" Laurence cried. "He's only trying to make you angry at me." He glanced at the third Kirkle in the room, his brother, Albert.

38

Albert was fifteen years old, and on his way to duplicating his father's stocky figure. He too was in formal clothes, though he seemed to strain against them with thick shoulders, dangling wrists, and constantly fidgeting hands. He was slouched against the marble mantel, now and again nervously cracking the knuckles of one hand with the other. On his lips was an ill-concealed smirk.

"Laurence," Lord Kirkle continued, "it is the custom of our nation, as it is the custom of the Kirkle family, that the first son"—he nodded toward Albert—"stands second only to the father. Albert shall carry our name forward as the future Lord Kirkle. Why must I remind you of that yet again?" There was weariness in his voice.

"You needn't, sir," Laurence replied sullenly. "I understand."

"Since he is my *elder* son," Lord Kirkle continued, "and you are the *younger*, he *may* make demands of you. It is your duty to oblige him. It will be so for the rest of your life."

"I'll never take orders from him," Laurence cried, noting his brother's mocking look.

"And I say you shall," Lord Kirkle insisted.

"I'd run away first," Laurence threw back in rage.

"Oh, stop this nonsense!" his lordship roared.

Laurence, unable to withstand his father's fierce gaze, cast his eyes about the study. It was a large ornate room, bursting with bulky furniture and, at the moment, very warm. Beneath an elaborately framed mirror, the coal in the marble fireplace glowed. Wall sconces blazed with wax candles, for the afternoon was dark. Heavy green velvet curtains graced the tall windows. On two walls, bookcases were filled with leather-bound, gilt-edged tomes. Thick rugs lay upon the floor. A huge table, which his father used as a desk, stood at one end of the room, from which could easily be read the Kirkle family motto chiseled below the mantel. Glumly, Laurence read it now:

On the wall hung portraits of the former Lord Kirkles from 1605 to the present day, 1851. Each was ruffed, wigged, or bearded in the fashion of the day. To Laurence, they all seemed to be glaring at him wrathfully.

With a sigh of exasperation, Lord Kirkle hooked thick thumbs into vest pockets, setting the gold chain to jangling. Turning to his elder son, he said, "Do *you* have anything to say?"

"My lord," Albert began, trying to force his voice into a lower register even as he rubbed his red blotched face, "all I asked him to do was blacken my boots."

"That's what the Irish servants do!" Laurence interrupted fiercely. "He only wants to mock me. To hold me down. It's not *fair!*"

"Fairness is not the issue here!" his father thundered. "We are considering privilege. It is not *your* privilege to determine what is right or wrong. Your elder brother, Albert, has the right to demand of you whatsoever pleases him."

"Sir," Albert interjected, "may I say something?"

Lord Kirkle scowled. "You may," he said.

"My lord, I didn't want to go into the details of this business with you. I was hoping, sir, it would stay a matter between my brother and me. I know you hate bickering."

"I do, sir."

"But since Laurence had the cheek to appeal to you, I think I should tell you the particulars of his crimes."

Laurence looked at his elder brother with astonishment.

"Continue," Lord Kirkle told Albert.

The young man stepped away from the mantel, turned to glare at his brother, then shifted around to look at his father. "Sir, I know the task I set for Laurence was low. I only did it to give him a taste of punishment. You see, my lord, though I told him not to enter my room, I discovered him there, snooping. The thing is, sir, I caught him taking a pen from my desk. Without permission. He was stealing, sir."

Stunned, Laurence reacted with fury. "Liar!" he cried.

"Let your brother speak," his father barked.

"But I never—"

"Silence!"

"I was thinking, sir," Albert continued—he kept glancing toward Laurence and smirking—"that if he *begins* by stealing my pen, my dear mother's gift, he might go on and do a lot worse if I didn't punish him. I was just trying to bring him to an understanding of right from wrong.

"I'm telling you this because Laurence is not merely a liar, sir. He's a scoundrel. And a thief. He *should* be punished."

Lord Kirkle glowered reproachfully at Laurence.

"None of it is true," Laurence insisted in a squeaky whisper. "None of it. You know how he hates me."

"Are you implying," Lord Kirkle rumbled, "that your elder brother has been untruthful?"

"*He's* making it all up, sir," Laurence cried hotly. "He is! You know he is! He's jealous of me."

"Jealous!" Albert roared. "What's there for me to be jealous of?"

"Because," Laurence shouted, "our father cares more for me than he does you!"

Red-faced, Albert stepped forward. "You're not just a thieving liar," he snarled, "you're a disgrace to the family! You ought to be kicked out of this house!"

In a rage Laurence flung himself at his brother and began to beat on him with his fists. Under the assault, Albert fell back.

"Laurence!" Lord Kirkle cried. Striding forward, he snatched at Laurence's collar, yanking the boy back with such force that he staggered, twisted around, became entangled in his own feet, and crashed to the ground.

The next moment Lord Kirkle was standing over him. "Face me!" he bellowed.

A terrified Laurence looked up.

"I will not have you attacking your brother!" their father said.

"But, sir, I—"

"You shall thank your brother on your knees for informing me of your wickedness."

Laurence, weeping copiously, sputtered, "I won't! *He's* the liar. He is!"

Lord Kirkle stiffened with anger. "Albert!" he thundered, thrusting the cane into the young man's hand. "You may strike your ungrateful brother four times."

Chapter 10
Albert's Response

I'm not ungrateful!" Laurence sobbed hysterically. "I'm not!"

Without a moment's hesitation, Albert lashed down with all his strength. The cane struck Laurence on the cheek, causing an instant bloody red welt.

With a shriek of pain, the boy covered his face and attempted to run for the door. Albert was too quick. Blocking his way, he struck again and again, forcing Laurence up against his father's massive table. With every cut, Laurence clutched his head, his arms, his chest with convulsive jerks and twists. "Please!" he cried. "Stop!"

"Enough!" Lord Kirkle shouted, finally restraining his elder son. "Enough, I say!"

Panting with exertion, Albert let himself be pulled away. In his hand, the cane twitched like an angry cat's tail.

Crying bitterly, Laurence lay in a crumpled heap. A red welt, from his right ear to his chin, oozing blood, disfigured the side of his face. His jacket was cut in many places. A sleeve had been ripped.

Lord Kirkle and Albert looked down at the miserable boy. Neither spoke. At last their father said, "Albert, you may leave the room."

"If I—"

"Albert! Go!"

"Yes, sir. But with your permission, sir, I'd like to keep the cane."

"You will *leave* it, sir!"

Albert started to protest but stopped when he saw how upset his father was. Instead of speaking, he flipped the cane at Laurence. It hit the boy and fell to the rug. With that, Albert bowed to his father and walked casually from the room, a smile fixed upon his face. Behind him, the massive door shut.

As soon as it did, Lord Kirkle pulled a silk handkerchief from his pocket and offered it to Laurence. The boy, kicking out furiously, scurried away, crablike.

With a sigh, his father turned to a window and looked out onto Belgrave Square, which the thickening fog was rapidly obscuring. His agitated hands clasped and unclasped. "Laurence," he said at last, "take your punishment like a man."

Laurence, whimpering, shook his head.

"You must learn to control your reckless temperament," his lordship said. "Albert is the elder. He stands before you. *Always.*"

43

Laurence, his crying slowed to an occasional sob, continued to shake his head.

"Besides," his lordship said soothingly, "it's all over now. Done."

"It's *not* done," Laurence muttered vengefully.

Lord Kirkle looked over his shoulder. "What am I to make of that?"

"I *will* run away."

"Oh, Laurence," his father responded with a burst of exasperation, "why must you talk such rubbish? It pains me to hear it."

"You let him give *me* pain!"

"It was necessary."

"I *will* run away!" Laurence shouted.

Lord Kirkle turned. "May I be so bold as to ask *where* you will run to?" His tone was softer, and a smile played upon his lips.

Laurence tried to recall the most distant place he'd heard of. India was the first that entered his mind. But that seemed too far, even for him. The name of another land sprang into his head. "America," he replied.

"Quite," Lord Kirkle snorted with sarcasm as he went back to the window. "The United States of America. Where no titled elder brother may lord it over you. Folly, my boy, but, to your credit, at least well-chosen folly."

Laurence, his body smarting with every move he made, stood up. "Albert did lie," he said.

At first Lord Kirkle made no reply. Then, very mildly, he said, "Why should he do that?"

"Because he knows you despise him. That you only defend him because he's the elder."

Lord Kirkle's fat fingers thrummed his waistcoat. But he remained silent.

"You always take his side to make people think it's *not*

so," Laurence pressed. "But you're . . ." He faltered, afraid to say what he felt.

"I'm what?" Lord Kirkle demanded, facing Laurence now.

"You . . . are the liar!" the boy finally blurted out. "You are!"

Lord Kirkle scowled angrily but said nothing. Emboldened, Laurence glared back.

"Go to your room," his father said, waving a weary hand of dismissal.

"I *will* run away," Laurence repeated in taunting fashion. "I *will*! To America!"

"Laurence, my boy, it is exactly that kind of hotheaded talk that continually undermines you. Run away! I shall not mention any of this to your mother. It's . . . balderdash!"

"I'm telling the truth!" Laurence screamed.

With a heavy step, Lord Kirkle moved toward the door of the room. At the threshold he paused. "Laurence," he said, "I try to do what's in our family's best interest. Unless, my boy, you accept your position, your life will be most unhappy."

"I will go!" Laurence shouted again.

"The only place you will go is to your room," his father replied firmly. "I will have your tea sent there." So saying, his lordship stepped out of the room.

Chapter 11
Laurence Alone

*F*or a moment, Laurence remained standing where his father had left him. Then he gave way all at once, weeping in earnest, covering his face with his hands to shield himself from the censorious eyes of his ancestors.

Fifteen minutes later the sobbing eased. Laurence smeared away the tears and, starting with the welt on his face, where his brother had first struck him, touched the raw wounds on his body.

He stared into the mirror. Not only did the red welt on his cheek look like it would last forever, but his hair was in disarray and his jacket was badly torn. His whole appearance was that of a street beggar, not the son of a wealthy lord, which he certainly was. "I hate Albert," Laurence said aloud.

He tried to take the jacket off, but it hurt so to twist about that he left it on. He did pull off his cravat—saw blood on it—and tossed it away with disgust.

Standing before the fire—the warmth soothed him—Laurence tried to think of ways of gaining revenge. No one else in the family would help him. As far as he could see, his mother *always* took Albert's side in disputes. The same went for his two sisters, three and five years older than he.

Laurence thought of what he'd said about running away. The idea was appealing. The whole family would be sorry and regret treating him so badly. If he reached America and if it were true—as his father said—that his brother could no longer bully him there, why, then . . . But, no, running away was impossible. He was doomed to a life of unfairness.

Suddenly very tired, Laurence sat in his father's chair behind the table. His feet barely touched the floor. Idly, he speculated as to how he might go to America. He had heard talk among the adults about the large numbers of people sailing there. They embarked—he recalled—from the city of Liverpool. He had only a vague sense as to where—or what—it was.

Regarding America, Laurence knew even less. He supposed it was rather like England, though different in ways he could not readily imagine. Something to do with a wild and rude people. He recalled someone saying that although

Americans had foolishly broken away from Great Britain, they did speak English. *Why* they broke away Laurence had no idea. Some quarrel. He wondered if it was like his quarrel with his brother. If so, perhaps the people in the United States would side with him. "It's so unfair! They *should*," he murmured.

While mulling over such random thoughts, Laurence stayed at the table, picking up papers, reading bits, putting them down. Most were business reports about lands his father owned throughout the kingdom, full of strange names like Dundee, Borking, Kilonny, Glasgow. All Laurence knew about these places was that his father never went to them. Agents looked after his interests. Sent him money. Lately though, his father had been grumbling about money. Things must have been rather bad for him to have spoken on the subject. Talk of money was considered grossly impolite.

Finding the papers uninteresting, Laurence put them aside and pulled open the table drawer. There lay a great stack of money in one-, twenty-, and one-hundred-pound notes.

Startled, Laurence stared at the bills. He touched them carefully, as if they were charged with sparks. Finally, he picked the bundle up and sorted it. Two thousand pounds!

Laurence wished he knew the worth of two thousand pounds. He had never handled money. On excursions, if he desired something—a toy, a book, food—servants always made the purchase for him. In all his eleven years, Laurence had never bought a thing.

A new idea filled him: Would this money in his hand be enough to take him to America? He had heard Cook say to one of his sister's upstairs maids that she earned twelve pounds a year. Whether that was a lot or a little, Laurence was not sure. Even so, it began to dawn upon him that if he really wanted to run away, here was the money to do it. Just the possibility brought a surge of excitement.

Laurence considered his reasons for going: He would *always* be beneath Albert. He would *always* be treated unfairly. He would *never* be believed. His father had not believed him when he'd said that he would run away—no more than he believed him when he spoke the truth about Albert.

"But if I did run away," Laurence reasoned, "Father would know I *had* spoken the truth about going. Surely then he would know I spoke the truth about Albert too!"

Laurence sat back in the large chair. Though he considered the idea from many viewpoints, what he found most appealing was the thought of his father admitting his error. Why, his lordship would *have* to come after him, *beg* him to come back before the whole family. In such a scene, Albert would be humbled while he, Laurence, would be triumphant at last.

It was the moment of returning that Laurence thought most about. How *wonderful* that would be! How much fun! Just thinking of it made him feel better.

He gazed at the money again. To take it, he told himself, would not *really* be stealing. After all, he had been accused of stealing when he'd not done so. Therefore, he reasoned, since *he* had been wronged, to take the money would not be wrong. Rather, it would enable him to run away, and the running away would prove he spoke the truth, that he was *not* a thief!

Laurence wondered how much he would need. Not all of it. *That* would be excessive. But perhaps half. . . .

With meticulous care, he divided the pound notes into two even piles. One he returned to the drawer. The second pile—of one thousand pounds—he stuffed into his jacket pocket.

Heart pounding, he went to the door of the room, opened

it, and peeked out. No one was in the hallway. He looked toward the gleaming mahogany front door. Not a soul stood between him and escape. Everyone was at tea. Once again he had been forgotten. They were ignoring him—*again*.

With a burst of determination, Laurence raced back into his father's study, picked the thrashing cane up from the floor, snapped it in two over his knee, flung it on the table, then ran out of the house.

Within moments, Sir Laurence Kirkle, aged eleven, was swallowed up by the fog-bound streets of London.

Chapter 12
Through London Fog

*L*aurence had no plan. Mindlessly, he ran down one street after another as if America were just a few blocks away. But though the boy had spent all of his life in London, he had never been on the streets alone. He had visited many places, from the Tower of London, where his ancestors had died, to the House of Lords, where his father sat whenever Parliament was in session. But always he had been with others: his nurse, his nanny, his brother, sisters, or parents. Now he was on his own.

What's more, the London fog into which he had fled was no sweet, soft mist but an eye-stinging murk, a yellow-black airborne stew of soot and ash. It turned the brightest street lamps into sickly glowworms. It hid one's hands from one's own eyes.

So it was that, thirty minutes after leaving his home, Laurence was lost—utterly.

Trying to catch his breath on a corner where the surrounding houses loomed like the shadows in a lantern show, Laurence made up his mind to find someone to tell him where he was. In that neighborhood of grand homes, however, the streets were all but deserted. Only a few people were brave enough to confront the January weather. These people, moreover, fairly flew by, their scarves, shawls, and hands over their mouths and noses as they tried to keep their lungs free of the rotten air.

"You there! Fellow!" Laurence called to an older gentleman who was moving by at a slower pace.

The old man stopped and peered at Laurence over half-spectacles. Through the veil of fog, he saw a boy with a torn jacket and a dirty, bloody face. Alarmed, he lifted his cane to defend himself. "Be off with you!" he cried, and scuttled away.

Laurence was shocked. Usually when he addressed people they paid elaborate attention to him. They'd stop, doff caps, bow or curtsy, and say, "Yes, Sir Laurence. How can we help you, Sir Laurence?" But when he approached two other passersby, they looked apprehensively at him and fled as well.

Bewildered that anyone should refuse his civil requests for help, Laurence wandered down one street, then another. At last he recognized what he took to be Lady Glencora's house. She was a friend of his mother's, and he had often visited her home.

He dashed up to the iron fence, clutched the bars, and tried to see in. "Hello!" he called. A snarling dog charged the fence and began to bark furiously. Laurence backed away in haste.

A carriage for hire burst out of the fog. Laurence sprang to the curb and tried to hail it by holding up a hand. He had seen his brother do so. But this driver, high in his seat, did not so much as glance in his direction. He whipped up his horses and clattered by, leaving Laurence spattered with mud and humiliation.

"Blockhead!" Laurence called after the carriage. "Dunce!" Though he tried to wipe himself clean, he did not accomplish much. And rubbing his right cheek caused him to cry out with pain.

Struggling to be brave, to think calmly, Laurence sat down on a curb beneath a street lamp. He chided himself for being so uncertain. Here he was, merely *starting* on his journey. But, oh, he wished he knew how far America was and how long it would take him to get there.

First, he had to find Liverpool—wherever that was. He was aware that many faraway places—even within England—were best reached by railroad, so he made up his mind to find a railway station.

Having a clear goal served to soothe him. Seeking further reassurance, he patted his jacket pocket, where he'd stashed his money. He took out the wad of bills and counted it carefully. One thousand pounds. He hoped it was enough.

After stuffing the bills back into safekeeping, Laurence looked up. A few feet away from him—like some ghost fashioned from the very fog itself—stood a man.

At first glance he appeared to be an old fellow, stooped with age, leaning on a makeshift crutch. An unkempt gray beard dangled from his chin. Over his rather broad shoulders was draped a tattered army greatcoat whose ragged hem hung to the tops of broken boots. The cap he wore, loose and ill fitting, was pulled so low it almost covered a patched eye. But the good eye—piercingly bright—was staring directly at Laurence.

"Yer there! Laddie!" the man called.

Not sure how to respond, Laurence ventured, "Were you addressing me?"

"I was," the man said. "And wot I'm wantin' to know is

this: Wot's all that ready clink yer got there!" With a hop
and step, his greatcoat flapping about him so he looked like
a crow with a lame leg, the man lurched forward.

Laurence sprang up and backed away.

The man leaned over his cane and leered wickedly.
"'Onest up, laddie," he sneered, "yer didn't prig that money
fair an' square, now did yer?"

Laurence noted that the man's lower lip was bruised and
puffy, as if he had been in a fight. And indeed, there was a
palpable air of violence about him.

"I—I—," the boy stammered. "I got it from my father."

"Did yer now? Well, then, *I'd* as soon be yer governor as
anyone. So, yer best 'and that money over to me." With a
sudden movement, he whipped up his crutch and flung it—
javelinlike—straight at Laurence's head.

Laurence saw the crutch coming just in time. He ducked,
whirled, and fled. Nor did he stop running until he had
passed ten streets. When finally he did look back—gasping
for breath—the old man with the eye patch appeared to
be gone. The fog, however, was too thick for Laurence to
be sure.

"Not fair . . . ," he murmured. "Not fair. . . ."

Ever more anxious, Laurence pressed on, hoping he would
recognize a building, a sign, anything that would tell him
where he was. Houses—those that he could see—were
smaller here. More people and carriages were passing on the
streets. No one, however, paid the slightest attention to him.
It was all very strange and shocking. He might have been
invisible.

The farther Laurence traveled, the more upset he became.
He veered from one confusing place to another more confusing. All the while he kept reminding himself that what he
needed was the railway station. But where to turn?

The fog was thickening. It slipped into every crack and

crevice until it seemed to swallow night itself. It grew colder too.

Sidewalks became narrow, clogged increasingly with stalls, stands, and people. Shops were forbidding in their busyness. Again and again Laurence had the sensation that buildings were about to fall on him. But when he darted past, they did not crash, only faded. People pressed in on him from all sides, stepping in and out of the fog like taunting imps. A few banged into him. Once, he was knocked to the ground. He cried out. No one bothered to help. No one bothered to care. In pain, Laurence picked himself up and sought refuge in a filthy alcove, where he stood and shivered.

A noise made him look up. Across the way—watching— was the patch-eyed lame man who had accosted him before. He had been following.

Laurence dived from his alcove and plunged into the crowd. He began to run, weaving frantically. A few blocks later, his side ached so severely he had to stop.

He had reached a crowded crossroad. The streets were jammed with a snarl of carriages, wagons, and carts pulled by snorting, prancing horses whose hooves clattered and banged on glistening cobblestones. The air was filled with the shouts and swearing of the men who drove the horses. The din was deafening.

Laurence glanced over his shoulder. The man with the crutch was there again. Terrified, Laurence raced across the street. He managed to avoid one wagon, then another, but almost ran into a third. The driver, trying to avoid him, swerved sharply only to lock wheels with a carriage. With an earsplitting crack, a wheel snapped in two. The wagon collapsed. From its bay, huge wooden barrels tumbled onto the street. One barrel smashed. The air filled with the stench of cider. Someone cheered. Another cursed. Three other barrels rumbled free. One struck a huge dray horse. The horse reared. Another, backing up, slipped and stumbled. People began to run and shout. Laurence, horrified by the pandemonium, felt petrified. Even as he stood there, unable to decide which way to go, he was struck from behind. Sent spinning, he tried to catch hold of something, failed, and fell. Hands gripped him, carried him up, set him down, and just as quickly vanished.

Confused, his body aching, Laurence leaned against a hitching post, gasping for breath. Impulsively, he slapped a hand against his jacket pocket. The money was gone!

He jerked his head up just in time to see the old patch-eyed man. The man, however, was no longer old. A false beard—half off now—was trailing behind him like a scarf. And, far from being lame, he was racing around a corner like a sprinter, clutching Laurence's money.

"Stop, thief! Stop, thief!" the boy cried. He tore after the man. A few heads turned, but no one helped. Laurence pressed on. He began to gain. The thief sped around a corner. Laurence followed, only to trip over the crutch. The man had turned and lain in wait for him.

Laurence spun headfirst into a muddy gutter. There he sprawled, stunned and coated with filth. When he did try to get up, he staggered and fell again, tearing a shoe.

It took a while for his head to clear of dizziness. Only then did he look about. The thief—and his money—had vanished.

Chapter 13

An Arrest Is Made

L aurence pressed clenched fists against his eyes in an attempt to slow his whirling fury. When he was a bit calmer, he reached again into his pocket. This time he felt a few bills. Something was left. Sighing, he closed his eyes with weariness.

A smack on his shoulder made him start up and look around. A police constable—enormous in his Wellington boots, wide belt and buckle, tall hat, and double row of bright buttons cascading down his blue swallow-tailed coat—loomed over him. In his hand he carried the heavy truncheon that he had used to strike Laurence.

"'Ere, what's this sittin' about for?" the constable demanded.

Greatly relieved to see a man of law, Laurence jumped to his feet. "Oh, Constable, I am glad you came! I don't think you're too late."

"Late for what?" the constable said, surprised by the boldness of the boy and his well-bred English.

"I've been robbed by a man pretending to be a lame beggar," Laurence explained with high-pitched indignation. "He was very deceitful. But I can describe him with accuracy. He followed me, you see, knocked me down, and stole a great sum of money from me. He's gone that way. I'm sure you'll be rewarded when you get the money back for me."

The constable gazed at the ragged boy with puzzlement. "What did you say?" he asked. He truly could not fathom what Laurence was talking about.

55

"Listen to me!" the exasperated boy cried. He stamped his foot. "I was set upon by a wicked man who stole a great sum of money from me."

The constable broke into a grin. "Is that the truth now?" he said with sarcasm. "Just 'ow much did he take from you?"

"I don't know exactly. Almost a thousand pounds."

"One thousand quid, you say?" remarked the constable with mock amazement.

"I was only able to save a little of it."

"I should 'ope you did!"

"Why are you looking at me like that?" Laurence demanded.

"I get it!" the constable exclaimed. "You've 'ad yourself a corkin' good time at the races, 'aven't you? Regular swell, you are."

It was Laurence's turn to be confused. "I beg your pardon. What do you mean by races?"

"Or maybe," the constable went on, "you were down visiting Her Majesty at Windsor, and she offered you up a 'andsome pension for yer noble deeds. Perhaps you killed a dragon, eh? Why, for all I know, you might be Saint George 'isself come back for an evening's stroll. One thousand pounds! Cor!" The constable laughed uproariously. "I'd be 'appy as a pig in muck to live on that for many a year."

"But it's *true*!" Laurence cried in his most shrill voice.

"Right-o," the constable returned, "and I'm the duke of York! Now, look here, laddie, come on out of the street and trot on your way so we'll 'ave no more nonsense."

"Why . . . you don't believe me, do you?" Laurence said. To prove he was telling the truth, he plunged his hand into his pocket. "There! You see. I *do* have money!" He held out his few remaining notes.

The constable's amusement ended. "'Ere now! Where did the likes of you get all that?"

"Why . . . why from my father."

The constable took a step forward.

"Come on then! 'Onest truth, now. You filched it."

Laurence, shocked by the accusation, backed away. "No, that's not true. I mean, don't you know who I am?"

"Am I supposed to?" the constable said, edging closer.

Laurence continued to back away. "My name is Sir Laurence Kirkle. I'm Lord Kirkle's son."

"Right. And I'm the sultan of all the Turks!" the constable roared. "You bloody thief!" Lunging forward, he attempted to snatch the bills out of Laurence's hand. The movement caught the boy unprepared. Pound notes exploded into the air. Laurence tried to catch them but managed to snare only one bill. The constable, with his truncheon raised, had prevented him from reaching the rest.

Laurence clutched the single note.

"Come on then! Give over the last of that money. And you can consider yourself under arrest."

Arrest! Laurence stared at the constable. The next moment, panic took hold. He turned and began to run. Behind him, he heard the ragged and repeated rasp of the policeman's rattle, summoning help. The sound made Laurence run that much faster.

Fifteen minutes later, he slumped against a gate. He could go no farther. Every muscle was in pain. His head throbbed. He was sick at heart. He had no doubt but that every policeman in London was searching for him.

Then, out of the corner of his eye, he saw—standing just a few feet away and gazing at him forlornly—a wretched-looking beggar boy with tattered clothing, ripped shoes, hands and arms caked with filth, and a bloody red welt upon his face. With disgust and fear, Laurence drew back. Here was another thief.

It took a few seconds for him to realize he was seeing his

own reflection in a shopwindow glass. He *was* looking at a thief. He *had* stolen money from his father. He had run away from home. He would be caught. He would be put in jail. He was disgraced. "It's all so *unfair*," he moaned.

He thought of returning home and taking his punishment—whatever that might be. But a vision of the constable standing at his father's door, preventing entry, rose up before him. He could not go home. Oh, why had he said he was Lord Kirkle's son!

But even that was not his worst thought. Far worse was a vision of his oafish older brother mocking him, telling the world that he, Laurence, *was* indeed a thief.

It was a humiliation Laurence could not face. Because of Albert more than anyone, he would not, could not, return. *Ever.*

He examined the money he had managed to keep. Of the thousand pounds he had taken only one pound remained! Would it enable him to reach America? It did not matter. What was important was that he get to Liverpool.

Chapter 14

An Investigation Is Begun

Albert Kirkle stepped into his father's study and closed the door behind him. His lordship, hands behind his back, head down, was pacing nervously. On the ottoman sat Lady Kirkle. She was a small woman, with the face of a china doll. Her hair was pulled back severely. The many layers of her long silk dress made her seem even smaller than she was, and every time she moved, she rustled like a delicate paper package. Now and again she daubed at her eyes with the tip of a handkerchief.

Albert, who was trying to appear solemn but was having trouble suppressing his elation, announced, "He's here." In his large hand he held a small card.

Lady Kirkle leaned forward. "Does he seem respectable?" she inquired. Her voice was full of alarm.

Albert shrugged. "As much as one might expect," he replied.

"Young, old?"

"Old to me," Albert said with a smirk.

Lady Kirkle addressed her husband, who was pacing up and down. "James?" she called softly.

Lord Kirkle, caught up in his own thoughts, stopped pacing and looked at his pocket watch. It was seven o'clock in the evening.

"James," Lady Kirkle said a little more loudly. "The man you sent for is here."

"Is he?" he said. He took a step toward the door only to stop and turn instead toward the fire.

"My dear, how much are we to tell him?" she asked his lordship carefully. Even as she spoke, she glanced at the long table upon which lay the broken cane and Laurence's bloodstained cravat.

Lord Kirkle was staring into the fire.

"My lord," Albert said, crunching his knuckles, "if this man were to be in any way indiscreet or . . . well, you know."

"I want the boy found," Lord Kirkle rumbled.

"Really, James!" his wife said soothingly. "We all do. What are you suggesting?"

With a handkerchief, Lord Kirkle blotted away the beads of sweat on his forehead. "I shall do whatever is necessary to find Laurence. I don't give a tinker's damn about what anyone thinks!"

"My dear! You must not swear!"

"I beg your pardon. I'm greatly troubled."

"What is this man's name?" Lady Kirkle asked her son.

Lord Kirkle held out a hand. Albert gave him the card he had been holding. His father looked at it.

MR. PHINEAS PICKLER
Discreet Investigations
For the Gentry

"The fellow's name is Pickler," Lord Kirkle informed his wife. "Phineas Pickler."

Lady Kirkle grimaced. "My dear, he's not Irish, is he?"

"I don't care."

"Who was it who recommended this man?" she asked.

"Lord Mulling."

His wife nodded. "Then he's sure to be trustworthy," she said.

Lord Kirkle frowned. "Albert," he said, "show the man in."

Albert exchanged a look with his mother. She nodded. "Yes, sir," the boy said, and stepped from the room.

Lady Kirkle sat very erect. "My dear," she said, "we *all* want Laurence home again. To think otherwise is positively wicked. At the same time—for Albert's sake, for his sisters' sake, for Laurence's own sake, I might add—the season *is* about to begin. We must avoid scandal."

"Beatrice, I want the boy found!" Lord Kirkle repeated.

Lady Kirkle took the measure of her husband with care. Then, very quietly, she said, "My dear, the cane."

Starting, Lord Kirkle snatched up the broken cane and the cravat and flung both into the fire. Just then the door opened, and Albert ushered Mr. Phineas Pickler into the room.

Mr. Pickler was a small potbellied man of some forty years. A smooth egg-shaped face with a sharp chin and pointy nose as well as round, slightly protuberant eyes helped give him the look of a sparrow. Indeed, the jacket he wore was of striped browns, his vest and trousers of brown checks. His boots were brightly polished. In well-manicured hands rested a brown bowler.

"My lady, my lord Kirkle," Albert announced, "may I present Mr. Phineas Pickler."

Mr. Pickler bobbed a bit of a bow—as if he were picking up crumbs—first to Lady Kirkle, then to his lordship. "My lady. My lord," he said. He spoke softly, without emotion. Lady Kirkle was relieved to find the man looking so mild.

Lord Kirkle, meanwhile, struggled to find the proper words with which to begin. "Mr. Pickler," he finally said, "you have been recommended to us by Lord Mulling."

Mr. Pickler bobbed his head again. "Lord Mulling has been kind."

"Recommended," Lord Kirkle continued, "as a man of discretion, with singular skills in . . . emergency family matters. We appreciate your willingness to come upon such short notice."

Yet again Mr. Pickler bobbed his head. Then he cocked his head and waited.

Lord Kirkle, feeling ashamed, mopped his brow. "The fact of the matter is, our younger son, Sir Laurence, aged eleven, has"—Lord Kirkle swallowed hard—"has *removed* himself from this home."

"I am deeply saddened to hear it, my lord."

"And," Lord Kirkle continued, "I have reason to believe—it sounds preposterous, I know—that he is trying to leave England for . . . for America."

"America . . . ," Mr. Pickler echoed.

"Yes, quite. I . . . We want him found and brought back. As soon as possible. This evening."

"Of course."

Lord Kirkle cleared his throat. "You seem to have some, what shall I say, experience in these matters of finding, returning . . . the young, and so forth. Eh, what?"

Once again Mr. Pickler nodded. "I have been allowed to be of use, sir."

Lady Kirkle leaned forward. "Mr. Pickler, we wish everything to be done with the utmost discretion."

The man placed his bowler over his heart. "The sole mission of my life, my lady, is to please."

"But I want him home!" Lord Kirkle burst out, pounding his table with a fist, causing Lady Kirkle, Albert, and Mr. Pickler to start.

"Well, sir," Lord Kirkle challenged. "Can you do it?"

Mr. Pickler looked into his bowler as if the answer lay there. "My lady," he said, lifting his birdlike eyes, "my lord, sir, in these matters—which are delicate indeed—much depends on two factors."

"We can pay you what you need," Albert put in.

"Thank you, sir. I have no doubt as to your liberality. But if you permit me, sir, the two factors I was referring to are, one, speed, and two, information. May I ask when the boy left?"

"This very afternoon."

"You have acted quickly. That bodes well. As for information . . ."

Lady Kirkle tensed. "What kind of information?"

"You see, my lady," Mr. Pickler said after a quick peek into his bowler, "my success in finding those who absent

62

themselves from good homes depends upon my knowledge of the circumstances that led to the young person's unfortunate departure. I should know what he looks like. What he was wearing. His character. Finally, sir—and here I fear I must intrude—I must know the . . . cause."

A deep silence filled the room.

On the ottoman, Lady Kirkle rustled her skirts. "You will have a full description of him," she offered.

"My lady," Mr. Pickler replied softly, "that will be appreciated. But with all due respect, a description, though vital, will not alone suffice."

Albert burst forth. "He's a hotheaded, impudent—"

"Albert!" Lord Kirkle barked. Albert stepped back and glowered. Lady Kirkle watched her husband. His lordship was staring at the fire again. Suddenly, he swung about. "Very well, Mr. Pickler. You shall have a full explanation."

"My lord," Mr. Pickler returned, "I am humbled by your trust."

"Albert, Beatrice," Lord Kirkle said briskly, "please leave me alone with Mr. Pickler."

Albert looked at his mother. She made a nod. "Perhaps," Albert suggested to his father, "I should stay and—"

"Albert," Lord Kirkle snapped, "you will leave as I asked!"

"My dear James . . . ," his wife protested.

"I prefer to speak to Mr. Pickler *alone*," his lordship said, his voice quivering with anger. Sweat trickled down the side of his face.

Albert opened the door. With an agitated rustling of her skirts, Lady Kirkle gathered herself up and swept out of the room. A pouting Albert followed her.

In the study, the only sound was the occasional settling of the burning coal in the grate. Mr. Pickler, eyes downcast, waited patiently while Lord Kirkle resumed his pacing. Finally, his lordship dropped himself into the chair behind his table.

Fussing nervously, he pulled open the table drawer. For a few moments he gazed absentmindedly at the pile of money that lay there. Suddenly he cried, "The Irish rents!" and plucked up the notes and began counting them rapidly. "My God!" he cried when he had tallied the pile a second time. In horror, he flung the bills down, sat back in his chair, and pressed his eyes with his hands.

"My lord," Mr. Pickler inquired—but only after making a quick search of his bowler—"did the boy take some money?"

For a long time Lord Kirkle made no reply. Then he whispered, "One thousand pounds."

Mr. Pickler was speechless.

Lord Kirkle sat up stiffly and, almost savagely, said, "Mr. Pickler, you may take a seat. I shall endeavor to give the full particulars. It is not a happy story."

"My lord," Mr. Pickler said, "if I have learned one thing from my efforts to find and return wayward youths who leave good homes, it is this: Young people do not have the best judgment."

"I want him returned, Mr. Pickler," Lord Kirkle said with a voice that came from deep within him. "I want my boy home!"

"My lord, I have no doubt we shall achieve that. May I ask some questions?"

"You may."

Mr. Pickler cleared his throat, as if to clear away something disagreeable. "Was there one particular happenstance, sir, that prompted the boy's departure?"

Lord Kirkle rose quickly, moved toward the mantel, and stared once more into the fire. His face was hidden from Mr. Pickler.

"It was a punishment," his lordship said without turning around. "The result of some dispute with his elder brother. They . . . they do not get along."

"Was it a . . . *specific* punishment, my lord?"

Lord Kirkle felt heavy. Old. Troubled. Absentmindedly, his fingers traced the family motto below the mantel.

FOR COUNTRY, GLORY—FOR FAMILY, HONOR

Lord Kirkle drew himself up, turned, and looked Mr. Pickler in the eyes. "Yes . . . the punishment," he said in the posture and voice he used when addressing his peers in the House of Lords. "Yes. Laurence was confined to his room for tea."

Mr. Pickler blinked in surprise. It was hard for him to keep from smiling. "My lord," he said, "I am moved by the confidence you show in me. But what you have said permits me to confirm what I said, to wit, young people lack good judgment. Your information encourages me to say that I will have your son home in a very short time."

"Do you think so?"

"My lord, you have honored me with your complete confidence. I shall repay it by bringing your boy back."

Chapter 15
Of Muffins and Names

Colder and colder. Laurence, without overcoat or scarf, was chilled to the bone. He was ravenous too. When the fog had lifted, it only gave way to a dreary freezing rain. From somewhere in the darkness, he heard the muted tinkling of a bell. It sounded to him like the mocking laughter of an elf. Once Laurence searched, he discovered it came from a small tentlike structure in which stood an old man selling muffins from a great wicker hamper. Gray lumps of knobby dough, they nonetheless smelled wonderful to Laurence. He approached timidly.

The muffin man, a toothless, weak-chinned fellow, peeped out from multiple wraps of shawls, capes, and mufflers. The wraps made his eyes appear, in the light of a street lamp, like two raisins atop a cinnamon bun. Now and again he struck the little bell that dangled from the tent's edge.

Laurence stopped just beyond the pool of lamplight. He said, "Can you tell me where the railway station is?"

The old man considered Laurence thoughtfully while flicking bits of muffin into his mouth. "Which one?" he finally said.

Laurence's heart sank. "Is there more than one?"

"Bless me," returned the muffin man. "'Course there is."

"I want to get to Liverpool."

The man gazed at Laurence. "Shippin' out, are yer?"

Laurence nodded curtly. "I'm . . . I'm going to America." He found the word still strange to say out loud.

The muffin man offered up a wide gummy smile. "To make yer fortune, I suppose, like Dick Wittington. And well yer might, says I. If I were younger, I'd join yer. What *yer* wants is *Euston* Station."

"Euston Station," Laurence repeated, trying to fix it in his mind. "Can you tell me where that is?"

"Bless me, yer a bit innocent to be aimin' so far. And yer got a fancy way of talking, yer 'ave. Just where yer from?"

"Somewhere," Laurence answered evasively.

"Right-o," said the muffin man with a sly smile. "Yer don't want to let on, do yer? As for Euston Station, 'tisn't that far neither, no more than a mile or two along Tottenham Court Road, which is but three streets over." He pointed in the general direction. "Yer can't miss it. Big as a blessed cathedral, it is. Now then, did yer want to buy a muffin against yer going?"

Laurence eyed the bread hungrily. The thought of food made his mouth water. He started to reach into his pocket for his money but hesitated. He was afraid to show it. It might be stolen. "Not now," he said, turning away reluctantly.

"'Ere then, lad," the man called after him. "Come on back."

Laurence turned. The man was holding a muffin out. "This one 'ere has gone flat stale," he said. "Bless me, yer can pay me after yer gets rich in America. Go on, take it. No shame to be poor and 'ungry, not in this world."

Laurence took the muffin.

"What's yer name then?" the man asked.

"Laurence."

"Laurence *wot?*"

Laurence was about to give his name but suddenly shut his mouth.

The man laughed silently yet so hard all his wraps quivered. "Right yer are, lad. Yer don't want to give *that* either, do yer? Not if yer've run away, and they're trying to catch yer back."

Laurence retreated a step. "What . . . what do you mean?" he stammered.

"That stripe on yer cheek," the muffin man said, "it's not what yer'd call natural, is it? Bless me, of course yer wants to run away. I don't blame yer. What I say is, God give yer luck! Now, look here, yer got me bread. Why don't yer take me name to America too? Bless me, it's mine. I've a right to lend it, I suppose, same as the muffin which yer already 'ave."

"But why?" Laurence asked.

"Look 'ere, lad, let an old man who knows naught but muffins give yer a bit o' advice. Keep yer real name close. A man's name is as much as his soul. Yer wants to protect it, don't yer?" He offered up a tiny wink. "All right then, Worthy is *my* name. Solomon Worthy. Yer can borrow 'alf of it and make yerself up to be, wot? Laurence Worthy. Bless me, but it's got a decent ring to it, don't it?"

"Yes, it does."

"Then it's yers."

"Thank you, sir," Laurence replied, confused but grateful. He turned abruptly and began to run.

"Worthy," the man called after him. "Don't yer forget it now! Laurence *Worthy*!"

No sooner did Laurence round a corner than he stopped and devoured the muffin in three gulps. He was certain it was the best food he'd ever eaten. He heard the tinkle of the muffin man's bell. How gentle and soothing it sounded. But the very next moment—as though to mock the tiny, tinny sound—a church bell boomed from somewhere in the dripping and dreadful darkness. *Ding-dong*, the notes echoed. To Laurence, it was his name being called. *Lau-rence! Lau-rence!* Deep solemn claps they were, as if tolling a death, his death. These first strokes were answered by yet another bell and then another and another, until the whole London night itself seemed to be shouting his name into the frigid dark. *Lau-rence! Lau-rence!* Then, in reverse order—one by one— the bells grew dim, then stilled until the city was silent. Now Laurence heard only the beating of his heart within his chest.

Chapter 16
Mr. Pickler Takes Action

M inutes after his interview, Mr. Phineas Pickler stood upon the sidewalk in front of Lord Kirkle's home. As the thick fog floated about him like a cold web, he turned to consider the dwelling from which he had just departed. How solid and secure it seemed to him, the home of a family that stood among the most powerful in England. And yet Lord Kirkle had turned to *him*—Phineas Pickler—to bring his son home. If Mr. Pickler had been a rooster he would have crowed: Could any man ask more of life?

From his pocket he took out and contemplated a small daguerreotype Lord Kirkle had provided of the boy. Mr. Pickler peered at it, trying to read young Sir Laurence's features. He saw the face of a healthy, happy boy. No willfulness. No stubbornness. It made Mr. Pickler smile to think how delicate these young aristocrats were. This one had run away from home because he'd been sent to his room at teatime! Such cases were easy. A kind but stern word from him, and the boy would be safely home.

All the same, Mr. Pickler decided it would be best if he assumed the boy was indeed trying to go to America. One had to give these young sirs their due.

Travelers to America generally embarked from Liverpool, to which a late train departed nightly. Mr. Pickler, noting the time, eight-thirty, upon his pocket watch—a recent birthday gift from his wife—hailed a hansom cab for Euston Station.

Chapter 17
A Secret Consultation

*H*ardly had Mr. Pickler taken himself from Lord Kirkle's home than the front door opened and Albert, the collar of his overcoat upturned, stepped into the evening cold.

A servant looked out after him. "Will you be long, sir?"

Albert looked about. "Going for a walk," he said.

"Very good, sir." The servant shut the door.

Albert proceeded down the steps, made certain the servant had retreated inside, then hurried to the avenue. Once there, he hailed a cab. "To the City," he commanded. "Watling Street." The driver, high up and behind the cab, watched the young gentleman clamber in, then flicked the reins. The horse trotted briskly off.

Not far from the great dome of St. Paul's Church, Sir Albert alighted. Through the murk of fog and rain, he called up, "Stay here," to the driver. "I'll need you again."

"Very good, sir."

Quickly, his boot heels beating loudly on the cobblestone pavement, Albert walked down Watling Street. The way was narrow, dark, and at the moment deserted, but he kept close to buildings to stay out of the rain. Those establishments that did business upon the street had long drawn their shutters. Even the public house was closed. Puddles of water were stiffening into ice.

Halfway along the street, Albert turned into Bow Lane, a passage even more gloomy, more constricted. At the farthest end stood a narrow stone building blackened with the grime and soot of years. It was five stories tall, barely visible in the fog save for a morbid glow from one window at the top.

Sir Albert pulled the bell next to a brass plate proclaiming:

BROTHER'S KEEPER, LTD.
Mr. Matthew Clemspool
Sole Agent

From deep within he heard a clanging noise.

Not long after, the front door creaked open. A rather portly man of middle age and height peered out. His smooth face was not unlike a cherub's, round, red, rosy. His head was bald but for a fringe of hair that ran ear to ear at the back, an incomplete halo. He held his plump fingers before him as if plucking—and sounding—the invisible strings of a harp. The cutaway coat he wore was gray, his cravat a fashionable maroon. When he recognized his young caller, he blossomed into an agreeable smile.

"Ah," the man exclaimed with enthusiasm, "Sir Albert! How very pleasant to see you again, m'lord."

"Clemspool," Albert said sharply, "I need to see you!"

"Sir, to make my point precisely, I am *always* available for you. Do be kind enough to step into my office." He wafted his hands as if unrolling a carpet.

The two climbed five flights, arriving finally at a small cubical room that contained, principally, a great rolltop desk lined with pigeonhole compartments, most of which were empty. An oil lamp stood atop this desk and cast a meager circle of sickly yellow light. There was a stool before the desk and a more comfortable second chair off to the side. Mr. Clemspool beckoned Albert to the comfortable chair. Albert sat.

With hands pressed together in a prayerful attitude, the cherubic man considered the youth before him. He did not

71

like Sir Albert. The young man was arrogant and often patronizing. But he paid well, exceedingly well.

Mr. Clemspool put on his most ingratiating smile. "What, Sir Albert, may I have the honor of doing for you today?"

The young man grimaced and cracked his knuckles. Then he said, "Clemspool, we've talked about a certain person."

Mr. Clemspool nodded agreeably. "Sir Albert, I am not a man who forgets. You are alluding to your brother, Sir Laurence."

"Look here, Clemspool," Albert said, "I'm not interested in your memory, just what you can do for me now."

Taking no offense at Sir Albert's rudeness, Mr. Clemspool said, "Sir Albert, I trust I have always been of good service, often suggesting various stratagems. Were you able to put the last one into play, my suggestion that you stage a small theft of some kind—?"

Albert shook his head to stem the flow of words. "Your idea worked well. Too well. Laurence has run off."

"Run off!" Mr. Clemspool cried with something like glee. "Surely you don't consider that a misfortune, do you?"

"That all depends."

"Ah, yes, depends on your famous father's will, the one, to make my point precisely, in which he leaves too little to you and too much to your younger brother."

Albert, who wished he had not told this man quite so much of his business, nodded disdainfully.

Mr. Clemspool wagged his head. "A second son *should* get very little," he said smoothly. "As I see it, it's a law of nature. The will—considering your father's position in the government—sounds almost treasonable. Do you read your Bible, sir?"

Albert drew back as if stung. "Bible?"

Mr. Clemspool placed his hands together as if in prayer. "Genesis. Chapter four. Verses five through nine. Cain and

Abel. 'Am I my brother's keeper?' Right from the beginning, Sir Albert, the *very* beginning, the second son has proved to be a problem." Mr. Clemspool let one hand go limp—as if it had died.

Albert shifted. Then, leaning forward out of his chair, he said, "What I want, Clemspool, is to make sure my younger brother stays gone."

"You wish to *encourage* his emigration."

"As far away as is possible."

"When did he run off?"

"This evening."

"Do you know his destination?"

"America."

Mr. Clemspool puckered his lips. "Do you know his route?"

"No. Of course not."

"Is your brother an experienced traveler?"

Albert snorted. "He hasn't even been to Kensington Park on his own."

Mr. Clemspool considered. "Sir Albert," he said, "the most direct way to America is to take a packet boat from Liverpool. Will he know that?"

"Maybe."

"Steerage goes for barely four pounds, and prices go up from there according to class of ticket. Will he have funds?"

"I don't know how much he's got with him."

Mr. Clemspool smiled. "I am sure I can be helpful."

"Mr. Clemspool," said Albert, "get proof to me that Laurence has landed in America"—he reached for his wallet and provided Mr. Clemspool with a wad of bills—"and you can count on more."

Without looking at it, Mr. Clemspool accepted the payment. "I have no doubt more will be required, sir."

"You'll get it when you do what you've promised to do."

73

Albert paused, then said, "Mind you, I want no foul play. Is that understood?"

Mr. Clemspool turned up his plump palms to show he hid nothing in them. "Of course," he said blithely.

"People say America is uncivilized. A violent place. . . ." The young man's voice trailed away.

Mr. Clemspool smiled. "You are, sir, a man of my heart. You have made your point precisely. I shall need a description, and *not* a general one. I know what he looks like. You have pointed him out to me. Now you must tell me what he looked like the moment you last saw him."

"Should I write it out?"

Mr. Clemspool wagged a finger. "No paper, young sir. Paper is evidence and evidence is bad. You don't want to end up in Chancery courts. In matters of law, m'lord"—Mr. Clemspool plucked his harp—"courts are to be *avoided*."

Albert described Laurence as he had last seen him upon the floor of his father's study.

"And you say you cut him about the face?" Mr. Clemspool asked.

"He deserved it."

"No doubt. Did you leave a mark?"

"A decent one."

"Which side?"

"Right."

"Making it much easier to snatch him out of a crowd. Well done, sir! If he is at Euston Station, I shall find him without fail."

Albert rose and stepped to the door. "Clemspool, I suppose I should tell you, my father has employed a man to find Laurence."

Mr. Clemspool frowned. "Has he?"

Albert sneered. "But he's Irish. At least his name is."

"Then we need not worry!" Mr. Clemspool plucked his harp.

Albert closed the door behind himself.

Once on the street he paused to savor a moment of satisfaction. All was in hand. But then, quite unexpectedly, a voice interrupted his thoughts: " 'Cuse me, laddie."

Startled, Albert looked up and automatically backed away. A powerfully built young man was standing a few feet from him. He was dressed shabbily in an old army coat whose ragged hem touched the tops of broken, turned-up boots. An ill-fitting cap was pulled so low it almost covered a patched eye, but the cap was not so low that it hid a fierce face, whose open eye was staring right at him. In the man's arms were a large number of parcels.

"Were you addressing me?" Albert asked, more than a little apprehensive.

" 'Oo do yer think I was talkin' to," the man snarled, "the Prince of Wales? Look 'ere, 'appen to know if Clemspool's in?"

Albert, discomforted by the notion that he and such another should have business with the same person, and that the man should somehow recognize the fact, considered him with alarm. The staring eye was particularly disquieting. All he answered was a curt, "I believe he is."

"Then if yer don't mind, laddie," the man said, "I'd like to get on by."

Albert moved.

"Much obliged," said the man as he plunged into the building with all his parcels.

Albert dismissed the man from his mind, hurried to his carriage, and ordered the near-frozen driver to take him back to Belgrave Square.

Chapter 18
Mr. Clemspool Has Another
Visitor

M r. Clemspool was sitting in his office, ruminating upon his talk with Sir Albert, when he heard a knock upon his door. It startled him. No bell had rung downstairs. There had been no sound of steps. Cautiously, he opened the door a crack, saw who his caller was, and frowned.

"Mr. Grout, sir," he said, "how many times must I tell you it's unwise to come to Bow Lane unannounced. You might be noticed. But," he added more graciously, "as it turns out, I have new and immediate work for you, and I was going—"

"Never mind yer work." The man chuckled as he pushed his way into the room. "I'm not the man I was. I've made me mint. From this 'ere day forward, I'm a bloomin' swell." No sooner did he say the words than he set his parcels down and rapped sharply on the wood door frame two times. "If me luck 'olds, that is."

"And how did you achieve such luck?" Mr. Clemspool inquired.

"Never mind the 'ow. Yer plays yer games, Clemspool, I plays mine. That's our rule, isn't it? We don't ask questions 'less we're workin' together. And I'm 'ere to tell yer that I won't be workin' for yer no more. I'm leavin' this miserable country. Emigratin' to America!" He dumped his packages on the desk and from his pocket ripped out a false beard and flung it at Mr. Clemspool.

"America!" Mr. Clemspool cried as he caught up the beard. "Just the place for a young man. Well then, Mr. Grout, I promise you there will be no questions about your good luck. But I do hope you are not entirely done working for me. I have one final job to offer you. Happily it pertains to America."

"Doin' wot?"

"Oh, my usual." Mr. Clemspool plucked some invisible strings. "Making certain that someone who has left England . . . does not come back."

Mr. Grout frowned. "I don't know as I wants to—"

"How often have we worked together? Fifty times? A hundred? I assure you, sir, this event shall pay you so handsomely that even in your new circumstance you could not possibly refuse. And, since you are so intent upon commencing your new life, what would you say to starting this very night? The Liverpool train leaves, let me think . . . Yes! Within the hour.

"Of course, Mr. Grout, as befits your new status, you must travel first class. I, in my more humble status, shall travel third. That way we shall cover both ends of the train. But in so doing we cannot fail to find our young man!"

Chapter 19

A Conversation Overheard

L aurence was so cold and hungry that as he trudged along Tottenham Court Road, he fancied he could smell food on every side. But the muffin man, as well as the muffin he had given him, was long gone. Once he reached Euston Station, the boy thought, he would find warmth and food. He did not care what it cost; he would get some.

But his exhaustion was growing. He was sore. He felt

bouts of dizziness. The welt on his face throbbed. Despite the cold, penetrating drizzle—which sometimes turned to snow—flashes of sweating heat burst upon him only to be followed by chills so sharp his teeth chattered. Blowing on his hands to keep them warm, he would have given anything to be in his own bed. Yet over and over again he told himself he had no choice—he must escape from London.

Laurence hardly knew which he feared most, thieves or the police. To protect himself against the former, he kept one hand thrust deep in his jacket pocket, fist tight around the money that remained. The image of the man with the eye patch, the one who had robbed him, kept rising before him. Even so, he pushed on, pausing only to step into an alley and—to his shame—relieve himself.

He resumed walking. And then, up ahead, he did see a police constable. Distinct in his tall stiff hat, the man was casually sauntering in Laurence's direction, whistling. Now and then he paused and held up a lantern to inspect doorways and dark alleys.

Laurence ducked down behind some ash bins. As he waited and watched—trembling—he imagined what the police would do if they caught him. They would put him in irons. A trial would follow and then the inevitable guilty verdict when his father and Albert testified against him. He saw himself standing before a periwigged judge, listening as the man meted out a sentence of transportation to the desolate penal colonies of Australia. Or perhaps he would be sent to the hulks, rotting ships used as prisons. No matter, the shame and disgrace seemed worse than any such fate.

Oh, why had he ever taken the money! Perhaps Albert had been right all along. Perhaps he, Sir Laurence Kirkle, was a bad person. . . . No, he had stopped *being* that person. He was Laurence *Worthy* now.

"Laurence Worthy." Laurence whispered the name out

loud through chattering teeth. Far better to disappear than to bring disgrace upon the Kirkle family. There was a hint of nobility in that. A martyrdom.

The constable had passed. Laurence moved on.

Twenty minutes later he came to Euston Station, grand with massive columns and an archway that reminded Laurence of a Roman temple his father had once shown him in a book. Horses and carriages kept coming to provide assistance to the crowds of passengers at the entrance. Boxes and trunks were piled everywhere, while porters carted goods in barrows, or on heads and backs.

Laurence slipped forward from one mound of boxes to another until he saw that he was heading right for another constable. Quickly, he ducked behind some crates, then peeked out through the drizzle.

The constable was just a few feet away and turning toward Laurence when he was approached by another man. This man wore a bowler and had drawn up the collar of his ordinary striped coat.

"Mr. Pickler, sir!" The constable greeted the newcomer with a crisp salute. "Pleasant to see you."

"The same, Mr. Griffin. . . ." The two men shook hands.

"Off on holiday?" the policeman asked.

"Not at all," Mr. Pickler returned. "I'm searching for another runaway."

Hearing the words, Laurence leaned forward to listen intently. The man in the bowler must be a policeman too. In disguise, the boy thought with alarm.

"Lots of runaways these days, eh?" Constable Griffin said. "You must be busy."

Mr. Pickler smiled grimly. "Young lord, this one."

"Heaven keep us! I'd like to know what *he*'s got to run from!"

"He's in earnest Mr. Griffin. He took a thousand pounds from his father."

"Crikey! One thousand! Did he really?"

"His lordship called me in. Informed me so himself," Mr. Pickler said with pride.

"You do get on with them swells, don't you?"

Mr. Pickler allowed himself a slight smile. Then he said, "The boy announced he would run off to America."

"Ah! That's what brings you here. You think the lad's heading for Liverpool."

"The late train."

"And traveling first class all the way," Mr. Griffin said laughingly. "Cheerful way to run off, I say, with all that lolly."

"We will stop him, Mr. Griffin," Mr. Pickler said with confidence. "Usual reward when we do."

The constable took out a notebook and pencil from a pocket. "All right then, Mr. Pickler, what's this one look like?"

"Eleven years old. The right height for his age. Sandy hair and blue eyes. Scrubbed pink cheeks. Dressed absolutely proper. When he left, he was ready for high tea. Answers to the name of Sir Laurence Kirkle."

"Kirkle?"

Mr. Pickler nodded.

The constable, impressed, made a low whistle.

"Here's a picture." Mr. Pickler held up the daguerreotype.

The constable eyed it. "Regular young swell, you might say, eh, Mr. Pickler?"

"Considering the money he took, I expect him to arrive in a carriage. Shouldn't be hard to spot."

"A young lord traveling alone, I should think not," the constable agreed.

"Exactly," Mr. Pickler said. "Keep the eye open for him, will you? If you see him, hold him. Use your rattle. I'll be about."

"I'll know him when I see him, Mr. Pickler." The policeman saluted. "His picture is part of my mind."

"Very good then." After another handshake, Mr. Pickler passed through the station entrance.

Laurence, having heard the conversation, felt ill. His worst conjectures had come true. Not only were the police looking for him, his father had called them in! It took all of the boy's willpower not to turn on the spot and run. Only the forbidding thought of spending the night on the cold London streets held him.

Laurence studied the constable, now pacing before the station entrance. Once the boy determined the pattern of the man's route, back and forth, he edged forward by keeping low and dodging behind carriages and carts. When the constable reached the far end of the station entrance, Laurence dashed from his hiding place and into the enormous building itself, then crouched behind a steamer trunk.

In amazement, he saw that the place was wide as a cricket pitch, lofty as a five-story building, crisscrossed with dark beams, and topped with a glass roof blackened by soot. Glowing chandeliers hung from above. Despite the lateness of the hour, the station was crowded. Laurence was glad of that. He would be less likely to be observed.

Before him, behind the low fence that functioned as a barrier, he counted fifteen railway tracks, on many of which waited locomotives painted bright greens and reds, and glowing with bits of polished brass. Some of the engines spewed steam and smoke like beasts ready to charge.

The carriages attached were of different colors: blue, green, yellow. Vaguely, Laurence remembered hearing Albert talk about the colors' representing different classes of travel: first, second, third. Unfortunately, he could not recall which was which.

Before some trains he saw guards standing. Passengers were approaching them and presenting tickets.

Laurence knew then that he had to buy a ticket before

he could pass beyond the barrier. Having no idea how much a ticket to Liverpool would cost, he furtively pulled his remaining bill from his pocket. He hoped it would be enough.

Surveying the station again, he noticed—over what looked like a series of holes in the far left wall—a sign that read TICKETS. He checked for the man with the bowler. Not seeing him, Laurence stood and moved to join a line of people facing the sign.

"My good man," Laurence said to the gentleman who stood just ahead of him, "is this where you get tickets for Liverpool?"

The man turned. When he saw who had spoken, he reacted with disdain. "Impertinent beggar!" he snarled. "Be off with you! Third class is over there!"

"But I want first class," Laurence protested in his high-pitched voice.

"Away with you, or I'll call the guard!" the man cried.

The threat was enough to send Laurence scurrying toward a long straggling line of the third-class passengers. They were dressed poorly. In their arms, at their feet, were all kinds of bags, bundles, and boxes. Laurence took his place at the line's end. Though no one paid him any attention, he felt better when someone came up behind him; he felt part of the crowd.

The line moved forward slowly. At last Laurence reached the ticket window. In order to speak to the agent, he had to stand on his toes.

"Where to?" the man demanded without even looking up.

"Liverpool, please."

"Shilling," the man requested.

Laurence offered his bill to the man.

"Here! Where did you get this?" the man demanded.

"It's mine," Laurence returned, blushing with shame at what he was saying.

The ticket agent glared at Laurence with distrust. "I'll bet me oysters it's yer money," he snarled.

"It is," Laurence insisted.

Making a sound that suggested otherwise, the man flung down a paper ticket and the change. Laurence scooped both up, pocketed the change, then slunk away, searching still for the man in the bowler. He wished he'd asked which was the Liverpool track.

Seeing a man who looked like a train guard standing by the barrier, Laurence approached timidly.

"Is this the train for Liverpool?" he inquired, offering his ticket.

"Track twelve," the man said, taking the ticket, tearing it in half, and returning the stub. He pointed to the far end of the station. "Leaves in four minutes. You better hop it!" He gave Laurence a helpful shove.

The boy began to run. Even as he did, he heard the cry, "All aboard for Liverpool!" and the sound of a whistle shrieking.

Mr. Pickler was lingering some fifty yards from track twelve. Intent as he was upon the entrance of the station, watching as hansom cabs unloaded their passengers, he had his back to the train. When he heard the cry and whistle, he began to fear that he had, after all, been wrong. Apparently the Kirkle boy was not going to be on the last Liverpool train tonight.

Quite casually, he glanced over his shoulder toward the track, observing the last few people heading toward the train. It was then he spied a boy racing toward it. With his clothing torn and filthy, he looked little more than a beggar. Mr. Pickler tried to imagine him without the fearful welt along his cheek. "Good Lord!" he suddenly exclaimed. "It's him!" He began to run. "Stop!" he cried. "Stop!"

Laurence yanked open the door of the first car he came to—a yellow one. He barely poked his head inside when a man cried, "Out! Out! First class only."

Confused, struggling for breath, Laurence backed out

frantically. A second whistle sounded above a distant cry of "Stop!" With a series of clanks, the train began to inch forward. Laurence fought to stay alongside. "Third class!" he yelled. "Third class!"

"Here you are!" A stranger stood on the step of a green carriage by an open door. As the train increased its speed, Laurence made a final burst. The man reached out, caught Laurence's hand, and hauled him aboard.

Mr. Pickler, running hard, reached the first-class carriages. He grasped for a handle only to have his hand shoved away. As he fell back onto the platform, he looked up, catching a glimpse of a grinning gentleman with an eye patch.

In the third-class coach, Laurence, panting for breath, his eyes closed, sat back on a hard wooden bench.

"There, there, my friend," said a voice almost into his ear. "Not to worry. You've made the train for Liverpool."

Laurence looked around to see the man who had spoken. He wore a tall hat and a cutaway frock coat with many pockets. His collar was high and stiff, wrapped about with a flowing maroon cravat. He wore the gloves of a gentleman.

"That was a near miss, wasn't it?" the man said.

Laurence, still gasping, only nodded.

"Going all the way to Liverpool?"

"Yes, sir."

"Good! I am too."

"I'm much obliged to you."

"I am, to make my point precisely, *happy* to help."

Laurence sighed. He was on his way to Liverpool. Tears came, of elation and grief. For the first time in hours, Laurence felt safe.

On the bench next to him, Mr. Clemspool struggled to keep from smiling.

Chapter 20
On the London-to-Liverpool Train

The train soon reached its traveling speed of twenty-five miles an hour, the carriage settling into a continual rattling, shaking, and lurching. Such light as there was came from a single oil lantern that swung erratically from the ceiling.

There was one long high-backed bench that ran full length down the middle of the carriage. Each side of the bench was packed with people bulked out with capes and cloaks, bundles and bags, making the carriage ripe with sweaty warmth. Still, since there were no windows, merely shutters, a cold smoky draft blew over them all.

Mr. Clemspool leaned toward Laurence. "You're young to be traveling alone, aren't you, my boy?" he asked in a friendly way.

"I'm all right," Laurence returned, wishing the man would not talk to him.

Just when Laurence thought the man would not speak again, Mr. Clemspool said, "If I may take the liberty—since we seem destined to travel together—might I inquire after your Christian name?"

"Laurence."

"Laurence," Mr. Clemspool repeated. "An *excellent* name for a boy." With a sidelong glance and a low confidential tone, he whispered, "Have a surname?"

Laurence opened his mouth to reply but checked himself. "Worthy," he said at last. Then, to make sure he had the name right, he repeated it. "Worthy."

Mr. Clemspool nodded solemnly. "Hard to remember your own name when going fast, isn't it?"

"Yes, sir," Laurence replied. He wanted nothing more than to sink into anonymity.

"Do you think you're going to be warm enough?"

"I think so," Laurence answered. His dinner jacket had, in fact, dried out considerably.

"If you are cold, Master Worthy, you need only tell me. I could share my cloak. We don't want you taking ill, now do we?"

Laurence shook his head and tried to look out through the shutter slats at the dark landscape. Now and again, he saw a streak of blurry light. He hoped the man would not ask him about the welt on his face.

"And where, Master Worthy," Mr. Clemspool pressed, "are you bound?"

Laurence considered the man and wondered at all his questions. He did have a pleasant round face. His smile was generous. His gentleman's manners inspired confidence. And he had, after all, helped him board the train at the last moment. "America," Laurence finally answered, trying to make this destination sound as casual as possible.

"America!" Mr. Clemspool returned with pronounced surprise—eyebrows raised, mouth agape, plump fingers extended as if to catch the word itself. "Master Worthy, you don't mean to tell me you're going to travel all that way *alone*!"

"I'm . . . meeting others," Laurence said, stumbling over the lie. "Friends. In Liverpool."

"Oh, well! To be sure!" replied Mr. Clemspool, sounding relieved. "A young fellow *needs* friends. You wouldn't want to be going so far on your own. I should think not. Not a soul in Christendom would recommend it. One hears dreadful stories. To make my point precisely, Master Worthy, it's neither safe *nor* prudent."

Laurence stared at him.

"Well now," Mr. Clemspool said, "you're free to close your eyes. We've got something of a passage here. You'll suffer no harm from me, Master Worthy. Count on me to be your traveling friend."

After a moment Laurence said, "Please, sir, can you tell me how long the journey will take?"

"To Liverpool? Oh, eight to ten hours, if there are no breakdowns, no sheep on the right-of-way, no rail washouts. God willing, we'll be there safe and sound by morning. So do try and get yourself some sleep."

"Yes . . . sir. . . ."

"And, Master Worthy, I beg you to remember, Mr. Matthew Clemspool—that's *my* name—is a friend to all youth. You mustn't forget that for a moment." He flourished his fingers as if soothing troubled air.

"No, sir, I won't," Laurence murmured, pushing aside any lingering suspicions of the man. It was far easier to blot out the world by closing his eyes.

Mr. Clemspool leaned forward. Thinking that Laurence was asleep, he allowed himself a grunt of satisfaction, drew his cloak about his shoulders somewhat tighter, then settled back against the seat bench. He was altogether pleased.

But Laurence was far from sleep. As he tried to imagine what lay ahead, his stomach churned with tension. To calm himself, he concentrated on the regular clacking of the wheels upon the rails, the swaying of the carriage, the swinging of the lantern, all of which created a symphony of droning monotony. Before long he felt drowsy. That drowsiness soon deepened itself into sleep and dreams. But in the dreams all he could see was himself flying blind through a midnight sky.

Chapter 21
Mr. Pickler at Home

*I*t was past midnight when Mr. Pickler returned to his apartment in the London district of Clerkenwell. There, in modest comfort, he lived with his wife, Mrs. Lucy Pickler, and their two children, Evelina and Thomas.

When he arrived, he found his wife—in nightcap and bed robe—waiting up for him. A round, careful woman, she always took the keenest interest in her husband's cases. Mr. Pickler, who drew considerable satisfaction from his wife's admiration, was pleased to provide her with the details, particularly those that involved members of the aristocracy.

"The enigma, my dear," he concluded after he had told her all that he knew while eating the supper she had kept warm, "is why a boy surrounded by such wealth and comfort should *want* to leave home."

"If anyone can find the reason, Mr. Pickler, you can," his wife said as she hovered about, making sure he ate well.

"But you see, my dear, Lord Kirkle informed me in private that the boy was piqued merely because he had been denied his tea. Now I ask you, does one run away from that kind of home because of such trivial punishment?"

"Mr. Pickler," whispered his wife, "am I hearing you suggest that something else might have happened?"

"My dear, the thing is, when I finally did see Sir Laurence at the station, he was not dressed at all in the way Lord Kirkle described. Though I had only the briefest of glimpses, I'm quite sure he'd been . . . well, disguised as a street urchin of the most contemptible lowness. A hideous welt had been painted on his face. What's more, he boarded a third-class carriage."

"How extraordinary," a shocked Mrs. Pickler cried.

Mr. Pickler put down his fork and knife. "Mrs. Pickler, you must not repeat a word of what I'm about to say."

"Merciful heavens, Mr. Pickler! You know I never would!"

"You see, though it all happened so quickly that I cannot be certain, it seemed to me that the boy was dragged forcibly onto that train."

"Dragged!" Mrs. Pickler cried. "But who would do such a dreadful thing?"

"My dear, the children are sleeping," Mr. Pickler cautioned. His voice sank to a whisper as he went on. "Moreover, when I attempted to board the train after the boy, it was as if I was pushed off."

"Pushed off!"

"By a gentleman with an eye patch."

"Mr. Pickler, it's a conspiracy!"

"My dear, please! I'm not certain. I can only say that if—*if*—Sir Laurence was abducted, the case is considerably altered."

"Do you think," his wife asked tremulously, "that the boy is being taken to America against his will?"

"I do not know," Mr. Pickler replied. "Nonetheless, my dear, I must travel to Liverpool by the earliest morning train to make sure it does not happen.

"My dear, Lord Kirkle is a man of enormous influence. If I am successful in restoring Sir Laurence to his proper home—"

"You will, Mr. Pickler, you will."

"The rewards could be enormous. A fine thing for us all.

However, if I fail to bring Sir Laurence back, my reputation—and chances for further employment—will suffer indeed. Having taken on the job, I have little choice but to be successful. It is best to proceed cautiously and tell Lord Kirkle nothing of these speculations of mine."

"I quite agree with you, Mr. Pickler," his wife said.

While his wife went to pack his traveling bag, Mr. Pickler, candlestick in hand, wandered into the nursery. Both his children lay asleep in their cots. Their father gazed at them fondly. So like angels. How could anyone abduct or harm a child? It was unthinkable! Indeed, the mere thought that Sir Laurence might have been badly treated so enraged the man, it made him even more determined than ever to save the boy.

At five-fifteen, after a fitful sleep, Mr. Pickler rose up, whispered a loving farewell to his wife—who insisted upon getting up with him—kissed Thomas and Evelina on their foreheads, and within the hour was on the early train to Liverpool.

Chapter 22
Maura and Patrick on the Liverpool Boat

*T*he journey from Kilonny had taken two days. On the *Queen of the West*, a low, mournful clanging of a buoy bell woke Maura O'Connell from her standing sleep by the bulwark. Bleary-eyed, she gazed about. The Irish Sea was calm but rolling. The air was a misty white. The great side wheels of the ship churned. Black smoke still flowed from the central stack. On deck the passengers huddled together, numb, wet, and cold. Many hunched beneath tarpaulins.

At Maura's feet Patrick lay fast asleep. Reaching down, she touched his brow and found it cool. Alarmed, she put a hand over his mouth. When she felt his breath warm, she whispered a prayer of thanks.

Gradually the mist began to lift. In the distance Maura saw a low strip of land. England. Ireland's Protestant master. It was everything she had learned to fear and hate. Tension knotted her belly. Unknown dangers, she knew, lay before them. She would have to protect them both until they boarded the packet ship to America. "Please, Jesus . . . ," she prayed, "make me strong."

Chapter 23

Laurence on the Liverpool Train

*A*h, Master Worthy! Awake, are you?"
The early light was dim and gray, the air fetid with a cloying clamminess that hinted of the sea. A jolt of the railway carriage reminded Laurence that he was on the train to Liverpool. Remembering now that Worthy was *his* name, he shifted about on the cramped seat. It was Mr. Clemspool who had spoken. A napkin was spread across the gentleman's lap, pieces of apple arrayed upon it like the open petals of a flower.

Trying not to stare at the food, Laurence stretched his stiff arms, legs, and back as best he could.

"And did you sleep well?" Mr. Clemspool inquired while

using a penknife to spear one of the apple pieces. Just before he bit into it, he glanced sideways.

Laurence was staring at him, his mouth open. "Not hungry, are you?" Mr. Clemspool asked.

"Yes, I am," Laurence whispered, feeling ashamed.

"Master Worthy," Mr. Clemspool cried, "why didn't you say so? Here you are." He held out the slice of speared apple. Laurence grasped it eagerly.

The man laughed at how quickly the boy swallowed it down. "Master Worthy, you *are* hungry. Here, help yourself." He offered the rest of the fruit. "As I've told you, I like young people, enjoy helping them, want them to trust me. You might say it's my calling."

"Yes, sir," Laurence mumbled.

"That welt on your face, Master Worthy. Does it bring much discomfort?"

Laurence put his hand to his right cheek. It was still sore, the blood a tight scab by this time. "No, sir," he said.

"I'm gratified to hear it. Now then," Mr. Clemspool pressed, "you informed me you are going to America. With friends, I think you said. So surely, Master Worthy, these friends of yours will know about getting tickets for the right kind of vessel, finding temporary lodging, arranging the proper medical exam, provisioning you for the long, hard voyage, choosing a proper berth—not any bed will do, you know—as well as securing suitable recreational and devotional readings to soothe the weary hours. All these details, my young friend, that—to make my point precisely—an experienced traveler knows about and attends to."

Laurence gazed at the man in bewilderment.

Mr. Clemspool smiled sweetly. "Of course, *you* knew all that, Master Worthy, didn't you?"

Laurence shook his head.

Mr. Clemspool wagged a finger. "Young man," he admonished, "that is unwise. Of course—and this is precisely my point—what every traveler *needs* is advice from time to time."

Laurence swallowed hard.

"So surely, Master Worthy," Mr. Clemspool continued in his most avuncular manner, "those people—the friends you alluded to—will meet you at the train and take you"—he fluttered his fingers—"as it were, under their wings."

Laurence peeked out at the passing countryside. The view flashing by made him dizzy. He closed his eyes. Everything that had happened unfurled in his mind: his dispute with his brother, Albert; the argument with his father. He remembered the caning, taking the money, running away from Belgrave Square, the one-eyed man, the pursuit by the police, and finally, the race to the train.

The day before seemed to belong to another time, another world. Gone now. What remained were feelings of rage and humiliation so thick they all but choked him. It was all so unfair! Tears trickled down his cheeks. He pawed them away. With effort, he turned back to Mr. Clemspool.

"I am not," he struggled to say, "certain my friends . . . will be . . . there."

"What!" Mr. Clemspool cried, apparently stunned by this news.

Laurence shook his head.

"I am shocked!" Mr. Clemspool exclaimed so loudly that four passengers turned to look at him and moved away a tad. "Absolutely shocked! Well then, I must hasten to assure you there will be at least *one* friend there for you!"

"What do you mean?" Laurence asked.

"Why, Master Worthy, to make my point precisely, *I* shall be your friend!"

By way of sealing the contract, he offered his large hand to the boy. Though not certain it was correct for him to shake a stranger's hand, Laurence extended his own small one. Mr. Clemspool shook it like a pump handle.

"Thank you, sir," the boy said, and meant it with all his heart.

"Master Worthy, you are not to mention it again. Instead, you must look to me for answers to all your worries. In fact, you must consider me, Matthew Clemspool, Esquire, your particular protector."

"Oh, yes, sir, I shall."

Mr. Clemspool positively glowed at the avowal. "I beg you to indulge yourself in more sweet repose. I will provide all the help you need to reach America in perfect comfort and safety."

Laurence, mumbling something that sounded vaguely like "Thank you," shut his eyes, gave himself over to the swaying of the carriage, and was soon asleep again.

Chapter 24
The *Queen of the West* Reaches Liverpool

*I*t was almost eight in the morning when the *Queen of the West* eased its way into the wide and muddy Mersey River. A bell on the ship began to ring. Someone cried, "Liverpool!"

On deck, the cold, sodden crowd of passengers stirred in hopes that relief was at hand. Wherever they looked, they saw boats of every size, from modest steam tenders to many-masted clipper ships, from small coastal ketches to large Atlantic barks. Some ships had their rigging hanging loose.

Smaller boats bore wind-puffed sails of red and tan. Steamers trickled smoke. Dories and skiffs skimmed the surface like nervous water bugs.

But the greatest number of vessels were moored within Liverpool's vast dock system of interlocking basins, each big enough to hold as many ships as fifty. Their masts and spars stood as thick as a forest shorn of leaves.

Just as extraordinary was the city of Liverpool itself, rising up on a hill beyond the docks.

Over the entire scene lay a thick, heavy air, rank with the smell of sea, tar, and decay. All in all, the Irish passengers found it nothing less than astounding. If Cork had seemed vast, Liverpool was twenty—fifty—times its size.

"Is it the biggest city in the world?" Patrick asked of Maura, his voice tight with astonishment at the jumble of wood, brick, stone, and marble buildings he saw.

Maura could only reply, "It must be."

"And are all the people Protestants?" Patrick asked, making the sign of the cross over his heart.

"I believe most are."

"Where will we go then?"

Maura put a comforting hand upon her brother's shoulder. "You needn't worry. Father Mahoney arranged for us to stay at a place," she reminded him. "It's called the Union House. Something of a vast inn, he said, for emigrants such as we. Mind, we'll only be stopping for a couple of days before we sail." She touched her dress where the packet of tickets and money was pinned.

"But where is the place exactly?" Patrick persisted.

"Ah, Patrick O'Connell, do you think I know? Look at the number of buildings, will you? But you need not worry," she said, seeking hard to suppress her own anxiety. "We can always ask the way."

On the *Queen of the West*, sailors raced about the deck.

Shouts and commands seemed to come from everywhere and nowhere simultaneously. Bells clanged. Whistles blew. The ship heaved back and forth by inches, creaking and groaning as though every timber were in agony.

Gradually, painfully, it eased past the other ships in Trafalgar Basin, threading its way through a maze of stone piers, turrets, open bridges, wooden piles, and brick warehouses, buildings so huge, they blocked the sky from view.

Then they were there. The ship's bell began to clang more furiously than ever. "All ashore!" came the cry. "All ashore!"

There was a rattle of chains as the gangway was run out. Patrick and Maura, along with all the other passengers, hastily snatched up their bundles. No one wanted to remain on the ship a moment longer than necessary.

"Stay close," Maura cautioned her brother as they were pushed along.

Seeing what looked to be an opening in the crowd, Patrick squeezed forward only to find himself thrown back and cut off from his sister. "Maura!" he cried.

She made a half turn toward his voice but was pulled away. Battling with all his strength, Patrick thrashed ahead frantically. The next moment his legs were kicked out from under him. Trying to keep upright, he dropped his bundle, realized what he'd done, and attempted to grab it; but he saw it swept away, pulled apart, and trampled underfoot. Then he himself began to go under only to be lifted up and hurled forward until he found himself at the top of the gangway. "Maura!" he cried again.

From somewhere he thought he heard a shout. "Patrick!" Before he realized it, he had been propelled down the gangway and now stood on the stone pier surrounded by a crowd of strangers. Maura was nowhere to be seen. His heart sank. Thinking he saw her, he tried to follow but was held back by someone gripping his arm. Struggling to free himself, he swung around. There she was! She met him halfway, and they reached the edges of the crowd, where the press of people was not so fierce.

"I was sure you were lost," Patrick panted when they were able to stop.

"I thought so too," Maura whispered. She was pale, her hair in disarray. "But where's your bundle gone to?" she cried.

"I dropped it," Patrick confessed.

Maura bit her lip to keep from rebuking him. She looked toward the mob of people. "Faith, I almost lost mine too," she said. "As for yours, we'll just be traveling lighter."

Patrick nodded, grateful for her forbearance.

They were standing on a stone-paved quay, part of an enormous rim of stone surrounding a pool of water in which many ships were berthed. On three sides of this basin rose five-story redbrick warehouses running the length of each side. The quay itself was crowded with the people from their own ship and hundreds more too. Never before had either Patrick or Maura felt so small, so isolated.

In need of reassurance, she reached for her packet of money and tickets and pulled it out.

"It's all here," she said in response to her brother's look of concern.

As she was preparing to repin the packet, a voice broke upon them. "Well now, you look like you're in need of some help." Maura hid the packet behind her skirt. Patrick grabbed up their bundle.

A few feet from them—arms akimbo—stood a ruddy-faced, bright-eyed young man. His wry smile was cockiness itself. He wore a seaman's tar hat at a rakish angle. Indeed, his loose striped shirt, his stiff wide britches, and his boots gave him the look of a sailor.

"Just in from Ireland, mates?" the young man asked. He touched the brim of his hat with his fingers to make a crisp salute.

Patrick took one look and knew whom he wished to be like.

Maura, however, hardly knew what to say or do. She was not used to being stared at by young men so brazenly, and this one couldn't have been more than her age. Even as she nodded, she looked down.

"And bound for America?" the fellow went on.

"Our father's there," Maura murmured.

"Well now, that's good for you," he said. "But even so, you'll need a place to stop until you sail."

Maura forced herself to look up. "Thank you, sir," she replied. "You're very kind, but it's all been done and arranged for."

"Is that so," the young man said. "Where are you headed?"

Maura, determined to say no more, simply looked away, tightening her grip on her money and tickets.

Fascinated by the young man, Patrick blurted out, "The Union House."

At the mention of the hotel's name, the young man's face clouded. He gave a somber shake of his head. "I think you'd better let me see your passes." He held out his hand.

Maura, taken aback, considered the young man with suspicion.

Patrick gave her a nudge. "Maura, show them to him. Surely he knows better than us."

"The lad's right. Let's see what you have."

Still Maura hesitated.

Patrick pulled on her arm. "Maura," he whispered urgently, "show them. We don't know where to go."

Against her better judgment, Maura sorted through her

packet and handed over the slips of paper pertaining to the hotel.

The young man gave the papers a cursory glance. "I'm afraid I've bad news for you," he announced.

"And what might that be?" Maura said.

"Just last night," he replied in deep and melancholy tones, "this Union House of yours burned to the ground. These are useless." Without so much as a by-your-leave, he tore the hotel papers up and flung the pieces into the breeze.

Appalled, Maura and Patrick could only stare.

"It's the truth," the young man insisted, putting hand to heart as though the gesture itself was proof of his sincerity. "But you're in luck," he went on quickly. "I know the perfect place for you." He paused. "You do have some money about you, I hope."

Maura hardly knew how to respond.

Once again it was Patrick who replied. "Yes, sir," he said, "we do."

"A good thing, mate," the young man said. "It takes money to get about here. This is England. Nothing comes cheap. I suppose it's English money you have, laddie? Not yet American dollars?"

Maura put a hand out to restrain Patrick. She was not fast enough. "It's all English, sir," he said. "And from a bank."

The fellow grinned. "All right then," he said with enthusiasm, "you're in luck. Toggs is my name. Mr. Ralph Toggs. And a good thing I found you. You can't be too careful in Liverpool. There are those who'd rob a blind man of his eyelashes if they could. But you can trust me. I'll treat you right."

Ceremoniously he took the bundle from Patrick. "Just follow me!" he cried, and began to march off with great speed.

For a moment Maura stood her ground, holding her

brother back. "Have you got to go telling our business to the first stranger we meet?" she whispered vehemently.

"Maura, you heard what he was saying. He's only being helpful. There's no call to be suspicious all the time!"

"We've hardly a choice to make now, do we?" she threw back. "Look at him. Off to a fare-thee-well, isn't he?"

They had to run to catch up.

Toggs strode boldly through the crowd, pausing briefly now and again to make sure that Maura and Patrick were following.

"Where are we going?" Maura panted. They were crossing a bridge from one boat basin to another, passing a small castlelike turret that held the bridge-lift mechanism.

"A place for emigrants like yourselves," Toggs called back. "The cheapest and best lodging in all of Liverpool!"

"We don't have that much money," Maura returned.

Toggs halted. "Well then, how much, exactly, do you have?" he asked, looking squarely into Maura's face.

She drew herself up. "Not so very much," she said.

Dissatisfied, Toggs looked to Patrick. "How much does she have, mate?" he demanded.

Flattered to be so addressed, Patrick told him, "Only a few pounds."

The young man grinned even more widely. "A few blinkin' pounds, he says! Spoken like a rich man without botheration. Don't you worry. If you keep following me, you'll get by." He started across yet another bridge.

All too aware that Maura was not pleased to be hustled along so, Patrick whispered, "Maura, he's being a friend."

"By the Holy Mother, I'm praying you're right," she snapped, and grabbing Patrick's hand, she rushed after Toggs.

For Maura and Patrick, the docks seemed to go on forever—Victoria Basin, Waterloo Basin, Prince's Basin, and

100

more. It seemed impossible that there could be so many people milling about, so many ships. Heedless, Ralph Toggs pressed forward, never slackening his pace.

At last they moved out of the dock area—passing sentry boxes manned by the dock police—and crossed the Strand, a wide boulevard. Here were warehouses far surpassing in size anything Patrick and Maura had yet seen.

Not that Toggs paid them any mind. Once across the Strand, he headed uphill along Lord Street for half a mile, then turned down Paradise Lane into the much narrower Gradwell Street.

"Look!" cried Patrick, pointing to a group of dark men in turbans. They were wearing ankle-length robes.

"Heathens," Maura whispered with a mix of fascination and alarm.

"What are they doing here?" Patrick wondered.

"I don't know," Maura replied. "But for heaven's sake, you mustn't let them see you staring." She pulled her brother along.

With the ever more congested streets came a roaring discord of shouts, cries, and calls, as people, horse-drawn wagons, carts, carriages, and barrows all jostled for passage amid the markets and liquor shops and dance halls. There was music. There were costermongers hawking their wares, vendors calling, children brawling.

Maura and Patrick were dumbfounded. It was hard to see. To hear. To think. Even so, they dared not stop. Ralph Toggs was pushing on.

Maura came to a dead stop. "Patrick!" she called.

"What is it?"

Maura was so alarmed that she found it hard to speak. "Blessed Jesus," she managed at last, "I'm swearing I saw a building with a sign on it that read 'Union House.'"

Chapter 25
A Liverpool Lodging

P atrick stopped short. "Where?"

"Some paces back," Maura cried, pointing. "Down that way."

Turning pale, he asked, "Are you certain?"

Maura shook her head. She was not sure.

As they stood there not knowing what to do, Patrick saw Toggs halt and look their way. After a moment he sauntered back, Maura's bundle slung casually over his shoulder.

"What's the matter now?" he demanded.

"If it pleases you, sir," Maura replied, struggling with herself to look up, "I thought I saw the Union House. The building you said had burned."

"Did you now?" Toggs said severely. "I thought you were strangers to Liverpool. You seem to know it better than me."

"Please, sir," Maura felt obliged to say, angry at her own tone of apology, "I didn't mean to question you, but—"

"You're doing it all the same," the young man replied as he dropped her bundle into the muddy street. "If that's the way you say thanks . . ."

"Wasn't I only thinking—?"

"Well, you might think less, missy," Ralph Toggs said sharply, cutting her off, "and pay mind to someone who's offering help. Mr. Ralph Toggs is not one to force a lady anywhere. You're free to go off on your own." He tapped the brim of his hat down, folded his arms over his chest, and glowered, challenging them to action.

Upset, Maura turned to Patrick. When she received a reproachful look from her brother, she felt further abashed.

"Forgive me, Mr. Toggs," she said, bowing her head. "I don't mean to deny your kindness. In Kilonny we were rudely used and here in Liverpool are at your mercy. Surely you'll forgive the confusion of strangers." She raised her face.

Her look of pain and sorrow caught Toggs unprepared. For an instant his own face softened. "Where in Ireland did you say?" he asked.

"Kilonny Village," Maura replied, finally gaining the strength to look into the young man's eyes. "But they've tumbled it. And our mother—just as we were leaving—decided not to come with us."

To which Patrick added bravely, "We're going to our father."

"Mr. Toggs," Maura said softly, "we do appreciate your kindness."

Toggs blushed in spite of himself, then shook his head to be rid of troublesome thoughts, to shake free of Maura's soft look and blue eyes.

"Follow me," he said gruffly, and picked up the O'Connells' bundle. Once more he set off, though no longer striding with his former energy.

It was not too long before they came into an even poorer district. Here, the muddy streets were narrower still and darker. Amid garbage, piles of ash, slops, and filth, people sat about in apparent idleness, slept, or staggered in drunken stupors. The stench was awful.

"And here we are," Toggs announced after they had traveled a few more dreary blocks. "Just about the best place for folks to stop."

Maura and Patrick looked to where he pointed. It was a decrepit three-story wooden building. Once it might have stood straight and tall, but no straight line was any part of its current posture. The windows—covered with paper, not glass—sagged dejectedly. The main door drooped. The steps to that door—five in number—looked like piled kindling, no two of them at the same angle.

Atop these was a ramshackle porch. The people sprawled upon it were a dismal lot, slumped like soldiers in defeat. It was hard to say which was closer to a final collapse, building or beings. They took not the slightest interest in Maura and Patrick.

"You can take my word for it," Toggs said, though, to Maura's ears, he spoke with little conviction, "in all of Liverpool, you won't find a better lodging to stay in than this. Shelter, bed, and food for no more than four pence a day. What's more, you can stay as long as you need to or"—he nodded significantly—"as long as your money lasts."

"We won't be staying long," Maura said finally, as much to herself as anyone else. "We'll be sailing in a few days."

"Then I'm sure you'll do well here," Toggs said agreeably. He moved toward the house. "Step up now. I'll introduce you to Mrs. Sonderbye."

"And who may she be?" Maura asked timidly.

"The kind lady who'll take you in." Toggs mounted the rickety steps. "Are you coming or no?"

Maura and Patrick looked at each other. When Patrick gave a tiny shrug, Maura started up after the young man. At least, she thought, it was a woman in charge.

"Mrs. Sonderbye!" Toggs bellowed at the doorway. "Are you about?"

The woman herself emerged. She was as large and round as a boulder, with massive arms, stocky legs, and a face as red as raw beefsteak.

"Who's calling?" she shouted, blinking her bleary eyes as if she had not seen daylight for a week.

104

"Ralph Toggs of the Lime Street Runners Association at your service, Mrs. Sonderbye," the young man announced, putting his fingers to his hat in salute. "I've brought some souls that need serving." He held up Maura's bundle and gestured to sister and brother.

Mrs. Sonderbye shifted her head ponderously in their direction. Contemplating the newcomers with ill-disguised contempt, she nonetheless closed her fat fingers around Maura's bundle. "Room and board, four pence a day, each," she announced. "Minimum stay, a week, payable in advance. You won't need no references."

"There, you hear?" Toggs enthused to Maura. "No references. Didn't I say the lady was kind?"

"Might we see the room?" Maura asked.

Mrs. Sonderbye did not seem to hear the question. "Do you want it or not?" she demanded while giving a backward toss to Maura's bundle. It disappeared into the house.

"You won't get better," Toggs pressed Maura. "You can trust me on that."

Maura was not sure what she had expected, but this was nothing of the kind. It was not the poverty of the place that upset her. She was used to that. It was the filth she found horrifying. But what else were they to do? Where else were they to go? And all the while Patrick was gazing up at her, waiting for her decision.

"Yes or no?" Mrs. Sonderbye demanded again.

Just two days, Maura thought, for in just that time she and Patrick would be on their way to America. She nodded.

"Money first," Mrs. Sonderbye sang out, "comfort second." She extended a fat hand, palm up. "You pays by the week."

"We're only staying two days."

"You'll get a refund."

Maura turned away, took out her packet, and extracted

enough coins to pay the first week's bill. They were swallowed instantly by Mrs. Sonderbye's grasping fingers.

"Come on then," the woman said. As she did, she reached out, and Maura thought she saw—though she wasn't certain—some of the coins drop into Toggs's hand. The next moment the landlady moved back through the doorway.

Just as they were about to follow, Maura turned to Toggs. "I thank you for your kindness," she said, looking squarely into his eyes.

He blushed to the roots of his hair. "You'll—do—well enough here," he stammered. "There are worse places. And—" Instead of finishing his words, he made an abrupt turn and ran down the street. Maura watched him go, then heeded Patrick when he tugged at her arm. Together, they crossed the threshold into Mrs. Sonderbye's house.

If the outside was in wretched repair, the inside was worse. Walls once plastered were pocked with holes, exposing lath and hair within. Even in the dim light, joists could be seen below the gapped and curling floorboards. The smell of refuse nearly caused Maura and Patrick to gag. As they made their way down the central hallway, they saw many rooms on either side. Each was crammed with people who appeared to be camping as they might in the open air.

Mrs. Sonderbye clumped to the far end of the hall. She yanked open a door. Having but one hinge, it barely clung to the frame. "Down the steps," she said. "Make yourselves at home. The loo is out back."

Patrick peered down the stairwell. It was too dark to see much of anything.

"And if you please, miss," Maura said to Mrs. Sonderbye, "our bundle." But the woman, paying no attention, was retreating ponderously along the hall.

Maura wanted to protest, but Patrick had already started

106

down the steps. With the greatest trepidation, Maura followed. Halfway there, they stopped.

Thin fingers of light poked in from cracks through the ceiling above. Scattered about on an earthen floor were stuffed bags and pallets. A dozen people were stretched upon these, eight men and four women, most asleep. Those awake sat on sparse straw. Few wore shoes or boots. None appeared clean or even healthy. They stared at the newcomers silently. Only one person seemed alive, and he was deeply immersed in a book.

But as Maura and Patrick gazed downward in dread, the man who was reading looked up. "Ah, new neighbors!" he cried brightly. "Welcome to you both! As the bard said, 'Small cheer and great welcome makes a merry feast.' Come right along!" Given the abject dreariness of the place, his cheerful greeting had the feel and sound of madness.

It was too much for Maura. She turned and pressed her face against the stairwell wall, a wall oozing with rancid damp, giving growth to patches of mustard-colored mildew.

Feeling equally wretched, Patrick looked on helplessly. He had but two thoughts: that it was he who had brought them to this place, and that they would never leave it.

Chapter 26
Some Troubling Thoughts

When Ralph Toggs rushed downhill away from Mrs. Sonderbye's, he was angry. He did not know why he was angry, only that he felt so. The very notion was itself mortifying. After all, he had done no more than he did every day—snapped up two ignorant Irish emigrants and led them to a place of lodging, for which service he received money. Three or four times a day he did it and had been doing so for five years as the best runner in the Lime Street Runners Association!

Sergeant Rumpkin, the association leader, had often told Toggs how good he was, praising him before all the others. At the age of fifteen, he had no rivals, except, perhaps, Fred, a boy without a last name. And Fred, in Ralph Toggs's opinion, was just a lack-brain brat.

And yet, this time, when Toggs had done his job, the girl had thanked him. It was confounding. And those eyes. . . .

Toggs could have sworn she knew he was misleading them. Had she not seen the Union House, where she and her brother were meant to stay, after he told them it had burned? Even so, she had trusted him, had *thanked* him! For Toggs, it was galling to be treated with such consideration! And from such a pretty girl!

As for Mrs. Sonderbye's home, Toggs knew how perfectly awful it was, knew the landlady's reputation for gouging her tenants in every possible way. It had not mattered to him before. Why should it matter now?

Distressed by such thoughts, Toggs took himself into a spirit shop and found a seat in a far corner. Once there, he wrapped himself in as deep a sulk as he had ever experienced.

Ralph Toggs was not usually given to thinking about himself. He did his job and lived his life with few questions asked and no answers demanded. Most of his friends did exactly the same. As far as he could tell, they never were troubled with questions or answers.

With his drink before him—it too had acquired a sour taste—Toggs began to admit that there was something about that girl. . . . He wished she had not believed him!

Was he getting soft? he asked himself. Being a runner

required hardness, and his hardness was something of which he had always been proud. After all, you had to take miserable, confused people right off the boats and make sure that what little they had was plucked away. They were not called pigeons for nothing. What did it matter to him? People should look out for themselves. The way he did. No one took care of him. He asked no one to pity him. And yet, he half suspected that the girl *did* pity him. It was galling!

If he was getting soft, he told himself, he should get out of the business altogether. There were always new fellows coming into the runners' trade ready to take his place, new ones like Fred. This Fred was nothing but a baby, yet hard as nails, mean as a rough stone. Worst of all, Sergeant Rumpkin had taken a liking to him. Brought him into the association. Praised him.

Toggs shook his head in disgust. He would be happy to take on Fred No-name anytime of the day or night. But as for this girl . . .

Maybe, he thought, he *should* get out of the business. Go to America like so many others. Not that it would take much money. Except that Toggs did not have money. What he got he always spent.

To prove this fact to himself, he reached into his pocket and took out the few coins Mrs. Sonderbye had given him. Perhaps if he gave them back to the girl, he would feel better. She might even tell him what she really thought of him. A good scolding or even a slap of anger would brace him up considerably. That was more what he was used to.

Toggs stood up, drained his drink, spit it out for the filth it was, and returned to the streets. His mind was made up: He would go to the docks and find a way to get some money. Exactly how, he had no idea. But one way or another, he was determined to have it. And with the money, win the girl.

With a confident tap to his hat, he started off.

Chapter 27
Laurence and Mr. Clemspool
Reach Liverpool

W
e are here, Master Worthy," Mr. Clemspool whispered into Laurence's ear. With a start, Laurence woke. Passengers were already clambering out of the railway carriage. The boy pulled himself up only to become aware of how much his body ached. He felt hot too.

"Push the door then," Mr. Clemspool urged.

Rather light-headed, Laurence did as he was told. Gingerly, he stepped onto the platform. Though not nearly as vast as the station in London, it was quite lofty and grand. Many people were pushing past.

Mr. Clemspool, in greatcoat and top hat, and carrying his traveling bag, extricated himself from the carriage. Once on the platform, he stretched. "Painful way to travel, isn't it?" he said. "Ah, but the sea, Master Worthy, the bracing sea. What pleasures are in store for you!" He patted Laurence on the back.

"First, however, we need to get you some food and proper lodging, wouldn't you say?" He glanced about. A few yards away a girl—not a day older than seven and dressed in rags— was selling sugar buns. Round like balls, large as a man's fist, and sprinkled liberally with sugar, they were heaped high in a shallow reed basket that the child held before her. A crudely lettered sign read SUGAR BUNS, HA'PENNY EACH.

Mr. Clemspool beckoned flamboyantly with his hat.

The girl hurried over. "Yes, sir!"

110

"One, two?" Mr. Clemspool offered Laurence.

The sight of food made the boy's stomach growl. "Two," he replied.

"Young Master Worthy desires two buns. *No!* Make that three!"

The girl curtsied and handed over the buns. Mr. Clemspool gave her two pennies, grandly waved away the change, then passed the buns to Laurence, who devoured the first in three bites and immediately started on the second.

The girl giggled, hand over her mouth. Mr. Clemspool laughed too. "Now then," he said, bending over the boy, "I'm supposed to meet an old friend for a brief chat. He was traveling first class. Ah! The clock! The very spot."

Upon the farthest wall of the station, a huge clock with Roman numerals had been mounted. The time was eight-thirty-five.

"Follow me," Mr. Clemspool said, wrapping one arm around Laurence so that the two of them moved in lockstep. Together, they made their way across a large crowded space amid bulky piles of boxes and trunks. Laurence saw many families—or so he thought they were—grouped around their possessions. He wondered if they too were going to America.

"There's my friend," Mr. Clemspool announced, deftly turning Laurence away so that the boy faced the way they had come. "Now, Master Worthy, I won't be but a twinkling. You *must* remain right here." He placed a firm hand on Laurence's shoulder and squeezed. "Do *not* move!" he ordered in a severe voice. "I intend to keep my eye on you. Once I return, I'll find a decent place for you to rest."

Laurence stood where he was and began to eat the third bun. It was much easier to have someone make decisions for him.

But once he had eaten the bun, Laurence grew impatient. Not entirely pleased to be relegated to waiting, he glanced

111

in the direction of the clock. Mr. Clemspool was still talking to the man he had referred to as his old friend. This gentleman was dressed in fashionable clothing that fairly glowed with newness. His tall top hat was brushed, his boots bright and shiny, his shoulder cape—with fur trimming on the collar—luxurious. One eye was covered with a patch.

Laurence fairly jumped. For one heart-plunging second, he thought he was looking at the scoundrel who had robbed him of his money in London the night before. He wished the man would turn so he could see his full face, but he did not. Then Laurence told himself this man could *not* possibly be the same person. That cad had been in London. This man was in Liverpool. The eye patch had to be merely a coincidence. Other men wore eye patches. Furthermore, the boy reminded himself, he had already made a number of bad judgments. He must make no more. With that thought, he made himself turn away.

Within moments Mr. Clemspool returned. "Very good then, Master Worthy," he cried. "You've done exactly as you were told. I *admire* that in a young man. Now, I shall give all my attention to you!"

Leaving the station, they stepped out into Lime Street. Facing them was a colossal stone building with many huge columns, guarded by two massive sculptured lions. Laurence gasped.

"Saint George Hall," Mr. Clemspool said with a casual wave of his hand, as if the building were an old acquaintance. "One of the marvels of this city of wealth!"

The building was as big as any Laurence had seen. Its size succeeded in making him acutely aware of his weakness and isolation.

Under Mr. Clemspool's guidance, they turned left and came upon a thoroughfare full of carriages, wagons, carts. Buildings of dark stone were festooned with bright commercial signs proclaiming where agents, packagers, shippers, deliverers, and a hundred more services pertaining to the ocean trade might be found.

"Liverpool!" Mr. Clemspool announced with an expansive gesture. "The second city in England! Half a *million* people, Master Worthy! *Not* a place—to make my point precisely—you'd wish to be adrift on your own, eh?"

"No, sir," Laurence replied truthfully.

At the curb, a row of hansom cabs waited for people emerging from the station. The first driver—a man with a stiff gray beard, a tall hat, and a long, trailing green scarf around his neck—peered down from his high perch. "All right, gents, where might you be going?"

"Royalton Hotel," Mr. Clemspool called up. "Grove Street."

The driver wrinkled his nose. "That boy there, he's a bit dirty and bruised, ain't he?"

Embarrassed, Laurence turned away.

"You are altogether correct," Mr. Clemspool replied briskly. "It's that wretched railroad. But be assured, my good man, there will be an extra shilling for you to wink the old eye."

"Right-o!" the driver returned with newfound enthusiasm for dirty passengers.

Mr. Clemspool held open the carriage door for Laurence to get in, which the boy did. Mr. Clemspool took the seat by his side. "Almost there!" he enthused.

The driver made a clucking noise and flicked the reins. With a clatter of hooves, the horse trotted off.

As Laurence sank back in the upholstered seat, Mr. Clemspool lifted the carriage blanket and tucked it about the boy's knees. The attention, the appropriateness of it, was all wonderfully familiar and comforting. This was life as Laurence knew it, as it should be.

With half-closed eyes, he considered his benefactor. He felt truly grateful to the man. But then, he told himself, why shouldn't Mr. Clemspool be kind? Was he not merely treating him the way he'd been treated from his birth?

But as the cab bounced over the cobblestone streets, the image of the man with the eye patch drifted back into his mind. Laurence now regretted having turned away without studying the man's face. He would have liked to feel reassured that this was *not* the man from London. But with a shudder and a shake of his head, he once again strove to dismiss the thought.

Mr. Clemspool noted the tremor. "You seem to be troubled by something," he remarked solicitously. "Are you?"

"No, nothing," Laurence replied, and shut his eyes. It was wrong, he told himself, to be suspicious of those who were treating you properly.

They soon reached the Royalton Hotel, a modest four-story brick building on a quiet street. Ordinary houses stood on either side. No great snarl of traffic or mobs of pedestrians crowded the way. Indeed, the place was quite isolated.

"Come along now," Mr. Clemspool urged, holding Laurence's arm firmly as he stepped from the cab. The boy was about to say there was no need to hold him so tightly when a uniformed attendant greeted them with a bow, called Mr. Clemspool by name, picked up his bag, and indicated the hotel door. Once inside, Mr. Clemspool let go of Laurence.

In the foyer was a table behind which sat a man, dressed formally. "Ah, Mr. Clemspool, sir," he said as he rose to his feet, "so good to see you again."

"Pleasure to be here," Mr. Clemspool returned, lifting his hat. His bald head gleamed. "My son," he announced, making a wave of his fingers that encompassed Laurence.

The man bowed. "Mr. Hudson at your service," he said to Laurence.

"We've just come down by railroad from London," Mr. Clemspool explained. "I must apologize for the boy's condition. Quite filthy, I know. He tripped at the station. Made a terrible mess. Ruined his fine clothing and bruised his face. Indeed, I fear the lad is none too well. Quite exhausted and overwhelmed by it all, you see."

A startled Laurence gazed at his protector. To be introduced as his son did not seem right. That was taking liberties. As for the reasons given . . . Laurence wished he were not so tired and disoriented. He hardly knew what to say.

Mr. Hudson seemed unconcerned. He made several references to previous visits, the weather, the tides, and inquiries as to the length of Mr. Clemspool's stay, as well as the nature of the accommodations needed. "The usual?" he concluded by asking.

"Quite sufficient," Mr. Clemspool returned.

In a matter of moments, Mr. Clemspool and Laurence were in their rooms. There were two rooms, both with beds. One was situated near the door, the other toward the back and reachable only by going through the first room.

"You shall stay there," Mr. Clemspool said, indicating the second, farthest room. "It looks out on the street and is pleasant and bright. I shall take this one near the door. Will that be agreeable?"

"I'm sure," said Laurence, bewildered by the ease of this business.

"I do hope you didn't mind my saying you were my son, Master Worthy," Mr. Clemspool offered with a generous swirl of his fingers, as if sweeping the air of cobwebs. "It saves explanations. For now, hasten yourself into bed. You don't look well, my friend. I shall procure some real food and some proper clothing for you."

Mr. Clemspool went on so briskly, Laurence had no time to respond. Besides, the thought of a bed pushed all worries

115

from his mind. He made his way into the farthest room. There, he used the basin and pitcher of water that stood upon a small table to wash his hands and face.

With a sigh, Laurence stripped himself of his dirty, tattered clothing, leaving them—as he usually did at home—in a pile on the floor. Then he slipped on the nightshirt that hung from a wall hook. Its softness was delightful. At last he crawled up on the high four-poster bed and crept deep beneath the covers. The delicious smell of clean cotton sheets was luxuriant. The fluffiness of three goose-down pillows, the gentle weight of wool blankets . . . like home.

Mr. Clemspool poked his head in at the door. "Comfy?" he inquired sweetly.

"Oh, yes, sir," Laurence purred with contentment. His eyes were already half-closed.

"Master Worthy," Mr. Clemspool announced as he came another step into the room, "I shall leave you to get some food." Glancing at Laurence and seeing that the boy's eyes were shut, he swooped up the soiled clothing. With practiced hands, he patted it down, finding and removing what remained of the money, then left the clothing on the floor where it had been.

Laurence, suspecting nothing, lay snug in bed. Half-asleep, he listened to the click of the lock in the door as Mr. Clemspool left the room. Did the locking bother him? Not at all. A locked door meant he was cared for, safe. Moreover, the sweetness of the bed proved to be so blissful that a sleep of total confidence was not long in coming.

Chapter 28
At Mrs. Sonderbye's Lodging House

D on't cry, Maura," Patrick pleaded. He was blaming himself for getting them into such a dreadful place. "You mustn't. We won't be here long," he promised. "We won't."

Even as he spoke, the man who had been reading stood up. "Welcome, welcome, welcome," he called across the dirt floor. "Do not lose hope," he added. "As the poet said, 'True hope is swift, and flies with swallow's wings; Kings it makes gods, and meaner creatures kings.' *Richard Three.*"

The very brightness of the greeting in such dismal surroundings made Patrick think the man was not in his right mind. But Maura momentarily forgot her wretchedness. She turned to consider the speaker.

He was a long, lanky man—thirty or so, she guessed—with so little flesh upon his bones that when he stood it seemed more an unfolding than a rising. His smile was as wide as his face. His large brown eyes and a thatch of straw-colored hair hanging like a tasseled curtain over his face and ears conspired to create the look of a simple fellow.

"My dears," the man said in a deep singsong voice, "you are distressed. The truth is, none of us would be here if we were not so." He spread his arms wide enough to encompass the whole world. "Do tell me," he coaxed, "what are the particulars of your grief?"

"Forgive us, sir," Maura said, ashamed to have been caught weeping against the wall. "We're emigrants just off

117

the boat. We meant to go to the Union House but were informed it had burned to the ground the night before. There was nowhere else to go but here.

"Ah-ha!" cried the man dramatically. "Who provided you with *that* information?"

"The fellow who brought us here," Maura explained. "No doubt he was meaning to be kind."

"Kind!" the tall man reacted with scorn. "If you trusted in *that*, you would believe the new year starts four times with each season because someone told you so. Let me assure you, my dear, that the Union House stood yesterday, stands today, and will stand tomorrow."

"But he told us—"

The man held up his long-fingered hands to cut Maura off. "My dear young lady, they will tell you *anything*."

"Who will?" Patrick asked, alarmed.

"The runners, dear boy, the runners. Like rats, they infest Liverpool." He wiggled his fingers like the galloping legs of a rodent. "Some work alone. Some are paid by houses. Others join associations. They will do anything to get people like you to lodge where it's profitable for *them*. Perfectly legal but *most* unfortunate. Believe me, there are hundreds of establishments such as this."

"But why?" Patrick said, beginning to grasp the extent of his folly in listening to Mr. Toggs.

"To get your money," the man replied. "And they'll keep you here until it's gone or you're in debt. Then, dear friends, you shall never leave."

Maura covered her face with her hands.

"Are you saying, sir," Patrick asked with growing resentment, "that this Mr. Toggs lied to us?"

"I know nothing about Mr. Toggs in the particular, but of course he lied," the man exclaimed with a grandiose gesture of arm and hand. "For a runner to tell the truth would be as miraculous as for the sun to shine at midnight. Avoid him and all his kind. I presume you are on your way to America."

Maura and Patrick nodded.

"I need hardly have asked. Nor did your Mr. Toggs. If you unfurled a banner that read 'Going to America!' it would be no easier to see. And from Ireland too, I'll venture. Of course you are," he added as the O'Connells nodded a second time. "But then most of Ireland and much of Germany and Scotland are going. All by way of Liverpool. All innocent lambs ready to be shorn of wool!

"My dears, I can guarantee it: You are not likely to see that young man again!" As if he had finished a speech on a stage, the man took a bow.

Patrick appealed to Maura with a look that begged forgiveness. Though she would not say, "I told you so," she would not forgive him either. Instead she turned away.

"But then," the man continued in his cheerful way, "you *have* gotten to Liverpool. And now that you are here, we must get you out. You've met Mrs. Sonderbye, I presume?"

"Was she the woman who took our money?" Maura asked wearily.

"You describe her to perfection!" exclaimed the man with glee. "Mrs. Sonderbye is a force to be reckoned with.

"But forgive me," he said suddenly, folding himself into another bow. "I've forgotten my courtesy. My name"—he touched his narrow chest—"is Horatio Drabble, actor. Late of London and the provincial stages, intent upon refurbishing my career in America. Mind, I do only Shakespeare, he who—as Johnson said—'was not of an age but for all time.'

"I do all the principal tragical parts," Mr. Drabble went on. "*Richard Three.* 'Now is the winter of our discontent.' *King Lear.* 'Blow, winds, crack your cheeks!' *Hamlet.* 'To be

119

or not to be, that is the question!' *Macbeth*. 'Is this a dagger I see before me, its handle toward my hand?' " With every phrase, Mr. Drabble struck a different dramatic pose.

"But," he continued apace, "since I have—at the moment—no proper stage to perform upon, I make every moment a performance." Mr. Drabble bowed as if expecting applause. When he received none—only stares of puzzlement from Maura and Patrick—he merely went on with the same good cheer as before. "But come along, my dears, we've got some mostly dry straw here. You can settle right down and be one with us."

Mr. Drabble fluffed up some rotten straw with his hands. "There," he offered, patting the top of the heap, "have a seat."

Patrick sat next to Mr. Drabble. After a moment Maura joined him.

"I'd offer tea and cake," the actor confided as he pushed the hair out of his eyes, "but the truth is, I have nothing but my talent. Have no fear, though. Dinner will be served eventually. I suggest we sup together, but first, might I beg the privilege of your names?"

"If you please, sir, my name is Patrick O'Connell. And this is my sister, Maura."

"Patrick and Maura. Excellent!" Mr. Drabble returned. "We've got a Bridgit here as well as a Sarah, Nell, and Kathleen. Then there is John, Roger, Godfrey, Brian, Jonathan, Peter, and Sean." He pointed to each person, whether awake or asleep. "Mostly from your Ireland. If you stay long enough—which I earnestly pray you do *not*—you'll know us as well as we'll know you."

"Mr. Drabble," Maura said stoutly, "we're intending to go to America in a couple of days."

"We have tickets," Patrick said.

Mr. Drabble quickly put a thin finger to his lips and

leaned forward. "Be careful what you say, dear boy," he whispered while glancing around at the other inhabitants of the basement.

"Once," he said, keeping his voice low, "we *all* had tickets. Don't you think a ticket is a metaphor for life? Who is born who does not have a ticket to somewhere? Alas, our tickets are lost or stolen. Gone, like so much confetti. Believe me, Liverpool is swollen with people without tickets. But enough, I wish to hear your story, truly."

Patrick was more than willing to relate all that had happened from the time their father left Ireland to their own arrival in Liverpool, including their meeting with Ralph Toggs.

Mr. Drabble, who listened intently throughout, sighed when it was done. "My dears, may I offer some advice?"

"Please, sir," returned Maura, "we'd be much obliged."

"Many people—myself included—are eager to go to America. Thousands do. But not these," Mr. Drabble said while gesturing to the others in the basement. "Not I."

"Faith then, sir, why not?" Maura asked.

"Poverty," Mr. Drabble replied. "It brought us here. It keeps us here. To be without money in Liverpool is to be lost. People pour into this city ready, nay, desperate, to go abroad. America. Canada. Australia. Ah, but this"—he used his hands to encompass the basement—"is a money trap. The longer you stay, the less likely it is you will leave, for your money will be siphoned away. If you are to meet your father as planned, we must act quickly! You said you have tickets. For what ship?" he whispered. "When?"

"The *Robert Peel*," Maura answered low. "It will be sailing in two days' time."

"God willing, we shall have you on it," Mr. Drabble said earnestly. "And I shall salute you from the quay. Of course, there is a medical exam to be accomplished first. You must have that."

"We didn't know," Maura said, quite alarmed.

"Not a thing to fear, my dear. But it must be done else your tickets won't be stamped. Without a stamp, you can't get on your boat. Many don't know till it's too late. I myself shall take you to the place where the exam is done. But for now, I think you need some rest."

Maura nodded. When Patrick—by way of atonement—grandly informed her that he would keep watch, she lay down on the straw. Within moments she was asleep. With a nod of his own, Mr. Drabble returned to his corner and—beneath shafts of faint light—continued his reading.

Just as he had promised, Patrick stayed by Maura. Staring into the gloom, his jaw clenched, his toes curled against the cold damp, he could not but reflect on their dismal circumstances. Anger filled him—anger with the deceitful Ralph Toggs and with himself for his own gullibility.

But what he felt even more keenly was fear, fear that they would, as Mr. Drabble had warned, be trapped in Liverpool. Oh, if only he could be like St. George!

Chapter 29
Laurence Awakens

At first Laurence could not remember where he was. All he knew was that his legs and arms were sore. His throat too. Then he recollected Liverpool, and a hotel. As for the man peering down at him, it was none other than Mr. Matthew Clemspool, the gentleman who had been treating him like a son—like a son, Laurence thought, should be treated.

"Awake, are you, Master Worthy?" Mr. Clemspool asked with unctuous kindness.

"Yes," Laurence murmured, still luxuriating in cozy sleepiness. "But I feel tired."

"Anything more than that?"

"I'm a bit sore," Laurence reported. "And my throat hurts some."

Mr. Clemspool reacted with alarm. "To put it precisely, Master Worthy, you are *ill*. I feared as much. You've been sleeping for hours. While you were in bed, I went to fetch you new clothes—I have them in my room—but came back to find you hot as a fresh loaf of bread. I tried in vain to waken you. Imagine my dismay when I could not! That is why I immediately sent for an apothecary to put you to rights. May I present Mr. Bungo."

Laurence raised his head from the pillow. Next to Mr. Clemspool was a very small man dressed in an overlarge and frayed green frock coat. With his pasty pale face, dull gray eyes, and pug nose, there was something doll-like about him save for the fact that he was badly in need of a shave and smelled of beer.

"Mr. Bungo," Mr. Clemspool said, "here is Master Worthy. We want him well enough to be able to travel to America soon."

Without a word the apothecary stepped forward and stared hard at Laurence. "Sit up," he commanded in a slightly slurred voice. Laurence did as he was told.

"Be so good as to look at my hand." Mr. Bungo waved his small trembling hand in Laurence's face. "Good. Now open your mouth wide. Yes. Tongue. Fine. Can you speak?"

"Yes, but my throat hurts."

"Seriously?"

"Some."

"Your pulse," Mr. Bungo requested.

Laurence held out his hand. The apothecary took the wrist briefly, then dropped it. "It is my duty to report," Mr. Bungo told Mr. Clemspool, "that rest and good food will revive him."

"Might you have some kind of restorative?" Mr. Clemspool prompted.

"Of course!" the small man cried. "I almost forgot." He swung a box upon the bed and flipped it open. The box contained three rows of bottles, labeled and corked, five to a row. The apothecary waved a finger over them like a vibrating magic wand until he found what he wanted. "This will do the job," he announced. "Tincture of rhubarb. One spoonful every two hours."

He handed the bottle to Mr. Clemspool and snapped his box shut. "When that's gone, you may apply for more. No charge for me, just the medicine." He extended a hand. "Two shillings, please."

Mr. Clemspool took the bottle and dropped the coins into the hand.

The apothecary pocketed the coins with something of a thank-you, made a curt bow, and scurried out of the room.

"There you are, Master Worthy," Mr. Clemspool said, holding the bottle aloft as if to check its purity. "We'll have you back in perfect health in nothing short. Tincture of rhubarb. No doubt it's what the queen—God save her—takes herself."

Laurence reached for the medicine.

"Not yet!" Mr. Clemspool cried. "I need to get a spoon."

Laurence sank back upon his pillow.

"Exactly, Master Worthy," Mr. Clemspool crooned with approval. "*Rest*, to make my point precisely, is exactly what you need. And of course, this restorative. Let me just fetch that spoon." So saying, he took the bottle and left the room.

Laurence looked around at the departing Mr. Clemspool

just in time to see him pull the door closed with a snap. Once again he heard the lock click shut. For a time he stared at the door, trying to imagine why Mr. Clemspool should bother to lock it when he was going only to fetch a spoon.

As he lay there, he thought he heard voices coming from without. One voice he recognized as Mr. Clemspool's. The other, he assumed, belonged to Mr. Bungo.

At first Laurence paid little mind. But when the conversation stretched on, he began to feel unsettled. Could it be, he wondered, that he was more ill than they had told him?

Unable to hear clearly from the bed, Laurence scooted his legs out from under the covers and stood upon the floor. For a few seconds he felt unsteady, but once the feeling passed, he moved softly to the door. Crouching down, he applied his eye to the keyhole. What he saw was Mr. Clemspool's back. Only when he shifted did Laurence see a face. But it was not Mr. Bungo's. It was the face of the man Mr. Clemspool had talked to in the Liverpool station, the man with an eye patch.

Greatly puzzled, the boy pressed against the door in an attempt to get a better look. What he observed was that the man's lower lip was bruised and puffy, as if he had been struck recently. Seeing it, Laurence's heart gave a tremendous thump. *There could be no doubt: This was the man who had robbed him in London!*

Reeling from shock, Laurence staggered back from the door. How could it be the same man? That was London. This was Liverpool. This man was dressed well, appearing for all the world to be a gentleman. *His* London man had been a common thief and looked like one. Then Laurence recalled that when the thief first appeared, he was bearded and leaned upon a crutch. But when he ran away with the money, the beard proved false and the man was in no need of a crutch at all!

Laurence returned to the keyhole. The man with the eye patch had moved out of view, but he and Mr. Clemspool were still talking. Laurence put his ear to the door and listened.

"As I told you, Mr. Grout, your good fortune—as you expressed it—has little to do with my affairs." It was Mr. Clemspool speaking. "I'm settled upon what I do, and do well, and there is no lacking for employment. Why gentlemen have so many more younger sons than they want is beyond the scope of my imagination. But since they do . . ."

"Ah," said the other man, "but yer could chuck it all and do the same show in the States."

"Mr. Grout," replied Mr. Clemspool, "my understanding is that things are not so arranged in America. No, sir, if you and I must end our partnership, so be it. I harbor no ill feelings. I wish you well."

"Same for me, governor. We've 'ad a good trot, yer and me."

"My only desire," Mr. Clemspool said, "is that you fulfill your final obligation to me in this little matter I have at hand. Only a question of overseeing the boy—my *son*," he added sarcastically, "until his proper destination is reached."

"I can 'andle it," Mr. Grout assured him.

"Indeed, he *likes* being taken care of. He expects it. I tell you, these rich boys are spoiled brats. They presume the world spins for them. *Want* someone to take care of them. Of course, he treats me like a servant. I don't complain. Makes my efforts so much easier."

Laurence, enraged, jerked back from the door. How dare they talk about him this way! He reached for the door to protest when he suddenly remembered it was locked. Stymied, he stood there.

"Don't yer worry none," he heard Mr. Grout go on. "Long as me luck 'olds, with no black cats, spilled salt, or cracked mirrors comin' along, I'll do the thing."

"Mr. Grout," Mr. Clemspool said with some exasperation, "now that you have risen in the world, you're going to have to put all these superstitions of yours aside."

"Just the opposite, Clemspool," he returned. "Now I've got something worth the 'avin', you'll see, imps, goblins, and ghosts will be tryin' to trip me up all the more. But I'm man enough to keep free of 'em."

"Good," Mr. Clemspool said, "that will be a considerable comfort to all concerned. Now let's go down to the lobby and send my bit of a message."

"Yer pleasure," Mr. Grout murmured.

The next moment Laurence heard the outer door closing. Quickly, he ran to his clothing and searched through the pockets only to discover that what had remained of his money was gone. Back he raced to the door and peered through the keyhole, then listened to make sure no one was there. Certain no one was, he yanked upon the door. It was indeed locked.

He had, in fact, become a prisoner.

Chapter 30

Mr. Clemspool Attends to Business

*I*n the lobby of the hotel, Mr. Clemspool, pen in hand, wrote a letter:

My dear Sir Albert Kirkle,

Sir, please be advised that the goods have arrived in Liverpool, have been secured, and will be shipped out on the

127

earliest possible conveyance. Once in the States, all proper attention shall be paid.

Yours faithfully,
M. Clemspool

When he was done, he offered the letter to Mr. Grout. "Yer know I can't read," the man growled, pushing the hand away.

"Ah, yes." Mr. Clemspool read the letter out loud.

"All fine and dandy," Mr. Grout observed, "but 'ow do yer expect to keep that there laddie cooped up in a room all the time without 'is gettin' suspicious?"

Mr. Clemspool smiled. "That's right, I forget this part of my business is new to you. Suspicion often does become a problem. But, as usual, the boy is exhausted, frightened. Running away seems to tumble the tummy. I tell them they are not well. They are glad to be told so. I call for Mr. Bungo. Mr. Bungo never fails to prescribe *something.*"

From a pocket Mr. Clemspool produced the bottle of tincture of rhubarb. From a second pocket he took out another bottle. He held it up while glancing left and right to make sure they were not being observed. They were alone.

With care, Mr. Clemspool poured some of the potion into the tincture of rhubarb. "This mixture," he explained, "will keep the boy sleeping until we get him on a ship."

Mr. Grout lifted an eyebrow, giving Mr. Clemspool the full benefit of a penetrating single-eyed stare.

"No, no, it won't harm him in the slightest," Mr. Clemspool assured his companion. "I made a promise to the boy's elder brother that nothing of that sort would happen to him—not, to make my point precisely, on *this* side of the Atlantic. For now I wish him only to sleep."

" 'Ow yer goin' to get 'im to swallow it?" Mr. Grout asked.

Mr. Clemspool laughed as he held up a spoon. "My weapon of choice."

"Yer think yerself double clever, yer do."

"Clever enough. And well-spoken enough, I dare say."

"What's the matter with my speakin'?" Mr. Grout demanded.

"You may have money in your pocket, sir, but you still have the street in your mouth."

Mr. Grout stood in anger. "Well then, I'm goin' out to see the street," he said in a huff, and strode away.

Mr. Clemspool shook the medicine bottle and smiled.

Chapter 31
Darkness in Liverpool

*M*aura O'Connell slept for most of the day. When she woke, it was to the harsh clanging of a stick upon a pot. The clamor brought the other people in the basement lumbering to their feet and straggling up the steps.

Mr. Drabble, a bowl and spoon in his hands, explained. "That's Mrs. Sonderbye's dinner chime. We'll need to get in line. She will do the honors, so for heaven's sake be careful. Don't," he admonished, "let the woman bully you. Above all, put no money in her purse!"

Maura and Patrick followed the actor up the steps. The hallway was crowded with people. In look and dress, they were no different from those in the basement, each and every one appearing depressed and defeated. There was hardly any talk, save guarded murmurs and mumbles.

"Who are they all?" Maura asked quietly as she, Patrick, and Mr. Drabble took their places at the end of the line.

"Mrs. Sonderbye's esteemed boarders, waiting for their dinner," the actor told them. "The lady herself presides. I urge you to take the basic menu. Your money will go farther."

"What is the basic?" Patrick asked. He was very hungry.

Mr. Drabble—brown eyes smiling—put a thin finger to his lips.

The line moved slowly, snaking its way down to the front of the house, then around and back again toward the kitchen. As they drew closer, they caught the smell of something strong and not altogether pleasant.

At last they could see their destination. In a doorway, an old table had been set up. Upon it was a large pot. Directly behind the table, in a high-backed chair like a throne, sat Mrs. Sonderbye, overseeing the operation. The serving was being done by an old woman and old man, one of whom was ladling from the pot, the other dispensing small pieces of stale bread from a basket.

When Maura, Patrick, and Mr. Drabble reached the kitchen door, Patrick eyed the contents of the pot suspiciously.

"What is it?" he asked of the woman serving.

"Cabbage soup," she replied. "Two spoonfuls is what you paid for. Two spoons is what you get. After that, it's a penny a scoop. Want it or not?"

"Of course they want it!" Mrs. Sonderbye cried from her chair. "They've just arrived. Give them as much as they'd like. And since you're newcomers," the large woman declared, "you'll rent some bowls, won't you? Or will you take your soup in your fingers?" She held out two bowls.

Maura and Patrick looked to Mr. Drabble for an answer.

"Dear, kind Mrs. Sonderbye," the actor said, "we three have chosen to form a company. We shall all sup from *my* bowl."

Mrs. Sonderbye's red face turned redder. "Don't do it!" she cried to Maura. "Take my word, as honest a woman as you'll find in all of Liverpool, that man is touched in the head. You don't want anything to do with him. I'd put him on the street if he didn't come up with his rent. These are clean bowls I offer, and good food. Only thruppence to rent. As good a bargain as you'll ever find."

"No, thank you," Maura managed to say.

"More fool you then," Mrs. Sonderbye returned with a scathing look at Mr. Drabble. "But don't come 'round and say I didn't warn you about him."

The woman servant took Mr. Drabble's bowl and poured in six scant ladles of soup. Then the old man handed each a small piece of hard bread.

"There, you see," the actor said, with a chuckle, when they were next to one another in a corner of the basement. "The woman would have flung me out a long time ago. But such is her greed, she'd rather have my irritating pennies than an empty hand."

"Is there no other place to go?" Maura asked.

Mr. Drabble blushed. "There's nothing cheaper," he said. "And as Hamlet said to his friend, 'Thrift, Horatio, thrift!' May I remind you, my name is Horatio.

"But as for supper, we shall share. As the reigning beauty amongst us, my dear," he said, offering the bowl and spoon to Maura, "you may start."

Blushing, Maura took them. The soup was nothing but cloudy and tepid water with a few wilted cabbage leaves floating about. She made a face.

"It's all we have, my dear," Mr. Drabble reminded her gently. "In America you'll eat much better. You know what is promised, gold in the streets. Cream in bowls. Blue in the sky. Consider this but the last bitter morsel of the Old World. It may weaken your body, but it will strengthen your resolve to go. May I suggest you dip your bread in the soup, to make it chewable."

Maura took a portion of the soup, dipped her bread, then passed the bowl on to Patrick, who had much the same reaction as she. Even so, he swallowed a spoonful, glad for something. Then it was Mr. Drabble's turn. Around and around they went until—after each had had his or her small lot—the bowl was scraped clean.

"Tomorrow then," Mr. Drabble said in his cheerful way, "we shall find your boat, make sure it's sailing, then arrange your medical exams. Does that sound satisfactory?"

"I'm sure you know better than we do, Mr. Drabble," Maura replied. She had decided to trust the actor.

"Good," he said. "Now, I suggest you repose here while I go off to work. Perhaps I'll earn a meager penny or two. One can only hope. I always do."

"What work can you do tonight?" Maura asked.

Mr. Drabble touched his heart. "I think I informed you," he replied with grave pride, "I am an actor. I offer the common people some touches of sublime art, which they might not otherwise expect to find upon the street. 'All the world's a stage, and all the men and women merely players.' Not a grand living, my dears, but so I live—perchance to die," he added dramatically. "But it is my art, and for an artist, that is *everything*. So make yourselves comfortable. I'll be back by midnight."

He stood up and brushed the straw from his clothing.

"Mr. Drabble, sir," Maura said. "If you'd be kind enough to allow it, might I go with you? I've slept long enough, and I'd take pleasure in watching you."

Mr. Drabble again put a hand to his heart. "You have touched my soul, my dear. Of course you are welcome. But I must warn you, it can be troublesome out there."

"In what way?" Maura asked.

"The streets are full, the competition is keen," the actor explained. "Not everyone appreciates art."

"You've been truly kind to us," Maura said. "If I could be of help to you . . ."

"I would be graced by your company," returned Mr. Drabble, making a deep bow. "And you?" he asked Patrick.

The boy looked to his sister.

"I think you'd best stay here," Maura told him. "Wasn't it you who watched over me before? Sure now, you can get yourself some sleep."

"Excellent," Mr. Drabble agreed. "No harm can come to him here."

So it was that at about seven o'clock Maura O'Connell and Horatio Drabble—the actor carrying a sack—ventured onto the street. Patrick went with them to the front door. After the two had gone, he loitered on the front steps, watching people pass by.

He was glad to be out of the basement. The crowds fascinated him. He wondered who they were, what they did, where they were going. That made him think of where he'd be a year from now. The question had never occurred to him before. Now he realized he could not really say. The thought excited him.

It was while idly watching the street that Patrick suddenly spied Ralph Toggs headed his way. On his back, the young man was carrying a trunk. Behind him were a man and a woman. Patrick could see they were Irish.

Feeling instant outrage, but not knowing what to do, he scrambled up the steps to the porch. Once there, he tried to slip behind the door, but a man was lounging against it and Patrick could not pass. Instead, he retreated into a corner and squatted near an old woman, drawing up his knees to make himself small.

Meanwhile, Toggs set the couple's trunk at the top of the steps and called, "Mrs. Sonderbye! Are you there?"

After a few requests, the woman emerged. "Who's calling?" she bellowed.

"Ralph Toggs, at your service, madam." He touched his hat in salute. "I've found some souls that need serving." He indicated the man and woman.

Patrick, watching from his corner, wondered if he and Maura had looked as dazed and bedraggled when they arrived.

Mrs. Sonderbye peered down at the newcomers, even as she clamped a possessive hand on the trunk. "Room and board, four pence a day, each," she informed them brusquely. "Minimum stay, a week, payable in advance. And you don't need references."

"There, you see," Toggs said to the man. "No references. I told you she was a decent sort, didn't I?"

The man and the woman exchanged worried looks. Patrick wanted to shout, "Don't do it," but dared not.

"Will you take it or no?" Mrs. Sonderbye demanded.

"You're not likely to find anything better," Toggs warned the couple. "Not at this time of night."

The man nodded. From his trouser pocket, he pulled out a purse and offered money to the landlady. She looked at it, then beckoned the couple into the house. As they passed her, she reached out and dropped some of the coins into Toggs's hand.

The young man took them but added, "Can I have a word, mistress?" Touching Mrs. Sonderbye's arm, he drew her off to one side.

"If you're asking for a bigger commission . . . ," the woman began to protest.

"It's nothing like that," Toggs assured her in a lowered

134

voice. "This morning I brought you two Irish ones, a boy and an older girl, his sister, I think."

"And I paid your part," Mrs. Sonderbye informed him.

"No, no, woman, I'm not asking for any money. Is the girl about? I want to speak to her."

Mrs. Sonderbye looked at him and smirked. "Got your eye on her, have you?"

"I might," Toggs said with a grin.

"They're all alike, these Irish," Mrs. Sonderbye went on. "She hardly arrived, but she hooked herself onto that troublesome actor fellow, Mr. Drabble. I seen them go off a while back."

"Did she?" Toggs returned, his face flushing. "What was she going with him for? Money?"

"I suppose he'll give her his earnings—not that he ever has much," the woman sneered.

"I can get more any day," Toggs bragged. "How much do you think it'll take to please her?"

"Her runt of a brother's about," the woman said with a laugh. "Go ask him."

"Never mind," Toggs growled. "I'll find her myself."

He gave a curt salute and started down the steps.

As Mrs. Sonderbye went inside after her new boarders, Patrick jumped up. As far as he was concerned, Maura was in danger. From the top of the steps, he saw Toggs moving quickly down the street. Hardly thinking about what he intended to do, he leaped to the ground and began to follow him.

135

Chapter 32
Laurence Reacts

*T*hough his heart was no longer pounding as it had been, Laurence was having difficulty absorbing what he'd discovered, namely that Mr. Clemspool knew he was from a wealthy family and was holding him prisoner. The man was also associated with the thief in London. Who was this Mr. Clemspool, and what was he up to? Laurence knew only that he had to get away from him.

He made a quick survey of his room, something he had not troubled to do before. It had two corner windows, adjoining. Each of these was draped with a single heavy curtain, drawn closed. A whale-oil lamp provided what light there was. There was too a clothespress and a closet for the commode. The only other furniture was a little table upon which rested several dishes of food.

Feeling weak, Laurence tested his arms and legs. They still ached. The pain made him think of the medicine Mr. Clemspool had promised. Perhaps it might make him stronger. He went back to the door and listened. The adjacent room was quiet. The door remained locked.

Laurence drew aside the curtain on one of the windows and looked down on the lamp-lit street. Very little traffic was passing, though as he watched, a horse and rider came along, as did a pony cart, a donkey, and two wagons. When a few pedestrians appeared, he decided to summon help.

Trying to make as little noise as possible, he pushed the window out. But he restrained himself from calling. What if Mr. Clemspool was nearby and heard him? He could not risk it. Dejected, Laurence started back to bed but stopped before the table. Hunger surged within him.

Snatching up some eggs, chicken, bread, he laid out a feast on his bed, then squirmed under the covers and propped himself against the pillows.

He was ravenous. Even when—twenty minutes later—Mr. Clemspool unlocked the door and stepped into the room, Laurence was still eating.

"Ah, Master Worthy," the man cried, "I see your appetite has not suffered. Good!"

Afraid to look at Mr. Clemspool lest his eyes betray what he knew, Laurence continued to chew upon a piece of bread.

Mr. Clemspool approached the bed. "Here's the very thing that will restore your strength in full measure." He held up the bottle of tincture of rhubarb and the spoon. "In fact, you should be dosed this very moment."

The smiling Mr. Clemspool made Laurence almost ill with distrust. No, it would not be wise to take the medicine. In any case, the food had revived him. With a curt shake of his head, he refused the bottle.

"Now, now, Master Worthy," Mr. Clemspool said soothingly, "let's not be foolish."

"I'll take it later," Laurence said, and held out his hand for the bottle.

After the slightest hesitation, Mr. Clemspool relinquished the medicine and spoon. "You do promise you'll take it, don't you?" he said.

"I will," Laurence mumbled.

"Good! I trust you. Now, Master Worthy, let us hope tomorrow you will be well. We need to arrange such things as your ticket."

Convinced the man was only lying, Laurence stared coldly at him.

Mr. Clemspool's smile never faltered. "Master Worthy," he said, "you do me an honor by letting me provide for you." He plucked the air. "Be assured I will do nothing to abuse your good faith.

"As for now, I leave you to your repast. Shall I return in an hour to make sure all is well? I think so. In the meanwhile, you *will* take your tincture won't you?" He wagged a cautionary finger.

"Yes, sir. . . ."

"Good-night then," Mr. Clemspool said as he executed something of a bow and retreated from the room.

Laurence listened for the click of the lock. When it came, he crept cautiously from bed and peeped through the keyhole. Empty and silent. Feeling slightly ill again from tension, he went back to bed and commenced to nibble on his food.

He glanced at the medicine bottle Mr. Clemspool had left. Perhaps, after all, it would be wiser to take it. He picked it up, pulled the cork, and sniffed. Its smell was most repellent. He studied the handwritten label: "Tincture of Rhubarb." The thought occurred to him that Mr. Clemspool had probably paid for it with the money he had taken from his clothing. Then and there Laurence resolved—as a matter of pride—never to take it.

Once again he rose from bed and pulled back the curtain across the street window. He was four stories high, and—as far as he could see in the twilight—there was no way to get below.

He went to the second window and pushed aside that heavy curtain. Below he saw the roof of the adjacent building, a flat roof, he noted excitedly. Even better, at its far edge a ladder stuck up. Where it led to, Laurence could not see. He hoped it reached the ground. If it did, he had found a way to escape. First, however, he had to get down to the roof.

One hand on the curtain, he leaned out from the window. His heart sank. The roof lay some fifteen feet below, too far to jump.

Laurence pulled himself back, let go of the curtain. Then an idea struck. The curtain was about seven feet in length. Could he not use it to lower himself out of the window and drop the rest of the way to the roof?

Looking up, he saw that the curtain was not directly attached to the window frame. Instead, it had been fitted with a series of loops along the top and threaded through a lengthy wooden rod. The curtain hung from this rod, which in turn rested upon wooden arms protruding from the wall. That rod, Laurence realized with sudden excitement, was longer than the window frame was wide.

In haste now, Laurence carried the side table to the window and climbed up on it. Reaching as high as he could, he took hold of the curtain and flipped it upward. The weight and force of its rising carried the rod off the arm on which it rested, causing curtain and rod to come tumbling down.

It was easy to lower the curtain out the window while keeping the rod inside. The curtain now dangled freely while being held securely by the rod, which was braced horizontally against the inside of the window frame.

Laurence dashed across the room to where his old clothes lay, stripped off his nightshirt, and pulled them on. They were damp and uncomfortable. He did not care.

Ready at last, he climbed up to the window and sat on the windowsill, his legs hanging out. With a quick twist, he rolled onto his stomach while keeping himself from falling by grasping the window frame.

Heart pounding, he gradually transferred his grip from the window frame to the curtain, hugging the cloth to his chest as tightly as possible. Half inch by half inch, he began to wiggle his way out the window. As his weight shifted off the sill, he began to slip. The next second he was dropping. He clutched the curtain to his chest. There was a jolt, but the curtain held. For a moment Laurence simply dangled. Then he relaxed his grip. Slowly, he slid down the full length of the curtain until he hung from its end. He was now some six feet above the roof. Holding his breath, he let go.

Chapter 33
Mr. Drabble Leads Maura through Liverpool

*T*his is a sailor's town, my dear," Mr. Drabble cautioned as he and Maura made their way through the streets. "There's considerable consumption of spirits at night. You must look about yourself with care."

It was a chilly night. People were bundled up. But the blaze from shops, open late, was more than enough to brighten the crowded streets. Everywhere Maura looked, she saw people selling goods, food, trinkets. People were buying too. But drink was being proffered more often than anything. It was sold in countless tiny spirit shops, most of which were packed with customers. There was a constant clamor, as though everyone was talking at once. Mobs of sailors roamed the streets in numbers greater than all the villagers of Kilonny. For Maura, the spectacle was frightening. As they moved through the throngs, she made sure she stayed close to her friend.

Mr. Drabble paid no attention to the hubbub but pressed on, now and again pointing out sights that he thought Maura should see. Having this young, pretty woman by his side filled him with delight. He was determined to perform well.

Maura had a vague sense that they were heading toward the docks. Sure enough, they began to move out of the narrow muddy streets and down into wider thoroughfares.

"Not long now," Mr. Drabble informed her.

They turned a corner and entered a large square bordered on all four sides by large buildings. Here the pavement was stone. In contrast to those on the streets from which they had just emerged, people here were of all classes, some whose bearing and dress suggested considerable wealth as well as those of middling and poorer means. The fact that it was a chilly night did nothing, apparently, to keep them from coming.

Maura soon saw that what attracted these people were musicians, acrobats, an organ-grinder with a begging monkey, even a puppet show. Someone was dancing. A magician was doing tricks. Hawkers were out in force too, offering fruit, ribbons, sweets, and newly printed sheets of songs. Maura, who had never witnessed such a scene, was fascinated.

"This way!" Mr. Drabble called, making his way directly across the square. She followed him to a large building with steps leading up to a recessed entrance set about with many columns. It was rather like a temple.

"What is this place?" Maura asked.

"The custom house," Mr. Drabble replied grandly, "the true heart and soul of Liverpool."

When they reached the building, they worked their way around a crowd of onlookers watching a juggler. The man was standing on the steps, tossing five wands into the air. A pile of burning wood at the base of the steps provided him with light.

"That's Mr. Bilikins," the actor whispered into Maura's ear. "A capital friend of mine. Soon as he's done, it will be my turn. We've all got regular times here, like the theater. Makes it all much more civilized. How I adore those columns. So Greek and Roman, don't you think? The proper background for my tragedies."

Even as Mr. Drabble spoke, the man he referred to as Mr. Bilikins concluded his act with a grand cascade of multi-colored balls. His efforts were met with polite applause, plus a few calls of more vigorous approval. The juggler gamely doffed his tall pointed cap, then held it before him, begging coins for his performance. He received some.

Mr. Drabble turned to Maura. "My dear Miss O'Connell, would you be willing to assist me?"

"Me?" Maura exclaimed, taken by surprise.

"Having the two of us will make something grand of my turn onstage. But only if you desire it."

Maura felt she could hardly decline. "If I can," she offered shyly.

"You have courage, my dear. I recognized it the moment I saw you," Mr. Drabble enthused.

Maura blushed at the compliment. "You're more than kind," she said.

The actor reached into his sack and drew out a small drum and stick. "If you will beat the drum, you'll draw people in. Usually I do it myself. Having you will help. You're very pretty, you know."

Maura colored again but this time said nothing.

"Come along then," the actor said as he trotted up the steps.

When Mr. Drabble reached the fifth step, he stopped and again reached into his sack, pulling out his book. Leather-bound, with gilt edging, it was nonetheless worn and torn. "My Shakespeare," he confided to Maura. "It sets the proper tone."

Holding the volume high in one hand, Mr. Drabble turned so as to present his profile to the audience, flipped the hair out of his eyes, lifted his other hand in salute, and called, "Give it a thumping, my dear."

Maura began to bang the drum.

"You'll want to do it so others might hear," Mr. Drabble suggested kindly.

Maura worked harder to produce a real beat.

Mr. Drabble smiled at her efforts, then turned to the square and cried, "Ladies and gentlemen! Gather around for some edifying culture. I, Horatio Drabble, late of the London stage, currently making a farewell tour prior to my imminent departure for America, shall perform a few selected and great tragical moments as written by the sublime William Shakespeare. His art will make you a better, finer person! It will raise you up in life. To hear his words is to breathe the very perfume of our culture. Beat the drum again, my dear."

A motley crowd of fifteen gradually assembled. There were a few children, but most were adults, a mix of the kinds of people Maura had already seen. To her eyes, most of them looked as if they could ill afford to spare the actor any money. She did notice, however, one man whose manner of dress had the appearance of real wealth. His clothing looked new, from his top hat and fur-trimmed cape to his shiny boots. The fact that he had a patch over one eye did not diminish the grandeur at all. If anything, it added to it.

"To begin," Mr. Drabble announced, "I offer, for your edification, the great oration by Mark Antony from the famous tragedy *Julius Caesar*."

So saying, Mr. Drabble turned to face his small audience. No longer smiling, his hair flicked back, his chin jutted forward, he lifted both hands, as if imploring the sky. "'Friends, Romans, countrymen, lend me your ears; I come to bury Caesar, not to praise him.'" On the actor went, pronouncing each word with meticulous care, so that every syllable could be heard and understood. With each phrase, he shifted his posture, so as to illustrate with his thin, angular body the particular dramatic emotion he was feeling—rather like a stick figure come alive.

Maura watched, fascinated.

At the end of his first speech, Mr. Drabble folded himself into a deep bow.

"How 'bout speakin' English?" shouted one rough-looking peddler, which brought some laughter from those around him. None came, Maura noticed, from the rich man with the eye patch.

Mr. Drabble ignored the remark. "I now wish to present to you the tortured soul of the prince of Denmark, Hamlet, in the immortal soliloquy 'To be or not to be.'"

"I already knows the answer," another onlooker bellowed, "and it's no."

Despite the disturbance, Mr. Drabble began declaiming as he had done before. His ardent gesticulation had rather the effect of a windmill. But all his effort produced was a rotten potato, which splattered at his feet.

Though Maura grew alarmed, Mr. Drabble seemed barely to notice. Instead, he went on to announce his final speech, a piece from *King Richard the Third*. Before beginning, he issued a warning to his audience. "Be advised," he told them, "that I am about to portray an evil man. A thief, a murderer. An upstart! I beg you not to faint. But pray take notice. Richard speaks well and thereby gets his way and becomes a king. Thus does culture lift a man!"

Mr. Drabble flung his hair out of his face a third time, opened his brown eyes wide, and tore into his final rendition.

As the speech drew to an end, Maura saw a man reach into a sack, pull out half a cabbage, and ready himself to throw it at the actor. But before he could, the man with the eye patch struck the cabbage from his hand, then sent the heckler flat onto the ground with a single blow. Those around him took one look at the well-dressed gentleman and melted away.

Bowing, Mr. Drabble addressed his audience of one, which was applauding loudly. "If, upon receiving this recitation, you have felt Mr. Horatio Drabble somewhat worthy, he would not be too humble to accept a penny or two for this, his farewell tour in England. Remember, ''Tis better to be lowly born, and range with humble livers in content, than to be perked up in a glistening grief and wear a golden sorrow.' *Henry Eighth*."

So saying, the actor descended the steps. Even as he did, another performer mounted them, a violin in her hands.

Mr. Grout—for it was he with the eye patch—offered the actor a whole shilling.

"Sir," Mr. Drabble said, unfolding from another deep bow and taking the coin, "you do me great honor."

"Don't yer worry," Mr. Grout returned gruffly. "I can spare it an' more too, if it comes to that."

"May the rest of mankind be so generous," Mr. Drabble returned.

"All the same," Mr. Grout said, "I'm wonderin' if I could 'ave a word with yer? Confidential like."

"Oh?"

"Right. I've been listenin' and watchin' yer and it looks to me—though I 'ave but one good eye—that yer could provide something as I'm needin' bad."

Chapter 34

Mr. Grout and Mr. Drabble
Have a Talk

*M*r. Drabble turned to Maura. "The gentleman wishes to have a brief conversation with me. Will you come along?"

"This 'ere yer gal?" Mr. Grout inquired with something of a leer.

Maura, made uncomfortable by both the look and the insinuation, took an instant dislike to the man.

"My companion in art, to be sure," returned Mr. Drabble gallantly. "Where do you wish to converse?"

"There's a pub over to the far side of the square," Mr. Grout suggested.

"Your name, sir?" Mr. Drabble inquired.

The man with the eye patch grinned. "Mr. Grout," he said. "Toby Grout. From London. Like yerself."

"My pleasure, Mr. Grout," Mr. Drabble returned, extending his hand and offering his own name.

Led by Mr. Grout, Mr. Drabble and Maura entered a spirit shop on the far side of the square. It was small and crowded, with the unpleasant smell of too many bodies consuming too much liquor. The publican, however, seeing money in Mr. Grout, quickly made room at a table in the back by forcing away the people who were sitting there.

"What do yer want for drinks?" Mr. Grout asked once they had all sat down.

"A dram of rum will do me," Mr. Drabble said politely.

Mr. Grout looked at Maura and winked his eye. "And you, gal?"

Maura shook her head, and though she kept her eyes averted, she studied the man. He was as powerfully built as a prizefighter she had once seen at a fair. His dark hair was cropped short, and his lower lip had recently been bruised or so it seemed. Maura guessed he had been struck in a brawl. It made her recall the savage blow that had felled Mr. Drabble's heckler. Indeed, though his clothing proclaimed Mr. Grout a gentleman, his manners and talk seemed crude and the bright eye positively threatening.

Requesting gin for himself, Mr. Grout placed the order.

As they waited for the drinks, he said, "I liked wot yer were doin' up there. All that fancy talk."

Mr. Drabble nodded. "You are more than kind to say so, sir."

"All that . . . What do yer call 'im?"

"Shakespeare."

"Right. Shakespeare. And is that wot yer said true," Mr. Grout asked, "just to know 'is words makes a man somethin' more? Is it?"

"It is my fondest hope," Mr. Drabble acknowledged.

The drinks were brought. Mr. Grout downed his gin at a gulp and ordered another. Mr. Drabble took no more than a polite sip. Maura kept her eyes down and her hands in her lap.

"Look 'ere," Mr. Grout said, slumping across the table toward Mr. Drabble in a confidential manner. "I'm a direct sort. Yer won't find me beatin' bushes. Yer see these togs I'm wearing?" He gestured to his cape with its fur collar and cuffs.

"Very fine indeed," Mr. Drabble said.

"A few days ago I didn't 'ave any such stuff. And now . . ." Mr. Grout winked his good eye.

"What occurred?" inquired Mr. Drabble.

Mr. Grout grew serious. "Mr. Drabble, do yer believe in spirits, ghosts, an' the like?" he asked in a low tone.

"I'm not certain. . . ."

"Well, I do. 'Cause all me life they've been a plaguin' me. Except now they've come around to treat me decent. Put a pile of money in me 'ands. Out of nowhere so to speak. Like magic, I'm a swell." Mr. Grout snapped his fingers.

" 'There is a tide in the affairs of men, which, taken at the flood, leads on to fortune. Omitted, all the voyage of their life is bound in shallows and miseries.' "

"Eh?"

"*Julius Caesar*. Shakespeare."

"Right. Exactly. See, what I'm doin' is—now that I'm a man of means—I'm goin' to America. Startin' a whole new life. Gettin' away from old ghosts, so to speak. It's money—not the way yer born—that makes yer way there, they say. And, as I see it, a man wants to be where 'e can have some respect."

"A worthy endeavor," Mr. Drabble agreed.

"But," continued Mr. Grout, "as yer can tell for yerself, I do speak low. I knows it. And I can't read a lick either. What I needs is education. For America, you see. To make something of meself."

"If I comprehend you," said Mr. Drabble, "you wish me to teach you some loftier ways of speech?"

"If yer can do it, I can pay for it. I 'eard yer say yer going to America too. Well, I've a few days. I'd be 'appy to put meself where yer can learn me something of the proper way of mouthin'."

"I approve of your desire, sir, I do. But, if I may be so bold, it is reading that should come first."

"Readin'!" cried Mr. Grout. "I would 'ave thought that was above me, don't yer think?"

"Not in the least. And once you learn to read, you will be able to peruse Shakespeare all on your own."

Mr. Grout considered Mr. Drabble suspiciously. "Look 'ere, sir, but do they read in America?"

"I believe they do, sir. At least, those of a better sort."

"Well then, I do wish to be a better sort. But do yer think yer can start me in the way of readin'?"

Mr. Drabble took his second sip of rum, then sat back and considered Mr. Grout. "I would require some . . . compensation," he said, choosing his words with care.

Maura, sitting close to the actor on the bench, sensed that he was trembling.

Mr. Grout waved his hand. "Like I told yer, I don't worry 'bout money no more. If yer can do it, I can afford it."

"Would . . . four pounds be within the realm of possibility?" Mr. Drabble inquired tentatively.

Mr. Grout fastened Mr. Drabble with his one-eyed stare as one might pin a bug to a board. "The price of a ticket to America?" he said.

Mr. Drabble turned pale. "I believe so."

Mr. Grout laughed and extended his large hand. "If yer can teach me to read, it's a done deal."

As Mr. Drabble shook the man's hand, his eyes sparkled, his smile grew very broad.

An appointment—time and place—was agreed upon for the very next day. Then again hands were shaken.

As Mr. Drabble and Maura walked toward Mrs. Sonderbye's, the actor was jubilant. "My dear Miss O'Connell, you have proved to be my muse. I have achieved—I think—salvation."

"I'm the first to be happy for you, Mr. Drabble."

"To think," the actor went on excitedly, "I shall have my ticket to America! Perhaps," he said, with a glance at Maura, "we shall locate in the same community. But you look glum, my dear. Can you not rejoice in my good fortune?"

"I do, Mr. Drabble. But it's not for me to say a word," Maura replied.

Mr. Drabble stopped. "My dear, say what you will. I'll not be offended."

"It's your own warning I'm hearing, Mr. Drabble. About money and Liverpool. I won't be saying I cared much for that Mr. Grout. He's more than a bit of brutish."

"My dear," returned Mr. Drabble, "you are an innocent. Take it from me, a man who knows the world. Mr. Grout is nothing more than a lucky man, a man who has chosen to touch me with some of that same luck. You saw the way he defended me from those rude people. As the poet said, 'All's well that ends well.' You may trust my judgment, my dear, as a man of great experience. We can trust Mr. Grout."

Anxious as she was to rejoin Patrick, Maura said nothing further all the way back to Mrs. Sonderbye's. Only when she reached the house did she discover that Patrick was not there.

Chapter 35
Laurence Moves On

*L*aurence sat on the roof of the building, slightly dazed but quite certain he had sustained no harm from the fall. As soon as he recovered his wits, he sprang up and rushed for the ladder. One glance revealed that it reached the ground. He swung onto it, made a rapid descent, and began to run. Nor did he stop until he had passed six streets.

Only then did he slow down. Panting, he kept on walking, feeling free and immensely pleased with himself.

The evening darkness was deepening rapidly. The air was growing colder too. With no particular place to go, Laurence wandered randomly. Some twenty minutes later he stopped, forced to acknowledge he had absolutely no idea where to turn. It did occur to him that he could go to the police and have Mr. Clemspool arrested for stealing the money from his clothes. Then he remembered the London police were looking for him. What if they had informed the Liverpool police about him? He could not chance it.

A lamplighter, long lighting pole over his shoulder, came onto the street and began to illuminate the gas lamps.

"You, there, fellow," Laurence called. "Can you tell me where the ships are?"

The old man paused in his work to scrutinize Laurence. "You there, yourself," he said with a snort. "You've got an uncivil tongue in your head, you do."

Laurence started to tell the man *he* was the one being uncivil when he remembered how he looked.

"Sorry," he said gruffly, short of a full apology. "I'm . . . I'm looking for the ships."

"Ships!" the lamplighter cried. "There are a million of them!"

"I don't want *any* ships," Laurence explained. "I want the ones that go to America. I intend to go there."

"Do you now?" the lamplighter scoffed. "Just like that, eh? A shrill-voiced ragamuffin like you? Well, why not, you and lots of others sail away every day, and the sooner the better, says I. Be well rid of your sort. But if you have to ask where the ships are, you've a far piece to go."

"But where are they?" Laurence said, not at all pleased to be so mocked.

"You're a fool, boy," the lamplighter said, "not to know

that before starting out. But if you'll leave me in peace, I'm willing to tell. Just head downhill, and you'll get to the docks." With those curt words, the old man turned his back on Laurence and resumed his work.

Regretting that he had not been more polite, but not knowing how to repair the damage, Laurence started off down the hill.

Everywhere he looked he saw posters for the United States and Canada. He examined one closely.

UNITED STATES
SNEED BROTHERS AMERICAN EMIGRATION
SERVICE
CLAYMORE BUILDING—KINGS STREET
The Following FIRST-CLASS PACKETS
Will Be Dispatched on Their Appointed Days
FOR NEW YORK, PHILADELPHIA, and BOSTON

A list of ships and their captains followed, including the size of each vessel, in tons, and the date of departure. Then the boy read:

The above ships are of the largest class, commanded by men of experience who will take every precaution to promote the health and comfort of the passengers during the voyage.

Fares from 3 pounds, 10 shillings up. Children half fare.

For further particulars, apply,

N. Sneed Ltd., Liverpool
R. Sneed and Co., New York

The Sneed Brothers' boats left for America twice weekly. When Laurence checked other posters, he found that there were departures virtually every day. On some days, many ships were sailing within hours of one another. All the posters listed the same base fare, thrée pounds, ten shillings. It was then that Laurence recalled his predicament. He had not a penny, nor the slightest idea where to get one.

Moreover, he began to grasp how much money he had taken—and lost. A huge sum. The realization deepened his guilt, his shame, his isolation.

With a sigh, he made his way into a large square. It was full of street performers, among them an organ-grinder making music with the aid of a red-capped gray monkey. Laurence stopped to watch. Tethered to his master with a long cord, the monkey begged for pennies with a cup. Whenever people dropped coins in, the monkey lifted his cap, then did a somersault. All the while, it grinned hideously. The creature did make Laurence laugh when it approached him, looking up with wide eyes and making ferocious chattering noises. Then the boy realized that the monkey had more money than he and knew how to find more. Upset with himself, Laurence hurried from the square.

The smell of the sea drew him. He began to fancy that someone on some vessel would note his nobility, take pity on him, let him board, allow him to sail away. He knew—vaguely—that such a stroke of luck was unlikely, but he drifted on, not knowing what else to do.

After crossing a wide boulevard, he came to a region of enormous buildings. The smell of the sea intensified. A few more steps, and the docks were before him. They appeared deserted.

But when he spied a police constable by a sentry box—ever-present rattle hanging from his belt—Laurence halted. Believing as he did that the whole world was looking for him, Laurence worried that the man would recognize him. For a long while Laurence remained still, trying to make up his mind what to do, go forward or retreat. If he went forward, he would have to pass the sentry box. If he retreated, he would be nowhere. Perhaps, he thought, it would be better if he *were* caught. At least he would be somewhere then, with someone watching out for him.

Arms pressed to his side, Laurence walked stiffly forward. The constable, a pipe clenched firmly in his teeth, turned slightly, looked down at him, nodded a greeting. Nothing more. Aware of keen disappointment that he had not been stopped, Laurence kept walking. Part of him wanted to turn and say, "My name is Sir Laurence Kirkle. Take me home." He was too fearful.

He had entered the dock area. Only an occasional quay lamp lit the deserted way. It felt colder. His breath misted. All about him rose ships whose countless masts, spars, and rigging made him think of a vast spread of the black lace his mother wore to funerals. Now and again he stopped to listen to the creaking and groaning of timbers, the occasional slip-slap of waves.

He walked to the edge of one wharf and looked up at the ship tied there. It was immense. He wondered if it would be going to America.

"Don't yer even *tink* of sneaking on," growled a voice from on high in the darkness.

Startled, Laurence jumped back.

"I'm here," the voice said, "an' I'm watching yer."

Laurence peered upward. He made out a man leaning over the bulwark of the ship. In his hand—the man made sure Laurence saw it—was a heavy belaying pin.

"Be off with yer now," the man warned. "Too much thieving 'round 'ere. Know what the punishment for thieving is?"

Laurence shook his head.

"Shipped to the penal colony—and yer can stay for fourteen years."

Laurence hurried away, craning his head to take one, then a second look back. The man brandished his club over his head and cackled.

For two hours Laurence wandered the docks. Four times he was chased away from ships. Chilled to the bone, teeth chattering, thoroughly discouraged and tired, he hunched deep within a coil of rope and stared up at the inky sky, where a moon now floated through scudding clouds.

I don't know what to do, Laurence said to himself. *I don't know what to do at all.* Exhausted, he closed his eyes and began to fall asleep till the sound of approaching footsteps startled him. Someone was standing over him.

"Well, well," Ralph Toggs exclaimed as he looked down at the wide-eyed Laurence, "just what I was looking for. A small boy to do a small job."

Chapter 36

A Way to Get Money

*L*aurence pushed himself back among the ropes. Toggs put out a hand and held him hard. "Don't you be so squirmy, mate. I want to talk to you. What's your name?"

"Laurence."

"Laurence, eh?" Toggs grinned. "Where you from?

"London."

"Long way from home, aren't you? Who you with? Come on, tell me."

"I'm alone," Laurence blurted out.

"Are you now? Can't say I mind. How about standing up so I can measure you?"

Trembling, Laurence sat up and pulled himself free of the rope coil.

"Empty your pockets."

"I don't have anything."

"Do it!"

Laurence did as he was told.

"All right now," Toggs said, "how'd you like to earn some money?"

"Money?"

"You heard me. Money. Clink. Lolly. Interested?"

After a moment, Laurence nodded.

"Good. 'Cause I've got a job you can help me with."

"What—do—you mean, job?" Laurence stammered.

Toggs reached out, put his hand about Laurence's neck, and squeezed it painfully. "No objections, mate," he snapped. "Just keep in mind I can pitch you into the water quick as a wink. Know when they'd find you?"

Laurence shook his head.

"Next week. *Maybe*. Understand?"

"Yes, sir."

"All right then, let's have ourselves a deal. I'm needing money, and I've found a way to get some. And you're going to do what I tell you to do. Can you follow that?"

Thoroughly frightened, Laurence nodded.

"Here's the pitch. Down the ways a bit, by Coburg Dock, there's a coastal trader easy on her moorings, the sniff of money fairly oozing from her. I watched as she came in, and I saw her crew—all five of them—when they went up to town. Thought they buttoned her down tight, but they didn't. Left one porthole open. Are you following me?"

"No, sir," Laurence said.

"You're as thick as a log. Listen carefully then. A boy

your size could wiggle in that porthole, see what they have, and pass it out to me.

"We'll make a deal. Nobody can say Ralph Toggs ain't decent. You can remember that name, Ralph Toggs, because whatever we get, we'll go shares. There might be as much as a few pounds for you. Depending. You might even make enough to ship off on your own, if you'd like. That's what I intend to do with mine, go to America."

Laurence, alarmed about what he was being asked to do, stared wide-eyed at Toggs. But with the young man's hand still tight around his neck, he could not move.

"Yes or no?" Toggs demanded.

Laurence could not speak.

"Oh, come on now, don't tell me you haven't ever stole anything. You didn't get that welt on your face licking up cream."

A deeply shamed Laurence shook his head.

"All right then," Toggs said, "so don't put on no airs. Only I want an agreement so I know we're square. 'Course, if we're not square, I can always whittle you until you are." From his back pocket, he pulled out a horn-handled knife. "You understand me now, don't you, mate?"

Laurence whispered, "Yes, sir. I'll do what you say."

"Now you've got it," Toggs said, releasing his grip as he put away his knife. "Come on. She's not far from here." He turned Laurence about and, with his hand resting heavy on the boy's shoulder, moved them along the quay.

Mindful of the knife that Toggs had shown him, Laurence kept walking.

"Do you know why I'm going to America?" Toggs asked.
"No, sir."

"You're too young for the girls, I suppose," Toggs said, "but I'm not. And I met a fair one today." He frowned. "Only she had nothing but pity for me. And when the girls

157

show pity, it's a sign you've gone soft and easy. When that happens, it's best to get away."

The docks seemed deserted. The only sound—aside from the shifting of boats and the lap of water—was their own footsteps. Once, twice, Laurence thought he heard others following. In hopes that the dock policeman he'd seen might be there, he tried to look back. Toggs slapped the side of his face. "Eyes front, mate, or you'll get a welt to your left cheek."

After fifteen minutes of walking, Toggs whispered, "Halt." Laurence stopped immediately.

"There she is," the young man said. "Ready for a plucking."

Moored against the quay was a boat about fifty feet in length. She had two masts and a raised cabin in the stern. The deck was clear, except for carefully coiled ropes and cables. Her sails were lashed along the booms. Small lanterns glowed at bow and helm, making the wood trim glisten.

"Turned out pretty nice, isn't she?" Toggs said. "Let's get ourselves a little closer."

They moved toward the stern cabin. "Here's the way we do it," Toggs whispered. "See that porthole up there?"

Laurence could make out that the boat's cabin had two round windows about five feet above wharf level. "Look carefully," Toggs went on, "like I did, and you'll see that window there is open an inch. Pull her, and she'll swing out.

"I'm going to boost you up. That way you can get the window open and wiggle yourself in. When you get there, you're to cast about for a cash box. Know what they look like?"

"No."

"Lord, what kind of a life you been living? It'll be a metal box, with a lid. No more than this long." He held his hands about a foot apart. "Half as wide. All these coastal boats use 'em. Seen 'em plenty of times. Mostly, they keep 'em in a cabinet. Find the box, throw it out to me. I'll be waiting right here. Can you understand all that?"

"Yes, sir," Laurence replied. Once again he thought he heard the sound of footsteps. Perhaps there *was* a watchman about. He tried to look behind Toggs.

"Eyes on me, lad," the young man warned, pulling Laurence's chin about sharply.

Laurence stared up at him with wide eyes.

"Have any questions?"

Laurence shook his head.

"All right then, quicklike," Toggs ordered. "The money box, understand?"

His hand on the boy's neck again, Toggs edged up to the side of the boat. "I'll make a stirrup of my hands," he whispered. "Don't you try to make a break for it, understand? I can run a lot faster than you. And besides—" He slapped his hand to his knife. "Don't think about doing nothing when you get in either. I can just as well stay here till the crew comes back. I'll tell 'em I caught a thief on their boat. So you do as I tell you." He bent into a stooping posture and linked his fingers.

Laurence, knowing he had no choice, placed his right foot in the hands, gripped Toggs's shoulder, and pulled himself up. As he did, Toggs lifted. Quickly, Laurence rose even with the porthole. He took hold of it. As Toggs had predicted, it swung open.

"That's it!" he called up. "Now haul yourself in."

The porthole was nearly two feet in diameter, wide enough.

"All right now," Toggs said, "I'm going to give you another boost!" This one enabled Laurence to thrust his arms inside, then his head. From below, he felt another sudden push. As if he were sausage meat being stuffed into its casing, Laurence was all but forced into the cabin.

He landed on the upper level of a bunk bed. For a moment he just lay there, trying desperately to still his heart. He looked about. The only light came from the outside helm lantern.

The little cabin contained two double bunks, one on either side. Against the stern wall was a table, over which a cabinet hung. In the middle of the floor was a small potbellied stove facing a doorway. Laurence guessed it led to the main deck.

"Are you there?" he heard Toggs say. "Can you hear me?"

Laurence closed his eyes. He wondered what would happen if he did nothing, just stayed where he was. But what if this Mr. Toggs came after him? And even if Toggs could not get at him and he remained in the cabin, what would he do when the crew came back—as surely they would? How could he explain what he was doing there?

"Did you find the box, mate?" his tormentor hissed. "Let me hear you!"

Laurence leaned toward the porthole. "I'm looking," he called in his high-pitched voice.

"Be quick about it!"

Laurence let himself down onto the floor of the cabin. From there he reached up to the cabinet door and gave a yank.

Inside were a few dishes and cups, a Bible, and a metal box, exactly as Toggs had described.

"Have you got it?" Laurence heard Toggs call with growing impatience.

Not answering, the boy put the box on the table. It was heavy. He slid back the hasp and flipped the lid open. The box was full of money, mostly coins, but with enough bills to remind Laurence of the drawer in his father's table. Tension twisted his stomach.

"I'll cut your throat if you don't get that box to me fast!" he heard from outside.

Still Laurence did not move. "It's wrong," he murmured. "It's wrong!" With a feeling of intense physical pain, he shut the lid and shoved the box back into the cabinet. Moaning with fear, he turned back to the porthole.

Just as he did, he heard the sound of a harsh rattle. It came three times. A constable!

In a panic, Laurence scrambled to the top bunk and peered out the porthole just in time to see Toggs fleeing down the quay. Not one but two dock policemen were in close pursuit, twirling their rattles and shouting. For a second Laurence watched, fascinated. The next moment he realized his opportunity and began to squeeze out the porthole, head-first. So quickly did he slip through that he tumbled down, making a complete somersault onto the dock and landing with an enormous thud. Dazed, he could not see. But he could hear.

"Get yourself up!" a voice cried into his ear. "Hurry!"

Chapter 37

Mr. Pickler Arrives
in Liverpool

It was late in the afternoon when Mr. Pickler stepped out of the second-class carriage in Liverpool. He stretched his legs, brushed his jacket, set his bowler securely upon his head, and, with birdlike eyes, looked about. What he observed were goodly numbers of people—some with children—traveling with trunks and bundles. Emigrants all, he presumed. Mr. Pickler bobbed his head. As far as he was concerned only failures emigrated. Their going could only make England a better place. Congratulating himself that he—and his family—were secure, he concentrated on the task at hand.

After noting the time on the large clock against a wall, Mr. Pickler set himself to observe the flow of porters, policemen, train guards, and ticket agents, as well as the variety of those selling food.

He began his interrogations with a ticket seller. "Can you tell me, please," he inquired, "when the first train from London arrived this morning?"

"The night train from London, sir? Well now, it usually gets in at about half past eight. Runs fairly to schedule too."

"Thank you, my good man."

Mr. Pickler approached a police constable. Having first determined that the man was on duty at the time of the morning train's arrival from London, he described Laurence and presented the daguerreotype, putting particular stress on the boy's ragged state. "Might you," he asked, "recall seeing such a boy this morning?"

The constable, even as he took the picture, replied, "Runaway, eh?"

"Let us just say he is not at home."

"No end to 'em, sir! Come from all over, they do. Like they were running from the plague. Which is just what our Inspector Knox thinks of 'em, sir, a plague." The constable handed the daguerreotype back. "I can't say I saw this one. If you want the truth, sir, they all look alike to me."

In all, Mr. Pickler interviewed fourteen people, not one of whom had the slightest recollection of the boy he de-

162

scribed. It was only when he spoke to a girl selling sugar buns that he met with success.

To begin he showed her Laurence's picture. "Did you happen to see a boy looking like this?"

The girl squinted at the image. "Maybe, sir, a bit. Though not nearly so fine as that there. Early this morning it was, and the London train just in. It was my first sale. And the one I saw had a welt here, sir." She touched the right side of her face.

"A welt, you say?"

"Looked nasty, sir. I shouldn't like to have gotten it. Must of had himself a nasty time."

"Can you recall anything else particular about him?" the investigator asked.

"Like I said, sir, he was ragged. And very hungry."

"Hungry?"

"Indeed he was, sir. The man he was with ordered three buns for him. My first sale and the best of the day. That boy—he looked very pinched, he did—swallowed the first bun in a gulp."

Mr. Pickler felt a stir of excitement. His judgment was proving right—the boy had been abducted. "And you say this boy was with a *man*?"

"Oh, yes, sir, and a very pleasant gentleman he was too. Took particular care of the boy, he did. When he saw how hungry the boy was, he ordered a third bun."

"Listen sharp now. Was it the man or the boy who paid?"

"The gentleman, sir. Tipped me jolly well too."

"Now then," Mr. Pickler said as he reached into his pocket and held up a shilling, "you've been most helpful. Can you tell me what the man looked like?"

At the sight of the coin, the girl positively glowed. She described Mr. Clemspool eagerly. "Very jolly he was, sir, plump and full of good humor. Top hat—but he was bald, sir, like one of these buns, if you'll forgive me saying so. Gloves and greatcoat as well as traveling bag. A gentleman."

"Any notion where the man and the boy were going?"

"I couldn't say, sir. Out of the station, I suppose. I just sell buns. I don't knows what happens to them who eats 'em."

"Lastly," Mr. Pickler concluded, still holding up the coin, "did, perchance, the boy refer to the gentleman by name?"

"If he did so, sir, it's nothing I can recall."

The investigator thanked the girl, gave her the coin, then rushed out of the station and onto the street. His first sight was of St. George Hall. For a moment he remained motionless, absorbed by its sheer size. England, he thought, at its greatest. And he was part of it! The thought made his spirits soar. Full of energy, he turned toward the commercial streets. They were thronged. Mr. Pickler was not sure what he expected to find, but when he looked about, it was difficult not to feel frustrated. Laurence, he now knew for a certainty, had reached Liverpool. What's more, he was with his abductor. Where had they gone? They could be anywhere!

Mr. Pickler had decided to make the rounds of ship ticket offices when he caught sight of the hansom cabs by the curb.

Might Laurence and the man have taken a cab? To ask the question was to have an answer. Of course they would have.

Briskly, he walked past a crowd of people to the head of the line. "Hello there!" he called up to the first driver on the line.

"You'll want to queue up like the others, mate," he was told sharply.

"I'm not looking to hire," Mr. Pickler returned. "I'm merely looking for information."

"What sort?" came the suspicious rejoinder.

Mr. Pickler described Laurence and the mysterious man.

"Did you, perchance, carry those two anywhere this morning early? They came in on the first London train."

"Never saw 'em" was the reply.

Two frustrating hours later, Mr. Pickler was still asking the same question. It was an older man with a gray beard and wearing a green scarf who remembered the pair well.

"I do recollect my fares, sir, the way your preacher recollects the pages of his good book. The boy was filthy and had a red welt on his cheek. Here." He touched the right side of his face. "Fact is, the man gave me an extra shilling to take him on."

"Did he?"

"Blamed the boy's filth on the railroad, for whatever that's worth. You don't want to question your passengers too closely, do you? Just enough to get an understanding."

"Might you remember where you took the pair?"

"Royalton Hotel. Grove Street."

"Can you take me there?"

"If you can pay the fare, sir, I'll trot you around the world."

"The Royalton Hotel would be good enough," Mr. Pickler cried as he leaped into the carriage.

The ride was not long. On the way Mr. Pickler studied his bowler. He was quite certain that the boy had very little—if any—of the money he'd taken from his father. His tattered clothing and the fact that the man purchased the buns and hired the cab suggested that. As for the man, he was a bounder, obviously. Probably took the boy's money too. No doubt it was he who had bruised his cheek. The mere thought of it stirred Mr. Pickler's wrath. What kind of scoundrel would strike a child!

Upon reaching the hotel, Mr. Pickler paid and tipped the driver well. Waving aside the uniformed hotel attendant, he stood on the curb and studied the building a moment: Four stories high, it stood to the right of a private establishment of approximately the same height. To the left was another such building but one less tall and flat roofed.

Next, Mr. Pickler took the precaution of strolling around the block to the Royalton's rear entrance. No sooner had he turned the corner than he caught sight of an open window on the fourth floor. Dangling out of it was what appeared to be a curtain. Mr. Pickler stared at it, then abruptly returned to the hotel's main entrance. In the lobby, he approached the man sitting behind the reception desk.

"Good afternoon, sir," the investigator began, trying to restrain the anxiety he felt. "I should like to speak to the person or persons who would have received guests this morning. Somewhere between the hours of nine and ten."

The man behind the desk looked at Mr. Pickler suspiciously. "And who might you be, sir?" he asked with some coolness.

Mr. Pickler inclined his head slightly. "I am here," he said, keeping his voice low, "on the authority of Lord Kirkle." He handed over his own calling card.

The man glanced at it, colored, and immediately came to his feet. "Mr. Pickler, sir, my name is Mr. Hudson. If there is some problem, perhaps I can be of help." He rubbed his hands together nervously.

"There is reason to believe," Mr. Pickler said, "that Lord Kirkle's son may have been abducted."

"Good gracious!"

"Further, there is a likelihood that he is lodged—against his will—in this very hotel."

The redness in Mr. Hudson's face drained away. "But, sir, how could that be?"

Mr. Pickler bobbed his head. "I'm not prepared to discuss the *how*, sir. I first need to know if you have any knowledge of a man who arrived with a boy this morning." He showed the daguerreotype. "Is this the boy?"

"It—it may be," stammered Mr. Hudson, deciding he had best cooperate. "I—I think you must be referring to . . . Mr. Clemspool."

"Clemspool?"

"From London. He's been . . . here before. A commercial traveler. He came up this morning. He said . . . the boy was his son."

"Did he?"

"I'm afraid you have only just missed the gentleman. He came in but left almost immediately. Some sudden business to attend to, he said."

"Was the boy with him?"

"No, sir, now that you mention it, he was not."

Mr. Pickler nodded. "I should very much like to inspect his rooms," he said. "Immediately!"

"Sir, I'm not altogether certain that we can allow—"

The investigator leaned forward. "Mr. Hudson," he all but whispered, "I believe that I have already mentioned my connection to Lord Kirkle. If that boy upstairs should prove to be his lordship's son, and if he were found to have been illegally detained in your establishment . . ."

Mr. Hudson held up a hand. "Sir, if you would be so good as to step this way, I shall be happy to show you the rooms."

Mr. Clemspool's rooms, however, were deserted. A quick search did allow Mr. Pickler to find a suit of new boy's clothes as well as a bottle of tincture of rhubarb. He held the bottle up.

"Ah, yes," Mr. Hudson said. "Mr. Clemspool informed us that the boy was taken ill. There was a need to send for the apothecary."

Mr. Pickler sniffed the contents. "I suspect there is more

here than the label suggests," he said, recorking and pock-
eting the bottle.

"Why . . . what do you mean, sir?"

"I suspect the boy has fled. Come." Mr. Pickler led the
way to the farther room. "You see the curtain. I believe he
went out that way."

"But why? And where?"

"I have no idea."

"Then what will you do?"

"Mr. Clemspool has not checked out, has he?"

"No, sir."

"And these other articles, clothing, traveling bag, they do
belong to him?"

"I believe so."

"Then there's good reason to believe this Mr. Clemspool
will return. I will stay here until he does."

"But . . ."

"Another question, Mr. Hudson."

"Yes, sir?"

"When I first asked you about Mr. Clemspool, you said
he had been here before. A commercial traveler, I believe
you said. Did he come with other young people?"

"He has a very large family and—"

Mr. Pickler lifted a hand to interrupt. "Mr. Hudson," he
said softly, "if I were in your position, I would find it prudent to cooperate to the fullest extent." He fixed his round
eyes upon Mr. Hudson's flushed face.

"Well, yes, sir, I am," the man said in haste. "Absolutely.
This is a respectable establishment. We wish to show our
full cooperation."

"Mr. Hudson, sir," Mr. Pickler said as he took a seat, "I
do hope that proves to be the case."

168

Chapter 38
Maura Is Distressed

"You must not fret, my dear," Mr. Drabble said to Maura soothingly when she had discovered that Patrick was not in the basement. "The boy may simply have wandered off to one of the upper rooms. If you sit here," he suggested, "I'll make the rounds above. I know the way. There isn't a room I've not occupied." So saying, he hurried off.

Full of foreboding, blaming herself for having left her brother alone on his own, Maura stayed at the top of the basement steps.

All too soon Mr. Drabble returned and admitted he'd found no sign of the boy. "Of course," he went on hopefully, "there are many rooms, and all are stuffed. Bodies here, there, everywhere. Mostly your countrymen. Do you know, they say 1851 will be a bumper year for emigrants. More than likely your Patrick is tucked off in a corner where I failed to notice him."

Maura shook her head. "Mr. Drabble, my brother's a mischievous lad. There's no telling where he's gone off to," she said.

"What do you want to do?" Mr. Drabble asked.

"I need some better air to think," she said. The two went to the front of the house and sat on the steps. The cold evening made her shiver.

"Perhaps he merely took to wandering, to see the sights," Mr. Drabble suggested after a while. "A young person's normal curiosity. Do you think that's possible?"

"It's as likely as not," Maura agreed, holding herself as

169

though the tension she felt might burst through her chest. "Why, even back to home, in Kilonny, which is—was—a tiny place, he'd trot off alone, roaming here and there with nothing like a by-your-leave. It drove my mother near mad, and it'll do the same to me." Suddenly she turned toward Mr. Drabble. "Do you think it possible someone stole him?"

"Did he have any money on his person?" Mr. Drabble asked, his voice low.

"I have it all."

"I should rather think—from what you say of the boy— it's more likely he followed us when we went off. I could return to the square and look about."

"Are you looking for a boy?"

"My brother," Maura exclaimed to whomever had spoken. "He's gone."

"A small Irish lad with big eyes and hair as black as coal?" the voice asked.

"That's him!" Maura peered into the dark. In the far corner of the porch, a woman was sitting propped up against the house, bare feet thrust before her.

Maura knelt by her. "Is it my brother you think you may have seen?"

"Well now, lass, perhaps I did. I can't say for sure, can I? But earlier this evening a runner came by, pulling in a man and his wife."

"A runner!"

"It was indeed. As soon as that boy—the black-haired one—seen him, he came clattering up the steps. So excited he was that he wedged himself into the corner, next to me."

"But why?"

"I supposed it was that runner."

"Did the runner try to catch him?"

"Oh, no, nothing like. I'll wager he never saw the boy."

170

A fearful thought came to Maura. "Can you tell me what the runner looked like?" she asked tremulously.

"He was young, you know," the woman said, "like most of 'em are. Tricked out in sailor's gob. Full of swagger and silver swift with his tongue. Bright too, with a hard smile, I'll give him that."

Maura turned to Mr. Drabble, who had come to her side. "Mr. Toggs," she said wretchedly.

"I didn't catch his name," the woman continued. "All I know is that as soon as he left his pigeons with Mrs. Sonderbye and went off, that boy—your brother, if that's the one—skipped right along after him. And that's all I saw, miss."

Maura murmured a thanks; then she and Mr. Drabble retreated to the steps to sit side by side.

"Do you think that's what happened?" he asked.

"Lord protect him," Maura sighed as much to herself as to him. "It must have been."

"Those runners can be repellent," Mr. Drabble felt obliged to say, hearing the anxiety in the girl's voice. "They move in gangs. And the worst of it is, my dear, what they do is strictly legal."

"But didn't he lie to us?" Maura cried indignantly, so angry her fists clenched.

"For sure he did," Mr. Drabble agreed. "I'm only pointing out that what they do is not against the law. Be honest, my dear, did this Mr. Toggs force you to come here?"

Maura had to shake her head. "It was his deceitful talk that led us to this dreadful place."

"It hasn't been all so bad, has it?" the actor asked with a tender sidelong glance.

Maura, caught up in worry, neither saw the look nor heard Mr. Drabble's tone. "Perhaps," she speculated, "Patrick was blaming himself for the way he was fooled by Mr. Toggs.

But, faith, what could he imagine doing if he caught up with the rogue?" she wondered out loud.

The actor had no answer.

Maura pressed her hands together tightly. Her head ached. Her heart was sore. "Mr. Drabble," she said, her voice shaking, "I don't know what to do."

"My dear, if I might offer a suggestion, I think it would be wise for you to get some sleep. We can't really search again until the morning comes.

"Tomorrow," he went on, "we'll use every waking moment."

"But you have your reading lessons to give to that man, Mr. Drabble," Maura reminded him.

"Never mind that! It's far more important that we find Patrick."

"But your fare money . . . ," Maura started to protest.

"Not until we find him," Mr. Drabble said resolutely.

"Mr. Drabble," Maura said, her breath coming hard, "you're a great mercy to me. Wouldn't I be altogether lost without you?"

The man placed hand to heart. His eyes grew bright.

The two returned to the dark basement.

"Come over here by this wall," Mr. Drabble suggested, stepping gingerly across two pairs of outstretched legs. "It's the driest area."

Maura crept toward the sound of his voice, raked some straw into a meager pile, then lay down on the cold ground. After a while she said, "Mr. Drabble, when we left our sad home in Ireland, we had three tickets for the ship to America. One for me, one for Patrick, and the third for my unhappy mother. Wasn't it my father's good money that's paid for it all. But with Mother choosing not to come, don't we have that extra ticket. You've been so very generous. And here you are now, passing up your own chance of emigrating by looking for my Patrick. Mr. Drabble, sir, it's to you I'd like to give the ticket."

"Miss O'Connell," the man stammered, "you cannot know how much you have touched my heart. For once I am at a loss for words."

"Merely say you'll take the ticket then," Maura pressed.

"My dear, I will if you wish it. But whose name is on the ticket?"

"My mother's."

"How is it written?"

"Mrs. Gregory O'Connell."

"Would you be offended if I took the *s* from *Mrs.*? I could pretend to be your father."

"No," Maura whispered.

"But more importantly, we shall find your brother," Mr. Drabble assured her. "Now do get some sleep. Good-night. And God bless you."

"God bless you," Maura returned.

Lying upon the ground, her head cushioned in her arms, Maura tried to think of everything that had happened that day. It was all too much. She could not hold it together. Instead, she stared into the dark and listened to the breath of sleepers. She tried to pray, but the words would not come. Is it my faith I'm leaving too? she asked herself tearfully. Her answer was a sob. "Oh, Mother, what if I have lost him?" Maura murmured as she fell into fitful sleep.

Chapter 39
Mr. Clemspool Makes
an Announcement

*T*he boy has bolted," Mr. Clemspool told Mr. Grout. The two sat in a small spirit shop not far from the elegant hotel where Toby Grout had established himself. He was propped lazily against his side of the bench, a glass of gin before him. He sipped it noisily, then wiped his mouth with the back of his hand. His eye was bright with amusement.

"Well now, there's a singular business," he drawled. "'Ow did that 'appen?"

"After we last spoke," Mr. Clemspool explained, "I went out. When I returned to my hotel room, everything seemed satisfactory. Nothing amiss. The boy's door was locked as I had left it. I called to him. 'Are you asleep?' I inquired. When there was no answer, I assumed he was. But, just to be sure—you know me, Mr. Grout, for the careful man I am—I entered his room. He was gone."

"And yer always tellin' me there are no imps and goblins," Mr. Grout declared ardently.

"There is nothing of the other world about it! He went out the window. Slid down a curtain to the next roof."

Mr. Grout whistled with admiration. "Regular gamecock, 'e is. I'd like to meet that laddie."

"I need hardly tell you I was shocked," Mr. Clemspool continued. "After all my care and consideration—and *expense*." He shook his head gloomily. "It's hard to accept, especially when you recall I am merely helping him do what *he* desires to do. Younger sons," he said with a disparaging wave of a hand, "you simply cannot trust them."

"And it don't speak too good for yer business, Mr. Clemspool, now does it?" said Mr. Grout with something of a smirk.

The bald man bridled. "How was I to know he might go out a fourth-floor window!"

Mr. Grout took another pull of his gin. "Wot about that sleepin' medicine 'e was supposed to be takin'?"

"I don't believe he even touched it."

Mr. Grout leaned over the table. "Think 'e came to know wot's in it? Yer know, *evidence.*"

Mr. Clemspool frowned. He was not enjoying the interrogation.

Mr. Grout, who *was* enjoying it, tapped his friend's arm. "Seems to me, Mr. Matthew Clemspool, this 'ere laddie 'as tricked yer game. I suspect 'e might 'ave some notion of the deck yer 'olding."

Mr. Clemspool shifted uneasily. "I don't know how he could."

"Lads on their own learn fast."

"Never mind what he's learned," Mr. Clemspool retorted with deepening gloom, "the point is, what does he intend to *do?*"

Mr. Grout laughed. "Depends on whether or not 'e's made the connection 'tween yer and 'is brother."

The very thought made Mr. Clemspool look up with dismay. "There is no way he could have!" he cried.

Mr. Grout grinned.

Now it was Mr. Clemspool's turn to lean across the table. "Mr. Grout, you know perfectly well I do absolutely *nothing* illegal. *Nothing.*"

"Wot kind of family does that boy of yers come from?"

Mr. Clemspool's eyes narrowed. "Mr. Grout," he said, his voice quivering with righteousness, "quite recently you came into a large sum of money, is that not correct?"

The other's smile grew broader. "Me magical in'eritance, yer meaning?"

"Your whatever-it-is," Mr. Clemspool said, pointing a plump accusatory finger at Mr. Grout. "I do not inquire about *your* business secrets. You need not inquire about *mine*. That has long been our understanding. I don't see why that should change now."

"All I'm sayin'," Mr. Grout replied laughingly, "is this: If that there boy's father is 'igh and mighty, it wouldn't matter much wot yer did or didn't do, would it? Give me a stack of cash over a stack of laws any day.

"Look 'ere, Clemspool," Mr. Grout drawled on, "it seems to me yer in a bit of a squeeze, ain't yer?"

"I don't believe the boy's gone back to London if that's what you mean," Mr. Clemspool answered sulkily.

"And why is that?"

"He has no money."

"'Ow do yer know?"

"Because I made sure of it."

Mr. Grout laughed out loud. "Did yer then, Mr. I-do-nothin'-illegal?"

Mr. Clemspool's face turned pinker than normal.

His companion went on. "Well then, stands to reason 'e's got to be somewhere in Liverpool, right? Let 'im be, says I. 'E won't be the first stuck 'ere. 'E won't be the last. All I'm sayin', Clemspool, is you might think of comin' to America with me."

"My work is here."

"As may be. But this time I've got the cash—a lot of it."

"Me? Work for you?" Mr. Clemspool asked with scorn.

Mr. Grout sat up very straight, staring with his one eye.

"Why shouldn't yer? I worked yer game. Now yer can work mine."

"Mr. Grout! To make my point precisely, I am a gentleman!"

"Well, I'm nearly one," Mr. Grout replied. "I'm on me way to bein' educated. Got me first readin' lesson tomorrow. I'll be talkin' like a regular shake-the-spear in no time."

Mr. Clemspool glanced toward heaven, as if only the powers there could bring off such a transformation. "The question remains, what shall *I* do about the boy?"

"Have yer thought of goin' to the police?" Mr. Grout inquired.

The absurdity of the suggestion was enough to make Mr. Clemspool rise from his seat. "Mr. Grout, I think it would be better if I left before we fall into serious argument. I'm going to walk about. Perhaps I'll see him."

Mr. Grout laughed. "Yer know where to find me if need be. And, Clemspool, me offer still stands! Off to America with Toby Grout! Yer'll be safe there."

Mr. Clemspool, as if he had not heard the remark—though he had—hurried into the street. Lanterns had been lit. Windows glowed with candlelight. It was not the darkness, however, that prevented Mr. Clemspool from setting off. He simply did not know where to begin his further searches.

For a while he even entertained Mr. Grout's suggestion that he go to the police. It was too risky. He did not wish to engage with the law in any fashion. He saw, therefore, only two choices. He could give the boy up as a bad job, return to London, acknowledge his loss, and pursue business elsewhere. There were plenty of sons to deal with.

Or he could invest more time in searching for the boy. Mr. Grout had made one good point—since Sir Laurence had no money, he had to be in the city *somewhere*.

Mr. Clemspool plucked his watch from his waistcoat and

consulted it. There was a night train to London at ten. But to rush off now seemed hasty. He could leave in the morning in more leisurely fashion. That meant he could continue searching for a few more hours. And by God, he told himself, if he caught up with the boy, he would not be so sweet.

Chapter 40
Laurence Hears a Voice

*B*estir yourself," the voice pleaded into Laurence's ear. "They might be coming back."

Laurence lay upon his back. His head was whirling. He had to force himself to open his eyes. Out of the darkness, a face peered down at him. It was Patrick.

"I heard what that fellow was saying," he whispered urgently. "So I ran back to the sentry box and called the police. Their coming scared him off. Only you best get away before they return. They're like to be after you too no matter what I say."

Laurence struggled upright and faced the boy kneeling by his side. To his eyes Patrick seemed nothing but a beggar, and—from the way he talked—an Irish one at that.

The boy extended a helping hand. For a brief moment, Laurence looked at it disdainfully. Then, with reluctance, he took it and hauled himself up on unsteady feet.

"They went that direction," Patrick said, pointing into the darkness. "We'd better be heading the other way."

Assuming Patrick knew the docks, Laurence made a murmur of assent. The two started off. Laurence ran a few steps, stumbled, steadied himself.

"Can you not run?" Patrick asked.

"I'm all right," Laurence insisted.

Too quickly they reached the end of the quay.

"Now where?" Laurence asked.

Patrick looked first one direction then another. It was hard to see far. What light there was came from the occasional dock lamp and the night lanterns on the ships. "I've no idea which way is best," he confessed.

"Don't you know where we are?" Laurence asked. There was annoyance in his voice.

Hearing the rebuke, Patrick looked around. "Do you?"

"No," Laurence was forced to admit.

"We can try this way then," Patrick said. "There's more light."

Ten minutes later, Laurence cried, "I need to rest."

A high lantern on a pole spread its yellow light in a circle about them. On two sides, dimly seen, floated ranks of moored ships, their masts, spars, and rigging a ghostlike forest against the dark sky. Not far from where they were, chests and trunks were piled high, waiting to be loaded.

Laurence sat down against one of the chests. It provided some protection from the chill wind, if not the damp. Patrick sat as well but not too close. After a silence, he said, "Do you have a name then?"

"Laurence."

"My name is Patrick."

Laurence grunted. For a while neither boy spoke. Finally Laurence said, "That man wanted me to steal."

"Faith then, it's true. I heard him."

"It was a metal box," Laurence said, as much to himself as to Patrick. "And full of money. I didn't want to take it." Fatigued, he closed his eyes.

"Did you know him at all?" Patrick asked cautiously. "The one making you steal?"

Laurence shook his head.

"I do," Patrick declared.

Laurence turned to him. "What do you mean?"

"Sure then, his name is Ralph Toggs," Patrick confided. "And he's a runner."

"What's a runner?"

Remembering Mr. Drabble's explanations, Patrick said, "They find people like my sister and me—just off the boat from Ireland—and tell a pack of lies to make you go to some wretched lodging place. You can't believe them. It's all for the money. There are lots of them in Liverpool."

Thinking he knew exactly the sort of man Patrick referred to, Laurence nodded.

"That was this morning," Patrick went on. "Then, this evening, didn't the same fellow come around again, bringing more people to the place he took us. Only this time he was asking for my sister, Maura. I was sure he meant to do her harm, so I had to follow him. All over town he wandered, until he came out here. Then I saw him catch hold of you."

"I was lost," Laurence said.

"So am I," Patrick allowed, staring into the darkness. "And, to tell the truth, I'll be needing to find my way back to my sister soon." He glanced around at Laurence. "We're going to America."

"So am I," Laurence murmured bleakly.

"Are you then?"

Laurence gave a small nod.

"So many are going," Patrick mused. "On the road, when we were coming up to Cork, the whole world seemed to be tramping. Where do you come from then?" he asked.

"London."

Patrick considered Laurence with discomfort. "Is it English you are?" Patrick asked.

"Of course."

"And a . . . a Protestant?"

180

"Church of England."

"I'm Catholic," Patrick felt compelled to say.

Laurence shrugged. He did not care. Patrick, however, felt ill at ease.

"Have you no family with you?" he ventured.

Laurence shook his head.

"Traveling alone then?"

"Yes."

"Sure, you've got it much harder than me," Patrick said. "I have Maura."

Laurence did not reply.

"You're right to go to America," Patrick said finally. "They say life is better there. Work and food in buckets. My father's gone and become as rich as a lord. When do you sail?"

"I don't know," Laurence said.

Patrick was surprised. "Don't you now?"

"I've no money."

Patrick looked at Laurence anew. He had never heard of an Englishman without money. "Have you none at all then?"

The grief Laurence felt rose to choke him. He could only shake his head.

Patrick felt a rush of sympathy. "Laurence, I don't think you're faring too well, are you?"

The boy shook his head again.

"If you have no money," Patrick asked after a time, "how do you expect to be getting on to America?"

"I don't know," Laurence whispered hoarsely, his eyes full of tears. He rubbed them away.

Patrick sighed. "My sister will be worried sick that I'm gone. I know she'll be."

"Are you going back now?" Laurence asked. He did not want to be alone.

"I should," Patrick said. "I wish you could stay at our lodging place, but the woman who runs it—a Mrs. Sonderbye—she won't let anyone in till they pay. I heard her say so." Patrick struggled to his feet. "I really should be off."

Laurence stopped him. "Would . . . would you mind if I went with you? I wouldn't have to stay there."

"You can if you want," Patrick said.

Laurence got up.

A thick fog had drifted in from the sea, wrapping the docks in swirling coils of cold mist and making it even harder to see than before. From the river came the occasional tinkling of a buoy bell.

"We might as well try this way," Patrick said, making a random choice.

For more than an hour, the two boys wandered over the docks, past row upon row of silent ships, bridges, closed warehouses, canal towers, dark waters. Discouraged, they stopped and sat again.

"I think," Patrick suggested, "it's only when the fog lifts that we'll be able to find our way."

Laurence, knowing the fogs of London, said, "They can last all night. And day."

Patrick stared into the murk. "Hello!" he called. "Is there someone about?"

"Ahoy there!" came an unexpected cry. "Were you hailing me?"

Unnerved, Patrick and Laurence peered in the direction of the shout. "Hello!" Patrick called again.

"Over here!" The voice seemed to come from one of the ships moored to the dock. The boys rose and crept toward it. Though obscured by the fog, a lantern could just be seen waving back and forth. They edged forward.

"Hello!" Patrick called again.

"You're getting there," came the reply. "I see you."

As they drew closer, the boys discerned a man on the ship before them. Even in the fog they could see this was no ordinary vessel. Of modest size, it had no rigging or masts. At midships, a houselike structure had been erected where the forward mast should have stood.

"Come on, lads," the man called, "you needn't be fearful. Haul yourselves over here."

Patrick and Laurence peered up from the edge of the quay. Looking down at them over the ship's bulwark was a gray-bearded figure in a sailor's jacket and hat.

"The hour is late, lads," the man said. "What brings you?"

"It's a way off the docks we're looking for," Patrick called. "Can you give us directions?"

"From what I can see of you, you're both in dire need of directions for your souls as well as your feet. Come along and board us. You can sup and sleep in peace."

Patrick and Laurence exchanged looks.

"And what kind of ship are you then?" Patrick called.

"This is the good ship *Charity*, a chapel ship. Reverend Gideon Bartholomew at your service. We don't sail worldly seas but venture on even greater heavenly voyages. We're tied up here for the glory of God so wayward sailors and all those who frequent these docks might find a sacred compass for their mortal wanderings. Step along. I've hot tea, a warm loaf, blankets, and the Gospels to share."

Laurence started to move forward but stopped when he saw Patrick was not following.

"What's the matter?" Laurence asked.

"He's Protestant!" Patrick whispered nervously.

"But it's food and warmth," Laurence said.

"If I go," Patrick said, "you must promise not to be telling him what happened."

"But why?"

183

"He won't believe us."

"I won't say anything," Laurence agreed, and started up the gangway, leaving Patrick on the quay. But as Patrick saw Laurence reach the boat, he found the offer of food and the chance to get out of the cold too tempting to resist. Though anxious for his soul, he followed.

Chapter 41
Upon the *Charity*

*T*he Reverend Gideon Bartholomew was a strong, burly man with a prominent nose, dark eyes, and a thick salt-and-pepper beard. With his lantern held high, he looked as if he'd just stepped from the pages of the Bible.

"Welcome to the *Charity*, lads," he boomed in a resonant voice. "Welcome to this floating house of God. All I need to know are your Christian names."

"Laurence, sir."

"P-p-patrick, Your Honor." He was afraid to look up.

"All right, Mr. Patrick and Mr. Laurence," the minister said with zeal, "this way to that food I promised." Lantern in hand, he guided the boys across the deck toward the ship's central structure, opened a door, and urged them to step within.

Inside was a simple chapel with a few old mismatched pews set before a Church of England altar. The walls were unadorned, the floor nothing but rough planking. Despite its meager furnishings, the room held a still, solemn air of sanctity.

Patrick, seeing the cross, automatically bent his knee and crossed himself.

"Ah, Mr. Patrick," Mr. Bartholomew said in kindly tones, "I see you're a Roman Catholic."

Patrick, fearing the worst, took a step toward the door as if to run.

"No, no, Mr. Patrick," the minister hastened to say as he held up a hand to block the boy's departure. "You need not worry. The *Charity* has been boarded by all faiths, and there's been no sinking yet, neither ship nor souls. Now, lads, step this way for tea and bread."

They went into an adjacent room, small and close, in the middle of which sat a rusty potbellied stove that radiated soothing waves of warmth. On the hob, a kettle was steaming idly. There were a few shabby chairs. On one wall a motto had been affixed. It read:

AM I MY BROTHER'S KEEPER?

"Sit yourselves down, lads," Mr. Bartholomew urged as he hung his lantern from one of the overhead beams. After removing his hat and hanging up his coat—revealing clerical suit and collar beneath—he went to a cabinet and took out two chipped mugs. Into these he sprinkled a liberal amount of tea, poured in some boiling water, then handed a mug each to the boys, who gratefully wrapped cold fingers about them.

"Now then, bread," the minister announced as he took a crusty brown loaf and a knife from another cabinet and cut two large slices, which he slathered thick with dripping molasses. The boys took the slices gladly and swallowed them in a few bites and gulps.

Looking on with contentment, the minister cut two more slices, but these he put aside—though, purposefully, not out of view.

"Very well, lads, more in a moment," he said, taking up

a position before them, hands behind his back, chin tucked in so that his beard looked like some vestment. "First you need to hear a brief sermon. As I told you, the *Charity* is a floating house of God. There are four of these ships at the Liverpool docks for all who choose to board. I'll not pass judgment on you. That's for Our Captain above. But if I'm to help you—and it's that I wish to do—I'll need to hear a true account of what brings you here. Mind, lads, I can tell a lie from the truth. . . .

"You," he said to Patrick, "have no doubt come from Ireland. Is that correct?"

Patrick, who had made up his mind to say as little as possible, mumbled, "Yes, Your Honor."

"And you, young man," he said to Laurence, "are English."

"Yes, sir."

"Very well, lads, straight to the mark. Were you on the docks for thieving?"

Flustered by Mr. Bartholomew's question, Laurence peeked over at Patrick, who made a tiny shake of his head.

The gesture was not lost upon Mr. Bartholomew. Assuming the worst, but recalling his vow not to judge, he struggled to contain his impatience. "Come, come, lads, if I'm to provide assistance, as I truly wish to do, I must know your story."

The boys stared at the floor.

"Well then, how did you two meet?"

Again no answer.

"Mr. Patrick," he said, "are you willing to tell me anything?"

Patrick, eyes averted, shook his head.

"So be it," the minister declared. Sensing that the English boy was not only the younger but the more vulnerable, he leaned forward. "What about you, lad, you're certainly not from Liverpool."

"No, sir," Laurence murmured. "I'm from London."

"And going where?"

Laurence hesitated. Then he said, "America."

Mr. Bartholomew considered the boy, taking particular note of the welt upon his face and the fact that the clothing he wore was—despite its soiled and torn appearance—of good quality.

Looking straight into the boy's eyes, Mr. Bartholomew said, "Mr. Laurence, I've piloted this ship for years. I can read faces as well as I can read the Gospels. So I ask you, lad, have you run away from home?"

As Laurence stiffened, a startled Patrick turned to stare at him.

"It's a sad but painful truth," Mr. Bartholomew continued carefully, "that runaways come to the Liverpool docks with great regularity. What led *you* to run from home?"

Laurence spoke to the floor. "I could not stay there any longer," he whispered.

"Mr. Laurence," the minister rejoined, "to cast away the anchor of family is a momentous act. You must have had a very strong reason indeed."

Laurence glanced up, but finding Mr. Bartholomew's scrutiny too heavy to bear, he turned and gazed at the words affixed to the wall: "Am I My Brother's Keeper?" They made him recall the words chiseled below his father's mantel: "For Country, Glory—For Family, Honor." Swallowing hard, he breathed, "I cannot say."

"That welt, my friend," the minister said with as much gentleness as he could muster, "did it come from home?"

Though Laurence colored with shame, he said nothing.

"I suppose," the minister offered kindly, "not saying is better than lying." He sat down. "Mr. Laurence," he said at last, "you are not the first to run away and, sadly, will not be the last. You spoke of going to America. Have you a ticket?"

"No, sir."

"Money for a ticket?"

Laurence shook his head.

"Well then, Mr. Laurence, may I ask, how do you expect to go?"

"I don't know," Laurence said quietly.

The minister—feeling he had come to an impasse—scratched his beard, cocked his head, wrung his hands. "Well then, here's another bit of bread," he said, handing the boys the other slices by way of signaling that the interview was over.

The boys ate the bread as eagerly as before.

Mr. Bartholomew stood. "It's late now," he said, "but I shall ponder what I can do to help you. In the meanwhile, you may both spend the night."

Patrick looked up. "And in the morning, Your Honor, may I be going?"

"To be sure, Mr. Patrick," the minister said evasively, "no one will compel you to stay. But it's late, and you may sleep here in safety.

"But first . . ." From a sea chest Mr. Bartholomew drew out a pair of worn canvas trousers and a jacket. He held them up before Laurence. "Mr. Laurence," he said, "your clothing will be of little help in this weather. I think these will serve you better."

Embarrassed, Laurence took the clothing.

"Go on now, get into them," the minister urged. "You'll feel more comfortable. I'll dispose of your rags."

Laurence retreated into a corner and changed into the new apparel. Compared to what he usually wore, the canvas material felt stiff, rough, and heavy. Both trousers and jacket

188

were big for him too, but Mr. Bartholomew bent over and rolled up the cuffs and sleeves. Laurence had to admit the clothes were warmer.

From the same chest the minister took two blankets and gave one to each boy.

"Now, lads, might we say a prayer for your momentary deliverance?"

"Can I be saying my own prayers, Your Honor?" Patrick asked anxiously.

"Mr. Patrick, you shall say whatever you desire!"

As both boys clasped their hands and closed their eyes, the minister recited a prayer concluding with, "And Lord, we thank You for guiding these poor lads Your way. May they find passage to homes both new and old. Amen."

The prayer done, Mr. Bartholomew banked the fire, retrieved his hat, coat, and lantern. "I'll be sleeping in my quarters," he informed them. "Morning service at six bells. Breakfast follows." Just before withdrawing, he looked sternly at them. "I expect to see you both here in the morning." Then he left, taking with him Laurence's tattered dinner jacket and trousers.

In the darkness, the two boys settled onto the floor and rolled themselves up in their blankets. For a while neither spoke.

"Patrick?" Laurence called.

"What?"

"Why couldn't we tell him what happened?"

"Well sure, it's his being an English Protestant clergyman, Laurence, and here I am, an Irish Catholic. More than likely, he intends to do me harm."

"He seemed friendly to me," Laurence said meekly.

"Faith, you can't trust them at all," Patrick insisted. "Back home, people would say it's better to hold your tongue in your head—else they'll use it to strangle you."

189

"I suppose," Laurence said, though he did not truly understand.

In a few moments Laurence heard Patrick murmuring his prayers. Then came silence, followed by the soft breath of sleep.

Though very tired, Laurence lay awake thinking about all that had happened to him. Yesterday he was living in one of the best homes in London. Now he was flat upon the floor of a floating church in the city of Liverpool without so much as a penny in his pocket. *What will happen to me?* he kept saying to himself. *What will happen?*

Chapter 42
Mr. Clemspool Pauses

Weary of fruitless meandering, Mr. Clemspool felt an urgent need to rest. Looking about where he stood, he spied a tavern called the Iron Duke and entered. There, in the farthest corner of the crowded room, he sat at a table, ordered himself a drink, and sat in gloomy isolation. The darkness of the spot matched his mood.

As Mr. Clemspool sat and sulked, a group of eight boisterous fellows ranging in age from ten to sixteen burst into the tavern. They were bubbling over with gibes and jokes, slapping backs, and punching shoulders.

Their leader appeared to be sixty years of age with gray hair tied back into an old-fashioned pigtail. Short and stout, he was wearing—from younger, slimmer days—a red military coat marked with sergeant stripes. The face was fleshy, with a plenitude of chins and jowls and a pendulous lower lip. Many rings adorned his fingers, which were long and strong, but almost delicate in appearance. In these hands he carried a small chest, its latch secured with a massive padlock.

The sergeant marched directly to an empty table at the rear of the tavern, not far from Mr. Clemspool. There he sat, placing the chest just so on the table before him. No sooner did his young fellows sit than a waiter arrived and set a large roasted chicken—brown and greasy—before the man. He tore off a leg with some savagery and began to chew upon it. The boys paid no mind but continued their chatter.

"Very well, gentlemen!" the sergeant barked with a booming military voice. "I herewith call the muster of the Lime Street Runners Association." So saying, he wiped one hand on a pants leg, produced a key, and with elaborate authority sprung the padlock on the chest and threw back its lid.

Immediately, the boys quieted themselves and gave full attention to their leader.

"Roll call," the sergeant announced even as he finished the chicken leg and began attacking the plump breast. "Mr. Young!"

"Here!" one of the young fellows replied.

"Mr. Spofford! Mr. Jones! Mr. Orkin! Mr. Thomas! Mr. Morris! Mr. Neal! Mr. Fred! Mr. Toggs!"

For each name called, there was a response of "Here!" until he reached Toggs. No one replied.

"And where is Mr. Ralph Toggs?" inquired the sergeant, wrenching off the chicken's second leg. "Absent without leave!" he pronounced. "Does anyone know his whereabouts?"

"Sergeant Rumpkin, sir," Spofford called out, "I saw him working earlier today. Had a couple of Paddies in tow as came right off the *Queen of the West*. That was this morning."

"Anyone else seen him?" Sergeant Rumpkin demanded.

"I did, sir," cried Orkin. "He had a twosome on the hook. Also Paddies. Late in the day, it was. Heading for Mrs. Sonderbye's, I think."

"Well then, at least he was in action," Sergeant Rumpkin said. "Perhaps he'll show up yet." He pulled his handkerchief from his pocket and with a flourish wiped some of the grease from his mouth.

"Now, gentlemen, let's see how the field looked today. Your reports, please. Advances. Retreats. Stratagems. And, not least, your victories." He looked about benevolently, his eye fastening on Fred.

Fred was a weasel-faced, sharp-nosed boy, with freckled cheeks and red hair. The youngest and newest member of the group, he had no last name.

In the association Fred and Ralph Toggs were well-known rivals. The fact rather amused Sergeant Rumpkin, brash Fred No-name (as he was called) against the cocky Toggs.

During the past few weeks, Toggs had seemed rather off his work. It had been the sergeant's policy deliberately to overpraise Fred so as to goad the older boy back to his former level of competence.

"Ah, yes, Mr. Fred," he said, "let's hear your report to begin." He sat back, poking randomly at the chicken carcass with his long fingers.

Fred stood, saluted crisply, and, in a high-pitched, almost squeaky voice, said, "All told, Sergeant, I brought in five pigeons."

"Five, Mr. Fred! Well done. Well done! I commend you."

The other boys chimed in with cries of "Hear, hear!" and "Good go, Fred!"

Young Fred's cheeks glowed almost as brightly as his hair.

"Proceed," the sergeant said.

"Soon as they came off the boat," Fred went on, "I

192

nabbed them. They were so bewildered, they gave me no lip. Brought 'em in easy. Like fish on a hook, they were."

"Any unusual circumstances, Mr. Fred?"

Fred grinned. "One old lady lost her bundle in the water. I jumped in, swum after to get it. She so took to me, I set her down at Grundy's."

There was much laughter.

"Mr. Fred," Sergeant Rumpkin cried approvingly, waving his handkerchief as if it were a flag, "I didn't know swimming was one of your many accomplishments."

"Like a fish, Sergeant. A bloody fish."

The burst of laughter this sally brought forth caused Fred's cheeks to glow even more brightly.

"And where, Mr. Fred, did you stash the rest of your brood?"

"Like you're always telling us to do, Sergeant. As far apart as possible." Fred reached into his pocket and hauled out a fistful of coins. "I made six shillings, four pence and a half today." He leaned forward and dumped the coins with a great rattle into the chest. That done, he stepped back and again saluted crisply.

"Very fine, Mr. Fred!" Sergeant Rumpkin cried. "You will go far. A credit to your family."

"I don't have no family," returned young Fred with smirking satisfaction. "That's why I've got no last name."

"Yes, well then, you're a credit to the Lime Street Runners Association, which I have the honor to command." Another wave of the flag.

This remark caused so much applause from his comrades that a beaming Fred felt obliged to stand up and bow.

"All right, who's next?" Sergeant Rumpkin asked as the waiter set before him a sizzling beefsteak. "Mr. Morris, may I have your report, sir?"

With Mr. Clemspool watching and listening from his table,

each of the young men reported in. Whatever the amount they had collected—some more, some less—each one dropped it into the sergeant's chest.

At times there was a setting forth of singular problems or difficulties. For these, Sergeant Rumpkin offered specific strategies and finished off a plate of mutton. Sometimes the handkerchief flag was waved; sometimes it was not.

When the reports were done and the money gathered, Sergeant Rumpkin made a rapid calculation, announcing the total and how much each boy had earned. Then he distributed the runners' equal shares, keeping a large percentage for himself.

"Sergeant, sir," one lad piped up to ask, "what about Toggs?"

"You know the rules, Mr. Neal. If Mr. Toggs is absent, he misses his pay," Sergeant Rumpkin explained patiently. "Of course, when he does come, we'll consider the matter on its own merits. I am fair, lads, nothing but fair. As for now, gentlemen, may I offer you something to drink?"

A waiter was hailed. Orders were placed. At this opportune moment, Mr. Clemspool approached the table.

"Good evening, gentlemen," he said. "May I have the pleasure of paying for your refreshment when it arrives?"

The entire membership of the Lime Street Runners Association swiveled about to look at the intruder.

"My name is Matthew Clemspool, Esquire, of London. A stranger here in Liverpool. I was sitting nearby and could not but overhear your conversation. To make my point precisely, I *admire* your venturesome spirits. Most enterprising."

The eight young men contemplated Mr. Clemspool with strict, silent neutrality.

"We are a charitable organization, sir," Sergeant Rumpkin said smoothly after a pat of his mouth with the handkerchief. "We offer to the confused and troubled traveler advice and accommodation, and we do this, moreover, without charging any fees whatsoever to the persons assisted."

"An admirable occupation," Mr. Clemspool hastened to agree. "With much to commend it as a charity. Indeed, it is not entirely unlike the kind of service my own business provides. But come now, shall I pay for your drinks? Then I will tell you of my need. Perhaps we may be of mutual benefit to one another."

The young runners looked to Sergeant Rumpkin. The older soldier motioned that a place for Mr. Clemspool be made at the table.

When they were all seated, Sergeant Rumpkin clasped his hands before him. "Well then, Mr. Clemspool, what might be your business?"

"Ever read the Bible, sir?" Mr. Clemspool began.

"I should hope every man reads his Bible," came the somber reply. For emphasis the sergeant looked around at his troops and nodded sagely.

"Genesis," Mr. Clemspool said, plucking his invisible harp. "Chapter four. Verses five through nine. Cain and Abel. Older and younger brothers. I'm concerned with both, with a particular inclination toward the older."

"The taller ground, sir," Sergeant Rumpkin approved. "Easier to defend and . . . that's usually where the money is."

"You take my point precisely," Mr. Clemspool agreed amiably. "Indeed, I am here in Liverpool on just such business. A certain young man—these days he goes by the name of Laurence Worthy—wishes to depart our green and pleasant shores for America. It is my desire to help him in the fulfillment of his wishes as quickly and as efficiently as possible."

"The truth is, sir," Sergeant Rumpkin cut in, "it's England's interest we serve. On one hand, we encourage the

195

failures amongst us to leave. Let America have the rabble! At the same time, we help the better sorts to remain. I dare say, before the year is out, I'd be surprised if we weren't commended by the queen herself"—Sergeant Rumpkin saluted his monarch—"for doing our public duty."

"You are a true patriot, sir," Mr. Clemspool allowed. "Alas, for reasons best known to himself, this boy has escaped my kindly ministrations. Alas again, he is bereft of friends—saving myself. Alas a third time, he has no money, though, I wish to assure you"—Mr. Clemspool raised a plump finger—"he is connected to a great deal of money. Sir, I want him back that I may speed him across the sea."

Sergeant Rumpkin clasped his long fingers together so that they looked like a locked trap. "And how, sir, do you imagine we humble foot soldiers might be of help?"

"The members of your organization seem to know the streets of Liverpool exceedingly well."

"They know the terrain, sir, every nook and cranny."

Mr. Clemspool asked, "Might they be willing, for a substantial fee, all being professionals in matters of business—might they be willing to conduct a search for this unfortunate young Laurence Worthy? If they found him and could return him to my protection, I would be most appreciative."

Sergeant Rumpkin looked around at his charges. "Well, sir, we're strictly military in organization. Here are the soldiers. I am, sir, their commander. I issue orders. They enact them. They trust me as their father. I treat them as my sons. No, sir, there are no democratic tendencies lurking here.

"If you will tell me what this boy—this Laurence Worthy—looks like, and assuming you and I can come to a satisfactory financial agreement, which I don't doubt, we can enlist the entire Lime Street Runners Association in single-minded pursuit of your young man."

"Excepting Ralph Toggs, Sergeant," Fred put in.

"Ah, yes, one of our lads is missing in action. But I harbor no doubts that when he returns, he will accept his marching orders like the rest."

Mr. Clemspool leaned forward on the table and provided a detailed description of Laurence. Then he made his offer: Four pounds to the association for locating the boy. A special bonus—two pounds—to the enterprising youth discovering him first. An additional two pounds to the organization once Mr. Clemspool had Laurence in hand. With such liberal terms, agreement was quickly reached. Drinks were raised all around, and the deal was done.

It was late that evening when Mr. Clemspool—once again feeling himself the master of his fate—entered the lobby of the Royalton Hotel. So absorbed was he in self-congratulatory thoughts that he entirely failed to note the nervous agitation his entry provoked upon Mr. Hudson at the reception desk. With candle in hand to light his way, and already looking forward to a good night's sleep, he mounted the steps to his room. Slipping his key into the lock of his door, Mr. Clemspool turned the catch and stepped inside. That was when he realized that a man was sitting in the darkness, a man wearing a bowler.

"Mr. Clemspool, I presume?" inquired Mr. Phineas Pickler.

Chapter 43
Mr. Bartholomew Ponders

*P*acing the floor in his quarters, Mr. Bartholomew tried to make up his mind about the boys. Patrick presented no great problem. There were hundreds, thousands of such beggarly Irish boys in Liverpool. They were not bad boys, merely abandoned, hungry ones. Impoverished when they arrived, they were hungry, and there was no employment for them. Hardly a wonder they took to thieving. And while the boys didn't say that's what they were doing on the docks, Mr. Bartholomew had little doubt on that score. In his heart he could not judge them harshly.

Fortunately, he knew of a fine place in Liverpool for such cases, the Catholic Society for the Protection of Abandoned Irish Boys. There, youths like Patrick were taken in, fed, protected, and taught a trade. The society was the making of many of them. Mr. Bartholomew resolved to bring Patrick to its door.

As for young Laurence, if that indeed was his name, he was another matter. Runaway English boys were common and came from any number of troubled situations. Many, in fact, did go off to America. In such cases, the question the minister always worried over was, Did the parents want them back? From his experience all too often they did not.

From Laurence's speech and bearing, the minister deduced he came from a family of considerable means. Now, upon further examination of the boy's discarded clothing, it was evident that the tailoring was of a very high quality indeed. Yet both jacket arms and back revealed long rips, almost as if they had been sliced. Mr. Bartholomew recalled the severe welt upon the boy's right cheek. The minister sighed. He was all too familiar with the evidence. The child had been beaten.

What, the man asked himself, were his responsibilities in the matter? Did Laurence's family want him or not? How could he be most helpful?

After further thought, Mr. Bartholomew went to his desk, placed a sheet of paper upon it, dipped pen into black ink, and wrote:

Inspector Knox
Metropolitan Police
Great Russell Street
Liverpool

Sir,

I feel obliged to inform you that a boy—answering only to the name of Laurence—*has come aboard my chapel. He was dressed in rags, is without any money, and has informed me he has run away from home.*

While I am aware that such cases number in the thousands, and you would not, therefore, ordinarily be concerned, this boy's speech and manner suggest that he comes from a family of means. I therefore wish to make you aware of the situation and await your advice, if any.

I remain, sir, your esteemed friend,

> *The Reverend Gideon Bartholomew,*
> *aboard the chapel ship* Charity,
> *Queen's Dock, Liverpool*

After reading over his words and blotting the paper, Mr. Bartholomew folded the letter, sealed it with a bit of sealing wax, addressed it, and put it aside until morning, when he would seek to find someone to deliver it.

At last the minister blew out the lantern, said his prayers, and retired to enjoy the sleep of the righteous.

Chapter 44
Mr. Clemspool Makes
a Discovery

I beg your pardon!" cried a startled Mr. Clemspool when he stepped into his hotel room and found Mr. Pickler sitting in the shadows. "Who are you, and what are you doing in my rooms?"

"My name, sir," the investigator returned quietly, "is Phineas Pickler, of London."

"London, eh?" Mr. Clemspool growled, perusing the small man before him in the candlelight, the round eyes, the jacket, the checked trousers, and the bowler. "Then I beg to inform you," he said, "your sense of geography is decidedly wanting. Out with you!" He held the candle high and the door open.

Mr. Pickler remained seated. "I am here," he went on calmly, "because I represent the Kirkle family."

Mr. Clemspool flinched, but in an effort to recover himself, he lifted his candle a little higher and considered Mr. Pickler, so to speak, in a new light. "Kirkle, eh?" he said, professing ignorance so as to collect his thoughts. "What's that to me?"

"Have you," Mr. Pickler inquired patiently, "some association with any member of that illustrious family?"

Mr. Clemspool, even as he tried to guess why this Pickler fellow was there, considered the question. "Look here," he blustered, "you have no right to be interrogating *me*. Or do you have some legal authority that gives you leave?" He puffed himself up. "To make my point precisely, I have *my* rights, and you are an intruder in my rooms."

Mr. Pickler removed his hat, stared into it for a moment, then looked up. "Mr. Clemspool, as an English citizen, I have the equal right to set forth certain information before the police."

Mr. Clemspool absorbed the remark in silence. Feeling the need to weigh his situation carefully, he set the candle upon a table and took a seat opposite Mr. Pickler. Only then did he say, "And pray tell, sir, what kind of information would that be?"

"It would appear that Lord Kirkle's son . . ."

"Are you speaking of Sir Albert?" Mr. Clemspool blurted out, grasping at the possibility that this Pickler fellow had come with a message from his employer.

Mr. Pickler gazed at him quizzically. "Sir Albert," he echoed. "Have you had dealings with him?"

"Oh, well," replied Mr. Clemspool, realizing he had blundered but trying to effect an indifferent manner. "Now and again, once or twice, sometime or other, I suppose I have. Nothing to speak of. Nothing." He removed his own hat and with deliberate casualness put it aside.

"But you did speak of it," Mr. Pickler pressed. "Would you be kind enough to provide me with the details of this connection?"

It was not particularly warm in the room, but the top of Mr. Clemspool's head began to glisten. "No, I don't think I will be so kind," he said. "Dealings between gentlemen are strictly private matters."

"Well then," the investigator continued, "perhaps the name Sir Laurence Kirkle will mean something to you."

"*Sir* Laurence *Kirkle*," Mr. Clemspool repeated with exaggerated emphasis. "No, I have never heard of such a personage."

"You arrived here this morning with a boy."

"Sir, you have no business meddling in the affairs of a private citizen who—"

"Mr. Clemspool," Mr. Pickler interrupted in a very quiet voice, "I should be perfectly happy to go with you to the Metropolitan Police office and present them with such information as I have. May I assure you, however, that Lord Kirkle is much more interested in the return of his boy to his proper home as soon as possible."

Mr. Clemspool began to see a spark of light upon an otherwise dim landscape. "Well, actually," he said, "now that you mention it, I did come upon a boy. It was in"—he plucked at the air as if snatching at old memories—"Euston Station, London. Yes! An unhappy boy. A boy dressed in rags. And with no money."

"None?" exclaimed Mr. Pickler.

"Not a brass farthing."

"I believe you took it, sir."

"Me! Take money from Sir Laurence Kirkle?" Mr. Clemspool replied with indignation. "*My* boy, Mr. Pickler, informed me his name was Laurence *Worthy*." Mr. Clemspool stressed the last name even as he put his hand to his heart. "I would swear to that fact on the tallest stack of Bibles in Creation."

"Laurence *Worthy*," Mr. Pickler murmured.

Mr. Clemspool went on, warming to the task. "Mr. Pickler, if I have a fault—and who amongst us does not?—I am too kind a fellow. Too given to charity. You might well ask, Am I my brother's keeper? To make my point precisely, my answer is *yes*. You might even go so far as to say my business is *helping* brothers. This boy, this Laurence *Worthy*, fairly begged my help and assistance. How could I"—Mr. Clemspool plucked at his airy harp again—"a man of profound sympathies, *not* respond?

"I found him exhausted. I provided lodgings in perfectly respectable circumstances. I found him ill. I brought him an apothecary who prescribed medicine for which I paid. I found him hungry. I fed him. His clothes were ragged. I purchased new clothes for him. All out of my own pocket, Mr. Pickler!" The more Mr. Clemspool tallied his expenses, the more indignant he became.

"Mr. Clemspool," the other man asked, "where is Sir Laurence Kirkle?"

But Mr. Clemspool was not yet done with his bill of particulars. "Laurence *Worthy* slept in the bed I'd provided, ate the food I'd fetched him. Then, to make my point precisely, he *left* without a word! Vanished. Disappeared."

"Out the window?"

"Very rude of him." Mr. Clemspool scowled. "Don't you think?"

"If you were helping him, why did he run away?"

"Sir," Mr. Clemspool cried, "I should very much like to know the answer to that question myself."

"Mr. Clemspool, I believe you informed the attendant at the desk below that the boy was your son."

"Did I? Perhaps the fellow misunderstood. Or a slip of my tongue, a reference to my fondness for youth. I do confess, sir, to treating him like a son."

"Mr. Clemspool, where is Sir Laurence Kirkle?"

"Mr. Pickler!" Mr. Clemspool bellowed, losing all patience. "I do not know! Haven't the foggiest. But if he were before me now, I should like to ask him why he gave me a false name and abused my hospitality. What's more, if he is of that highly esteemed family you mentioned—the Kirkles—I intend to lay down the specifics of my expenses so they may know how much the young impostor has cost me! Mr. Pickler, to make my point precisely, *I* have been taken advantage of!"

Mr. Pickler studied his bowler in search of a response. Gradually, he came to the opinion that, whatever his intentions, Mr. Clemspool no longer knew where Laurence was.

"Sir," said Mr. Pickler, "do you have an office in London?"

"I do."

"Might I have the address?"

"By all means," Mr. Clemspool replied with an air of a man who felt he had acquitted himself on the whole so skillfully that he was no longer in any danger. "The City. 12 Bow Lane."

The investigator committed the information to memory, then said, "Mr. Clemspool, I am myself searching for Sir Laurence Kirkle at his father's behest. You understand that speed is of the essence. From here I am going to the headquarters of the police."

"Mr. Pickler—!"

The man held up a hand and rose from his chair. "I shall ask the police to help me find the boy. On the assumption that I am successful, the boy will be questioned closely about your role in his disappearance from the city of London."

Mr. Clemspool opened his mouth to protest, but Mr. Pickler hurried on. "Furthermore, I intend to inform Lord Kirkle of what I have learned, along with my suspicion that there has been some connection between you and his elder son, Sir Albert Kirkle, in regard to this case. Finally, sir, I intend to ask a chemist to analyze the contents of this." Mr. Pickler reached into his pocket and held up the bottle of tincture of rhubarb.

Just the sight of it was enough to make Mr. Clemspool sag.

"If you think you are frightening me," a frightened Mr.

Clemspool returned, "you have, to make my point precisely, utterly *failed*." He mopped his brow.

"I was merely informing you of what I intend to do," Mr. Pickler replied. So saying, he set his bowler on his head and walked past Mr. Clemspool out of the room.

Mr. Clemspool watched him go, shut the door, locked it, again wiped his brow. The next moment he rushed to his wardrobe, pulled out his traveling bag, and began to stuff it with everything he had brought with him from London.

In the lobby, he paused briefly to speak to Mr. Hudson. "Urgent business requires me to leave," he announced. "Send a bill to my London address!"

"Whatever you say, sir," replied Mr. Hudson, greatly relieved that the man was going. As Mr. Clemspool rushed away, Mr. Hudson made a mental note not to make rooms available to him again.

Twenty minutes later, Mr. Clemspool was pounding upon Mr. Grout's door at the elegant Mayfair Hotel.

The door opened a crack. Mr. Grout peered out with his one good eye. "Oh, it's yer, is it?"

"Let me in immediately!"

Mr. Grout pulled back the door.

"America!" announced Mr. Clemspool as he swept into the room. "I must leave for America as fast as possible."

"Must yer now. Wot's the rush?"

"I am in danger!"

"'Oo from?"

"It doesn't matter who from," Mr. Clemspool cried. "There can be no delay."

Mr. Grout grinned. "Is that so? Well, it so 'appens I've got me education startin' tomorrow."

"Hang your education! We must leave immediately."

"No 'arm in yer goin' yerself."

"Mr. Grout, considering the nature of the emergency, I have insufficient funds!"

The one-eyed man laughed. "Oh, now, so that's wot it is. Yer beggin' me for some 'elp."

Mr. Clemspool waved his fingers about as if clearing away a cloud of frustration. "Yes," he said through gritted teeth, "I am in need of your help."

"All right then, if yer willin' to say that, Toby Grout is not a man to let yer down."

Chapter 45
The Liverpool Metropolitan Police

*T*he Liverpool police headquarters was to be found at the back of City Hall, down a circular iron staircase. These offices consisted of one large whitewashed room illuminated by the glare of two rather noisy gas jets. Aside from a few paper notices pinned to one wall, and a large pendulum clock on another, the only decoration was a shabby picture of Queen Victoria.

For prisoners, a small cagelike structure had been erected. Two constables lounged on a bench nearby, their greatcoats partially unbuttoned, their hats low over closed eyes.

At the rear of the room, facing the door, stood a high desk behind which sat the duty officer, one Inspector Knox. Having already been on duty for twelve hours, Mr. Knox was bleary-eyed. His pug nose, thin unsmiling mouth, and bristling muttonchop whiskers all conspired to give him the appearance of a rather cross hedgehog.

Though Mr. Pickler walked right to the inspector's desk, Mr. Knox chose to continue reading his official papers. Only after some minutes had passed did he lift his eyes. "Can I help you, sir?" he inquired in a tone so sour, it was perfectly clear he did not think he could nor did he wish to.

"My name, sir, is Phineas Pickler, late of the London Metropolitan Police."

"You say *late*, sir," the inspector snorted as if he were accepting a confession of guilt. "What might you be doing presently?"

"I am functioning as a private investigator."

"Are you now?"

"Indeed, sir," Mr. Pickler said quietly. "Currently under the private employ of Lord Kirkle."

The inspector lifted one eyebrow. "Is that . . . Lord Kirkle of the Treasury Bench?" he inquired.

"The same," Mr. Pickler replied with a modest bob of his head.

The two constables on the bench opened their eyes and sat up. One of them began to button his coat.

The inspector leaned back in his chair and peered down sardonically at Mr. Pickler. "Well now, it's not often we have exalted ones up from London asking for our help. What can we do for you?"

Mr. Pickler glanced about the room. The eyes of the constables were upon him. He turned back to Mr. Knox. "Sir," he said in a hushed voice, "it's a rather private matter."

"Tingley! Baker!" Mr. Knox barked. "You're not wanted! I've matters of state here that are above you. Get yourselves outside."

The two men, grinning sheepishly, lumbered to their feet, then stepped from the room.

"Now then, sir," Mr. Knox observed, "you've got your privacy."

Mr. Pickler was perfectly aware he was being mocked. He did not care. He had a job to do. "Mr. Knox," he said, "I am looking for Lord Kirkle's son."

"*The* Lord Kirkle?"

"Yes."

The inspector pursed his lips. "Are you now?" he allowed.

Refusing to be provoked, Mr. Pickler cleared his throat. "Yesterday Sir Laurence Kirkle ran off from his illustrious London home, saying he was going to America. Of course, he did not really mean it. But hard upon his saying so, there is reason to believe he was abducted and brought to Liverpool. He must be found immediately."

Mr. Knox shook his head glumly. "I dare say you do want to find him," he said. "And you'll forgive me for remarking, Mr. Pickler, but it's many a father who comes to stand before me in search of a runaway son. Abducted, you say. That's what all fathers claim. It's the rare one who'll admit his boy's a runaway. Instead they insist their darling has been stolen or tricked away. But between you and me, sir, there is no abductor."

Mr. Pickler bridled. "You are speaking of Lord Kirkle's son!" he exclaimed. "And I have found the abductor."

Mr. Knox rubbed his tired eyes. "If you've found the abductor, where's the boy?" he asked.

"He escaped before I could get to him," Mr. Pickler admitted.

"That's not very original either," Mr. Knox said.

"It's true!"

The inspector clasped his hands before him, leaned over his desk, and stared down at Mr. Pickler. "Sir, since the boy is now free—as you yourself admit—then surely he'll hasten back to his laudable home or he will come here looking for help. No need for us to do a thing."

"I must find him," said Mr. Pickler firmly.

Mr. Knox shook his head in a most melancholy fashion. "Sir, do you know Liverpool?"

"Only slightly."

"To find one boy—even Lord Kirkle's son—will be extremely difficult."

"I'm perfectly aware of that, sir. But I needed to bring the matter to your attention."

"I do appreciate your confidence, Mr. Pickler," Mr. Knox said dryly. "And considering who the boy is, I suppose we must do everything possible to merit that confidence. If you'll be good enough to leave us with his description, I shall share it with everybody on the force and commence a search.

"Perhaps someone will report your boy. But, speaking from experience, sir, it's not likely. Have you inquired at the ticket agencies?"

"Why should I do that?"

"It is there one gets a ticket for America."

"Mr. Knox, I repeat, the boy does not wish to set sail. He was abducted. As for money, all evidence suggests he has none. It is my belief it was taken from him."

"Well then, do you think he would attempt to steal money so as to purchase a sailing ticket?"

"You don't seem to have heard me!" cried a shocked Mr. Pickler. "We are speaking of Lord Kirkle's son."

"Yes, of course," Mr. Knox said with the hint of a smile, "and unlike other mortals."

"Inspector," Mr. Pickler exclaimed, "not only did his abductor take all the boy's money, but he beat him, leaving a cruel mark upon his face!"

"Mr. Pickler, do you know these things as facts?"

"I believe them to be facts!"

Mr. Knox shook his head. "Not the same, sir. Not the

same. Well then, since the boy has no money, do you think he might attempt boarding a ship as a stowaway?"

"Sir!" Mr. Pickler cried out with as much heat as he could muster. "How many times must I repeat myself? The boy was brought to Liverpool against his will! He does not wish to leave his family."

"That's as may be, sir," returned Mr. Knox. "But all the same, if I were you, I'd pay some heed to my experience."

"But—"

"There are as many as a dozen ships sailing for America every day. I'll be more than happy to provide you with a list. By posting yourself on the quay at the time of embarkation, you just might catch your young fellow. But, considering who the boy is, we'll set up a watch ourselves. I suggest you come back in the morning to speak to the officers yourself."

Deeply unhappy, Mr. Pickler wrote out a description of Laurence and promised to return in the morning. But he would hear no more about departing ships.

From police headquarters, Mr. Pickler took a cab and returned to the Royalton Hotel. When he arrived, Mr. Hudson informed him that Mr. Clemspool had only recently checked out.

"Was the boy with him?"

"No."

Mr. Pickler fixed his birdlike eyes on Mr. Hudson. "And did you, sir, discuss the situation with him at all?"

"Not in the least," Mr. Hudson hastened to say. "I swear I didn't."

Mr. Pickler was too tired to do anything but believe him. "May I have a room, sir?"

"Of course, sir. No fee. Complimentary."

Once in bed—dressed in his flannel nightshirt and cap—Mr. Pickler pulled the blankets up to his chin, closed his eyes, and tried to sleep. He could not. He kept reviewing the events of the day. In many respects, he had made great progress. But it was Mr. Knox's insistence that Laurence had *not* been abducted, that he had really run away from Lord Kirkle's home, that rankled. The impertinence of the man!

And yet . . . Mr. Pickler was troubled. The inspector's words were not so very different from what Mr. Clemspool had claimed. What if it were true that Laurence had *not* been abducted . . . that the boy had given a false name and truly wanted to flee the country? Such an unhappy circumstance. What of Sir Albert? In some fashion *he* was involved here. Mr. Clemspool had admitted that. Mr. Pickler sighed. Surely, this was the most frustrating, upsetting case he had been called upon to solve.

Chapter 46
What Happened to Ralph Toggs?

The dock police who chased Ralph Toggs from beneath the porthole of the coastal schooner did not pursue him for long. Though they whirled their rattles loudly and demanded with angry authority that he stop, Toggs was too fast for them. They hurried back to the quay. When they reached the ship, no one was there, Laurence and Patrick having already fled.

But then, as far as the police were concerned, they had done their task. A theft had been prevented. After closing up the boat's porthole, the two constables returned to their posts and thought no more about the incident.

As for Toggs, he simply moved on to his favorite hiding

place, an old warehouse in a serious state of ruin. He knew that, once inside, he was quite beyond discovery.

Though it was black as pitch past the entry, he easily made his way down a crumbling hall to a little room once used for coal storage.

Over a period of time, Toggs had furnished the room with an old rug, a few candle stubs, a blanket, even a small sack of cotton, which he used as a pillow.

Now he lay down on the rug, pulled the blanket over his body, and sat back against his pillow. With his hands behind his head, he thought over the day.

He would have been happier if that boy with the welt on his face had been successful in handing out some money. Since he had not, he, Toggs would have to find another way to impress that Irish girl.

The girl . . . Toggs did like to think about her. She was a comely lass, so slim, with her thick dark brown hair and blue eyes. He even liked it when she had been upset. Her face seemed pitiful then. He did wish he knew her name and wondered if she remembered his.

If he was going to impress her, he had to have money in his pocket. He considered his day's takings from running emigrants. It was not much, and in any case, most of it was supposed to go to Sergeant Rumpkin.

Ralph Toggs sighed. Yes, she was the girl for him. And he was determined to win her over. The question was, How? It was while thinking such thoughts that he fell asleep.

Chapter 47
Maura Awakens

The dawn was still dim when Maura O'Connell woke. She rose up immediately and, in hopes that her brother had returned while she slept, searched the basement corners. All she discovered was what she most feared: Patrick was not to be found.

Greatly troubled, she made her way up the rickety stairs to the porch, stepping carefully over the sleepers in the halls. Outside, early morning light glimmered through the chill city haze, enough to reveal that Patrick was not on the porch either. Nor did Maura believe, as Mr. Drabble had suggested, that he was elsewhere in the house.

Shivering—more from tension than the raw frost—the girl sat upon the top porch step, drawing her shawl tightly about her head and neck.

Why ever did Patrick go? she kept asking. What had happened to him? Had that Ralph Toggs done him harm? Or was Patrick simply lost, wandering somewhere in the city? Maura was almost afraid to know the answers. And when she reminded herself that they were meant to embark the next day, her dread increased. "*Patrick, where are you?*" she whispered to the air, and pressed a hand against her aching heart. If she lost him, surely she would die.

She must search for him. Yet she held back, wondering if it might not be wiser to wait for Mr. Drabble to awaken. The next moment she decided she must act alone. It was not prudent to be always depending on the actor's kindness. All in all, he was still a stranger. She could only hope she'd done nothing improper by being so much in his company. Though it was a small worry compared to her concern about Patrick, the thought troubled her.

Clutching her shawl around her, pushing her hair away from her worried blue eyes, Maura stepped into the muddy street. The cold morning air smelled foul. Walls of tall tenement buildings rose up and vanished into noxious mists that stung her eyes. It was hard to see far. Every few yards she paused to look around, struggling to memorize signs, shops, buildings, whatever might help guide her back to Mrs. Sonderbye's.

Despite the early hour, many people were passing. Their shoulders were hunched, their eyes hardly open. Hands were thrust deep in pockets. Maura kept wondering where these folk were going. Was it to work? What sort? The only work she knew was the work of home, the tending to fields, or the jobs in shops such as the one in Kilonny.

Maura had never been one to conjure visions of hell, but Liverpool, she thought, must be something like it. "Jesus, Mary, and Joseph," she whispered, shuddering and making the sign of the cross, "protect us all." How, she wondered, could people live their lives pressed together so tightly in such a place? How utterly unlike her home.

She thought of Kilonny, so small, so tucked away in its ignored cranny of the world. What an insignificant spot it was! The thought startled her. Was that what she truly thought, that Kilonny was insignificant? Yes, she told herself, it was true. But how painful to acknowledge that one's own home mattered only to those few souls who lived there! A short time ago her entire life lay marked before her. With utter certainty she could have recited every task, every obligation, every stage of life until she became an old woman and died. Now, she realized, she could neither predict nor guess what she would be doing the next hour. The notion frightened her, not the least because she knew it excited her too.

She wandered on downhill, scrutinizing faces of strangers as they passed. Who were they? What were their lives like? It was not that she thought they might be Patrick in disguise. Rather, she kept wondering if their eyes had rested on him without their even knowing it and had retained—in some way—a hazy image of her dear brother. More than once she had to suppress the desire to look into their eyes, to ask if, indeed, any had seen him.

She stopped at a sign that read:

CATHOLIC SOCIETY FOR THE PROTECTION
OF ABANDONED IRISH BOYS

She wondered if she should make inquiries within, only to scold herself—Patrick was lost, not abandoned.

Half an hour later Maura came upon two constables on a corner, a sheet of paper between them. They were talking earnestly, now and again pointing in one direction then another as if trying to decide which way to go. Maura decided to ask if they had seen Patrick.

Eyes cast down, she stood off a few paces, patiently waiting until they noticed her.

"Yes, miss, what can we do for you?" one of the constables asked finally.

"If it please Your Honor, it's my brother."

"What about him, miss?"

"He disappeared last night and hasn't come back. I've been searching all over for him."

The other constable laughed. "Ah, Miss Paddy, if we had to look for every Barry, Brian, and Bridgit who disappeared in Liverpool, it'd take an army of us. And what's more, we still wouldn't find them."

"Faith, sir," Maura pressed, "he's only twelve years old and a stranger to the city."

The first constable, struck by Maura's earnestness, said, "We don't mean to banter, miss, but here we are already looking for a boy. It's a useless task."

"What boy is that?" Maura asked, her hopes rising.

The constable held up the paper they had been consulting. "What's your brother's name?"

"Patrick, sir. Patrick O'Connell."

"Well now," the constable said, checking his paper, "this one's named Laurence. An English boy. They're making a point of not telling us much. No last name given but eleven years of age. Sandy hair. Fancy clothes gone ragged. A nasty welt on his face, right side. That wouldn't be your brother, would it?"

Disappointed, Maura shook her head.

"Are you sure your brother hasn't signed on some ship for crew?" the second constable asked.

"He'd never do such a thing!" Maura cried.

The constable grinned. "There are plenty that do, miss."

Offended by the idea, Maura recoiled. As if Patrick would run away! Restored by something close to anger, she turned back toward Mrs. Sonderbye's. Perhaps, while she was gone, Patrick had returned. Folly to think so, she told herself. Folly not to, her heart cried.

The next moment she made herself stop and once again reversed herself. She would look for Patrick awhile yet before turning back.

Chapter 48
Concerns Fred of the Lime Street Runners Association

*F*red had a history no more lengthy than he was tall. His mother died when he was born. His father shortly after. They left him nothing, not even a last name. At eight he ran away from the Yorkshire workhouse in which he had been placed and came to Liverpool. For two years he had pursued many occupations: old-wood gatherer, dog finder, crossing sweeper, rat catcher, and finally, at the age of ten, runner. Considering his age and size, membership in the Lime Street Runners Association was not just an achievement, Fred felt it a great honor.

As far as he was concerned, he had but one rival and that was Ralph Toggs. Toggs was not just older, he was considered smarter. He knew how to read and was generally acknowledged as the wiliest at catching up emigrants. These attributes had made Toggs Sergeant Rumpkin's favorite. Fred's great ambition was to take Toggs's place in the sergeant's esteem. What's more, Fred was convinced he now had a way to achieve just that: He would find the missing London boy, a challenge about which Toggs knew nothing.

Fred lived in a dustbin at the end of Tumbler's Alley, a loose thread of a street that ran off Dunn's Court. Though he was one of six in the dustbin, it was usually Fred who left his bed of straw first each morning. Since he slept in his clothes, he could be on the street in a matter of moments. So it was on this Thursday. The city was still dark when, hands in pockets, breath steaming, he set out to find this Laurence Worthy.

From his experience, runaway boys who came to Liverpool headed straight for the docks. Accordingly, Fred headed there too, but only after pausing to purchase a breakfast of boiled black coffee and a stale roll.

In the two years since Fred had come to Liverpool, he had learned the docks wonderfully well. He knew countless shortcuts, dodges, and back ways. But that morning his knowledge was to no avail. He found no sign of Laurence in any of those places.

Moving on, he began searching among the many piles of goods on the quays. Perhaps the boy had holed up for the night. There were hundreds of these piles held up for want of customs clearance and fees or because of shippers' mistakes. It was while he was prowling along Queen's Dock that he suddenly heard a shout.

"Hello there, lad!"

Fred halted, looked about, and saw that a gray-bearded man was hailing him from the deck of a ship. It took another moment for Fred to realize in the misty dawn that the vessel was one of the chapel ships and the man hailing him a minister.

"You calling me, governor?" Fred called.

"Yes, you, lad," Mr. Bartholomew said. "Might I have a word with you?"

Fred, curious though wary, strolled over. "What did you want?" he asked cheekily.

The minister, choosing to ignore the rudeness, said, "Young man, I wonder if I could entice you into doing a small favor. It's a matter of some importance." He held up the letter regarding Laurence that he had written to Inspector Knox.

"If you would be so good as to deliver this, there will be a whole penny for you."

Fred eyed the letter suspiciously. "Where's it going?"

"City Hall. The police headquarters."

Fred, wanting nothing to do with the police, backed away.

"You see," the minister confided in a whisper, "I have some lads on board whom I would rather not leave."

The mention of lads brought a quick stop to Fred's retreat. Perhaps this was something worth investigating. "Well, I might deliver it," he allowed.

"I cannot thank you enough," Mr. Bartholomew enthused.

Fred made his way up the gangway. Once he was on deck, the minister handed him the letter with one hand, the penny with the other.

"Obliged, sir," Fred said with an obedient tug to his ginger hair by way of respect.

"Now, lad," the man said, "I would be derelict in my duty if I did not urge you to join us for morning service."

Sensing Fred's hesitation he added, "I'm sure you can spare a few moments to hear the word of the Lord. And you won't be alone. Those other lads I mentioned will join you."

That he might see these other lads was something Fred could not resist. "All right," he agreed. "I will."

"Good for you!" the minister cried, and led the boy into the chapel. "Take a seat. I'll return in a moment." Suddenly he paused. "Young man," he said, "if you could put that letter away . . . I'd much prefer it not be seen."

"Yes, sir," Fred said.

Fred stared at the letter, but since he could not read, he angrily shoved it into a pocket.

In moments Mr. Bartholomew returned herding a sleepy Patrick and Laurence before him. "Here we are, here we are," the minister bubbled as he guided the two boys into seats. Rubbing their eyes and yawning, they slumped down.

Fred swiveled about to catch a look and, remembering Mr. Clemspool's description of the missing boy, knew he had found his prize.

"All right, my lads, I think we can begin," Mr. Bartholomew said. He moved to the front of the chapel and prepared for the service.

Fred kept stealing glances at Laurence and Patrick. They looked so very ragged, he found it hard to believe that Laurence was connected to money, though it was true that he was, for one, wearing shoes.

Fred felt for the letter in his pocket. Could it have something to do with this Laurence? The minister had said he did not want it to be seen.

Mr. Bartholomew's deep bass voice filled the small chapel. Fred tried to be patient. But instead of giving his mind over to the sacred words, all he could think of was getting news of Laurence to Sergeant Rumpkin. So it was that halfway through the service, at a moment when the minister's back was turned, Fred bolted.

He did not stop running until he was a full quarter of a mile away from the chapel ship. When he paused, it was to think of where Sergeant Rumpkin would be at such an early hour. Presumably at breakfast at the Iron Duke.

That was a problem. It was a standing order in the association—an important order—that the sergeant was never to be troubled during meals. Fred was sure, however, that his news and, perhaps, the letter were important enough for a breaking of the rule.

After thinking through the fastest route, one that snaked in and out of some of the older warehouses and then out of the dock area, Fred took off at a hard trot.

Chapter 49
Reverend Bartholomew
Concludes the Service

With loving care, Mr. Bartholomew removed his surplice and turned a smiling face upon his youthful congregation. Only then did he realize that Fred was gone. He sighed. How difficult these young people made his work! Now, moreover, he had to worry if the red-haired boy would even deliver his letter to Mr. Knox at police headquarters.

The minister berated himself for having given the boy the penny before the task was completed. Perhaps, though it was painful to acknowledge, he had been too trusting. But far, far better for a man of the church to have too much faith in people than too little.

The thought put him in a more suitable humor to set about helping the boys still sitting before him. First, he would take Patrick to the Catholic Society for the Protection of Abandoned Irish Boys. Laurence he would leave on the chapel ship, giving the Liverpool police some time to respond to his letter before acting.

"I fear our other young friend has slipped his moorings," Mr. Bartholomew said as he came down the aisle. "That you boys remained pleases me greatly. I do hope the words of the Lord were a comfort."

During the service, Patrick had kept his eyes squeezed shut and murmured his own prayers as protection against the minister's words. Now that the service was done and he found himself intact, he felt like St. George. Emboldened, he looked up. "Please, Your Honor," he said, "it's time I was going."

"Going? Perhaps I can first interest you in breakfast?"

Laurence, who had been staring morosely at the floor, wondering where he would go next, lifted his face. "Yes, thank you, sir."

Patrick, with a glance at his friend, agreed.

The minister led the boys back to the room where they had slept. There, he put the kettle on, cut slices of bread, spread them with molasses, and offered each boy two pieces. Laurence bolted his down. Patrick ate more slowly. Soon they were sipping at their tea as well.

"I'll just fetch my coat," Mr. Bartholomew told them.

As soon as the minister left them, Patrick leaned out of his chair. "Laurence . . . ," he whispered.

A dejected Laurence looked around.

"Now that it's daylight, I think I'll be able to find my way back to my sister."

Laurence said, "Perhaps I'd best go home."

"To London, do you mean?"

"Yes."

"Will it be hard for you there?" Patrick asked.

Laurence nodded.

"What do you think might happen?"

Laurence lifted his shoulders, then let them drop. "I suppose I'll be arrested."

"How will you be getting there?"

"I don't know."

Patrick gazed at Laurence. He had never met anyone like him before. It was not that the boy was younger than he or that he reminded Patrick of Timothy, his little brother who had died. What was amazing was that an *English* boy should be worse off than he.

Patrick ran a finger around the edge of his cup. "Laurence," he said, "when my sister and I set off for Liverpool, my mother was coming too. But then, just as we were boarding the boat, she stayed. So you see, my sister still has her ticket. For America. What I'm thinking, Laurence, is, since it won't be used, it might as well be yours."

Laurence, not sure he had heard right, looked up. "Give your mother's ticket to me?" he asked.

"To be sure, it'd be a shame to waste it, now wouldn't it?"

A tremor of excitement passed through Laurence. "Do you really think your sister would?"

"To be sure. When Maura sees you have nothing, she's bound to say yes. She can be fierce, but for all of that she's kindness itself."

Laurence asked, "When are you to sail?"

"Tomorrow."

"I know you said I couldn't stay at that lodging place. . . ."

"Mrs. Sonderbye's."

"But if I had a ticket, it wouldn't be so bad to sleep out one night."

"It couldn't do much harm," Patrick agreed.

"Then I'll go back with you to that Mrs. Sonderbye's," Laurence said. "I will."

Mr. Bartholomew, wearing coat and hat, returned. As soon as he appeared, Laurence stood up.

"Please, sir," he said, "I'll be going too."

The minister frowned. "Now, now, Mr. Laurence," he said severely, "I'm not sure that would be wise."

"But I can't stay here."

"I'm not suggesting that you stay permanently, but . . . I'll tell you a secret. I have written a note to a friend, a gentleman who might be helpful to you."

"But I've got a ticket to America!" Laurence blurted out.

"Mr. Laurence," the minister said harshly, "last night you did not have one."

"And it please, Your Honor," Patrick cut in, "it would be my mother's ticket, which we're not using. I just offered it to my friend."

Mr. Bartholomew could barely keep from laughing out loud. The notion that an impoverished Irish boy would have such a valuable article, much less give it to an equally impoverished English boy, was nothing less than preposterous! "A ticket to America?" he exclaimed. "I thought we agreed I'd hear no lies from you, Mr. Patrick."

"But, Your Honor, it's true!"

"Very well, Mr. Patrick, if you have such a ticket, be so good as to show it to me."

"Faith, it's my sister who has it."

"Sister now! This is the first I've heard of a sister."

"But I do have a sister!" Patrick cried in exasperation. "And isn't she waiting for me at Mrs. Sonderbye's lodging house."

"Mr. Patrick," Mr. Bartholomew said with great patience, "if this is true, why did you not tell me last night?"

"I . . ."

The minister wagged a finger. "Mr. Patrick, I am trying to help you. Lies will only make me cross. Now pay heed. I'm going to take you to the Catholic Society for the Protection of Abandoned Irish Boys, run by your own countrymen. And a very fine establishment it is too. You'll be fed, clothed, taken care of."

"But I don't want to go to any place but where my sister is!" the boy cried in horror.

"Mr. Patrick," the minister replied in his most soothing voice, "you need to learn to trust those who know what's good for you."

"Your Honor," Patrick pleaded, his eyes suddenly brimming with tears, "I am telling the holy truth. Maura's waiting for me!"

224

"Mr. Patrick, please don't try my patience. I'm doing you a good turn."

Patrick started to protest again, but fear froze him. What was happening was exactly what he had most dreaded.

Mr. Bartholomew, taking Patrick's silence as acceptance, turned to Laurence. "As for you, Mr. Laurence, you will remain here until I return. I want you to give me your promise on that."

"Yes, sir," Laurence answered, not knowing what else to do. "I'll wait."

"Very good then," the minister said. "Now then, Mr. Patrick, let's be off." He stood by the door.

Patrick and Laurence stared at each other for a moment.

"Bye," Patrick murmured.

"Bye," Laurence returned.

"All right, lad, come along," Mr. Bartholomew said, and clamping his hand firmly on Patrick's shoulder, he led him away.

Chapter 50
Ralph Toggs Is Woken Up

*T*he night had passed quietly for Ralph Toggs in his warehouse chamber. Indeed, he slept so well, it was only the sound of footsteps in the old hallway that woke him.

Up in a flash, he took a quick look, realized whose steps he had heard, waited, then jumped out in front of Fred.

"Well, well." Toggs sniggered. "It's little Fred No-name, the Yorkshire marvel. What brings you here?"

Fred, with Mr. Bartholomew's letter in hand, had been loping along, caught up in daydreams about how he would spend the reward money he got for finding Laurence. Toggs took him completely by surprise.

He stopped in his tracks. Trying to recover his composure, he eyed his rival with fear and anger. "Just looking for pigeons," he said.

"In here?" Toggs said scornfully. "Not likely."

"Well, what are *you* doing here?" Fred threw back.

"I was waiting for you."

"Me?"

"Sure," Toggs said, enjoying the boy's uneasiness. "I knew you were coming."

Fred looked at Toggs suspiciously.

"What's that you got there?" Toggs demanded.

Fred had quite forgotten the letter. The moment Toggs asked, he thrust it behind his back. If the letter had something to do with Laurence, the last thing he wanted was his rival getting hold of it. "Message for Sergeant Rumpkin," Fred said.

"Who gave it to you?"

"A clergyman."

"A clergyman! What's it about?" Toggs wanted to know.

Fred took a step back. "None of your business," he answered.

"You don't even read, do you?" Toggs sneered. "So you wouldn't know whose business it is, now would you?"

"I do know!" Fred cried.

"Well, *I* can read," Toggs pressed. "So you can hand it over now." He reached for the letter.

Fred took another step back.

"Well then, keep it yourself," Toggs said. "It's likely rubbish." He turned away.

Thinking he had deflected Toggs's curiosity, Fred relaxed his guard. The next moment Toggs whirled, made a lunge, and snatched the letter away. Fred tried to retrieve it, but

Toggs held him off and read the address on the paper. Out came a derisive whoop. "Going to the police, were you?"

"Wasn't!" Fred cried. "I was taking it to the sergeant."

"Liar!" Ralph Toggs said as he unfolded the letter and read it hastily.

"Let me have it," Fred cried. "I have to take it to the sergeant!"

"Well then, we'll both take it to him," Toggs returned. "Unless you can get it back from me."

Fred glared at Ralph Toggs with all the hatred he had ever felt for anyone. But there was little choice. "All right," he muttered. "We'll both go."

Chapter 51
Fred and Toggs Have a Race

The streets of Liverpool were already crowded with the morning's latest emigrants. With bundles, bags, and trunks in hand, they were pouring into the city. But neither Fred nor Toggs paid them any mind, so intent were they upon their current purpose. Each was thinking furiously. Fred was wondering if he could outrun Toggs and reach the sergeant first so as to claim the discovery of the boy. For his part, Toggs was puzzling over the Laurence referred to in the letter and why Fred should be so anxious to carry information about him to the sergeant. He was not, however, going to ask.

One hundred yards from the Iron Duke, Fred could not restrain himself. He broke into a run. His advantage lasted barely ten seconds. Toggs's longer legs quickly enabled him to catch up so that he burst through the doors of the Iron Duke five steps ahead of his rival.

The main room was crowded, mostly with dock laborers. A few called familiarly to Toggs. Ignoring them, he pushed toward the rear.

In the back room, sitting in isolated splendor, Sergeant Rumpkin was partaking of his regular breakfast. Beneath his many chins was tucked a grease-spotted napkin. On the table before him were plates of eggs, ham, chicken, beef, and venison pie. There was also a pitcher of ale, a bottle of wine, three loaves of bread, and a great pyramid of yellow cheeses. In the fireplace, a roaring fire gave off such heat that even the food was sweating.

Toggs dashed up to the table, flung down the letter, and cried, "Fred's gone informer!"

"Liar," screamed Fred as he came up fast and attempted to shove Toggs away. The two boys were red faced, panting hard.

The startled sergeant, a half-eaten lamb shank in one hand, a drink in the other, looked from Fred to Ralph Toggs, then down at the letter.

"I caught him going to police headquarters," Toggs exclaimed. "Carrying a message from some clergyman."

"I found that boy," Fred barked. "The one we're looking for."

"Attention!" the sergeant roared. "Attention!"

The two boys stopped their clamoring and stood as stiffly as their excitement allowed.

"Do you think we're in Bedlam?" the sergeant cried with vexation. He flung down his food in disgust, then wiped his hands and chins with the napkin, all the while glaring furiously. "Mixing *your* business with *my* viands is against all regulations," he growled even as he snatched up some ale and swilled it down to make clear that he, at least, intended to follow the proper rules of conduct. "It's not to be condoned! How many times must I tell you boys, I am not to be disturbed during my meals!"

Fred, almost beside himself with rage, blurted, "But I—"

"Mr. Fred!" the sergeant cried, "did I or did I not command you to be still?"

"It's only that Toggs—!"

"Silence!" the sergeant thundered.

Reluctantly, Fred shut his mouth.

"Now then," the sergeant said as he leaned back in his chair, "there seems to be some kind of skirmish here."

Holding them silent with his stern gaze, he plucked up a hard-boiled egg, cracked it with his sharp knuckles, peeled it slowly, then flicked away the shell bits with his narrow thumb like so much confetti. Only when he had stuffed the entire egg into his mouth, crushed it, chewed it, swallowed it, belched, and patted his lips and chins again with his napkin did he pick up the letter.

"Is this the letter you're speaking of, Mr. Toggs?" The sergeant dangled the paper before Toggs like some unclean thing.

"He was running errands for the police," Toggs repeated.

"I was bringing it to you!" Fred shouted.

"One at a time!" the sergeant shouted. "All right, Mr. Toggs, you arrived first. Let's hear your report."

"I was laying low," Toggs began, "in the Duke of York's warehouse on account of some problem I had with the dock police. That's why I couldn't make muster last night. Though I did bring my money." So saying, he took out his earnings from the day before and, with a great rattle, dumped the money before the sergeant who, with a swift swirl of his hand, scooped it up and put it in his pocket.

"Go on," he growled.

"Then here comes this No-name pegging through, letter in hand. I hails him and asks him, perfectly friendly, where's he going. 'None of your business!' says he."

229

"Not true!" Fred cried.

"In turn, Mr. Fred, in turn!" the sergeant roared.

Toggs grinned—further infuriating Fred—and then continued. "Well, I saw right off he was up to no good. So I took that letter from him—he's not much of a fighter—and read the cover and saw it was for the police. 'What're you going to the police for?' I asks. 'None of your business,' says he. 'Don't you think you better go to the sergeant first?' says I. 'Go where I want,' he retorts.

"So I opened the letter, read it, and saw it was all about some boy. Laurence is his name."

"*Laurence?*" the sergeant exclaimed with new interest.

"That clergyman was telling the police all about a Laurence."

"Was he!"

"Read it for yourself," Toggs suggested.

"Is that the end of your report?"

"Except that, since he wouldn't bring it to you, I thought *I* should."

"That's all lies!" Fred cried in exasperation.

"Very well, Mr. Fred," the sergeant said. "What's your account of this fracas?"

Fred was so upset, he could barely talk. "I got up this morning. Early. Wanted to search out that boy we're looking for. The one we talked about at muster last night. Which Toggs didn't come to. When I was passing by the chapel ship *Charity*, the clergyman there hailed me and dragged me to his service. Before he did, he told me to take a letter to the police. Offered me a penny to do it." Fred held out the coin as proof.

The sergeant extended his hand. Fred dropped the coin into it and saw the fingers close.

"I said I would," he continued, "only intending to bring the letter to you. Next thing is, the clergyman brung in that boy, the same as we're looking for. So I took a guess, figuring the letter had something to do with him. I was bringing it to you when Toggs grabbed it."

"He was taking it to the police," Toggs sneered. "You can see for yourself that's what's written."

Sergeant Rumpkin studied the letter's address. Then he unfolded it and read it once, and again. After the second time, he did not put it down. Instead, he held the letter before his eyes, considering which boy to believe.

On the face of things, he was rather more inclined toward Fred. Not only was it like the youngster to be up early to search for the missing boy and earn the reward money, but his anger seemed the more genuine.

As for Ralph Toggs, Sergeant Rumpkin knew him for the bully he was. All the same, if he sided with Fred, there was a danger that Toggs could do something rash, perhaps even absent himself from the association. On the other hand, if he sided with Toggs, though Fred might go on a sulk, there was little else the weasel-faced youngster could do. Besides, now that he had built Fred up, was it not time to cut him down? That was sound strategy. And finally, since Toggs had not been at the meeting the night before, he had no claim to Mr. Clemspool's reward money. As far as Sergeant Rumpkin was concerned, that meant he could pocket it all.

The sergeant lowered the letter. "Mr. Fred," he began, "it is my understanding that you don't know how to read. Is that correct?"

"No, I don't, but I . . ."

"Since you can't read, you couldn't know the contents of this letter, could you? To take it to the police would have been a tactical mistake. An ambush. A defeat. It seems to me, Mr. Fred, you've made a serious breach in our rules of combat."

231

"But I wasn't taking it to the police!" wailed an outraged Fred, his face as bright red as his hair.

"Sure, he was," Toggs said, sensing his victory.

"I wasn't!"

"Gentlemen, gentlemen," Sergeant Rumpkin interrupted. "I choose, in this instance, to believe Mr. Toggs. Mr. Fred, I'm deeply grieved that you would even consider consorting with the police and—"

"It's a lie! An awful lie!" Fred shouted, so livid that tears started in his eyes.

"Look at him!" Toggs mocked. "He's crying like a baby!"

The insult was too much for Fred. Furious, he leaped at his tormentor. But the older boy's weight and strength proved too much for him. Toggs threw Fred off with ease. Fred, sprawling, recovered and crouched low, ready to spring again. Toggs in turn whipped out his knife and held it before him.

The sergeant leaped from his chair. "Cease-fire!" he roared, waving his napkin wildly. "Cease-fire! Truce! No brawling at my breakfast. Instead, we'll all go and fetch this Laurence boy. Though you've made a mistake, Mr. Fred, I'm willing to overlook it this once. But you must promise not to go on any more errands to the police. And no more attacking comrades."

A smirking Toggs held his hand out to Fred. "I'm willing to forgive him, even if he don't have no last name."

His face contorted with rage, Fred cried, "I'll get you back for this, Ralph Toggs. I will!" And he raced from the room.

"Mr. Fred!" the sergeant called after him. "Halt!" It was of no use. Fred had dashed out of the Iron Duke.

Toggs laughed. "Not to worry. He's young. He'll be back."

"Be that as it may," the sergeant rumbled, "I think I had best lay immediate siege to this Laurence. Come along, Mr. Toggs. Step lively. We've a forced march to make to the *Charity!*"

Chapter 52
Mr. Bartholomew Endeavors
To Be Helpful

Y ou will find the society home a great blessing, Mr. Patrick," Mr. Bartholomew said, his hand firmly upon the
boy's shoulder. As they passed through the docks, he was
keeping to a fearful pace.

Patrick barely listened to the minister's words. He was trying
to decide the right moment to break away and run for freedom.

"Father Kiley, the principal, is a generous, bighearted
man," the minister went on. "All the lads are quite devoted
to him. And, Mr. Patrick—no small thing—not once have I
heard any complaints about the food. So you see it will be
a happy time for you, I'm sure."

"Yes, Your Honor," Patrick said.

After passing by the last of the dock police stations, they
paused before crossing the wide congested street known as
the Strand.

Patrick looked about. He was sure he remembered buildings and signs from the time they had followed Ralph Toggs
to the lodging house.

"As to how long you will remain there, that's for Father
Kiley to decide," the minister went on. "Generally, it will
be until he finds you suitable employment. That usually
takes two months or so. But it can be the making of you,
Mr. Patrick. I've seen it happen many times."

"Yes, Your Honor."

"He may even teach you to read."

233

Patrick looked around. "I can read," he said.

"Can you? Well, Mr. Patrick, I'm both surprised and gratified to hear it," Mr. Bartholomew said as he moved them forward, threading their way through the wagons, carts, and carriages that crowded the road.

A hansom cab loomed up before them. The horse came so close, Mr. Bartholomew had to step back. In so doing, his grip on Patrick loosened, just the chance Patrick had been waiting for. Giving a sudden twist to his shoulder, he freed himself. Instantly, he darted forward, cutting in front of a large wagon filled with bales of textiles all labeled "Shagwell Cotton Mill." Clearing the wagon, Patrick skipped across the road. Once on the other side, he plunged into a narrow street and began to race up through the city.

Mr. Bartholomew was taken entirely by surprise. "Mr. Patrick! Stop! Halt!" he cried. "You mustn't go! I'm trying to help you!" He attempted to follow, but the wagon blocked his way. Endeavoring to sidestep it, he was stopped by a man pushing a barrow. By the time he reached the other side of the road, Patrick had vanished.

Winded, frustrated, the minister looked up and down the busy street. He had lost Patrick for sure. The thought made his heart heavy.

Then he reminded himself there was still a chance to do some good. That is, there was Laurence. He hesitated, wondering if he should just go back to the *Charity*. The question was, did that red-headed boy deliver the letter or not?

After looking about to take his bearings, the minister realized he was closer to police headquarters than to the chapel boat. Would the English boy wait as he'd been told to? There was something about the boy—better breeding perhaps—that suggested he would indeed keep his word. It seemed, therefore, most efficient to go to the police. With renewed vigor, the Reverend Mr. Gideon Bartholomew set off uphill.

234

Chapter 53
Laurence Makes a Discovery

On the *Charity*, Laurence remained in his chair for a long time. Periodically he sipped at the remainder of his tepid tea, but the silence that surrounded him contributed to his feeling of being very alone.

Slowly, painfully, he weighed what had just happened: First he had found a solution to his problems—Patrick's ticket to America—only to have it snatched away. Though he knew he should feel upset, he gradually became aware that he did not. He wondered why. Was not the chance to go to America *exactly* what he had desired? Yes, he kept telling himself, *yes*. What then was the matter with him? Why was he feeling . . . relieved not to have it?

Bit by bit, Laurence began to grasp the truth. *Going to America would be a mistake*. He did not want to go. He wanted to be home. He wanted to beg forgiveness of his father. His brother, Albert, might bully him again, but nothing that happened at home could be as bad as what he had experienced since running away. He wanted to be Sir Laurence Kirkle, not Laurence Worthy.

"Sir Laurence Kirkle," he said out loud. It felt good to say it.

Laurence took a deep breath, the freshest he'd drawn since leaving home. He felt taller. Lighter. Happier. If only the minister were not taking so long to return!

Itching with impatience, Laurence made his way out on the deck of the chapel ship. Observing the docks by daylight, he saw for the first time how vast they were, how many ships they could accommodate. And people. . . . Everywhere he looked, there were milling crowds! Their numbers, their beggarly state alarmed him. What a relief it was that he need have nothing to do with any of it. No longer Laurence Worthy, he was Sir Laurence Kirkle, who stood beyond and above it all.

"Sst! Hey, boy!" came a call.

Laurence needed a moment to realize that the call was directed at him and that it came from the quay below. He looked down. There was Fred.

"Were you calling to me, boy?" Laurence demanded in a voice tinged again with a tone of superiority.

"I was," Fred cried, "if your name is Laurence. Is it?"

"It is, yes. And why do you ask?"

"Don't you remember me?" Fred said. "I was in the chapel with you and your friend before. Fred's the name."

"It was impolite of you to run off," Laurence informed him loftily.

"Well, if I were you, I wouldn't stay around either. Not for a minute."

"What are you talking about?" Laurence asked, annoyed at this ginger-haired boy's presumption.

"They're coming after you."

"Coming after me?" Laurence echoed. "What do you mean?"

"Ever hear of the Lime Street Runners Association?"

Laurence shook his head.

"Well, you know about Sergeant Rumpkin, don't you?"

"Is this some kind of jest?" Laurence snapped, and started to turn away dismissively.

"Then how about Ralph Toggs?"

Laurence stopped short. "What—what about him?" he stammered.

"They're all out to catch you, that's what."

"*Catch me?*" Laurence echoed again. "What are you saying?"

"Ever hear of a Mr. Matthew Clemspool?"

Laurence leaped back to the rail. "How do you know of him?"

"He's a London gent, ain't he? And didn't he go to the Lime Street Runners Association—which is Sergeant Rumpkin, Ralph Toggs, and a whole flock of stupid sheep—and say if they got hold of you and handed you over, he'd give a whole two-quid reward?"

Laurence's mouth fell open with shock.

"And Sergeant Rumpkin and Ralph Toggs and all the Lime Street runners said they'd find you for him. Why, I'd bet you ticks to tumblers they're galloping here right now. So if you don't move, and move quick, they'll snatch you certain and hand you over to that Clemspool bloke."

"They're coming *here?*"

"That's what I'm telling you."

"But . . . but how do you know this?" asked Laurence.

"Never mind how," said Fred grimly. "I just do. And what I'm saying is you better move unless you want to be catched."

"But where can I go?"

"Don't you have any friend to hide you?" Fred asked.

"That other boy who was here," cried an increasingly panicked Laurence, "the Irish one. Patrick. He said he had a ticket for me so I could go to America. But now he's gone."

"Where?"

"Some . . . society. A society for Irish boys."

"Did he have the ticket with him?"

"He said his sister had it."

"Where's this sister at?"

"At a . . . a Mrs. Sonderbye's."

237

"Mrs. Sonderbye's! Nothing to it. I can take you there easy. Come on!"

Laurence, not sure what to do, felt unable to move.

Fred charged halfway up the gangway. "Can't you hear me!" he shouted. "I'm telling you they're coming!"

Laurence looked back toward the chapel. Should he not wait for Mr. Bartholomew? Surely the minister would protect him. But what if those others arrived first?

"I'll not answer for it if you don't move fast," Fred pressed.

"But the minister . . ."

"Fiddle the minister! He's no better than the others."

"Why, what do you mean?"

"He was informing the police on you."

"Mr. Bartholomew . . . informing the police?" Laurence gasped, hardly able to breathe much less speak. "On me?"

"Didn't he give me a letter for them that was all about you?"

Laurence was flabbergasted. "But—but," he stammered, "why?"

"That Clemspool fellow said you were connected to money."

"But—"

"Well, any boy I ever knew who had money stole it," Fred said. "Isn't that what you did? Steal money?"

Fred's words struck like a sledgehammer on Laurence's heart. He turned deathly pale. His legs all but buckled.

Fred went up to the deck and plucked at Laurence's sleeve. "All I'm saying is you better get that ticket from your friend and sail off. It's your only hope. They're coming for you, all of 'em! Right now!"

Chapter 54

Sergeant Rumpkin Leads
Toggs to a Siege

D o you think Fred went to warn that Laurence off?" an impatient Toggs asked when the sergeant, wheezing and red faced, bade him stop yet again for a rest. They still had a distance to go before reaching the docks.

"Not a chance," the sergeant replied as he mopped his sweating brow with his handkerchief. "He may be angry, but he's loyal."

"Maybe I should go ahead and check," Toggs suggested. All he could think of was taunting his rival again.

"You're not to do it," the sergeant ordered. "I need to be there myself." *He* had fixed his mind on the reward money and wanted to make sure the boys' feud would not interfere.

"What's so special about this Laurence anyway?" Toggs wanted to know.

"A good soldier doesn't ask," the sergeant replied. In fact, he had wondered as much himself, but he was not about to share that with his underling. "All you need to know, Mr. Toggs, is we have to get him."

"You might tell me what he looks like."

Sergeant Rumpkin mulled over the suggestion while purchasing a paper twist of nuts from a vendor. "Eleven years of age," he said, cracking a walnut in his hands and prying out the meats with his slender fingers. "In fancy clothes but ragged. With a long welt on his face, here."

"Welt!" cried Toggs. "Crikey! I had that boy last night."

Sergeant Rumpkin, momentarily neglecting the nuts, looked up. "Mr. Toggs, be so good as to make a report."

"Remember I told you how I was hiding from the dock police last night? Well, it was because of that boy."

"More, Mr. Toggs, more!"

Toggs told his story, but as he related it, the theft from the boat was all Laurence's idea. As for the police coming and giving chase, that too was Laurence's fault, though how it happened Toggs hardly made clear.

Having listened to the tale, Sergeant Rumpkin shook his head and mopped his chins. "Look here, Mr. Toggs, I don't like that sort of thing. The running profession is fine enough. No one interferes. We don't need the trouble common looting brings. Discipline in the ranks, Mr. Toggs. It's what worked at Waterloo. . . . It will serve us well in Liverpool," he concluded as he finished off the nuts and scattered the shell bits to the wind.

"It was only a lark," Toggs replied. "Besides, it wasn't me on that boat. Didn't even touch the cash box. That boy done it."

"Did he get the money?"

"Must have."

"Well then," Sergeant Rumpkin said thoughtfully, "no wonder that minister was informing the police. He probably caught the boy out. Go on now, I'm ready."

As they continued on, Toggs asked, "What if that minister is holding the boy?"

"Leave that to me."

After some minutes of hard walking and more and more frequent stopping, the two came upon the chapel ship. "There she is," Toggs said.

Sergeant Rumpkin held up his hand. "Halt and reconnoiter," he commanded.

They paused to study the boat. "Ever been on her?" the sergeant asked in a low voice.

"Never!" Toggs replied as if the question were a serious insult.

"Now mind, Mr. Toggs, no advances on your own. Strictly under orders. Do you understand me? The boy might be desperate."

"Don't worry about me," Toggs said. "I can handle any boy."

"All right then, let us lay siege."

With Sergeant Rumpkin in the lead, they crept up the gangway and onto the *Charity*. Once on deck, however, they stopped. There was no one to be seen.

"He must be below," Toggs whispered.

The sergeant nodded and moved forward, treading softly.

Toggs eyed each and every place big enough to hold a boy but saw no sign of Laurence.

Sergeant Rumpkin rapped on the chapel door. "Anyone here?" He edged the door open and stuck his head inside. The chapel was deserted.

They entered cautiously. When the hall proved empty, they proceeded into the adjacent rooms.

"Think he could be hiding in the hold?" Toggs asked.

"You can look if you care to, Mr. Toggs," the sergeant answered, "but I should doubt it. I think the minister took him prisoner and hauled him to the police on his own."

"Or maybe Fred took him," Toggs suggested.

Frowning, the sergeant considered the idea. "Wouldn't dare," he decided.

Toggs hastened away to the hold but soon returned.

"Report!" ordered the sergeant.

"Just this," Toggs said. In his hands was Laurence's torn clothing. "I think it's what he was wearing when I saw him."

The sergeant swore under his breath and returned to the deck to stare out over the busy docks.

Toggs, following, said, "I'll bet you anything Fred went to the police just to spite you." He dumped Laurence's clothing on the deck.

"The police!" the sergeant growled. "If he's done so, it's grounds for a court-martial."

"You saw how hot he was when he ran off," Toggs reminded him. "Keen to do something."

Sergeant Rumpkin, his sense of indignation growing, puffed himself up. "Mr. Toggs," he pronounced, "if that Fred has committed such a vicious act of treason, he will be punished for it or I'll take my pension and retire!

"Here are my orders. I shall return to the Iron Duke. Once there, I'll call in the troops and make sure they don't interrupt me at breakfast again. Then they can redouble their search for this Laurence. And for that rapscallion Fred too.

"As for you, Mr. Toggs, you are to go to police headquarters, where that minister was sending his letter. Maybe you're right and Fred went there. Reconnoiter. Determine the lay of the land. Then come back to me."

Toggs saluted and started down the gangway.

"Mr. Toggs!" Sergeant Rumpkin called.

Toggs looked back over his shoulder.

"If you see Fred, you're to capture him and march him to me. No more! No less! Discipline! That's an order."

"Yes, sir," Toggs agreed with a grin, and hurried off at double time.

Chapter 55
A Meeting on the Streets

*M*aura was doubting she'd ever get back to Mrs. Sonderbye's when she caught sight of Patrick running up the street.

"Patrick!" she shouted.

Patrick stopped, turned, and saw his sister. With a whoop of joy he raced back and embraced her.

"Oh, Patrick, I thought I'd lost you for sure."

"I was only at the docks, Maura."

She took hold of her brother by his shoulders and gave him a shake. "Patrick O'Connell," she said, "you had me near bled of life last night when I couldn't find you. Where and why, in the name of glory, did you go?"

"I thought you were in danger," Patrick explained. "It's you I was thinking of."

"What danger?"

"Wasn't that runner, that Ralph Toggs, asking after you at the lodging house."

Maura was taken aback. "*For me?*" she cried.

"It was right after you left with Mr. Drabble. Who should come along but that Ralph Toggs, the one that brought us to Mrs. Sonderbye's. And he was asking about you, Maura."

"Me?"

"Faith, he was. And when he learned you'd gone, he said he'd find you. So off he went. I was that fearful I ran after him."

"Patrick O'Connell, promise me we'll never leave each other's side again. Not for an instant!"

"But I need to tell you all of what I was doing," Patrick said, and told Maura not just about Toggs but about the English boy, the attempted theft from the ship, how he himself summoned the dock police, how he and the boy fled until they came upon the *Charity*, where Mr. Bartholomew took them in. "So you see, Maura, I was perfectly safe all the time."

"And with a Protestant clergyman."

"But didn't I get away from him?"

"Jesus, Mary, and Joseph," his sister said sternly, "why would you be doing all that for an English boy? Have you forgotten so quickly? What have we to do for the English when they lord it over us?"

"Ah, Maura, you can hardly believe how bad off he is. Worse than us. Not a penny in his pocket. And hasn't he run off from home. Wanting to go to America. That's why I offered him the ticket."

"What ticket?"

"The one Mother won't be using."

"Patrick," Maura replied, "there's no ticket to give."

"Where's it gone to then?" he asked.

"I've given it to Mr. Drabble. Sure, I could do no less. Last night he helped me look for you. In fact, we should be getting back. He'll be wondering if I'm lost too."

Patrick was beginning not to like Mr. Drabble. "Isn't Mr. Drabble English?" he asked.

Maura drew herself up with indignation. "It's not the same at all," she said.

"Why?"

"Because he's been kind to me. Now come along," she said, and set a fast pace.

Patrick, hurrying after, was now sure he didn't like the actor.

Suddenly, Maura stopped. "This English boy, might his

244

name be Laurence, and him dressed in rags and with a welt on his cheek?"

"Why, that is him. How did you know?"

"Patrick," his sister said, "it's the police themselves who are looking for him."

"The police!"

"It's true. When I was searching for you early on, I met some of them. Didn't they give me his name. 'Laurence,' they said, reading his name from a paper. They're searching everywhere for him. The Lord knows what that means. By the Holy Mother, Patrick, have you thought that that boy might not be so innocent as you'd believe?"

"Maura, I don't know why they're after him, but you've only to see him to know he's done nothing wrong."

"Well, it no longer matters," his sister said as they set off again to the lodging house. "You'll not be seeing him again."

Chapter 56

Other Meetings at the Liverpool Police Office

*T*oggs needed little time to reach City Hall and the police headquarters. After loitering a bit outside while deciding what he might say if questions were asked, he started down the circular staircase. Trying to look as nonchalant as possible, he strolled into the office, hat set rakishly, hands in pockets.

The room was busy. Inspector Knox was at his place behind the high desk, leafing through papers. A number of blue-coated constables were seated on the bench engaged in earnest conversation with a man in a bowler hat. A poorly dressed fellow lay sprawled upon the floor of the prisoner's holding dock, fast asleep. As for Fred, Toggs saw no sign of him. Whether his rival had come and gone was another matter. He approached Inspector Knox.

At first the inspector ignored him. Toggs was patient. Finally Mr. Knox looked up. "Yes, lad, what is it?" he asked curtly.

Toggs snatched off his hat. "Begging your pardon, sir," he said, "but I'm looking for a friend."

Mr. Knox was stern. "Someone taken in?"

"Not that I know, sir," Toggs said. "He left in a rush, if you know my meaning."

"That him?" Mr. Knox asked, pointing to the man in the holding cage.

Toggs considered the sleeping man as if the possibility were real. "No, sir, it's not."

"What's your fellow's name? He might have been charged."

"Fred, sir, Fred. Nothing but a chit of a boy. Doesn't even have a last name. Weasel faced and nasty, to tell the truth. Ginger hair."

"Not here," Mr. Knox said, and continued sorting through his papers.

Toggs put on his hat and turned to leave just as Mr. Bartholomew entered the room and approached the desk.

Mr. Knox looked up. "Here, young man," he barked at Toggs, "stand aside and let the gentleman approach."

Toggs did so.

"Good morning, Mr. Bartholomew," the inspector said, reaching over his desk and shaking the minister's hand.

"A good morning to you, Mr. Knox."

"Is the *Charity* still afloat then?" Mr. Knox asked.

At the word *Charity*, Toggs, who was halfway to the door, stopped and looked around with interest.

"Sitting pretty, sir," the minister replied.

"And what brings you to us this morning, sir?" Mr. Knox inquired.

"I'm sorry to trouble you, Inspector, but I need to determine if you received my message. I sent it with a boy earlier this morning."

Toggs edged closer.

"You might have sent it," Mr. Knox said, "but it never reached this desk. Gentlemen!" he called out to the constables. "Any of you take in a message from Mr. Bartholomew this morning?"

There was a general shaking of heads. "Not me, sir."

"I'm afraid not, Mr. Bartholomew," said Mr. Knox.

"Disappointing," said the minister with a sad shake of his head. "One wants to trust these lads, but . . . most unfortunate."

"What was it about then?" Mr. Knox asked.

"Last night, quite late," Mr. Bartholomew said, "two boys boarded the *Charity*. One was Irish, the other English. Both adrift."

"Indeed, sir."

"Naturally, I took them in. I tried to get the Irish boy to the Catholic Society for the Protection of Abandoned Irish Boys, but he would have none of it. The other lad, however, the English one, is a different problem. His accent, his manner, suggest someone of better class. He did admit to having run away from home. And the bad welt upon his cheek seemed to indicate why."

Mr. Knox leaned forward. "Excuse me, sir. Did you say this boy had a welt on his cheek? His right cheek?"

"I did. Very pronounced it was too."

"Was his name, by any chance, *Laurence*, sir?"

"Why, yes, how did you know?"

Inspector Knox swiveled about in his chair. "Mr. Pickler, sir!" he cried.

Toggs, who had been listening with great attention, now looked across the room and saw the man in the bowler glance up from his conversation.

"Mr. Pickler," cried Mr. Knox. "Be so kind as to step over here, will you?"

Mr. Pickler immediately broke away from his group and approached the desk.

"London luck, Mr. Pickler, sir," said Mr. Knox sarcastically. "Here's Reverend Bartholomew, coming to answer your prayers. Claims he's seen your boy. Mr. Bartholomew, you can have it on my authority that this Mr. Pickler is actually an honest man, and does us the singular honor of being here on behalf of a most illustrious family."

Mr. Pickler and Mr. Bartholomew shook hands. "I'm gratified to meet you, sir," the investigator said. "If you have news of Laurence, I should be most pleased to hear it." He offered up the daguerreotype. "Here's a picture of him."

Mr. Bartholomew studied the image intently. "Well, yes," he said, "that's him, more or less."

"And you say you know where he is?"

"Even as we speak he's waiting for me on my chapel ship."

Mr. Pickler felt a surge of well-being. "His family will be very appreciative for his return, sir."

"Well, now," Mr. Bartholomew said, "this is good news indeed. Most fortuitous, sir."

"And is the boy safe?" Mr. Pickler inquired.

"A bit worn, but, yes, safe. I shall be delighted to pilot you to him."

Mr. Pickler made a little bow. "At once, sir, if that's not too much of an inconvenience."

Mr. Bartholomew, after thanking Mr. Knox for his help, gestured toward the door. Mr. Pickler moved to it, and the two men left the police office.

"Mr. Broderick!" Inspector Knox called as soon as the two men had gone. One of the constables hurried forward.

"Yes, sir?"

"This morning I sent a directive to the force, concerning a boy named Laurence," Mr. Knox explained. "Please be so good as to send out a second notice. No further searching is required. We've had a little miracle. That London boy has been found." With a shrug of his shoulders, the inspector went back to his papers.

As for Toggs, he had followed Mr. Pickler and Mr. Bartholomew out of the building.

Chapter 57
What Mr. Pickler Learns

*H*ow much, sir," Mr. Pickler asked the minister as they strode along toward the *Charity*, "did Laurence inform you about the circumstances that brought him to Liverpool?" Behind them, Ralph Toggs kept a careful distance.

"I was only able," Mr. Bartholomew replied, "to gather that he had run away from home."

Mr. Pickler stopped. "Did he say that?"

"Not in so many words. But understand, Mr. Pickler, I have had considerable experience with runaways. One comes to see common elements."

"He did not say he was abducted?"

"Not a hint."

"No mention of a Mr. Clemspool?"

"Never heard the name."

"What did he speak of then?"

249

"When I asked the boy to explain the nasty welt upon his face—"

"Ah, yes, the welt."

"He colored up, became very agitated, and would say no more."

"What did you make of that, sir?"

"I assumed the welt and his departure from home were connected."

Mr. Pickler halted again. "Sir, what are you suggesting?"

"While it pains me to say so, Mr. Pickler, all my experience in these matters leads me to believe that boy was thrashed with excessive violence at home. His clothing was of a superior quality but quite cut up. One might almost say *sliced*. I've seen it any number of times. If one is thrashed with a cane, that's the result. I shall show it to you."

Mr. Pickler was beginning to feel ill.

"I can't imagine," Mr. Bartholomew went on, "what the boy might have done to provoke such a beating."

"Tell me," Mr. Pickler said at last, his pace slowing, "about the boy he was with. I believe I overheard you say—"

"A poor Irish lad."

"An unlikely companion."

"Perhaps. But I suspect they had one thing in common."

"And what was that?"

"They seemed desperate enough to become thieves."

Yet again the investigator halted. "Explain yourself, sir."

"It's part of the runaway saga, I fear. Full of bravado when they leave home—whatever home it might be, Irish or English—these boys become isolated, frightened, desperate by turns, and all too easily turn to acts of a criminal nature. To survive, sir. Or they take their own lives. I'm afraid I see it every day. My ministry is designed to offer other choices."

The investigator remained silent for a while. Finally he

said, "Mr. Bartholomew, you cannot truly think that the boy ran away from his home of his own free will."

"But I do."

It was too much for Mr. Pickler. "Sir, the boy's father is Lord Kirkle!" he cried.

A shocked Mr. Bartholomew stopped and stared at the investigator. "I am truly sorry to hear it," he said softly. "But, sir, life has taught me that people do not run away from happiness."

For the rest of the way to the docks, Mr. Pickler, caught up in distressed speculation, remained silent. But upon reaching the chapel ship he said, "Mr. Bartholomew, I may well have underestimated the boy's desire to run away. I now fear there might be some resistance to being returned to his father's home." He looked about. Some forty feet away, Toggs lurked, watching the two men.

He had been enjoying himself immensely. He could not help but think he would enjoy telling that Irish girl of his adventures.

"That young sailor over there," Mr. Pickler said, "perhaps I should ask him to guard the gangway. Just in case. I don't want Laurence to escape."

"If you wish," Mr. Bartholomew agreed. "Here, young man! You there!" he shouted.

"You calling me, mate?" Toggs replied.

"I am, my good fellow. Would you be good enough to come closer?"

Toggs, swaggering slightly, sauntered over.

"Look here, young sir," Mr. Bartholomew said to Toggs, "we're in need of some assistance. My friend here"—he indicated Mr. Pickler—"is about to go aboard to secure a runaway boy. Would you be kind enough to stand guard at the gangway and catch the boy if he eludes us?"

Toggs grinned. "Happy to give a hand, mate."

251

"Excellent," Mr. Bartholomew said. "We shall be most grateful. All right then, Mr. Pickler, shall we go on board?"

Mr. Pickler allowed himself to be led up the gangway. When he reached the deck, he called down to Toggs. "At the foot of the gangway, if you please. The boy might try to jump off the ship." He was thinking of Laurence's departure from the hotel.

"I can handle a skiff, mate, but I don't swim," Toggs admitted.

"I don't think it's likely he'll go into the water," Mr. Pickler replied. "But he might try to leap to the dock."

"Don't you worry none," Toggs said, giving a salute. "If he blows, I'll nab him."

"Well, sir, this is curious," Mr. Bartholomew declared.

Mr. Pickler turned. In his hands the minister was holding Laurence's torn clothing. "This is what the boy had been wearing," he said. "I can't imagine why it's here on deck. I did give him some better clothes. But do look at the rips, sir. Perhaps you'll agree with me as to their cause."

Mr. Pickler examined the clothing. In dismay, he shook his head. "May I keep these?"

"Of course. Now just follow me, please," Mr. Bartholomew called to Mr. Pickler. "The boy should be along here." The minister led the way to the room where he had left Laurence. It was empty. "Perhaps he's gone to the chapel," the minister said, inwardly pleased by the thought. But Laurence was not there either.

"If you will return to the deck," an increasingly upset Mr. Bartholomew said, "I shall look into my own rooms." He hurried off.

Already certain that Laurence would not be found on the *Charity*, Mr. Pickler went to the deck even as he plunged into a whirl of self-recrimination. Could it be that this boy—from one of the grandest homes in the nation—truly wished to run away?

252

Mr. Bartholomew returned to the deck. "Unless the boy has gone off for a stroll, I am afraid he's bolted. I'm deeply embarrassed."

"Nothing to suggest where or why?"

The minister shook his head. "What can I say?" he said woefully. "He promised to remain."

"You mustn't blame yourself," Mr. Pickler assured him, though he was in truth seething with frustration. "You had no idea who he was. And if he gave you his word . . . He appears to be a most determined lad."

Mr. Pickler gazed across the docks and beyond, up at the city. To have been so close to success so many times only to have the boy slip past him yet again . . .

"Mr. Pickler," Mr. Bartholomew said, "I do have one small idea."

"I should be grateful for anything."

"The other fellow, that Irish lad, claimed that he and his sister were staying at a lodging house in the city. A Mrs. Sonderbye's. Patrick wanted to take Laurence there. Claimed he would give him a ticket to America."

"Did he!" Mr. Pickler cried.

"I chose not to believe any of it, of course. For this impoverished Irish lad to give away a ticket to America, why, it was absurd. Typical Irish blarney."

"Did he mention the name of the ship?"

"I fear not. But now that I reconsider all this . . . You see, I was taking the Irish boy to a charity home when he ran off. Perhaps he did have a sister and she was staying at Mrs. Sonderbye's lodging house. True or not, perhaps your Laurence believed that ticket was possible. If so, he might have gone to that lodging house. I should be happy to take you there."

Mr. Pickler considered the offer. What Mr. Bartholomew had told him made him very uncomfortable. The truth was he wanted to get away from the minister. He leaned over the bulwark. "You there, young fellow!"

"Still here, mate," Ralph Toggs returned.

"Do you know of a lodging place in the city run by a Mrs. Sonderbye?"

Toggs grinned again. "Know it like the palm of my hand, mate."

"We think the boy we are looking for might have gone there. If you could show me the way, I'd be willing to pay you well. Could you?"

"Nothing to it!"

"I'll be happy to pilot you there myself," the minister offered again.

"I appreciate that, sir," Mr. Pickler replied. "But I suppose there's a chance the boy will meander back. If so, please take him to the police office. No, this young man will guide me to that lodging. Quite sufficient." He held out his hand. "You have been very helpful, sir."

Mr. Bartholomew shook it warmly. "I do wish I could have provided more success."

Eager to move on, Mr. Pickler, with Laurence's torn clothes bundled up in his hands, hurried down the gangway. Toggs was waiting for him.

"Mrs. Sonderbye's, you say, mate?"

"Is it very far?"

"All you have to do is follow me," Toggs assured him. And off they went.

As Ralph Toggs led the investigator away from the docks and up through the city toward Mrs. Sonderbye's lodging house, he was thinking about Maura. How nice it would be if she saw him with this gentleman. He might even offer her protection. Get some decent food for her. But only for her, not her brother. She'd have to drop him. He had no use for tykes.

254

For his part, Mr. Pickler kept thinking over what the minister had told him regarding Laurence. The thought that his lordship had lied to him proved very upsetting.

But then the city, with its squalid, filthy streets and jostling crowds, depressed him. To think that Sir Laurence Kirkle should be part of this!

"Do you mind my asking," said Toggs as they turned a corner, "who's this bloke we're looking for? He got a name?"

"His name is Laurence," replied Mr. Pickler stiffly, not feeling particularly inclined to chat.

"What's so special about him?" Toggs pressed.

Mr. Pickler considered his companion. The young man— cocky, swaggering—was not the kind of person with whom he liked to associate. With a stab of bitterness, Mr. Pickler wished once more that he had never taken on the case. But then, there was his own family to consider.

"Just take me to the lodging house," he said.

Toggs touched his hat and started off. "In case you were wondering, my name is Ralph Toggs. You the boy's father?"

"Oh, no!" Mr. Pickler replied indignantly. "I am simply trying to find him."

Toggs said no more.

Chapter 58
Maura, Patrick, and Mr. Drabble
at Breakfast

Along with the other occupants in Mrs. Sonderbye's basement, Maura, Patrick, and Mr. Drabble sat on the floor and ate the breakfast the landlady had provided: a cup of tea and one piece of stale bread each.

"As soon as we're finished," Mr. Drabble explained, his voice low so as to keep their affairs private, "we must proceed to the medical exam."

"What is it?" asked Patrick, who had never dealt with any medical man.

"It's nothing to worry about," the actor assured him. "Merely tedious. The lines are long for those who go steerage like us."

"What's steerage?"

"The very lowest class of ticket, Mr. Patrick," Mr. Drabble said. "The way we mortals are obliged to go. In any case, once the doctor stamps our tickets, we must secure provisions for the voyage, take ourselves to the dock, board the ship, and bid farewell to fair England!"

"How long will the voyage take?" Patrick asked next.

"From one to two months—"

"Two months!" the boy cried.

"Shhh. . . . It all depends on the ship, the tides, the winds."

"They say many perish going over," Maura said.

"But, Miss O'Connell," the actor said, "didn't your father get across?"

"By all that's holy, it's true," Maura said, ashamed at her worry. "And I for one shall be glad to leave this terrible lodging house. It's more cemetery here than a place fit for life."

"My dear," Mr. Drabble said, "I can assure you, America will be like paradise. And when we—"

"Is there a girl who has a brother named Patrick down there?" a voice called from the top of the basement steps.

Patrick, taken by surprise, looked around.

"Anyone know about a Patrick below?" the voice demanded again.

Mr. Drabble unfolded himself and went to the foot of the stairs. "And who, my good man, desires to know?" he asked.

"There are two boys in the street, wanting to see the sister of a boy named Patrick, and they won't go till they do. They insist she's here."

Maura looked at her brother. "Patrick, do you know what this is about?"

"It must be that Laurence," Patrick answered. "The English boy. He'll be asking about the ticket I promised. He didn't know I'd be here."

Feeling suddenly threatened, Maura said, "You need not see him."

"But shouldn't I at least be telling him that I'm safe and the ticket is not to be his?" Patrick asked.

"I suppose you should if you truly did promise," Maura allowed. "But I'll go along to make certain you say what needs to be said. Tell them we're coming," she informed Mr. Drabble.

The actor relayed the message.

Fearful about what the English boy might do, Maura said, "Mr. Drabble, would you be kind enough to come with us? You just might be needed. . . ."

"Of course, my dear, of course."

It was Patrick who led the way up the old steps. The three picked their way through the crowded hallway and stepped onto the porch.

Laurence and Fred were waiting on the street. Fred was all energy, looking this way and that as if danger might appear from any direction. Laurence, completely disheveled, bore a face showing nothing but fear.

"You're here!" Laurence cried with relief when he saw Patrick.

Patrick grinned sheepishly. "I got away."

Maura gazed at Laurence with surprise. He was merely a

wretched, frightened boy, not at all what she expected. She found herself moved to pity.

"This your friend?" Fred asked. "The one you told me about?"

Laurence nodded.

"Look here," Fred called up to Patrick on the porch, "this here boy, Laurence, says you've got a ticket for America to give him. That the truth?"

"I'm afraid it's gone," Patrick said, pained to say it.

Laurence gasped. "Gone?" he said. "But you gave your word!"

Patrick came down a step. "You must forgive me, Laurence," he said. "I shouldn't have offered. Remember, I was telling you I couldn't be certain. The ticket was already bespoken. My sister gave it away." He darted an angry look at Mr. Drabble.

Fred shook his head. "This boy here needs to get out of Liverpool."

Maura descended the steps. "Mr. Laurence," she said, "it was Patrick who told me your name. . . . It's not for me to be your judge. But did you know the police are searching everywhere for you?"

Laurence recoiled. "The *police?*" he cried.

"It's true," Maura said. "They read your name from a paper to me."

"It's all Ralph Toggs's doing," Fred cried.

"Why, what about Mr. Toggs?" Maura demanded.

"He's the one causing all this trouble."

"But how?" she asked.

"Because he's a thief and a swindler," Fred exclaimed. "And if you know what's good for you, you'll clear yourselves out of this place. That Toggs will track you down and do you harm like he's done me and this boy here."

"But . . . what am I going to do?" Laurence said, wholly consumed with his own plight. "I have to get away!"

"Don't you worry none," Fred said. "I'll keep you from Toggs."

"See here, my good fellow," Mr. Drabble joined in, "what is this all about?"

"This boy needs to get on an emigrant ship, fast," said Fred. "Before they grab him."

"*Who* will grab him?" Mr. Drabble asked.

Fred ticked them off on his fingers: "There's Sergeant Rumpkin, there's Toggs, there's that Mr. Clemspool, there's the minister, and, like this lady says, there's all the police in Liverpool."

Mr. Drabble looked at Laurence with astonishment. "But, good heavens, my boy," he exclaimed, "what ghastly things have you done?"

Laurence, too stunned, could not reply.

"Sure, he's done nothing," Patrick insisted. "It's what this boy says. It's all that Toggs's doing."

"Isn't that the runner who led you here?" Mr. Drabble asked of Maura.

Deeply upset by Laurence's anguish, she could only nod. The fact that he too was a victim of Toggs only intensified her sympathy.

"This boy may be right, my dear," Mr. Drabble said with some agitation. "These runners can be quite ruthless. It might be wise to heed his warning."

"Ruthless ain't half of it!" Fred agreed. "When it comes to Toggs, I'll not answer for it if he gets his hands on anyone here."

Patrick turned to his sister. "Maura, we have to help him."

"Patrick," she reminded him, "we're leaving tomorrow."

"What ship are you going on?" Fred asked.

"The *Robert Peel*," Maura said without thinking of the consequences.

259

"All right then, I'll get this boy aboard her," Fred announced. "You can take care of him once he's there."

"What are you talking about?" Mr. Drabble demanded. "You heard the boy say there is no ticket."

"He don't need a ticket," Fred said. "I'll get him on as a stowaway."

"But that's against the law!" Mr. Drabble cried.

Laurence's heart tumbled.

"Don't you worry yourselves about it," Fred insisted. "It's been done before. It'll be done again. Nothing to it."

"And I for one will help you," Patrick said to Laurence.

"Bully for you," said Fred. "Stowaways can't work proper unless they've got a friend on board."

"I'll do it," Patrick vowed to Laurence. "I give you my word I will."

"Good enough," Fred said. "I'll make arrangements."

Once again Mr. Drabble tried to intervene. "But, see here, boy, we can't take responsibility—"

"Maybe you can't, but we can," Fred insisted. He turned to Laurence. "Come on. We won't lay about here."

"We're going to the medical exam," Patrick said.

"That will be Ransom Street," Fred called as he began to drag Laurence away. "I'll find you there!"

"You must keep your promise this time!" Laurence shouted over his shoulder to Patrick. "You must!"

"I will!" Patrick returned. He stood watching the two until they turned a corner.

No sooner had they gone than Maura approached her brother and laid a hand on his shoulder. "Patrick," she said softly, "why are the police looking for that poor boy? What's he done?"

"I don't know," Patrick said. "And I don't care. Wasn't that Mr. Morgan looking for me when I did no wrong? He's depending on me, Maura. I won't be failing him again."

"But, Jesus, Mary, and Joseph," Maura pleaded, "we mustn't have trouble with the police here too. The boy is unfortunate. I could see it with my own eyes. But don't we need to be taking care of ourselves first? I shouldn't have told him the name of the ship. Promise me you'll do no more for him."

Before Patrick could respond, Mr. Drabble interceded. "Now, now, my dears," he said, "what I'm concerned about is your Mr. Toggs. We don't want any of his mischief to stand between us and our departure, do we?"

"It's true what that other boy said about Ralph Toggs," Patrick insisted. "He is a villain."

Mr. Drabble turned to Maura. "Have you the tickets with you?"

Maura put a hand to where her packet was pinned. "I do."

"May I suggest we go immediately to the medical examiners? There's no saying how long the lines will be."

"Will it be the Ransom Street place?" asked Patrick.

"There is no choice," Mr. Drabble informed him.

The three set off at once.

Chapter 59

Toggs Brings Mr. Pickler
to Mrs. Sonderbye's

Here it is," Ralph Toggs announced. "Mrs. Sonderbye's." Mr. Pickler gazed with dismay at the wretched building. "And you say people live here?" he asked, finding it difficult to believe that anyone should desire to stay in such dismal conditions.

"One of the best," Toggs assured him. He stood before the porch steps. "Mrs. Sonderbye!" he called. "Are you about?"

The red-faced landlady emerged, blinking at the daylight. "Who you got this time?" she demanded.

"Not that at all," Toggs said quickly. "This here gentleman is looking for someone." He gestured toward Mr. Pickler who, reluctant to draw closer, had remained standing on the street below.

Mrs. Sonderbye considered the investigator suspiciously. "What do you want?" she asked.

"The name is Phineas Pickler, madam. I am from London but working closely with the Liverpool police."

Mrs. Sonderbye's face turned dark. "This is a respectable house," she cried. "Nothing illegal here."

"I'm not suggesting anything of the kind, madam. I am merely looking for a boy by the name of Laurence."

Mrs. Sonderbye turned to Toggs. "That someone you brought?" she asked.

"Not me," the young man replied.

"I don't have anyone by that name," the woman declared to Mr. Pickler. "But you can search for yourself. I've nothing to hide."

Though loath to enter the building, Mr. Pickler, with Laurence's clothing still in hand, forced himself up to the porch. Toggs—in hopes of finding Maura—started to follow. Mrs. Sonderbye blocked his way with an arm. "Where are you going?" she demanded.

"I'm his assistant."

"Is he?" the woman demanded.

The investigator had been staring down the hallway with deep disgust. The chaos, the smell, and the filth assaulted him.

"Would you tell her I'm your assistant, Mr. Pickler!" Toggs called.

The man swallowed his revulsion. "Yes, I suppose you are," he murmured.

Mrs. Sonderbye let Toggs pass.

A half hour's grim search yielded no Laurence for Mr. Pickler, no Maura for Toggs.

Once outside again the investigator felt obliged to use his handkerchief to wipe off his hands and face. He felt as if his very soul had been dirtied.

"Where are we going to look now?" Toggs asked him.

"Somewhere else in Liverpool," the man confessed gloomily.

Toggs touched his hat with a finger. "Happy to be of help, mate," he said.

The two set off. A deeply despondent Mr. Pickler—having no idea what to do next—could barely hold his head up.

"What you need, mate," said Toggs, "is lots of eyes."

"The police, you mean. Yes, I suppose I should return there." Mr. Pickler recalled the list of ships that Inspector Knox had offered the day before. Though it would be uncomfortable to ask for it, he knew now he had need of it.

"No, sir, I was thinking something better. Know anything about runners?"

"I'm afraid not."

"You see," Toggs explained, "lots of emigrants come off the ships here in Liverpool. Mostly Irish—and an ignorant, filthy lot they are. Can't speak the language proper and don't know where to stop before they board the packet ships. We runners find them lodgings."

Mr. Pickler, suppressing the urge to inform Toggs that his own mother was Irish, only said, "Do these people pay for this service?"

"Not a farthing, mate. It's all Christian kindness on our

part. It's the lodge keeper who pays the fees. All up and up, and perfectly legal."

"And Mrs. Sonderbye's is just such a lodging place?"

"It is, sir, but it's a scurvy one. There's lots better to be had. That's the whole point. We runners guide the folks to decent places. Not that the Irish care."

Mr. Pickler wished he could walk away. But he could not. "What exactly do you have in mind, Mr. Toggs?"

"There are a troop of us runners—the Lime Street Runners Association—who know the city like the inside of our boots. Led by Sergeant Rumpkin, who fought at Waterloo next to the Iron Duke himself. You could hire us out to help find your boy. We'd find him, sure as daylight."

Mr. Pickler, kneading Laurence's old clothing in frustration, felt himself on the verge of tears. There was Inspector Knox. . . . But he had been so sarcastic, so unhelpful. The investigator looked resignedly at Toggs. That he must turn for help from such . . . And yet . . . "Perhaps you are right, Mr. Toggs. If you could take me to this Sergeant Rumpkin of yours, I would appreciate it."

Chapter 60
In Search of a Hiding Place

W here are we going?" Laurence asked. Fred had rushed Laurence through one twisted, crowded, and muddy street after another. Now they stood in a dank narrow alley, surrounded by buildings on the verge of collapse but nonetheless reaching high enough above them to blot out the winter sun. Laurence felt he was in a long narrow room. But they were hardly alone. Vendors were hawking rags, rotten vegetables, and stale bread from pushcarts everywhere. And to Laurence's astonishment, people were buying.

"We need to find a place where you can hide while I work out the rest," Fred said.

"What's the rest?" Laurence asked.

"You're getting on a boat for America, aren't you?" an exasperated Fred returned. "Isn't that what we're about?"

Laurence leaned against a wall, uttering a small moan.

"It's either that or you'll be caught up by all them people looking for you," Fred reminded him.

"But *why* are they all trying to catch me?" Laurence wondered tearfully. "What do they *want* with me?"

Fred could not hide a look of scorn. "Because you've got money stuck all over you, that's why."

"*But I have nothing!*" Laurence wailed.

"Come on," Fred said, "don't go waxing the truth. How much did you snap?"

"Snap?"

"Steal."

Laurence stared at his feet. Then he murmured, "One thousand pounds."

"*One thousand quid!*" Fred cried in astonishment. "Where is it?"

"It was taken from me."

Fred stared at Laurence. "I'll admit, you don't act like a thief. But I don't care. All I want is that you don't get caught by Toggs. You don't want that either, do you?"

Laurence looked up and down the horrid street. The narrow alley gave him the feeling of being crushed while the swarms of people pressing by, oblivious to his presence, intensified his feelings of isolation. Everything seemed terribly wrong. If he could only find a place to stop, he might think out what to do. "I need to rest," he said.

"I'll take you to a place where you can rest all you want."

"All right," Laurence said.

"This way then," Fred said.

They soon reached the dock area. It was as crowded as ever with people, carts, horses. Laurence hardly looked where they were going. So it was that when Fred came to an abrupt stop, Laurence banged into him.

"Hold it!" Fred warned.

Laurence looked over the younger boy's shoulder. Standing some fifteen yards before them were four boys side by side, blocking the way. "Fred!" cried one of them. "Sergeant Rumpkin wants you!"

"Tom Spofford," Fred shouted back, "I'm off the association. And you can tell Sergeant it's because of Toggs!" Fred grabbed hold of Laurence and began to pull him back the way they had just come.

Laurence glanced over his shoulder. The four boys were in pursuit.

"Here!" Fred yelled, making a sharp turn and racing through a maze of barrels and boxes into a small shack, only to burst out its back door. A slow-moving horse and wagon was passing by.

"Jump on!" Fred called. He leaped on the wagon, spun about on his knees, and held out a hand to Laurence, who, running frantically behind, grabbed the offered hand and allowed himself to be hauled on.

"Now lie flat!" Fred ordered in a hard whisper. "And don't you move or talk none!"

Laurence, terribly frightened, did as he was told.

With the driver unaware of his passengers, the cart rumbled on for a while.

"Now off," Fred cried, and he scrambled down onto the road. Laurence obeyed, only to tumble and fall to his knees. Fred jerked him up. "This way," he cried. They staggered behind a building. Fred crept to the corner of the building and looked out. "Good, we've lost 'em."

"Who were they?" Laurence managed to ask. He was completely spent. One of his knees was bleeding. "Why were they after me?"

"The Lime Street Runners Association," Fred said. "It's Toggs again."

Laurence closed his eyes.

Fred glanced up at the sky to determine the time. "Tides are low," he said. "I can take you to my best spot. Skip the docks entirely."

Laurence shook his head. He did not want to move.

"Come on now," Fred said more kindly. "You can rest all you want when we get where I'm taking you."

Laurence still didn't move.

"Don't you trust me?"

Laurence shook his head.

"Who else you gonna trust?"

"Patrick."

"First me," Fred said with a grin. "Then your Patrick."

They turned south along Grafton Street. The farther they went, the less grand grew the buildings. Crowds thinned. Now and again an open patch of land was to be seen and beyond that the river. The street had become a muddy track. Crumbling cottages and broken shanties lined the way. As they pressed on, Laurence saw what looked to be fishermen's nets spread to dry. There were also small boats hauled high. The city was behind them.

They came upon a ridge overlooking the Mersey River. The river itself lay roughly two hundred yards beyond tidal flats of rocks and black sand. The stench of seaweed and rotting fish was intense. A brackish stream wound its crooked way from land to river, where rickety wooden docks had been built.

Midway between where the boys were standing and where the river flowed lay what Laurence thought was no more than a vast mound of tangled planking, spars, and rope. But when he stared at it, he realized he was seeing the remains of beached and broken sailing ships abandoned to rot.

"The hulks," Fred proclaimed with triumph, pointing to the old ships, "that's where we'll hide you. No one will find you there."

Laurence's heart sank. "Hulks!" he cried. "Are they prison hulks?"

Fred shook his head. "Not these. But the best hiding place in the world."

Laurence gazed at the hulks bleakly. "How long will we have to stay?"

"Got to find that ship—the *Robert Peel*—they're sailing on," Fred explained. "Find out when she's going. Then I'll find a way to get you on and let your friend know how and where I'm doing it. Takes time, all that.

"Come on," he urged, and he skittered down the ridge. Laurence hesitated for a few moments but then followed. They moved across the flats. Though now and again they had to skirt puddles of water, the black sand was firm beneath their feet.

From the ridge, the hulks had seemed one mass. As they drew closer, Laurence realized how distinct the old ships were, standing more than fifty feet over his head. There were, in fact, three ships heeled over, hulls sprung, their masts and spars intertwined in a tangled mass of ropes and tackle like discarded bird's nests. Patches of seaweed and algae grew everywhere, glossing the rotten wood with a sickly green sheen.

"Here we go," Fred called. He was standing by a ship's bow that was, in part, staved in. Above it rose an old figurehead in the shape of a great bird. Only half a beak remained.

Its colors were faded. The ship's name—*Seahawk*—was barely legible.

Reaching high over his head, Fred pulled out a board and removed a candle. He lit it with a match.

"We'll need to climb some," Fred warned. Reaching up, he took hold of a jagged end of wood and hoisted himself high, then disappeared within the hulk.

For a second Laurence considered running away. But he could see for himself there was nowhere to go. Besides, he had no energy left. Resigned, he grabbed the same jagged piece Fred had used and hauled himself into the ship.

By the light of Fred's candle, he saw great ribs of wood encircling him, ribs that stuck out from what looked like a monstrous backbone that ran down the length of the open area. Laurence's first sensation was that he—like Jonah—had entered into the dim belly of a giant fish. He could see that the planking of the hull had given way in numerous places, enough to let light, sand, and seaweed seep in.

"Over here," Fred called. He was standing by a ladder that dangled from above. The next moment, he scampered up and disappeared.

Clumsily, Laurence made his way to the same ladder and began to climb. It brought him into another cavern, one darker than below and, as far as he could see, smaller. He had to search for Fred.

"Keep coming," the boy called. He was on another ladder and moving up again. Laurence did the same. Fred waited at the top. It was hard to stand there, the broken deck being at a slant.

"Here you go," Fred said, gesturing toward a door. He worked his way forward and yanked the door open. Its hinges were rusty. They stepped inside the gloomy space, and Fred stuck the candle to the floor with a blob of wax.

"Perfect, ain't it?" he said with pride. "My special hiding place. The captain's quarters."

Laurence peered around the small room. Its rear portholes were crudely boarded over. A bunk—no more than a ledge built into a wall—could be seen on one side of the room. Where the bowed wall met the raked floor, a collapsed table lay. A few cabinets—interiors empty—had their doors gone. All else had been stripped away. The angle of the decking made it impossible to stand properly.

"Am I to stay here?" Laurence asked, looking about with dread.

"If you don't want anyone to find you, you are."

"But . . . but, there's nothing," Laurence said.

"Just a few hours," Fred assured him. "Then I'll come back and fetch you."

Laurence leaned against one wall and covered his face with his hands. "I can't do it," he said. "I can't."

"And let yourself be caught by Toggs?" Fred cautioned. "You don't mean it. Not by half!"

"But what if you don't come back?" Laurence asked.

"Don't you worry about that. I'll be back quick enough. Just blow out the candle, pop yourself onto the bunk, and take yourself a snooze while old Fred does all the work." He was already halfway out the door.

"Please, don't go!"

"Just a short time," Fred insisted. The next instant he was gone.

"Please, you mustn't leave me . . . ," Laurence cried. He tried to follow, but, forgetting he was not on a level, he slipped and fell. He hit the floor hard, then rolled until he tumbled in a heap against the wall. There he lay, crying.

Outside, Fred scampered across the tidal flats, pausing only to look back when he got to the top of the ridge. To his satisfaction he saw that the water was rising. The tide was coming in. No one would be able to get onto the hulks—or off.

Chapter 61
Fred Returns to the City

*A*ware that the Lime Street Runners Association was eager to find him, Fred slipped into the city with caution. As it was, he did spy one association runner—Mr. Orkin—on the prowl, but Fred avoided him without being seen.

Upon reaching the docks, he approached a sentry box where a dock policeman was standing.

"Excuse me, sir," Fred asked, "can you tell me who's running the packet *Robert Peel*? I'm to lead a gentleman over to her tomorrow."

The policeman ducked into his sentry box and returned leafing through a sheaf of papers. "That's a Lazarus Brothers ship."

"Right then," Fred cried. "Clarence Basin."

Near the northern end of the docks, Clarence Basin was big enough to berth thirty ships or more. There was a narrow portal to and from the Mersey River, with a pair of lifting bridges so that pedestrians and navvies could move around the ships with ease. On three sides of the basin—close to the ships—rose great warehouses.

The basin was crowded with three-masted, full-rigged packet ships. Thousands of feet of rope, crossing and crisscrossing, gave the appearance of a gigantic spider's web in whose midst sailors—like spiders—worked, tarring, splicing, and tying lines.

From the quay Fred tried to pick out the *Robert Peel*. At first glance, all the ships seemed very much alike, the standard packet having three masts, copper-sheathed hulls, a short billethead, and an extended, steeply angled bowsprit. But finally by asking he found the *Robert Peel*. Looming tall, she was snug against the dock, her black-and-white bulwark newly washed and bright, a contrast to the dull copper of her hull. On the adjacent quay were bales of textiles and wooden crates. These were being taken out of the warehouse bale by bale, crate by crate, on barrows that men were rolling onto the ship.

"You've got lots to load there, mate," Fred called to one of the workers who was momentarily resting.

"Aye, she sails tomorrow on the early tide," the man replied. "We'll be going all night." He stood up, approached a crate, and from a pocket pulled out a piece of chalk. He made an X mark on the box.

"The X means bottom hold, doesn't it?" Fred asked.

"Right-o. Sure thing. Any lower, and you'd have to swim it across. Top, bottom, fore, or aft—you want the weight distributed evenly, you know."

Fred watched the men work. When he saw a piece of chalk lying on the ground, he picked it up and pocketed it. Then he wandered among the crates and pulled at some of their slats, finally sauntering away as if nothing was on his mind. He approached one of the warehouses but was chased away. It did not matter. Fred had already decided how he would sneak Laurence on board.

Chapter 62

Mr. Clemspool and Mr. Grout
Make Travel Arrangements

*A*t 115 Waterloo Road, a wide avenue directly across from the docks, stood a large building with many windows and an elegant facade of architectural fancies.

At street level, a door had been wedged open. Arranged in a lengthy line, shabbily dressed people were attempting to make their way inside. Most were encumbered with trunks and bundles, as well as children. An air of intense if silent agitation pervaded them all as they waited. From the look of them—weary, half-asleep—some had been in line for hours if not days.

Across the front of the building was a large sign.

LAZARUS BROTHERS—SHIPPING AGENTS

With his one good eye, Mr. Grout gazed at it. "Wot's that sign say?" he asked.

Mr. Clemspool read it to him.

"Right then," Mr. Grout replied. "It's wot we want, isn't it?"

"I suppose," Mr. Clemspool said, looking about furtively. Fearful that some policemen would notice him, he had insisted that they take a cab to the building. Now that they had arrived, he was being made anxious by the sight of a constable patrolling the fringes of the crowd.

"Look at them Irish beggars," Mr. Grout said scornfully.

Mr. Clemspool sniffed. "I feel I am about to be reduced to traveling among cattle."

"Don't yer worry none," Mr. Grout assured him. "Mr. Grout only travels first class these days. Yer can 'ope for the same."

Mr. Clemspool waved away the insinuation. "I have an intense dislike for waiting in lines," he said.

"A flash of the old coin changes all that," Mr. Grout assured him with a laugh. He started to move forward.

Mr. Clemspool restrained him. "Do you think that constable is looking for *me*?"

Mr. Grout grinned. " 'Ere now, Mr. Clemspool, yer've grown wonderful sensitive, 'aven't yer? Never noticed yer to be so worried about the law before."

"You know perfectly well what concerns me," Mr. Clemspool snarled. He was finding it exceedingly difficult to be so dependent upon his former subordinate. "That Mr. Pickler may well have gone to the police about me. I don't intend to wait upon the consequences."

"We 'ave got to get tickets somewhere," Mr. Grout reminded him, "don't we? These 'ere Lazarus Brothers seem to have ships sailin' today and tomorrow. Are we goin' or not?" Mr. Grout took a few coins into his hand and held them there in readiness.

"I must," Mr. Clemspool said with an air of heavy resignation.

As the two men approached the line, the constable began to move toward them. Mr. Clemspool froze. The policeman, however, merely saluted. "Morning, gentlemen. Will you be needing to get inside?"

"Right yer are," Mr. Grout called. "We're buyin' first-class tickets."

"Step right this way," the constable said. He moved toward the crowd and began barking orders. "All right now, make way for gentlemen! Stand aside here! Let them through!" Cowering under the commands, most of the people moved. A few resisted. These the constable shoved aside with his hands or stick. A way was soon cleared. The officer turned. "Gentlemen," he called, with a tip of his cap.

"Thanks," Mr. Grout replied, and led the way, dropping a coin into the constable's hand as he and Mr. Clemspool passed into the building. Mr. Grout, catching sight of Mr. Clemspool's apprehensive face, said, "Ain't no better mask than a bit o' coin, is there?"

The two men stepped into a vestibule with a vaulted ceiling, marble floors, and walls of fine wood paneling. A sign on the wall read:

TICKETS—STEERAGE

A man could be seen through the ticket window. To its immediate right was a placard that listed the date, destination, and captain for each departing Lazarus Brothers ship for the next two weeks.

Standing before the ticket window was an attendant trying to keep order among the jostled and harassed people in line. It was not easy. Those who had finally reached the window kept consulting the placard, their friends, and their purses, as all the while hopeful passengers were pushing and shoving behind them.

As soon as Mr. Clemspool and Mr. Grout appeared, the attendant hastened to them. "May I help you, gentlemen?"

Mr. Grout extended a hand, thereby transferring a coin, and said, "We'll be needin' some tickets to America."

The attendant pocketed the coin without looking at it and bowed. "Please step right this way, gentlemen." He beckoned to a door.

They were led to an elegant room with fine wood floors and windows draped in velvet. The walls were covered with framed sea prints of stately ships under full sail. A few heavy upholstered chairs stood before a table, behind which sat a meticulously dressed man. A closed folder—bound in polished leather—lay before him. When Mr. Grout and Mr. Clemspool entered, he stood immediately.

"Gentlemen, welcome to Lazarus Brothers. How may I be of service?"

Mr. Clemspool stepped forward. "We have pressing business. What's the first ship departing for America?"

The man consulted his folder. "Well, sir, we have the *Valiant*. She leaves today, flood tide, which I think should be about seven P.M. She goes to New York. Very fast. Very good accommodations. First-rate captain. We have some places remaining, but, unfortunately, second class only."

Before Mr. Clemspool could assent, Mr. Grout said, "We're only wantin' first class."

The agent behind the desk eyed Mr. Grout momentarily. Then he murmured, "Very well," and turned a page of his folder. "The *Robert Peel,* for Boston, leaving with tomorrow's morning tide, approximately seven A.M. British registry. Captain Rickles in command. A first-rate packet. Very fast indeed—has made the crossing in thirty-five days. Alas, only two first-class cabins, and one has been taken by an American. If you want the remaining room, you must share it."

Mr. Grout shrugged. " 'Ow much?"

"Twenty-four pounds each, sir. I presume you gentlemen will share quarters. All meals included, and dinner at the captain's table."

"I've got one question," Mr. Grout said. The man looked up. "Anyone ever report a ghost on this 'ere ship?"

"I beg your pardon?"

"A spirit, or some such like?"

"I never heard of such a thing," the man behind the table said with some indignation.

"Just makin' sure," Mr. Grout said. "All right then, we've got a deal." He slapped his hand on the table and, after a look at Mr. Clemspool, gave their names.

"One formality," the agent advised. "The medical exam. A government requirement, I'm afraid. They will stamp your tickets. And the ship's officer at the point of embarkation is required to inspect all tickets to make sure the stamp is there. You need only indicate that you are traveling first class. Naturally, that speeds things along. Just a few steps away. On Ransom Street."

"I never thought I'd be required to leave the land of my birth," Mr. Clemspool complained as they left the building.

"America's the land of promise, or so they calls it," Mr. Grout informed him.

"Land of safety," Mr. Clemspool replied in his best sulky fashion, and reached into the air as if to pluck strings. But there were none, and he trudged along in gloomy silence.

Chapter 63
The Medical Exam

R ansom Street," Mr. Grout announced shortly.

It was a narrow mews, muddy underfoot, hemmed in upon three sides by stone buildings whose walls were plastered by posters announcing ship departures. At the far, closed end of the street was a building upon which was a sign:

GOVERNMENT

MEDICAL INSPECTOR'S OFFICE
HOURS 10 TO 4

The mews was choked with emigrants, all trying to enter the office at the same time. No police constable was there to enforce order.

"Just follow me close," Mr. Grout said. "I'll get us in quick enough." He waded into the crowd, crying, "Make way for gentlemen! Make way for gentlemen!" With Mr. Clemspool at his back, Mr. Grout moved forward. Suddenly he stopped.

" 'Ello," he cried. " 'Oo do we 'ave 'ere?"

Pulled at rudely, a startled Mr. Drabble reached for Maura and Patrick even as he looked about. When he saw it was Mr. Grout, he immediately began to bow.

"Mr. Grout, sir, I do apologize for not meeting you as planned, sir. Unfortunate circumstances—"

"Don't yer worry none, Mr. Drabble," Mr. Grout assured him grandly. "I weren't there meself."

"I am much relieved."

"Too much goin' on," Mr. Grout allowed. To Mr. Clemspool he said, "This is Mr. Drabble, the bloke who was goin' to give me an education."

"A worthy task," Mr. Clemspool muttered with disinterest. His sole desire was to get through the business at hand.

"Are you here for the medical exam?" the actor inquired.

"Leavin' tomorrow, early tide," Mr. Grout said.

"So are we," Mr. Drabble replied. "These are my friends the O'Connells."

Patrick, close to Maura, kept looking up at Mr. Grout, fascinated by his eye patch. Maura, who had formed a dislike for the man when she had met him with Mr. Drabble, kept her eyes averted.

"Wot ship are yer takin'?" Mr. Grout asked.

"The *Robert Peel*, I believe. Is that so, my dear?" he asked Maura.

"It's so," she murmured.

"Well, there's a piece of good luck," Mr. Grout enthused. "We're goin' on that one too. Yer can give me lessons as we go."

Mr. Drabble bowed again. "Nothing would give me greater pleasure."

"All right then," Mr. Grout said. " 'Ow yer travelin'?"

"Steerage."

"We're first class," Mr. Grout said proudly. "Not to worry. We'll find each other." He was feeling the pressure of Mr. Clemspool's hand upon his back, urging him to get on.

"My pleasure, I assure you," Mr. Drabble insisted, folding himself into a final deep bow.

With Mr. Grout calling, "Make way for first-class passengers!" the two men pushed on until they entered the building.

"Now *there* is a piece of uncommon fortune," Mr. Drabble declared when the two had gone. "To think, Miss O'Connell, I'll be earning some money as we sail. I'll be able to repay you for the ticket and still have enough to start us off in America."

Maura, hearing the *us* among Mr. Drabble's words, blushed. She feared the actor's presumption but did not wish to say anything hurtful. Instead, she bit her lip and turned away until she recovered her composure. All she said was, "Mr. Grout is not a man I care for."

After another hour, Maura, Patrick, and Mr. Drabble were able to enter the medical building. They stepped into a large, long, and bare room where the emigrants were divided into two lines. These lines worked their way to the end of the room, where two small tables had been placed. Behind each of these tables sat a medical examiner.

There was another half hour to wait before Mr. Drabble reached the table and faced the examiner. He was an older man, with small eyeglasses perched upon a thin red nose.

His sparse gray hair was in shambles and the suit he wore was spotted with stains.

"Ticket!" he demanded, slurring the single word.

Mr. Drabble handed his ticket over. The examiner took it with a shaking hand but did not even look at it. "What's your name?" he demanded.

"Gregory O'Connell."

"Are you well?" the examiner barked even as he scribbled the name Gregory O'Connell on the ticket.

"I should think that on the whole I—"

"Hold out your tongue! So I can see it!" the examiner demanded.

Mr. Drabble bent down.

The examiner barely glanced at Mr. Drabble's protruding tongue. "All right!" he murmured. Picking up a stamping bar, he pressed it into a pad of black ink, then slapped it on Mr. Drabble's ticket. With a pen he covered the mark with a scrawling signature.

"Next!" he cried.

Mr. Drabble was not sure he understood.

"You're healthy!" the examiner said. "Be off with you. Make room for the next."

Surprised, Mr. Drabble stepped away. In his place came Patrick. The examiner asked the boy the same questions he'd asked Mr. Drabble, passing him just as swiftly. Maura took no longer. Within moments all three were out the exit door and back on the street.

"There, you see?" Mr. Drabble said. "No trouble at all. Now we must purchase some provisions, then take ourselves to the quay and wait."

"Don't they feed us on board?" Maura asked, remembering the *Queen of the West*.

"They do, my dear. But from what I've been told, it's never enough. All a question of what we can afford. Now that I'll be earning as we go, we might get more." He made a move to leave Ransom Street.

It was then that Patrick said, "I have to wait for that boy."

"Whom do you mean?" Mr. Drabble asked.

"The boy who's helping Laurence. Didn't I tell him I'd be waiting here."

"Mr. O'Connell," said Mr. Drabble sternly, "haven't you made enough trouble for us already?"

Patrick was about to reply angrily when Maura took his arm and tried to lead him away. "Patrick," she said, "I saw for myself the poor boy was wanting help. I'll not begrudge him any. But you don't know what kind of thing he's tarnished with, do you? I'm fearing it will come down on us."

"Maura, I promised I'd wait," Patrick said stubbornly. "I'd be going back on my word if I didn't."

Mr. Drabble refused to be excluded from the debate. "A stowaway is strictly illegal," he said.

"What would happen?"

"He'd be at the mercy of captain and crew. His very life would be in jeopardy. It should not be encouraged."

Patrick shook his head. "The two of you can go off," he said. "I'll not budge until you get back."

"Patrick O'Connell," Maura said, "didn't we agree there would be no more separations?"

"Then can't we wait a bit?" Patrick begged. "If that boy doesn't come, then we can go on."

"A short time only," Mr. Drabble replied.

Though reluctant to set any limit, Patrick agreed. The three found a place against a wall not too far from the medical hall. Thirty minutes later, Fred arrived.

Patrick rushed forward. "Have you got Laurence on board yet?" he asked.

Fred grinned. "Not yet. But I will."

Patrick looked over his shoulder. Maura and Mr. Drabble

were watching. "They don't want me to help," Patrick said quickly, keeping his voice low. "But I will. Only you'll have to tell me what to do."

"Right you are," Fred agreed. "We'll keep him from Toggs, that's for sure. And here's the way: I'm going to put him in a crate on the *Robert Peel* myself."

"A crate?"

"It's the only way," Fred said. "Then, when you get on the boat—once it's well off—you open it up and out he pops."

"But how will I be knowing where the crate is?"

"There's always a crowd of emigrants waiting to board the ship. You'll be part of it. I'll find you and tell you where I put him."

Mr. Drabble was advancing on the boys now. Maura, not wanting a row, hastened after.

"Be off with you," Mr. Drabble shouted at Fred even as he tried to pull Patrick away. "He's not going to have anything to do with your friend."

Patrick tore himself free. "It's none of your business!" he cried. "None!" He was sure he hated Mr. Drabble.

Maura hastily stepped between the actor and her brother. "Mr. Drabble," she said, "I'll take care of things."

A laughing Fred danced backward. "Make sure you're at the quay," he called to Patrick. "I'll find you."

"I promise!" Patrick returned.

Fred turned and ran off.

Maura was greatly relieved to see Fred go, but once he had, she cried to her brother, "Patrick O'Connell, what have you promised to do now?"

Patrick gazed at her fiercely. "Nothing," he said. "Nothing at all."

Maura looked at him. Then she decided she did not want to know.

Chapter 64
Mr. Pickler and the Lime Street
Runners Association

O nce again Sergeant Rumpkin could be found at his table at the Iron Duke. Once again the members of the Lime Street Runners Association were in attendance. Once again one member was missing. This time, however, the missing one was Fred. And, instead of Mr. Matthew Clemspool asking for assistance, it was Mr. Phineas Pickler, with Laurence's torn clothing on his lap. As for Toggs, he sat next to the investigator, grinning for all he was worth.

"You see, sir," Sergeant Rumpkin explained to Mr. Pickler, "we're strictly military in organization. Here are the soldiers. I am, sir, their leader. I set the strategy and issue orders. They enact them. No democratic tendencies lurking here, sir!" The sergeant blotted his lower lip with his handkerchief.

The boys, hearing this declaration, allowed not the slightest hint that they had ever heard anything like it before.

"I am much obliged for your explanation," Mr. Pickler said to the sergeant, "and given the urgency of the matter, I'm willing to work out an understanding. I must find this boy. He may be using the name Laurence Worthy. Though it appears he has not so much as a penny in his pocket, he is, in fact, Sir Laurence Kirkle."

"A Kirkle," cried Sergeant Rumpkin, his eyes sparkling with joy. "This boy is a prince! Worth his weight in gold! So be it!" He sat back with a smile. "And what would you say, sir, if"—he paused for effect and even lowered his voice—"if I was to tell you that your boy has been observed?"

Mr. Pickler sat bolt upright. "What do you mean?"

Sergeant Rumpkin winked, took up a biscuit, snapped it in two, and ate each piece deliberately. Only when he'd brushed the crumbs from his chins did he say, "Your boy was seen—by four of my runners here—in the vicinity of the docks some hours previous."

"Are you sure?" Mr. Pickler demanded.

"I'd bet my rank on it."

"How did you know him?"

"Mr. Pickler," the sergeant replied with another wink and nod, "the Lime Street Runners Association, which I have the honor of commanding, knows what needs to be known."

"But . . . but what has happened to him!" cried Mr. Pickler.

"He got away. It is my judgment he was trying to ship out as a stowaway."

"A stowaway!"

"I am truly grieved to say so."

"But how can you be so sure?"

"Deep experience, sir. That's to say, why else would a penniless boy be lurking about the docks?"

"But what am I to do!" Mr. Pickler cried.

Sergeant Rumpkin leaned forward. "Sir, there are nine ships leaving for America tomorrow. I keep a listing of such ships. You shall be provided with one. Each ship is owned by a different company. Each sails from a different dock. We are but eight. Mr. Pickler, might I inquire if you will be securing the help of the police?"

Once again Mr. Pickler recalled the unhelpful Mr. Knox. "Do you think it would be useful?" he asked.

"Being upstanding citizens," the sergeant informed the investigator, "we much prefer to cooperate with the police."

Mr. Pickler sighed. "If I were to ask them to work with you, I think they would."

The sergeant considered Mr. Pickler carefully. "You speak of powerful influences, sir."

Mr. Pickler bobbed his head. "I believe I represent them."

Sergeant Rumpkin slapped the table hard. "Excellent! We shall all work together to serve the queen's subjects!" he cried out.

"May I propose," he continued, "the following plan of action: You, sir, shall arrange to have the police posted at the gangway of every one of the departing ships so that they might observe and detain—if necessary—all suspicious boys who go aboard. Meanwhile, I shall have these eager young troops of mine"—Sergeant Rumpkin extended his hand so as to include his soldiers—"posted up and down the docks, patrolling those ships. They too shall be on the alert.

"Now then, when and if the police see your boy, they will alert a runner. The runner shall speedily inform all others up and down. All then shall join forces in a siege. It will be impossible for your young man to escape!" He rattled his finger rings upon the table for emphasis. "There, sir, what do you think of that?"

Mr. Pickler studied his bowler. "If the police will cooperate, it might work. But where, do you think, should I be posted?"

"In military matters, sir, one should never assume victory. No, sir. Never underestimate the enemy. Never!

"You, sir, shall station yourself at the northernmost point of the docks. That would be Sandon Basin. It's undergoing some repairs so it won't be occupied. Mr. Toggs shall serve as your assistant as he has already ably done. At his disposal shall be a skiff. A small boat, if you will. He is adept with the oars, is Mr. Toggs. Is that not right, Toggs?"

"Right-o," Toggs acknowledged.

"If, sir," the sergeant continued, "as a misfortune of war, your boy eludes us, Mr. Toggs can intercept any vessel you choose from that most northern position. You can board the ship and capture your boy. Is there anything beyond all this?"

"You will wish to be paid," Mr. Pickler said.

"Well, yes," agreed Sergeant Rumpkin amiably, his eyes positively smiling. "Soldiers cannot be expected to work on empty bellies, sir. Never have. Never will. Never should be!" He patted his own stomach as proof of this policy.

Mr. Pickler's offer was accepted. Four pounds to the Lime Street Runners Association for taking on the task. Six more pounds when Mr. Pickler had Laurence in hand. A list of departing ships was provided. Mr. Pickler stood up and shook hands with Sergeant Rumpkin.

Toggs, catching the sergeant's quick nod, followed the investigator out of the Iron Duke.

Sergeant Rumpkin remained at the table with his seven young runners. "Any questions?" he asked, looking about. "Yes, Mr. Orkin. You have something on your mind?"

"Sergeant, that gentleman who was here last night, Mr. Clemspool. Was I confused, sir, or did we have contrary orders regarding this boy, Laurence? I mean, are we trying to keep this here boy *here* or are we trying to ship him *there*?"

"Gentlemen," the sergeant returned, "in war as in life, it is not victory that matters, it is loyalty! Do you not see, Mr. Orkin, that boy has great profit in him. Great profit. When we get him, I shall auction him off to the one who wants him most. All shall benefit.

"But, gentlemen, there remains the question of loyalty. So there is something I want as much as I want that boy."

286

"What's that?" Mr. Orkin asked.

"Fred," said Sergeant Rumpkin. "I want him too." And he laid one hand upon the table and curled up thin fingers so that they resembled a claw.

Chapter 65
Mr. Pickler and Toggs Confer

Where to now, mate?" Toggs asked Mr. Pickler when they emerged from the meeting.

Mr. Pickler was studying the list of departing ships that Sergeant Rumpkin had given him.

FRIDAY, JANUARY 24, 1851

Name of ship	Company	Captain	Destination
MISS INDIA	Ruse	Bright	New York
DUCHESS OF KENT	Cunard	McOsker	New York
LIZA KAY	Tapscott's	John	New York
ROBERT PEEL	Lazarus Brothers	Rickles	Boston
SUFFOLK	Red Ball Line	Rayfield	New York
QUEEN CHARLOTTE	Raplinger	Churchill	New York
BISHOP BERKLEY	White Star	Rabkin	Philadelphia
WEBSTER	Armistead	Collins	Boston
CAESAR	Black Ball Line	Trollop	New York

The list depressed him. If Laurence was attempting to stow away, he could be on any of them. With a sigh he said, "I shall return to police headquarters and make arrangements with Inspector Knox. You will meet me at my hotel, the Royalton, tomorrow morning, five-thirty."

"You're the early bird."

"You will take me to that most northern place on the docks as your sergeant suggested, Sandon Basin. You'll have a skiff in readiness. Is that all understood?"

"All set," Toggs assured him.

"Tomorrow morning then." Mr. Pickler, feeling less confident than Toggs sounded, bobbed his head, tucked Laurence's clothing under his arm, and went off toward police headquarters.

Left alone, Toggs thought he might prowl the streets on his own in search of Laurence. But he was feeling too pleased with himself to spend time on others. What he decided to do was go back to Mrs. Sonderbye's. It would be fine to tell that Irish girl about his exploits. He was sure she'd be impressed.

Chapter 66

On the Hulks

South of the city Fred sat on a rock by the water's edge, put aside the loaf of stale bread he had snatched from a baker's cart, and pulled off his old boots. Overhead, the sky was still clogged with clouds, but here and there patches of blue appeared, hinting at better weather. On the sand, just above high water, small white birds raced about on sticklike legs, then stopped and pecked furiously. The hulks, which had been mired in mud, were now surrounded by the tide.

Boots in one hand, bread in the other, Fred waded into

the water. If he had waited any longer he would have had to swim.

Reaching the hulks, he made his way inside, then up the ladders. He peeked into the captain's cabin. By the dim light he saw Laurence lying on the bunk, eyes open, staring blankly before him. He looked dead.

"Laurence?" Fred cried.

"Yes," Laurence murmured. Since crying his eyes dry, he had lain all morning upon the bunk.

"Told you I'd come back," Fred said.

Laurence said nothing.

"Got it all worked out with your friend."

"What friend?"

"The Irish boy."

"Patrick?"

"I'm going to stow you away on the same ship he's going on. The *Robert Peel*. You'll be in America in spit time."

Laurence turned his face to the wall.

"Don't you want to go?" Fred asked, puzzled.

"I don't care," Laurence said.

Fred snorted. "You'd care a lot about going if Toggs was standing here instead of me, wouldn't you?"

Again Laurence said nothing.

"Can you read?" Fred asked.

"Yes. Why do you ask?"

"You'll see." Fred stretched himself. "I've half a mind to go with you to America," he said. "What's it like?"

"I don't know."

"Don't know?" Fred replied with surprise. "What you going for then anyway?"

"Because all those people are after me."

"There's your reason," Fred said as he sat on the floor with his back propped up against the bunk. "But we've got to wait till dark. Then we can get moving."

"I'm hungry," Laurence announced.

Fred held up the bread loaf. "Thought you would be." He broke the bread in two and offered half to Laurence over his shoulder. Laurence took the bread and began to gnaw on it.

"Where do you come from anyway?" Fred said.

"London."

"London . . . What's it like?"

"All right," Laurence said indifferently.

"Lived on your own, did you?"

"With my family," Laurence said rather wistfully.

"Did you?" Fred said with new interest. Having no family of his own, he was always curious about them. "Do you have a mother or a father then?"

"Both."

"Crikey!" Fred said, impressed. "What happened to them?"

"Nothing."

"Alive then?"

"Yes."

"My mother died when I was born," Fred explained in a matter-of-fact way. "Then my father ups and does the same. Not very helpful, was it? When no one would have me, they put me in the workhouse. Didn't care much for that so I runs off and came here, where I could take care of myself. You live in a room in that London?"

"A house."

"That's got rooms?"

"The whole house," Laurence said.

"A whole one?" Fred asked with disbelief. He swung around on his knees the better to consider Laurence.

"Yes."

"How many rooms?"

"I don't know."

"Can't you even guess?"

"Twenty . . ."

"*Twenty!*" Fred cried in astonishment. "Wool in your eye. That's a warehouse! What did you do with all them rooms?"

Laurence shrugged. "Lived in them," he said.

"Why, how many of you are there?"

"Six."

"Six people in a whole warehouse of twenty rooms?"

"There were servants too."

"What do you mean, servants?"

"Twelve of them."

"Get off! If that was so, why would you ever want to leave?"

Laurence looked away. "I'm a thief," he said.

"Oh, right. I forgot," Fred said, giving Laurence a sympathetic poke. Then he twisted around to resume his seat. "And someone took it from you. That's the world for you," he allowed. "Big thieves stealing from us little thieves. Your name's Laurence, isn't it?"

"Yes."

"Got a last name?"

Laurence hesitated. "Kirkle," he said softly.

The name meant nothing to Fred. "I don't have a last name," he said. "Once I asked a man why folks have two names, and he says, ' 'Cause it tells to who you belongs.' But, there you are, I don't belong to anyone, do I, so there's no point in having one, is there?" They ate the rest of the bread. But there was no more talk until Fred sighed, "I'm tired." So saying, he stretched out and without any ceremony soon slept.

Laurence lay in the bunk, thinking about what he had described to Fred: the house he lived in, the servants. It was untrue now, all past. He was no more than a thief trying to run away from everyone. In pain, he closed his eyes and dozed.

When Laurence awoke, he lay awhile contemplating what he was about to do, get on a ship and stow away to America. "I don't want to go," he whispered to himself.

When he saw that Fred was still asleep, he stood up. The raked floor was hard to walk on, but he made his way out of the room.

Once beyond the room, he could discern the forecastle but little else beside rotten rope and wood debris. When he saw some steps, he climbed them and found himself standing on the forecastle deck.

Standing by a broken capstan, Laurence looked about. The land between the hulks and the shore had vanished. Now there was only water, upon which a pale sun glinted. To the immediate west lay two other hulks, seeming in worse condition than the ship he was on. Beyond these, at some distance across the river, he could see the western shore. The eastern shore was closer.

Laurence went back down the steps and worked his way down ladders until he was at the bottom, in the broken hull. He found it full of water. When a stick floated by, he used it to probe the depth—at least as high as his neck. It was impossible for him to walk away. A sense of grief engulfed him.

Clinging to the ladder, Laurence contemplated leaping into the water. Drowning was, he thought, the only way to save himself, his name, his family. "I don't want to be me," he whispered. "I don't." He remembered Fred's words, "I don't belong to anyone." That was the way he felt.

But he did not want to die.

From deep within the boy came a sound, half-sigh, half-moan, the sound of something breaking. He began to weep. The tears began softly but soon became deep racking sobs of bewilderment. "I can't be me anymore," he cried to the darkness. "I can't!"

He knew then that if he were to live, he could no longer be the person he'd been mere days ago. He'd have to become someone else, though who he had no idea. If he could get to America, he thought, perhaps he could be that someone.

Wiping his face clear of tears, Laurence climbed once more to the captain's quarters. Fred was still asleep. Laurence crawled back into the bunk, picked at a few crumbs that lay about, and chewed them, all the while wondering who it was he might become.

Chapter 67
The O'Connells Prepare
for Departure

Not far from the open-air food stalls in the Haymarket, Maura, Patrick, and Mr. Drabble squatted by three cloth bags, one each of rice, oatmeal, and flour, as well as an open tin can.

"I do hope you were right to buy these things, Mr. Drabble," Maura said to the actor. "We have only a few pennies left us."

"My dear, let me assure you again, it's money well spent. We will need these provisions for the voyage."

"Besides, Maura," Patrick said, "hasn't Da grown rich? He'll not begrudge us any."

Maura shook her head. "It's being short of cash and only just starting that troubles me. I was certain Father Mahoney said they would feed us on the boat," she said.

"And so they will," Mr. Drabble explained. "Be so kind as to show me your tickets."

Maura unpinned her packet and offered them to Mr. Drabble. "There, you see?" he said, holding up one ticket. "Here's what they promise:

" *'Every day each passenger shall receive three quarts of water. And each week the same passenger shall get two and a half pounds of bread, one pound of oatmeal, two pounds of rice, one half pound of sugar, one half pound of molasses, and two ounces of tea.'* "

"That's more than we had at home, Maura," Patrick reminded his sister. "We're like to grow fat on that."

"True enough," Mr. Drabble agreed. "Though much depends on the ship's master. As for these"—he waved his hands over the food—"you know me for the optimist I am, my dear, but one can never be certain how long the voyage will take. Better to have too much than too little." He touched the can. "And something to hold the water."

"On the boat from Ireland, they gave us nothing," Maura told him. "And kept us in the open all the way, even though it stormed."

"It will not be so on *this* voyage," Mr. Drabble assured her. "I can give you my word about that."

She glanced up. The sun was sinking rapidly. "I only wish we were on our way."

"Maura," Patrick suddenly asked, "are we not getting our bundle from Mrs. Sonderbye's?"

Maura looked at him. "Why, that's true," she said. "I had forgotten. She took it when we arrived."

"My dear," Mr. Drabble cautioned, "I'm not certain it's wise to go there. You heard what that boy said about the runner—"

294

"Ralph Toggs," said Patrick.

"Exactly. If he's lurking about, we wouldn't want to meet him, would we? Not in the dark."

"But those are things we'll be needing," Maura protested.

"Now, Miss O'Connell, I think you'd best take my advice on this. I'm here to protect you."

Maura bridled. "Mr. Drabble," she said, "haven't I listened to you in much of this? And no doubt you know more than I. But surely that woman has no right to our things. It's all we have. As it was, we lost one bundle."

"Very well, my dear, if you insist." Mr. Drabble sighed. "But I shall go with you. It will be safer."

With that, they gathered up their provisions and set off for the lodging house. But no sooner did they turn the last corner onto the street where the house was than they saw Ralph Toggs standing on the porch steps, talking to Mrs. Sonderbye.

"It's him!" Patrick cried.

"Who?" Mr. Drabble asked.

"The runner Ralph Toggs."

Mr. Drabble held out his arms to keep the others from advancing. "My dears," he whispered, "I really think—"

Maura ducked around him. "Mr. Drabble," she said, "I can deal with that one myself." Tossing her hair away from her face, she moved to the foot of the steps. Ignoring Toggs, she called, "Mrs. Sonderbye!"

Hearing her name called, Mrs. Sonderbye looked down. Toggs, when he realized it was Maura, snatched off his hat. "There you are, missy. You're the one I was asking about," he said.

"And why would you be doing that?" Maura demanded.

"Toggs's the name. Did you forget? I met you at your boat and brought you here. You and your brother."

"Of course I remember. But my business is with Mrs. Sonderbye and not you."

Toggs paid no mind to her words. "I'm glad you recall me. After I left you, I thought of a better place for you to stay. It's probably something you'd find more to your liking. I'd be happy to take you there."

Maura, her blue eyes fierce, stared right at him. "And why, Mr. Toggs," she said, "should I be listening to you after the things you told us were nothing but lies?"

"What lies?"

"That this was a decent place and that the Union House was burned to the ground."

"Now see here, miss," Toggs replied, coming partway down the porch steps, "I was only doing my business. You needn't have paid heed to me."

"Lurking about and making trouble for the likes of poor strangers like us," Maura went on. "You should be ashamed of yourself for taking advantage. You're nothing but a trouble-maker!"

Toggs slapped his hat back onto his head. "Is that what you think?" he returned. "I suppose that's why I'm working for the police."

"The police?"

"Came to me special, they did. So, Miss Paddy, if you don't take care, I'll just make sure you won't get on any ship soon."

Maura paled. "What do you mean?"

Toggs, sensing his advantage, grinned wickedly. "There are ways and ways to keep a body off a ship. If I were you, I'd mind my manners. I was only trying to show you some kindness." He reached out and put his hand on Maura's arm. She froze.

"Keep your hands off that young woman!" Mr. Drabble cried, taking a prizefighter's stance and holding up his fists.

Toggs glared at Mr. Drabble menacingly.

"Step away from her," Mr. Drabble insisted, making a few feints.

Toggs smirked, took a step forward, cocked his arm, and threw a punch that landed on Mr. Drabble's chest. The actor, spun about by the force of the blow, tumbled to the ground. Toggs stood over him, threatening to strike again. Mr. Drabble cringed.

"Maura!" Patrick cried. "Get away!"

A laughing Toggs gave Mr. Drabble a kick. Then he turned back to Maura. "If that's the kind of fellow you prefer, you can have—" Toggs did not finish his words. Maura slapped him hard across the face with the flat of her hand.

"Be off with you!" she cried in fury. "You're nothing but a brute!"

Taken more by surprise than pained, Toggs turned scarlet and backed away. "Stupid Paddy!" he spit out. "Don't think you'll be leaving Liverpool by any ship soon. Not if I have anything to do with it!"

"Be off with you!" Maura cried again, and stamped her foot. "Or you'll get yourself a slap to the other side of your lying face!"

Toggs turned and ran off.

Patrick watched him go with glee. Then he turned back to Maura. She was kneeling by Mr. Drabble's side.

"Are you all right?" she asked. She could hardly keep from crying.

"My dear," the actor replied tremulously, "I can cast a spell upon the stage, but in life I'm no more than a useless prop. You have saved me when I thought I was saving you."

"Wasn't she positively fierce with him!" Patrick crowed.

"I'm sure she was," Mr. Drabble said.

With Maura and Patrick's help, the man climbed to his feet and brushed himself to hide his embarrassment.

"Stay here," Maura said. "I'll fetch the bundle."

"Wait!" the actor called. "I must get my Shakespeare."

Maura stepped toward the porch only to find Mrs. Sonderbye blocking the way, her beefy arms folded over her great bulk.

"That's all you Irish is good for, fighting," the woman cried, her face redder than ever. "Well, I won't have you staying if you're like that. This is a respectable, law-abiding house."

"If you give me the bundle you took from us when we arrived yesterday, mistress," Maura replied, "we'll go."

"It's in the front parlor. You can get it yourself, and then be off. All of you. You'll get no refund either. As for you," Mrs. Sonderbye said to Mr. Drabble, "you call yourself an actor, but you're only a conceited fool, knowing nothing but words from a book. No bloody use to anyone." She stepped aside.

While Patrick stayed on the street to guard their food, Mr. Drabble hurried toward the basement. Maura went into the parlor, which was filled like a refuse bin with bundles and boxes. Though it took time, she was able to find hers. She carried it out to Patrick. Not long after, Mr. Drabble appeared with his own small bag.

"Now get away from here!" Mrs. Sonderbye cried. "The lot of you!"

"Maura," said Patrick, as they crossed the street, "what if Ralph Toggs can keep us off the ship?"

"Preposterous!" Mr. Drabble sputtered. "It can't be done. An Englishman has his rights!"

The chilly night was already upon them when, forty-five minutes later, they reached Clarence Basin. Illuminated by warehouse lights, the *Robert Peel* lay on the northern side, looking not very different from the other packets.

Two gangways had already been deployed, running from

the ship to the quay. On one, navvies were hauling kegs, bales, chests, and boxes into the ship's hold. Some of these things they carried on their backs. Others required barrows. On the second gangway, more men, empty-handed except for their barrows, returned to fetch more goods.

Mr. Drabble, Maura, and Patrick moved as close to the ship as they could, then searched for a place to wait. Some seventy people had already set down their bundles and were camped about the quay. From the look of them, Maura and Patrick assumed most were from Ireland.

Mr. Drabble found space at the base of a gas lamp. There they settled down for the long wait.

"And when will they be letting us on board?" Maura asked.

"Tomorrow morning, early," Mr. Drabble assured her.

"If that Ralph Toggs does nothing," Patrick added gloomily. He had noticed a police constable standing guard by the gangway.

Chapter 68
Laurence Prepares for Departure

*H*olding a newly lit candle in his hand, Fred woke Laurence. "Should be about time now."

Laurence sat up sleepily. "But there's water all about," he said.

"Should be low tide again," Fred said. "We'll be able to walk it easy."

"Where are we going?"

"We're going to get you on the *Robert Peel,* that's where.

299

Far away from everybody as wants to get you. Come on now, we've got a ways."

Laurence rolled off the bunk and followed Fred into the hull. In the candlelight, Laurence saw that, as Fred had predicted, the water was almost all gone.

They splashed through the hull. Once they emerged from the boat, Laurence looked up. A bright moon cast a shimmering light over the river and made the path before them seem almost on fire. Fred blew out the candle and put it in its hiding place.

"This way," he said. Laurence followed.

Just before reaching the shore, Fred bent over and scooped up some black mud. "Come here," he called.

"What for?" Laurence asked.

"Your welt is too particular. You'll want to muck it a bit." With a few strokes of his hand, Fred smudged Laurence's face on both sides. "There you are," he said. "Now you look like a regular nobody."

They headed north back into the city. Hardly speaking to each other, Fred always in the lead, they made their way through dark streets. Only once did Fred stop.

"That's where I live," he said, pointing into a shadowy alley.

Laurence looked. All he could make out was a muddy lane worming between decayed buildings on the verge of collapse. "Where?" he asked, truly curious.

"Down at the end. Nothing much. Not like your house. I'd like to see that."

Laurence shook his head. "You can't."

Fred looked around. "What do you mean?"

"I made all that up."

Fred studied Laurence, trying to decide if he was being teased. But the grimy sadness that filled Laurence's face would admit to no fancy. Grinning, Fred gave him a playful

300

poke. "Well, I didn't think it was true. Too fine for the likes of us. But I don't care, I'll get you away from Ralph Toggs anyway."

They pressed on, stopping again when they came upon a crowd of sailors, shouting and laughing as they danced around a street fire to the wild strains of an old fiddler. White-haired, his back bent no less than his elbow, the man tore after his tune as though to challenge the dancers to see which would drop first, he, they, or the melody.

The two boys watched. "Like tykes, aren't they?" Fred said.

When they came down out of town and neared the docks, Fred halted again. Now the only light came from the dull gas lamps placed fifty yards apart and from dimly lit windows across wide Regent Street. "You might as well know," Fred cautioned with a sly grin, "this won't be all that easy."

Laurence felt his heart skip. "What do we have to do?"

"First off," Fred said quietly, "we got to get you into the warehouse."

"Why?"

"You'll see. Ready?"

"I suppose."

"Come on then."

Fred approached a wall built of great stone blocks. It extended without gaps in both directions along the road for as far as Laurence could see.

"Think you can climb it?" Fred asked.

Laurence had to lean back to look up. The wall was at least twenty feet tall.

"Not so hard," Fred said encouragingly. "The way the stones fit, it's almost like a ladder." He pressed Laurence's hand to the wall. The wall surface was jagged, with the mortar between the stones set deep. "Like steps. Now mind, sometimes there are guards. So we have to do it fast."

"What if they catch us?"

"Don't you worry none. I've climbed the like so many times I could do it with my eyes closed. I'll go first. That way I can pull you over."

After checking to make sure they were not being observed, Fred reached high and sprang up. Lizardlike, he slithered to the top in a matter of seconds. Once there, he swiveled around, belly flat, and peered down.

"Now it's your turn," he called. "Just do it right quick."

Laurence reached over his head, curled his fingers around the edges of a stone, and pulled while scrambling with his feet. Up he went.

"That's right!" Fred encouraged. "You're doing it just fine!"

Clinging to the rocks with one hand, face pressed against the rough, cold stone, Laurence stuck out his other hand and again pulled, kicking and clambering until he felt Fred's hand grip his hair.

"Got you!" Fred said, pulling until Laurence reached the top. Once there, he lay panting for breath.

"You're a good one," Fred insisted. "I thought you'd be. But fast now, roll on down." Fred did as he said, dropping below on the inside of the wall.

Laurence stared after him. Fred's pale face gazed up from the darkness like a pale moon.

"Come on!" Fred cried. "Good as before!"

Laurence twisted about, let his feet dangle, then dropped. Failing to push himself far enough away from the wall, he scraped against it, then fell, landing so hard, he toppled onto his back. The shock took his wind away.

Fred hovered over him. "You all right?" he asked.

"I . . . think so."

"That's all the hard part there is," Fred assured him as he offered a hand to help Laurence get back on his feet.

"Where are we?" Laurence asked.

"Clarence Basin. We could have walked in, regular. But bet you double farthings it's being watched."

"For what?"

"*You.* Come on now. The rest is old bread."

Before them rose the basin warehouse, an immense red-brick building with only a few windows. Behind some of these, lights flickered faintly.

Fred took them along one wall of the building. At ground level there were many iron doors. He kept trying them until he found an open one. "In here!" he called. Before Laurence realized what Fred was doing, he was pulled inside.

They found themselves in a long iron-beamed hall. The tiny flames of lofty oil lamps seemed to create more gloom than light below the thirty-foot-high brick ceilings. Piles of crates, barrels, and bales were shadowy presences looming on all sides. At the far end of the warehouse, where the light was better, Laurence saw men busily coming and going.

Fred pointed to a nearby crate. "See this label?" he whispered. "Everything here has one. You said you could read. You got to read the labels for me. Find one that says which ship it's going on. We want the *Robert Peel.*"

Laurence moved quietly up and down the dim aisles, squinting at the crates and their labels. "Here's one," he called in a whisper.

Fred hurried over. "Stand up against it."

"Why?"

"So we can see if you fit."

"What do you mean?"

"You're going inside."

"*Inside?*" Laurence cried, aghast.

"Shhh! Don't need to worry none. It won't be for long. But this here is too small. Find another. Go on, do it." He gave the suddenly reluctant Laurence a shove.

Laurence kept looking and soon found a bigger crate. Made of rough wood, it was about two feet wide and five feet tall. Fred pushed Laurence against it.

"That should do," the younger boy said. "Now go fetch that barrow over there."

Laurence went to a heavy barrow, swung it about, then wheeled it to where Fred was hard at work, pulling at one of the crate slats. It barely budged.

"Give a hand," Fred summoned.

The two pulled together. The board groaned.

"Not too fast," Fred cautioned. "We'll need those nails."

They worked three boards out gradually. Once they were pulled free, Fred leaned into the gap and fished inside with a hand. "Hats!" he exclaimed. He plucked out a tall one and, giggling, dropped it on his head. It came down over his nose.

"Look like a bloody swell, don't I?" Fred said, imitating upper-class talk while walking with mincing steps. As Fred snatched off the hat, Laurence smiled—the first smile Fred had seen from him. "But we can't fool now," Fred said. "Come on."

Together they took out all the other hats and hid them behind another crate. As soon as the first crate was empty, Fred said, "Got to put the boards back on."

"I thought I was getting in it," Laurence said.

"Not now."

They replaced the boards. "All right then," Fred instructed, "we got to get the box on the barrow."

With much pulling and shoving, the boys maneuvered the barrow close to the crate, then tipped it in. Though the crate fit awkwardly, it stayed.

"What we want to do," Fred explained, "is get this thing on your boat."

Working side by side, they readied the barrow with the

crate on it. Under Fred's direction, they wheeled it down the long warehouse corridor.

"Don't you say a thing," Fred cautioned. "I'll do all the talking."

They trundled toward the brighter end of the warehouse. There was little talk as the workers, sometimes in pairs, sometimes alone, hoisted the heavy goods and hauled them out of the building into the darkness. Fred and Laurence, looking not so different from the others, attracted no notice.

On the shadowy quay, Fred paused and scanned the ghostly ships. As a workman passed, he called, "Where's the *Robert Peel*, mate?"

"At the end," the man said, not even pausing to look at his questioner.

Fred called a casual thanks. "This way," he murmured to Laurence, his voice low. "And keep your face down."

Despite the warning, Laurence kept stealing quick glances to see where they were. Off to one side, he thought he caught a glimpse of a crowd of emigrants sitting among their possessions. "I think I see Patrick," Laurence said.

"Keep your face down!" Fred hissed. Laurence did as he was told.

Approaching the gangway, they were forced to stop. A man with a lantern and a sheaf of papers was examining every load going on board. Standing next to him was a police constable.

Chapter 69
On the *Robert Peel*

Not a word," Fred reminded Laurence.

The boys halted the barrow at the bottom of the gangway. "What you got there?" the man with the papers demanded.

"Hats," Fred said.

The man looked at the label on the box, riffled through his papers, then made a mark on them. Finally, he marked an X on the box with a piece of chalk. "You're on," he said. "Keep moving."

"Hold it!" the constable barked. He leaned forward and peered at Fred. Then he turned to Laurence, who was looking down and away, and chucked him under the chin so as to raise his dirty face. He studied it.

"You're holding everything up," the other man objected.

"Never you mind," the constable growled, but even so, he drew back and nodded to the boys. "Get on with it, you filthies."

Leaning into the barrow, the two boys pushed up the gangway and onto the ship. "Glad we dirtied you," Fred said under his breath.

At the top of the gangway, they were met by another man. He peered at the mark on the box. "Bottom hold," he said. "Keep on movin'."

Laurence, who had never been on a ship before, was astonished by the complexity of decks and rigging.

"You'll have time enough to gawk later," Fred cautioned as a navvy shouted at them, pointing to where the cargo

306

hatch had been pulled back. It left a gaping hole on the ship's deck through which goods meant for the hold were being lowered by block and tackle attached to the lowest spar on the main mast.

No sooner did the boys take their crate out of the barrow than deck workers flung ropes around it and tied them fast.

"We got to set it right!" Fred called. "Come on!" he shouted to Laurence as he leaped on the box and clung to the encircling ropes.

Laurence, seeing what Fred had done, hardly thought but jumped too, just having time to get a grip before the entire crate was yanked into the air, swung about, then dropped almost instantly into darkness. It happened so fast Laurence had to gasp for air.

"Hang on!" Fred called.

They landed with a harsh thump. Fred leaped off. Laurence fell. He looked around him. A few oil lanterns revealed that they were in the bottom cargo hold. Beams of dark wood crisscrossed overhead, not unlike those he'd seen in the hulks, but here the air was murky and so rank with the stench of sewerlike filth that he gagged.

Not far from where they stood, he could see workers hauling already deposited cargo and lining it in rows much as in the warehouse.

As Laurence stared about, Fred was working fast to untie their crate. "Come on!" Fred cried. "Give a hand!" Laurence hurried over.

When the crate was clear of ropes, Fred took hold of them and gave them a jerk, a signal that the lines were clear. Up they flew.

"Have you been here before?" Laurence asked.

"Rather work here than the workhouse," Fred spit out. "Come on now, let's get the thing in place," he said. The boys pushed and shoved the crate along the floor, wedging it as far as possible into the ship's most forward section. No other boxes could be fitted in before it.

"All pretty," Fred said, looking about furtively. Reassured that they were alone, he began to pull off the boards they had previously loosened. As soon as the three were partly off, he turned to Laurence. "There you are. In you go."

Laurence had known what they were doing, but now that the moment was at hand, his fear burst upward in him. He stared at the crate. "It's like a coffin," he whispered. "How long will I have to stay in there?"

"Ship's supposed to slip by the morning tide," Fred answered. "Soon as she clears the Mersey, your friend can get you."

"But what if he doesn't?"

"He promised he would."

Laurence looked around. "What if they put another box against it?"

"No chance," Fred assured him. "That's why I put it here."

"You're sure Patrick will come?" Laurence said. His heart was thudding.

"You said you saw him on the quay, didn't you?"

Laurence nodded.

"I'll tell him where you are soon as I leave. Get in now."

Laurence had to force himself into the box. He could stand up, but it was impossible to sit. "Wait!" he implored, holding a board out with a hand. "Swear that you'll tell Patrick where I am."

"Of course I swear. Just don't you worry. It'll be fine."

"But what will I eat?"

"You can go without for a day. I've done it lots of times."

Laurence closed his eyes and tried to breathe slowly. He did not want to see Fred replace the third board. All the same, he heard the nails inching in.

He opened his eyes to darkness and ran his fingers over the rough, splintery wood. Only a faint glimmer of light glowed through the cracks in the boards.

"You all right in there?" Fred whispered through a crack.

"I think so." Laurence kept swallowing hard. He was panting for breath.

"I'm marking the box now." Fred took the chalk from his pocket and circled the X. "You're all set now," he cried. "I'm going."

"Tell Patrick *exactly* where I am!"

"I will."

"Good-bye," a tearful Laurence called.

"And when you come out of it," Fred said, laughing, "you'll be in heaven."

Or hell, Laurence thought.

Chapter 70

Final Arrangements

F red made his way out of the hold and down the ship's exit gangway without attracting any attention. He searched the quay—it was quite dark now—and saw the crowd of emigrants. More than a hundred were already there. He worked his way through them, trying to find Patrick, whom he finally spotted sitting under a quay lamp with his sister and her friend.

"I'm here," Fred said, slipping up to Patrick.

Patrick jumped up. "Where's Laurence?" he asked.

"Not so loud," Fred cautioned, looking around to make sure no one had heard. Only Maura and Mr. Drabble had noticed him.

"Listen hard now," Fred said, keeping his voice low. "He's on the ship in a crate for hats. Bottom hold. You can't get any lower. Can you remember that?"

"Bottom hold," Patrick repeated.

"Right. And he's as far forward as we could go. I marked it. Made a circle around a cross mark. When you're away from Liverpool—out to sea—find it and open it up, and he'll be there. Now don't you forget him," Fred warned, "or your friend won't be breathing much."

"Fred!" The call came from across the quay.

Fred turned. Mr. Orkin of the Lime Street Runners Association was pushing his way through the crowd.

"Don't you forget him!" Fred repeated to Patrick as he backed away. The moment he reached open ground, he began to sprint. The other runner, impeded by the crowd, struggled to pursue him.

Patrick watched them go even as he tried to absorb what he had heard. The next moment, however, he was grabbed by the shoulders.

"Patrick O'Connell!" Maura cried. "I'm begging you. There's too much danger with that boy. Wasn't it bad enough to have our home tumbled, Mr. Morgan chasing you, and our mother abandoning us? Do you want English law crashing down on our heads too and we barely finding our way!"

"But, Maura," Patrick cried, "it's too late. He's there, on the ship, waiting for me! If I don't get him out, he'll die!"

Maura closed her eyes tightly and pressed her hands in prayer. "Dear God," she prayed with the deepest fervor, "in all the goodness of Your sacred heart, protect us now!"

Chapter 71
Fred Prepares for Departure

*F*red slipped away easily. But once free he had to decide where to go. It was clear to him that the whole Lime Street Runners Association was now out in force trying to catch him. He needed a place to hide for a while.

He considered going back to the hulks. But he wanted the satisfaction of seeing the *Robert Peel*—and Laurence—clear Liverpool first. He would deal with the rest later.

His mind made up, he headed north along Regent Street toward Sandon Basin. There, at the outlet to the river, he would have a sweeping view of the Mersey, a perfect spot from which to watch the *Robert Peel* when it came downstream.

After a fast trot through the dark, Fred crept behind one of the towers built to contain the machines that opened the basin bridge. Some work was being done on the tower, and building stones were scattered about the ground. A small workman's shed had even been constructed to keep tools from the rain. A perfect hiding place.

Fred eased the shed door open, crawled inside, and made room for himself to sit. After barricading the door, he leaned back against the wall. He felt content, certain he had done everything possible to thwart Ralph Toggs. As for Laurence, it was up to the Irish boy now.

Chapter 72
Mr. Pickler Faces the
Early Morning

*I*t was barely daybreak when Mr. Phineas Pickler, bowler upon his head, a bright brass telescope tucked under his arm, stepped out of the Royalton Hotel's doorway and squinted into a murky sky. On the curb, waiting next to a hansom cab, was Ralph Toggs.

"Morning, mate," Toggs said, offering up a lazy salute. "Hope you passed the night in comfort."

Mr. Pickler turned to consider the young man coldly. "I did," he replied.

Toggs laughed. "I was having a rousing good time myself and—"

"Mr. Toggs," the investigator interrupted, "I am not the least bit interested in the way you spent your evening. Is everything in readiness as ordered?"

"Got the boat you wanted," Toggs replied, somewhat chastened. "She's a skiff, and she can buzz if you need it."

"Good. Then, please, let us get on with it!"

"If you say so."

"I do say so," Mr. Pickler returned stiffly. "You may ride with the driver," he said, and pulled himself into the carriage.

Mr. Pickler settled himself upon the seat and laid the telescope to one side. Then he removed his bowler and stared into it. It was profoundly empty. But then he was not happy with the day, himself, or, for that matter, anything. He would have given a great deal to be home with his family.

The cabdriver turned to Toggs. "Where we going, mate?"

"Sandon Basin."

Chapter 73
The O'Connells at Clarence Basin

At Clarence Basin, Maura, having passed the chilly night in fitful sleep, woke to the sound of a clanging bell. Through the swirling gray fog, she made out other emigrants who—like themselves—had been waiting to board the *Robert Peel* since the day before. They too had passed the night on the cold, wet stone pavement, propped one against another. She sensed immediately that there were more people now. Their clutter of possessions, close to hand, served as pillows or as barriers in the attempt to make some private space for themselves or their families.

Then Maura realized that some passengers were already pressing toward the boat. Only then did she grasp that the bell she was hearing came from the *Robert Peel*, summoning all to board. People were scrambling to their feet.

"Patrick!" Maura called excitedly. "Mr. Drabble! They're boarding the ship!"

Patrick woke at once and snatched up their remaining bundle and the tin can. Mr. Drabble unfolded himself more slowly, stretching and craning his neck, smoothing back his hair.

"We'd better hurry," Patrick urged.

"I am ready, my boy," Mr. Drabble assured him. He had his own bag as well as the food provision sack slung over his back. "Miss O'Connell," he warned, "may I advise you not to take out your tickets until they're asked for."

She nodded her understanding.

Trying to stay together, the three joined the great wedge of people pressed toward the ship's gangway.

Remembering what had happened when they came off the boat from Ireland, Patrick clung to their bundle with two hands.

Suddenly there was a shout. A man was attempting to board the *Robert Peel* near the stern. Hardly did he make his leap than two other men followed. On the deck of the ship, sailors armed with belaying pins rushed to the railing to meet them. The emigrants on the quay ceased pushing forward as all eyes focused on the drama being played out before them.

When the first man reached the bulwark, a fierce struggle erupted. But the sailors, outnumbering the intruder five to one, easily managed to throw him off. He fell to the quay. As for the two other men, they too were repulsed savagely. No one else tried.

As soon as the disturbance was quelled, the crowd surged toward the gangway again.

"You see," Mr. Drabble said in a low voice, "how desperate people are to go."

It was not just passengers who were struggling to get aboard. Crowds of hawkers had appeared. They were crying out their dire predictions as to what might happen if travelers did not purchase their food, their blankets, their medicines.

Despite the great desire of the passengers, movement forward was painfully slow. Only one of the two gangways had been deployed, and at the base of it a police constable was staring intently at each and every young boy who came along. To further hinder progress, the ship's first mate—Mr. Murdock—stood at the top of the gangway, double-checking all the tickets. He was a man of middling height, but menacing with bulging muscles, massive hands, and hard eyes. Upon his stern, swarthy face a scowl seemed fixed. And if he were not imposing enough, two burly sailors stood by his side. Another man entered names in a ledger book.

As Maura watched, she saw the mate turn one passenger away. He'd not had the medical exam. Though the man protested with anger, it was to no avail. Mr. Murdock picked him up bodily, carried him down the ramp, and flung him to the quay.

"Make way for gentlemen! Make way for gentlemen!" came a cry from the back of the crowd. Led by a ship's officer, Mr. Grout and Mr. Clemspool forced their way through the press of people.

"It's your friend," Patrick informed Mr. Drabble.

"So it is," the actor acknowledged. "Maura, look who's there. Mr. Grout. And a blessing too, my dear. It's not every man who benefits from employment while crossing the sea."

"Make way for gentlemen!" the officer cried again. As people gave way, Mr. Grout, reveling at being the center of attention, walked grandly up to the gangway. Behind him crept Mr. Clemspool, his face averted so as to avoid the scrutiny of the constable.

At the foot of the gangway, Mr. Grout lifted his beaver hat in salute and addressed the crowd. "Good riddance to England!" he called to no one in particular. "From this 'ere moment on, Toby Grout can say America is me 'ome!"

"Do move on," Mr. Clemspool insisted. "I don't like these crowds." To his enormous relief, the constable was showing not the least bit of interest in him.

At the top of the gangway, Mr. Grout displayed his tickets

like a gambler producing his winning hand. Barely checking them, the first mate saluted with elaborate respect, then called upon a sailor to escort the two men across the deck.

They then mounted some steps that in turn led to a small pulpitlike deck before the main mast. Here stood Captain Rickles—the *Robert Peel*'s commander—who had posted himself to oversee the proceedings. A large square-chested man with a flamboyant red mustache, he stood proudly in his splendid gray captain's uniform, gloves, and cap.

As Mr. Grout and Mr. Clemspool reached the deck, the captain offered a crisp salute. "Welcome to the *Robert Peel*, gentlemen," he cried out. Removing his gloves as a gesture of respect, he shook the two men's hands with zest.

On the quay, the boarding of the steerage passengers continued with painful slowness. The crush of people was suffocating. It was a strain just to keep upon one's feet. Maura and Patrick managed to stay close together until they arrived, finally, at the gangway.

"You there!" the constable cried, slapping the flat of his hand hard on Patrick's chest to keep him from moving. "What's your name?" he demanded.

An alarmed Patrick tried to stand firm. "Patrick O'Connell, Your Honor."

"Where you from?"

"It's Ireland, Your Honor."

"Kilonny, county Cork," Maura intervened.

"Let him talk for himself," the constable insisted.

"Ireland. Kilonny," Patrick repeated.

"Where's your ticket?"

Maura, straining to hold her own against the shoving of the crowd behind her, struggled to unpin her packet of tickets. These she showed to the constable. He inspected them carefully, looking repeatedly from the name on Patrick's ticket to Patrick himself.

"Let's see your cheek," the constable ordered, and he twisted Patrick's face about, examining it intently.

"All right then," he said, clearly disappointed. "You can board."

Mr. Drabble, next in line, was quickly passed through. So was Maura.

"Faith, Maura, I'm sure that constable was looking for Laurence," Patrick whispered.

"Shhh!" Maura hissed. "I don't want to know!"

The trio reached the top of the gangway. Once again tickets were asked for, produced, and accepted. "Get to the forecastle deck," came the order.

Under the watchful eye of several surly faced sailors, the three hastened to the short flight of steps that led to the forecastle deck, already crowded. Under sailors' orders, all passengers were required to leave their piles of sacks, bags, trunks, chests, and mattresses on the main deck. The O'Connells were no exception.

Patrick kept straining to take in the ship. Everything was very much bigger than on the boat from Ireland. But it was much more important to sleuth out some means of getting to Laurence.

"Not so very difficult, was it now?" Mr. Drabble cried, his cheeks red with excitement. "To think I'm really here! And it's to you, my dear Miss O'Connell, I am so deeply indebted for it all."

"Mr. Drabble," Maura returned coolly. "We're not yet safe upon the sea."

"It will happen, my dear," Mr. Drabble cried. "It will happen!"

More and more people kept crowding upon the forecastle deck. Babies screamed and children cried. Some adults wept openly.

Patrick, leaning over the forecastle rail and looking into the ship's waist, called, "They're closing off the gangway!"

No more passengers were being allowed on board, although some twenty, still on the quay, protested vehemently. Their cries—some screams—went unheeded.

With a helping hand from the first mate, a top-hatted man climbed upon the rail. In his hand he held the ledger book.

"All right! All right," the man cried to the crowd before him. "You must listen to me now. The ship won't sail until this is done." He held up the book. "As a representative of Lazarus Brothers Shipping, I have in my hand the names of all passengers who have paid their way. I shall call these names. When you hear your name, step forward. I shall call your berth number too. Remember it. It will not be repeated. You may then go down the steps and wait upon the main deck.

"All those who remain—whose names I do *not* call—will be summarily removed from this ship. There will be no arguments. You will go off! If you do not, you will be thrown overboard."

Without further fuss, the officer began to read names. "Albertson, Terrence!"

"Aye!" cried a man.

"Berth number one. To the deck!"

With three hundred and fifty names to be called—and many to be mispronounced—the roll took considerable time.

The merchants and hawkers who had managed to slip on board departed without ceremony. But when the roll call was done, five people remained on the forecastle deck. Their names had not been called. The two men, two women, and a boy of nine all insisted with great passion and tears that they had paid their passage money. Two even produced tickets that, they claimed, proved they had a right to be there. It made no difference. Sailors stepped forward and, taking hold of the begging, rejected passengers, forcibly ejected them from the ship.

Captain Rickles looked over the scene with calm amusement. "Raucous, isn't it?" he said, turning to Mr. Grout and Mr. Clemspool, who stood by his side, also looking on.

"Is it always like this?" Mr. Clemspool asked. He was finding the embarkation distasteful.

"Always," insisted the captain in the mildest of tones. "And often worse."

" 'Ow do yer mean, worse?" Mr. Grout asked.

"Take my word for it, gentlemen, there are those who try to steal their way across."

" 'Ow can they do that?"

"Stowaways," Captain Rickles replied smugly. "There's not an emigrant ship out of Liverpool that isn't plagued by 'em. You'd be amazed at how they try and hide themselves away."

"And how do you find them?" Mr. Clemspool inquired.

"Actually, my crew—under the orders of my first mate, Mr. Murdock—enjoys hunting them down. Singular mind, Mr. Murdock's. He watches them board, and from then on he'll remember all their faces. If one appears later who isn't regular, he'll spot him."

"What 'appens when yer nab 'em?" asked Mr. Grout.

"It all depends on when we find them," the captain replied with a smile. "If we are still in the river here, we can toss them overboard. They can swim home. A little farther out, we can send them back with the pilot boat. But if we're already upon the seas when they're discovered, we can make them work their passage over. Or, for that matter, tar and feather them."

"Yer don't!" Mr. Grout cried.

"If they are scurvy enough, sir, I've done so and with pleasure."

"Serves them right too," Mr. Clemspool agreed. "Every man should pay his way."

Mr. Grout turned to look at his companion with irritation.

"Perhaps," the captain said, "you'd like to go along with Mr. Murdock when he leads the search party. Only a matter of moments now."

Mr. Grout laughed. "I'm game for it. Bit of sport, yer might say."

"It is that," the captain agreed with a laugh. "They take pikes to poke into sacks and barrels, as well as hammers to get into crates. Great sport. I'll have the first mate take you along. What's more, gentlemen, if we catch anyone, I shall let you decide what we do with them."

"Be some fun in that," Mr. Grout agreed with a grin.

"Just pitch him overboard," Mr. Clemspool grumbled.

Sailors were swarming all about the ship, hauling in lines, casting them off. A bell began to sound again. This time, however, the bell came from a steam lighter that was approaching the *Robert Peel*.

Once the lighter took on lines from the ship, she commenced to back up. Trembling, the packet began to move. The passengers, even those with tearstained faces, gave a shout.

Mr. Drabble suddenly leaped upon the bulwark and, holding on to the ratlines with one hand while gesturing with his other, proclaimed, " 'Thus I turn my back. There is a world elsewhere!' *Coriolanus*."

Under her breath and with eyes closed, Maura began to pray. Impulsively, she reached out, took Patrick's hand, and brought it to her mouth to kiss. She had remembered her mother's words: "It would be better for me to die at home. The earth will know me there."

"Oh, Patrick," Maura murmured as much to herself as to her brother, "what earth will know me?"

"Sure, Maura, it doesn't matter what earth," Patrick replied. "It's where Da will be waiting."

"Let me have your attention, please," the first mate cried out from the forecastle deck. "In a short time you'll be allowed to go to your berths below. But first, we'll be making our search for stowaways. Let me warn you people now, if any of you have hidden someone among your possessions, or have assisted a stowaway, both you and he will be returned to Liverpool. There will be no exceptions. What's more, if you know of any stowaways on the boat, you'd best come forward now, and it will go a bit better for them."

Patrick felt Maura's hand clamp down upon his shoulder and squeeze. He trembled.

Chapter 74
Two Endings and a Prayer

At the far northern end of the Liverpool docks, Mr. Pickler paced up and down along the quay of Sandon Basin. With each turn, he stared nervously out at the river, now and again applying the telescope to his eye and scanning the passing vessels. Though many boats had already gone by, he was quite sure no emigrant ships had sailed. Even so, he felt tense, his mood swinging wildly between hope and frustration.

All that morning, he had been receiving reports from the police that they'd had no sightings of Laurence. Twice, some boys ran up and spoke to Toggs. Mr. Pickler recognized them as members of Sergeant Rumpkin's association. He tried not to notice them. Why had he allowed himself to work with such riffraff? Because he had failed, he told himself miserably. And he had failed because he had been too willing to believe Lord Kirkle. I do not question others enough, he said to himself. Then he added, I do not question myself. Deeply agitated, he resumed his pacing.

Would he have done things differently if Lord Kirkle had told him the truth, he fretted, had admitted that the boy ran away because he'd been beaten? Mr. Pickler did not know. Perhaps he might not have taken on the case. It certainly would have been better if he had not.

For a while he continued to stare glumly at the river. Small boats, with their red-and-tan sails, seemed to be flitting about aimlessly, like his thoughts. Now and again he thought of his own children. It soothed him to think they were safe with their mother.

He turned to look reproachfully at Toggs idling in the little skiff—oars at the ready—on the basin side of the bridge. The young man, with his brash cocky manner, was an affront to him.

One hour later, yet another boy rushed up and yelled down to Toggs.

Mr. Pickler hurried over.

"This is Orkin," Toggs called. "You remember him. Seems he saw Fred last night. Tried to catch him. But couldn't."

"Fred?" asked a puzzled Mr. Pickler. "Who is Fred?"

"The one who took your boy off."

Mr. Pickler blinked. "What are you talking about?"

"You know," Toggs said, "the one who got your Laurence off that chapel ship, the one who's trying to get him stowed on a packet. Sergeant told you about him."

"Sergeant Rumpkin never spoke such a name to me," Mr. Pickler snapped. "This is the first I have heard of any Fred!"

With a shrug, Toggs looked to Orkin. "Better tell the gentleman what you knows."

"Yes, sir," Orkin said. "Begging your pardon, but this here Fred—"

"Who is *Fred*?" cried Mr. Pickler, completely exasperated.

"Used to be in the association."

"And you say Laurence was connected to him?"

"Yes, sir. The thing is, I saw Fred hanging about the ship *Robert Peel.*"

"The *Robert Peel*?" Mr. Pickler echoed dumbly.

"Yes, sir, he was."

"Did you see Laurence?"

"No, sir. It was Fred I was trying to get at. But he probably knows where your boy is. Except Fred got away."

"When did you see him?"

"Like I said, last night, by the *Robert Peel.*"

"Last night?" cried Mr. Pickler. "Then why am I learning about this only just now?"

The boy backed away. "I was waiting on the sergeant, sir, for him to be up this morning. See, he's most particular about being disturbed at his meals. We all knows that. Told us so again last night. It's one of his major orders. But when I finally did tell him—after his breakfast—he told me to trot double time here, which I just did."

Mr. Pickler shouted down to Toggs. "And you say this Fred has been the one helping Laurence get away? And you knew it?"

"That's how Sergeant figures it," Toggs said sheepishly.

Mr. Pickler whirled about and stalked back out to the end of the quay. As he watched, a packet ship, pulled by a steam lighter, approached midriver. The lighter dropped away, and the packet's sails began to unfurl and fill with wind. Heeling slightly, the ship glided down the choppy river.

Mr. Pickler lifted his telescope to an eye. By the ship's

bowsprit he could just make out the name, *Robert Peel*. "Toggs!" he cried. "Come here."

The young man clambered out of the skiff and onto the quay.

"I believe that's the *Robert Peel*!" Mr. Pickler cried, thrusting the telescope at Toggs.

Toggs looked for himself. "That's it," he agreed.

"We must reach it." Mr. Pickler snapped. "I have to board it."

They ran back to the skiff. Toggs climbed in first, taking up the oars from the center seat. Mr. Pickler all but jumped into the stern.

"Push us off," Toggs called to Orkin. The boy did, and the moment they were cleared, Toggs leaned into the oars and began to row.

"Hurry!" Mr. Pickler cried.

The skiff shot forward, as Toggs, using deft short strokes, drove them toward the narrow basin entrance under the bridge. Just before they reached the bridge, a voice hailed them. "There you are, Ralph Toggs! I knew I'd get you!"

Mr. Pickler looked up. So did Toggs. Standing on the bridge above was Fred. In his hands, high over his head, he held, tremblingly, a large building stone. Even as Mr. Pickler and Toggs spotted him, he hurled the stone down. It struck the skiff just inside its bow, punching a hole right through its wooden bottom. Water began to pour in. The skiff foundered.

Toggs leaped up, only to have the boat shift beneath his feet. He tumbled into the water, splashing about frantically. "Help!" he cried. "I can't swim! I can't swim!"

Mr. Pickler, who could swim, clung to the boat. His bowler floated away. He started to reach for it only to let it go. Instead, with his free hand he snatched at one of the oars floating by and thrust it toward Toggs, who grabbed it.

Kicking, Mr. Pickler struggled to propel them back toward the quay. As he did, he turned, just in time to see the *Robert Peel* sail by.

Upon the bridge, Fred leaned over, shouting, "Huzzah! Huzzah for them who has no names!" then rushed away.

Upon the *Robert Peel*, deep within the bottom hold, in the dark crate, Laurence waited. Had it been a day, less than a day, or two days? He hardly knew. Sometimes he was awake, other times he slept, though he was never quite sure which was which. For long stretches of time he thought—or did he dream?—of nothing but food and water. Other times he remembered his London home and family. He cried then. Most generally, his thoughts drifted from notion to notion without connections or conclusions. At times he was certain he was seeing Fred before him or Mr. Clemspool or the man who had robbed him in London or Toggs or Patrick. And with each sighting came an endless drift of anxiety, frights, and regrets.

Now, at last, he began to sense that something was happening. The crate was swaying gently. Did that mean the ship was under sail? Would Patrick be coming for him now? "Please, please," Laurence prayed out loud, "let Patrick come. If he doesn't, I'll die in here. I know I will."

To be continued in
Book Two: Lord Kirkle's Money

Look for All the Unforgettable Stories by Newbery Honor Author

★ AVI ★